SWORDS & STONES

DESCENDANTS OF THE ROUND TABLE
BOOK ONE

KIMBERLY LYNN HANSON

CASPIAN
PUBLISHING

SWORDS & STONES

DESCENDANTS OF THE ROUND TABLE
BOOK ONE

KIMBERLY LYNN
HANSON

CASPIAN
PUBLISHING

CASPIAN PUBLISHING, LLC.

Text copyright © Kimberly Lynn Hanson

Cover illustration © Aes Munandi

Cover design © Kimberly Lynn Hanson

Names: Hanson, Kimberly Lynn, author

Title: Swords & Stones / by Kimberly Lynn Hanson

Description: Caspian Publishing, LLC | Colorado, 2025 | Summary "In a war-torn world after the death of King Arthur, the teenage children of the Knights of the Round Table embark on a quest to save Camelot while cleaning up the mess their disastrous parents left in the kingdom." —provided by publisher

ISBN 979-8-9926538-1-6 (paperback) | ISBN 979-8-9926538-0-9 (eBook)

Subjects: Fantasy — Fiction. | Myth and legends — Fiction. | Magic — Fiction

For my parents, who taught me to dream and always make room for everyone at the Round Table.

AUTHOR'S NOTE:

This story is written for a mature young adult audience. As a medieval fantasy novel, this book includes depictions of violent battle, fight scenes, blood, and severe injury. It also contains mental health episodes (panic and anxiety), death of a parent (on and off the page), underage drinking, and some darker themes. Readers who may be sensitive to these topics are advised to proceed with caution.

"This is the oath of a Knight of King Arthur's Round Table and should be for all of us to take to heart... I will speak the truth at all times, and forever keep my word, I will defend those who cannot defend themselves... I will be faithful in love and loyal in friendship... I will live my life with courtesy and honor from this day forward."

—*Le Morte d'Arthur*, Sir Thomas Malory

"You wear your honor like a suit of armor…You think it keeps you safe, but all it does is weigh you down and make it hard for you to move."

—*A Game of Thrones*, George R.R. Martin

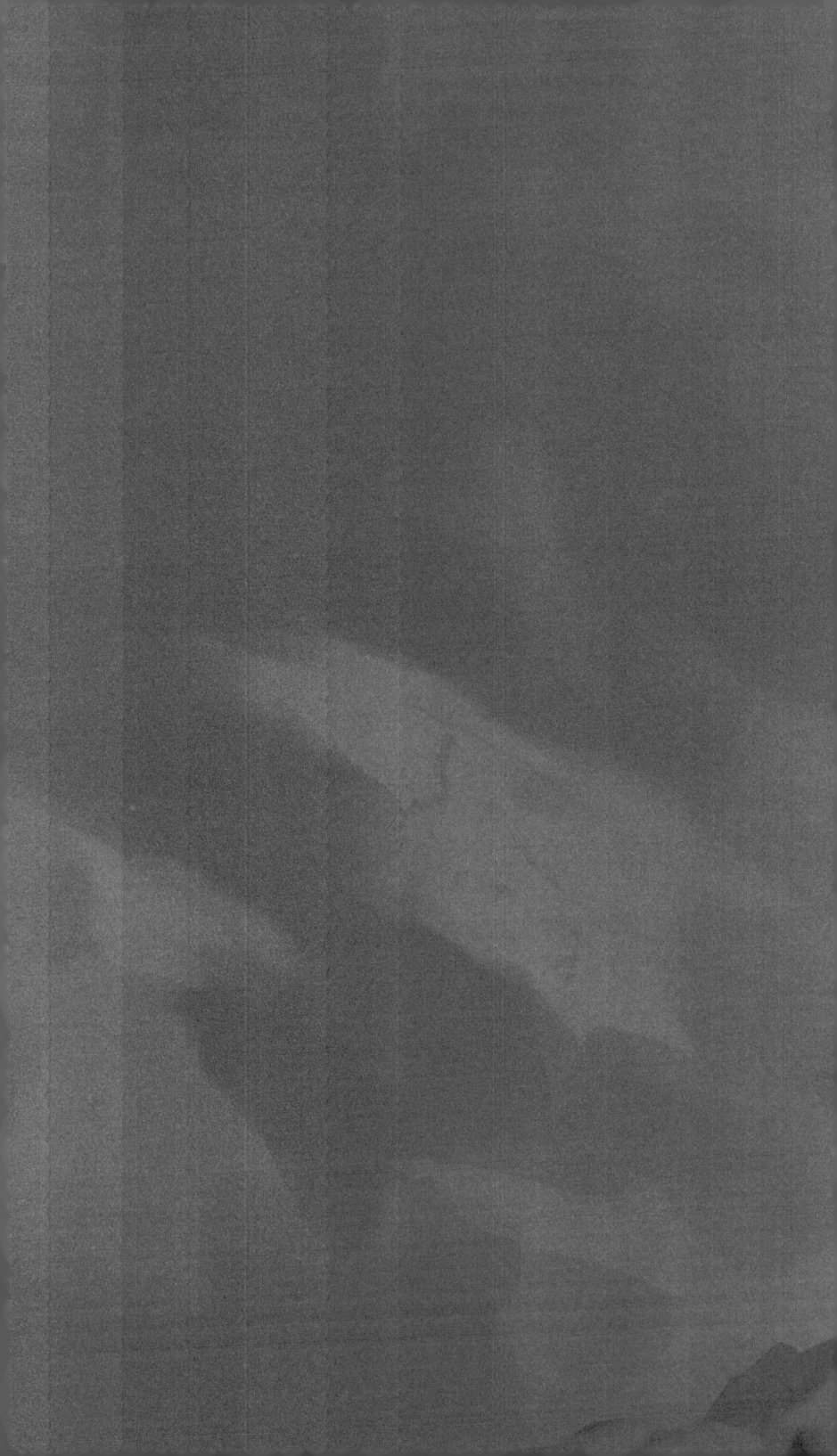

PROLOGUE

It began with a sword. And it will end with one, too.

CHAPTER

ONE

CAMELOT WAS THE MOST BEAUTIFUL AT NIGHT.

Ren walked along a cobblestone street as fiery bursts of orange and gold sparked on the horizon. He gripped the worn leather hilt of the sword strapped to his hip—a steadying habit to ease the twisting nerves making a mess of his insides. But it wasn't working tonight, and he stopped against a house with a thatched roof and a curl of smoke billowing from its chimney.

He let out a long sigh and tugged at his rust-colored tunic to tame the wrinkled fabric. Over his arms were tarnished steel bracers and matching shoulder armor.

The sun disappeared behind the far eastern stone wall, the lights from small houses glowing like twinkling fireflies. Tonight, instead of admiring the beauty of his town, Ren was too distracted by the looming ceremony. Tonight, Ren would become a knight. He'd spent most of his life preparing for this. Seventeen years. *No big deal.*

The training pit used to be his favorite place within the castle's high walls, but he'd seen too much of it in recent days and was still finding mud in places it shouldn't be. He winced as he adjusted the armor over a blooming bruise on his bad shoulder, sprained last year but never quite healed. Now the bruise only made the pain worse, but those were the sacrifices he had to make.

Sacrifices.

That's what being a knight of Camelot meant. That's what his father, Sir Bedivere, one of the last remaining Knights of the Round Table, always told him.

You must sacrifice for the good of the people. For the kingdom.

Ren was happy to do it most days. Well...some days. Even when the best knight in training beat him repeatedly, and even while his best friend Geret gave him a hard time because the best knight in training happened to be Ren's girlfriend, Gwen.

Stopping at the end of the street, he shoved a hand into the pocket of his trousers. His fingers met with the edges of a silver rose brooch with glittering cobalt petals. He'd bought it for Gwen.

"You are ready, Ren," Gwen had told him during one of their training sessions. "They already know you are knight material." She'd leaned against the wooden fence encircling the gritty sand and straw training dummies of the sparring pit. A rosy flush bloomed on Gwen's ivory cheeks as she caught her breath between sessions.

She knew how nervous he was for the ceremony. He was the first of the group to come of age. It was a burden he felt every day, but some of the weight lifted while he exchanged blows in the training pit. He could breathe again and forget about all of it.

"I wish you could stand up there with me. You deserve it." Ren had approached her, tucking his sword into the leather scabbard at his hip. Her long, blonde curls were braided into plaits, but Ren caught a stray hair fallen over her face and tucked it behind her ear. He'd allowed his fingers to linger there a moment.

She was radiant, even with sweat staining her clothes and mud marking her exposed skin. Her beauty had mesmerized him since they were kids.

She caught his hand in hers, her mouth melting into a frown. "It's not my year. My father isn't on the counsel like yours."

"He would be if he were still here," Ren said.

"You know that isn't true. My father made his choice, and now I'm the one who must live with it." A twinge of disdain laced her words.

She was right, though. It wasn't fair Gwen should suffer because of Lancelot and Guinevere's betrayal. He knew it. The rest of their group knew it. When would the counsel see it?

"Perhaps next year." He gave her an optimistic smile.

Instead of responding, she'd leaned in and planted a kiss on his lips before twirling back to the center of the pit. "Come on, let's get back to it."

That was weeks ago, and Ren had barely seen her since. When he did, there was an awkward tension between them he couldn't place. Blaming it on the flurry of activity surrounding the ceremony, he hoped his gift would set it right. He squeezed the brooch in the palm of his hand, slipping it back into his pocket.

Ren gripped the sword at his side before sucking in a breath and turning down an alleyway, cutting through to Merchant Square. A large tent bursting with colorful blooms exploding from baskets stood at the center of the square. A wave of people drifted into the tent wearing their finest attire and sparkling jewels. Ren ran a hand through his locks in a futile attempt at taming the brown strands hanging haphazardly over his ears.

As he walked through the entrance, a shadowed figure caught his eye. The flash of a dark cloak disappeared around one side of the tent. The muscles in his neck tensed. As he stepped over to peer around the edge, the bellowing laugh of a familiar voice drew his attention, and a strong grip yanked him inside the entrance.

"Would you look at this!" His friend Geret stood before him with an enormous grin spread over his dark cheeks.

He slapped Ren a little too hard on his bruised shoulder, and Ren winced against the sting. If Geret noticed, he didn't show it because his eyes were alight with excitement. He wore his finest tunic in forest green with shining armor over his chest and shoulders. Even his wild curls were tamed into tight ringlets tonight. He had put in an effort.

"It's something," Ren returned, thoughts of the shadowed figure from outside feeling silly now.

He scanned the room full of unfamiliar faces, taking in the aroma of smoked meats and spiced wine. A flute carried an enchanted melody through the crowd as people swayed to the music. Colorful flags danced along the ceiling, and lanterns emitted a soft glow from the corners of the tent.

"All these people turned up. They had a juggler earlier, and you just missed the town falconer who brought his sparrowhawk. I swear it had glowing yellow eyes," Geret said.

"You mean Ranulf?"

Geret turned to him with a puzzled expression. "The hawk's name is Ranulf?"

Ren chuckled. "No. The man. I've seen him in Merchant Square before. He has like six birds. My father used to invite him hunting. I guess they are really good for that."

Geret shrugged. "I can't keep track. But Ren, look...." Geret's eyes landed on a group of young women in silken gowns. They gathered at the back tables, where candles dripped wax amongst a towering display of steaming meats, stacks of cheese, and bright fruits. Ren's stomach growled, and he wet his lips.

"I know, right?" Geret nodded, biting his bottom lip.

"I'm hungry," Ren snapped, knowing his friend too well.

"I'm just saying. This is more people than all the year's feasts combined."

He was right. Even their Beltane feast was sparse last year, and it felt like they invited fewer and fewer allies from neighboring towns with every event. Or perhaps fewer and fewer had shown up. Ren wasn't sure, but it did feel like Camelot's friends were disappearing. But here they were.

All for tonight. Ren's throat went dry.

The girls at the food tables emitted a series of giggles, commanding Geret's gaze.

Ren shook his head. At least his friend lightened the mood, and he could use a bit of fun to take his mind off things. "I thought you only had eyes for Camelot women." He elbowed Geret in the side. The girls leaned in, whispered to one another, and flashed them both wide-toothed smiles.

"Why would you say that?"

"Because rumor has it you asked every single maiden in Camelot to come with you tonight, and they all said no. Including my sister." Ren's eyebrows shot up.

"Lies. All of it. Besides, your sister will come around. They all do."

"I'm going to pretend I didn't hear that."

Geret drifted over to the food table while Ren walked through the space searching for anyone else he recognized. From afar, the guests' attire appeared luxurious, but as he got closer, he noticed frayed edges on sleeves and jewelry encrusted with tarnished metals and hazy jewels. Some even sported lighter garbs made from common linen instead of lush velvets and silks. Camelot hadn't had a feast like this for ages, and it showed.

Ren found a spot at the side of the tent, exhaling the breath held in his chest, and put a hand to his sword. The closer it got to midnight, the more his pulse raced to the beat of the pounding music. A whirl of thoughts raced through his mind— was he truly ready to join the other knights? What would his father think? What if he failed? Or worse, what if he endangered someone? One by one the thoughts beat stronger and stronger until sweat beaded on his brow and his heart raged inside his rib cage.

Luckily, he spotted Gwen at the entrance of the tent, which was a temporary relief. He needed a distraction. She strolled in on the arm of a castle guard (knights who were trained with protecting the town and castle of Camelot, but not a part of Arthur's Round Table knights), and whispered something into his ear. He nodded and left her standing alone. Catching Ren's eye, she smiled and glided over. A stunning metal corset hugged her waist over silky, flowy layers of sapphire and cobalt. The line of her bodice, strung with shiny metal twisting temptations around her neck, cut deep, showing a hint of her chest.

She was a distraction, alright.

"Whoa." Ren's eyes lingered on her chest. *Her neck.* His eyes lingered on her neck.

She cleared her throat, drawing his eyes upward. Her hair was a waterfall of silky, golden hair pinned in ringlets behind one shoulder. Ren's cheeks caught fire with yet another un-knightly thought.

He straightened his spine and grasped her hand in his. She had long, delicate fingers, and her nails were shredded into jagged shapes. She'd been chewing them again. A nervous habit of hers. But what did she have to be nervous about tonight?

He planted a kiss at her knuckles. "Shall we, my lady?"

She giggled, lifting his head with the tips of her fingers and drew him in close. Ren breathed a sigh of relief. It was as if the last few weeks hadn't happened, and they were just Ren and Gwen again. All the pressures of the ceremony floated away into the symphony of flutes. Ren went in for a kiss but was interrupted by the one person a guy would not want to hear while trying to woo his girlfriend.

"Amren?" Ren's mother, Lady Roslyn, broke the spell.

His mother was dressed in a modest velvet gown with puffed sleeves and jewels in her hair. It was a much different look than the usual linen dresses and aprons she donned around the house. He gave her a hug, noting the floral notes clinging to her red hair.

Emeli, Ren's younger twin sister—only by forty-two minutes, as she constantly reminded him—stood by their mother's side shooting Ren a knowing smirk. She beamed in a copper silk gown with flowers running along the neckline and rust-colored arm bracers at her wrists. She'd been talking about this dress for weeks, to the point that Ren might have tossed it out the window to avoid hearing about it again. But seeing her practically glowing in it tonight made all the fuss worth it.

"Behave, you two," Emeli ordered, looking between Gwen and Ren.

Gwen gave her a jilted glare before bursting out laughing.

Those two were always teaming up on him.

Ren ignored the giggles and turned toward his mother. "You did a wonderful job on the feast. It's incredible."

"Thank you, love. The people deserve a celebration. These past few years have been difficult for everyone. It was a challenge to convince some of our neighbors to show."

"But it looks like they did. Even the Southerners," Ren commented, eyeing the crowd.

Most of Camelot's allies were to the south, but making the journey these days was harder than in the past. Lands were divided and allegiances threatened. Camelot needed something to unite them before it got worse. That's what counsel had said when they announced they were finally having a knighting ceremony after all these years.

"They are all looking forward to seeing our newest knight."

Ren recognized the voice of his father and turned to find him approaching. Greying hair and chiseled cheek bones shaped his face behind a wide smile—the biggest one he'd seen him wear in a long time.

"Father." Ren gave his father a customary bow since they were in public. "I missed you at breakfast this morning. Were you out?"

Dark bags hung under his father's eyes, and weary lines etched deep into his forehead. Still, he resembled every bit the shining image of a knight in his polished armor and Pendragon crimson cape embroidered in golden thread.

"Your father has been gone for two nights. Honestly, Amren," his mother sighed.

Ren exchanged glances with Emeli, but she shrugged like she hadn't noticed, either.

"A structure fire in Willowdale threatened the entire village. It took us half a day's ride to get there. All we found upon our arrival were ashes. Three buildings lost. We stayed for the cleanup."

"A structure fire?" Ren's eyebrows lifted.

"It seems it was intentional, but we didn't catch whoever set it."

"Oh," Ren responded, not knowing the right thing to say. Was a single structure fire truly worth all the trouble?

Ren's father leaned in closer, allowing the others to drift into their own conversations. "I know you don't understand why we answer these things, but we will always go to those who call for aid." He straightened his neck. "I will be generous to the poor and to those—"

"Those who need help," Ren finished. "I know the Knight's Code." A tight knot twisted in his stomach. He'd been reciting the code since he could speak. It was second nature. But tonight, it took on a whole new level of meaning. It was soon to be *his* Knight's Code.

His father grasped his good shoulder as if knowing to avoid the other, and he gave it a squeeze. "You would do well to take the code seriously. It's in your blood."

Ren nodded and let out a heavy sigh.

His father's eyes softened. "All you see are old men breaking up street brawls and putting out house fires, but there was a time, Arthur's time, when this meant something." He peered around the room full of guests and at all the fanfare that came with the ceremony. Musicians strummed their instruments, and people danced and stuffed their plates with rich foods. The energy felt different than in the Merchant Square or at the smaller feasts. This was... hopeful.

Ren's father leaned in closer, and his words whispered in a serious tone. "The day will come again when you may find yourself called to that duty. Like tonight." He gave Ren a wink, releasing his shoulder. "Believe me. We need good knights like you, son. For the kingdom."

"Come, my love. Let the kids have some fun before they start." His mother looped her arm through his father's and pulled him through the room, stopping to greet the guests.

Gwen cleared her throat next to Ren. "Shall we?" She grabbed his hand and led him to the dance floor before latching his arms around her waist and swaying to the music. "You need to forget all that nonsense from your father and just enjoy the night. Alright?"

He opened his mouth to tell her she was probably right. He hoped they would have a chance to talk, and he felt for the brooch in his pocket, but Geret's boisterous voice interrupted.

"Ready to get the party started?" Geret made his way over carrying multiple pewter cups, and Emeli trailed behind with an annoyed wrinkle in her nose. Geret handed everyone drinks.

Ren sniffed the contents, the scent burning his nose, before they all cheered and downed the liquid. Even Emeli, with her lips puckered. Dancing and laughing, the group found the fun for a little while, and Ren did feel lighter, forgetting all about the pressures of the night.

A slight buzz raced through his head as Geret let out a belly laugh, bending over himself. "Remember when we tricked old Mrs. Tilly into giving us extra cake for the poor orphaned girl we found wandering the streets of Camelot in the rain?" He locked an arm around Ren's shoulder, tugging him into his side and ruffling his hair. "Ren had to wear one of Gwen's dresses because we thought she would sooner give sweets to a little girl than a boy."

Emeli burst out laughing, her face turning bright red. "And

Gwen was taller than him in those days, so he stumbled over the hem, knocking his head against the counter. Knocked out two baby teeth!"

Ren chuckled. He looked at Gwen, but she didn't seem as amused as the rest. Her cup was still full of liquid even though she kept pressing it to her lips. Something was bothering her. He hoped she wasn't upset about the ceremony, though she insisted she wasn't. Maybe being a knight meant more to her than she let on.

He turned to Geret and Emeli, who were still laughing, tears squeezing from the corners of their eyes. "There was blood everywhere! She was so angry," Geret said a little too loudly, drawing glares from several nearby ladies.

Ren clasped him on the back, readying to reign him in, when a horn drew everyone's attention to the entrance of the tent.

A herald dressed in bright patches of Arthur's colors puffed his chest and announced, "I present to you the noble order, Arthur's Knights of the Round Table, protectors of Camelot."

Through the entrance marched the knights led by Ren's father, escorting his mother by his side. She winked at the group as they passed. Next was Sir Bors, an older gentleman with a graying beard and round belly, and his nine-year-old son Elian trotting alongside him. Eli's mother had died during childbirth. She was Sir Bor's third wife and first to bear him any children. That they knew of. Rumors around the kingdom hinted at more than one illegitimate child sired by Sir Bors over the years, but nobody would outwardly accuse him of such a thing.

After Bors, a tall man with deep wrinkles, Sir Percival, walked in with his much younger wife Lady Blanchefleur, along with their new baby girl, who bounced on the lady's hip while fussing at the crowd.

Sir Galahad entered alone, wearing shining armor with a plum-colored tunic complimenting his warm brown skin. Galahad was the youngest of the remaining knights, only ten years older than Ren, and was responsible for training everyone. Ren had countless bruises and sore muscles to prove it. The one currently itching under his armor was one of them.

The knights arranged themselves at the front of the tent as the crowd erupted in applause. Once a mighty force of twelve, their number had diminished to four. However, their presence still inspired awe in the people. They were the closest thing to royalty since the death of the king twelve years ago.

Percival's young wife helped her husband to his seat with a hand to his lower back, while Sir Bors ripped into a turkey leg at the nearest table, juice sliding from the corners of his lips. Galahad leaned into the shadows and crossed his arms over his chest. His expression hardened into the grumpy facade he usually wore.

The party resumed and the nerves in Ren's belly came alive again. He headed for the exit to get fresh air, but Gwen intercepted him, dangling a berry tart in one hand.

"Where are you going?" Her brows shot up.

He ran his hand through his hair, and his eyes darted toward the exit. "I just needed a moment." Sweat slid down his temples. Why was it suddenly so hot in here?

Gwen pushed him by the shoulders a little too hard and he winced against the throbbing bruise.

"Sorry! It's just... don't leave. You haven't tried any of the food yet."

"You've been watching me?"

An innocent smile slipped over her lips, and she batted her long eyelashes, something that always did it for Ren no matter how ridiculous it may have looked to others.

"Here, try this. It's delicious." She offered him the tart.

The top glistened with browned sugar over ripe berries and sweet dough. Despite its allure, his nervous stomach flipped.

He put his hand up in protest. "No, I really don't want to."

Gwen tucked him into a private corner of the tent. "It's your birthday. Your mother worked so hard to secure these all the way from the eastern coast. They use special berries that give it a subtle sweetness but then a punch." She licked her lips and leaned in next to his ear. "Right at the end."

She had him. She'd had him all along. Gwen and Ren had been tethered by some invisible rope since they were kids.

He gave in, taking a bite. The buttery pastry melted in his mouth, followed by a creamy explosion of bitter berries and sugar. It was just what his brain needed to settle. A smile crested his lips as he reached into his pocket. Now was the perfect time, he decided, and he pressed the brooch into her palm. "Listen, I know you said it wasn't important, but I wanted to thank you—"

The shrill sound of trumpets cut him off before he could finish, sending their gaze darting in the direction of the dais at the front of the tent.

Gwen's eyes flicked to the exit before she tucked the brooch into the pocket of her dress. "Come on, there will be time later. It's starting." She tugged on his hand, pulling him through the crowd gathering at the dais.

"Welcome back to Camelot!" Percival announced in a booming voice, completely unexpected from the older knight. The crowd erupted in cheers. "As you know," he cleared his throat, "we have not had a proper knighting ceremony since King Arthur. But our children are coming of age, and the kingdom needs them." His eyes flicked to his wife, and his baby let out a small cry. Then he looked at Ren and the others—Geret, Emeli, and Gwen—all huddled together in the crowd. Emeli knocked Ren's shoulder with her own, and Gwen squeezed his hand.

"It is my greatest honor to present to you our newest knight," Percival continued, but his voice melted into a haze as Ren struggled to stay in his body. He grounded himself with his boots planted and pulled his shoulders back. He'd seen his father do it countless times when he was preparing for something.

"Gwendolyn Marie, of Lancelot," Percival announced to the cheering crowd.

All the air left Ren's lungs. He exchanged looks with Emeli, but the astonished expression on her face confirmed he had heard correctly.

He wasn't going to be a knight.

CHAPTER
TWO

REN DIDN'T KNOW WHAT TO DO. SEVENTEEN YEARS OF training and listening to his father recite the Knight's Code and what was it all for if not for this moment? And it wasn't even his.

He looked at Gwen, horror striking the features of her face. "I'm so sorry, this wasn't part of the plan," she said, dropping his hand.

As the eyes in the room bore down on them both, Gwen shook her head, pushing people aside and darting for the back of the tent. Right for the exit. At the same time, a loud crash sounded, followed by screams.

People darted in every direction, the commotion intensifying as chaotic fighting broke out. Fighting? Who would be fighting?

Ren pushed through the crowd, spotting his father with his sword drawn, clashing with a man with dark hair. He couldn't see his face but caught a crow symbol stitched into the swish of his cape. On the other side of the tent, Percival ushered his wife and child outside. Bors had disappeared completely.

Whatever was happening must have been planned because there was too much chaos in every direction. They must have already been inside the tent. Maybe disguised in cloaks or other party attire? It was the only explanation he could devise. He spotted Galahad dueling with a burly man with blonde hair tied back in a bun, and another lunging in his direction.

Ren drew his sword and jumped into the fray. All his training surged through him, muscle memory taking over. He dodged blades, swinging his sword and lunging at the strange fighters. Their numbers grew and he was quickly overwhelmed, even with Galahad at his back.

As Ren continued fighting, his eyes scanned for his friends. Emeli. Geret. Anyone. And of course, Gwen. Burning air filled his lungs, and his throat grew raw thinking of her. He had to find her and make sure she was okay.

A man came barreling at him, and he used his boot to kick him away. Tables were upturned, and drinks and food splattered over the floors. People raced in all directions, most of the guests funneling out the exit, but still no sight of Gwen. What would he even say to her? That it was alright her name was called and not his? That it was normal to be scared? Because that must be why she fled.

Screams echoed through the tent as more Camelot guards joined the fighting. Another shattering yell rang through the space. It was a voice Ren recognized. *Emeli.*

He turned to the back of the tent where thick black smoke swirled to the ceiling, coating everything in a thick haze. Galahad tapped his shoulder. "Go! I got this." He slammed his body into a fighter and Ren swore a grin splashed across Galahad's face. Galahad hadn't seen this kind of action for some time, and he guessed it was a lot more energizing than sparring with teenagers in the training pit.

Ren spotted his sister in the corner, and he bounded through the bodies. The candles from the food tables had tipped over, and fire crawled up the side of the tent, devouring the fabric. Nearby, Emeli fought off the two men who had trapped her with their mother close behind.

Emeli held her own, but not for long. Ren rushed over, barreling into one man's backside, knocking him to the ground as Emeli slammed the blade of her sword into the other intruder. When the chance arose, they all rushed to the exit.

Once outside, Ren broke out in a coughing fit, expelling the smoke from his lungs. All the color drained from his mother's pale cheeks, her eyes widening. "Your father." She took a choking breath. "He spotted him."

Ren squeezed her shoulders. "Who? Who are they?"

A flurry of emotions washed through her expressions, and while she tried to explain, she couldn't string together a coherent sentence.

"Stay here," Ren urged, tugging on his sister's hand. His head gestured toward the tent.

"Don't you think we should let Father handle this?" Emeli asked. Her eyes darted from their shaking mother and back to the black smoke billowing from the tent.

Ren's stomach turned. He didn't know where their father was, but he did know there were still people back by the tent, and small fights had broken out all over the square. Clanging swords rang out between chaotic screams.

"They need our help, Emeli." His eyes pleaded with hers, and she gave him a reassuring nod.

They both ran toward the tent but couldn't get far as the crowd of people barreled outside. The flames ripped through the fabric, setting everything in a blaze. Smoke burned Ren's nose and made his eyes water, but he jumped into the crowd and met up with Geret, who was helping a family with a small child. They shuffled them safely away from the flames, directing them to an alleyway. A line of guests had run in that direction, as well.

The night had not gone the way Ren imagined.

He searched for his father and Gwen, scanning the crowd amongst the chaos, but found neither.

Geret tugged on his arm and pointed to a fountain on the other end of the square where a crowd had gathered. His father's voice boomed through the bodies, and Ren took off running, pushing through people until he spotted his father's sword.

"Give it up. It is pointless. You are outnumbered here." His father's gaze traveled to the center of the commotion and Ren's stomach dropped.

A group of dark knights with silver armor surrounded Gwen with her hair disheveled and dress ripped. The delicate ropes once holding her bodice in place hung in strands by her side.

But the most heartbreaking of all was the sword she held. It was the one Ren had grown to know as well as his own. The one he sparred against countless times. It was the sword that had become just as much a part of her as he had. But he didn't recognize this sword anymore because it pointed directly at his father's chest.

"Gwen, what are you doing?" Ren cried out.

Her eyes fell upon him. "I'm sorry Ren, but this isn't about you. It's not about any of us. It's about them." She pointed a shaking finger at the circle of knights, including his father.

"They betrayed us long before we were born. They betrayed all of us." She gestured around the square at the wide eyes of the people staring back. "They killed one another. They slept with each other's wives. They waged wars against brothers. Where does it end?"

Her eyes turned glassy, and a wild look took over her face as she turned to Ren, sword still held at attention. The sword and the girl he no longer knew.

"I grew up without my parents and for what? A ruined kingdom and a divided country? Holding onto the memory of a dead king who left us in ruin?"

She looked to Geret, who hung his sword at his side, shrinking into the crowd.

"Geret? Where are your parents right now? They should be here. But they aren't because my father killed your father. They were best friends like you and Ren. How can we stand here day after day and worship the ground they walk on when they have caused so much pain?"

Geret clenched his teeth, his eyes falling to the ground, but he said nothing. He never talked about his parents.

"Gwen. Please don't do this." Ren stepped forward drawing his sword to meet hers.

Please.

But there was an emptiness iced over the crystal blue of her eyes when she responded. "You don't know the truth, Ren. Nobody here is innocent."

He leaned forward as his father called out, "Ren, don't!"

Gwen cemented her lips together, blinking a tear down her cheek.

Then, a man dressed in midnight entered the circle. He wore a black leather vest adorned with a barrage of buckles climbing up his chest. Black crow feathers fanned over a half cap floating over his shoulder armor. This was the same man he'd seen fighting his father earlier. A sword floated in the man's one hand, and he grasped Gwen's waistline with the other. She didn't even flinch, as though his touch was familiar.

A fire erupted in Ren's chest.

"Gwendolyn is right. There is nothing left in Camelot but the wicked. It's time for a cleansing. And a new reign." The man sneered.

"What gives you such a claim?" Galahad demanded from the circle of knights.

The dark stranger looked past Galahad, though, his eyes locked with Ren's father's. His father's face hardened, his jaw tight and his eyes narrowed into a scowl so dark and unfamiliar that Ren didn't recognize him.

The stranger sucked in his cheeks, curling his lips in satisfaction.

"He is from house Orkney," Ren's father declared with a dangerous edge in his voice.

Hushed gasps erupted through the crowd.

But Ren was still confused.

"Morin, Son of Sir Mordred." The dark stranger took a bow.

Ren's stomach dropped for the second time. Mordred. As in Arthur's illegitimate son, who declared war upon Camelot. The man who killed the king. Morin was that man's son, and until now, nobody had known he existed. None except...

Ren's eyes met his father's, but they gave nothing away as to how he knew. They both knew what this meant. Mordred was Arthur's only child, so he had a legitimate blood claim to the throne. Maybe the only one. And if this man really was his son...

Sweat dribbled down Ren's temple as fire burned in his veins. In that moment, he felt everything ripped from under him. Knighthood. Gwen. All the good Camelot had once been. Everything he worked for. It all disappeared in a moment.

"No!" Ren growled, narrowing his eyes at Morin, and he lunged in his direction, his blade aimed at the man's throat. His swing met a clang of metal that sounded through the square when Gwen's sword blocked his. She pushed him away, sending him stumbling backwards.

The action sprung everyone back into a barrage of fighting. Ren's father jumped in front of Ren, meeting with the blade of Morin's sword.

Ren pushed through the crowd, clashing swords with Gwen as the rest of the fighting scattered through the square.

"Was this your plan all along? Help me train for knighthood while you were doing this behind our backs? Why?" Ren dodged a blow as sweat poured from his forehead.

A furious red burned her cheeks. "You don't understand. It was different for you growing up. You had your parents. And the counsel. You don't know what it's like." Their swords danced until they were fighting in front of the burning tent. Townspeople worked to put out the blaze with buckets, but it was already out of control. Just like the fight.

"You are right. I don't know, but I know there has to be another way. You have to stop this, Gwen!" Ren paused in the middle of the action, catching his breath and locking eyes with her.

She clenched her teeth, blowing a controlled breath through her lips. "There is no other way." Letting out a scream, she landed an unexpected kick square in Ren's stomach, and he doubled over, gasping for air. Gwen was always fierce in training, but he didn't recognize this anger. How long had she felt like this and never told him? He thought they'd shared everything, but now he wasn't sure he knew her at all.

"Gwen, I—"

But he couldn't finish because a swirling fury arrived as Morin and his dark knights rushed the area.

Galahad arrived at Ren's side, squaring off with the others. But they were outnumbered, and the other knights were nowhere in sight. Even the castle guards were busy fighting their own battles.

Ren searched for his father, his sister, Geret. But he didn't see any of them. They were on their own.

"You've put on a good show, but it's time to accept defeat with honor," Morin said, sliding his bloodied sword into its sheath.

Ren looked at Galahad, who shook his head.

"You no longer have a claim here." Galahad spit, heaving in breaths.

"I have the only claim here." Morin turned to his band of knights, confirming his words with hollers.

"Camelot will never belong to a traitor, and that is what your family is. Your father paid for his sins with his life." Galahad squared his stance, pointing his sword at Morin.

Morin laughed. "My father, the traitor. You all love that story, don't you?"

"Story?" Ren asked. Galahad refused to meet his eyes.

Ren rounded his shoulders, taking in a deep breath. At least he would go out defending Camelot like the other knights, even if he wasn't one of them yet.

As they prepared to engage in battle with a dozen men, a charged pop shot through the sky, drawing their eyes upward.

Colorful lights erupted like fireworks, slicing through the gray smoke billowing from the burning tent and clearing the way for the twinkle of stars in the dark sky. Through the veil, a figure emerged, pounding through the air in a jolt of fiery energy. It landed on the ground between Ren and Morin's men.

The man, whom Ren did not yet recognize, wore tight brown leather trousers, his bare chest covered in clunky talismans peeping through an unbuttoned shirt. A long coat lined with fur hung loosely around his shoulders as he surveyed the scene.

"What a mess," he said. "I'm gone for a few years and utter chaos ensues."

Morin's eyes went wide, a snarl cracking his lips. "And who are you?"

The man smiled, pulling a wooden, cylindrical object from his pocket. Swirls of glittering metal laced the dark wood. He held it out in his palm as everyone's eyes fixed on the glowing object. Two wooden staffs shot from the side, and he twirled it around like a sword.

Suddenly, Ren knew who this was, but where had he been all this time?

Morin cried out something that Ren couldn't hear as a

powerful explosion ripped from the staff into the space, sending Morin and the rest of his men flying backward.

As they scrambled to their feet, a look of recognition dawned Morin's face. "Merlin."

With a signal, Morin commanded his men to retreat, and they headed away from the square. Meanwhile, Morin ripped through the buckles on his tunic, exposing his chest. Underneath, dark ink painted his pale skin with a tattoo centered over his clavicle in the shape of a black crow.

The charcoal ink churned and burned into the flesh of his chest until a black vapor erupted from the figure. Wings flapped violently, emitting more dark vapor clouds. Then Morin's skin faded, merging with the smoke until he was nearly translucent. One final smirk and he disappeared in a cloud of smoke, transformed into the winged bird. He sailed upward into the dark sky, disappearing out of sight

Ren searched the crowd for Gwen, but she must have fled on horseback with the rest of Morin's men. The sound of their brigade clacked over cobblestones away from the square.

"That was a neat trick," Merlin said, reaching into his coat pocket and retrieving a pipe. His staff glowed again, snapping back into its original form. A blue flame sparked at one end, which he used to light the pipe in his other hand. He took a long puff, blowing out white smoke.

Ren raised his sword. "We have to go after them!"

Everyone stared back at him, beaten and tired. He couldn't believe what he was seeing. Camelot's finest had given up. He found Galahad tending a wounded guard on the ground.

"Galahad. We have to rally everyone and pursue them. Morin can't attack us and get away."

Galahad, who had always been outspoken in their training, barking orders and pushing them to their limits, was now eerily silent. He shook his head and stood.

Merlin glanced at Galahad with bright eyes, passing the pipe his way. Galahad scrunched his face in disgust.

"You look different," Galahad said, pushing Merlin's hand away.

"As do you. The last we met, you were a wee boy with your voice cracking."

"And you were an old man with a silver beard and a bad back."

"Yes. Well, aging backwards for a wizard does have its advantages." He gave Galahad a playful onceover before turning his back and casually walking through town as if on a nighttime pleasure stroll.

Ren's blood boiled. A scream from the square caught his attention. A familiar scream belonging to his mother.

Running toward the sound, a small crowd had gathered next to a fountain again, but this time, their hushed mouths forced a shiver down Ren's spine. At the center, his mother kneeled over the body of Ren's father, violent sobs shaking through her.

A gurgle escaped his father's lips as he struggled for breath.

"Father!" Ren fell to his side, grasping at his tunic. "Get a healer! Now!" He yelled into the crowd and several people fled.

A dark stain at his father's side made Ren's stomach turn with sickness.

"Amren," his father's voice strained.

Ren leaned over him. "Yes, father."

He let out a groan, mustering the strength to speak. Ren shut his eyes and searched for the strength to listen. "Remember the code."

Ren nodded. "I will. I promise."

His father groaned, licking his pale lips, and whispered weakly, "It was supposed to be you."

A sticky wet tear slid down Ren's face, and he realized he was crying. "Father?"

His father blinked, his gaze wandering to Ren's mother and then to Emeli, who had found her way into their mother's arms. Then, he looked to the unseen space between this world and the next before his eyes went dark.

Ren shook his shoulders. A healer arrived and gently pressed him aside, but it was too late. He was already gone.

Above, the stars continued to wink behind passing clouds like the world hadn't stopped. Ren's eyes searched for something in them that would make it make sense, but the sky was an endless sea of black and the stars too faint to burn through the depth of despair.

CHAPTER

THREE

LINA

Lina hadn't slept soundly for weeks. She rolled over, knees curled into her chest, and a hushed groan escaped her lips. Tall pines rose up around her, and the last curls of smoke rose from glowing coals in the fire next to her bedroll. Her eyelids were heavy, and she fell back asleep, drifting into a battle as another nightmare laid siege to her mind.

Angry fire burned through the woods, turning a blooming canopy of trees to flying ash. It spread through the field surrounding the town of Camelot and crawled up their protective stone walls. Panic surged through the streets and people abandoned their homes as they choked on black smoke.

Lina was there, standing on the edge of the forest, watching the chaos. Sweat glistened along the hairline of her dark chestnut waves, sliding down her temple. But it wasn't only the town in danger. Echoed screams rose up behind her and she turned on her heels to find the fire consuming the forest. Her home. She wanted to run, to help her people escape the invading flames, but she couldn't tear her gaze from Camelot.

An army of castle knights marched out front the gates carrying buckets of water with their swords swinging from their hips. They doused the flames, but it did nothing to stop them, only spurred the fire on further as it devoured the walls, eating the town, home by home.

Beyond, the castle towered above the smoke, but the licking flames were at her feet, threatening the stronghold.

Lina turned to run, but something caught hold of her wrist. Someone. A boy, not a child, but not yet a man either, stood at the edge of the trees. She couldn't make out his face, which blurred into the smoky haze. He pointed at something behind her, and her gaze followed to the place where the fire circled a tower of stones nestled in a field of creamy white flowers.

The people's screams and the hissing of the fire faded behind her as she approached the stones. Veins of honey and slate swirled through the surface. It was beautiful, but she didn't understand what was so special about it.

A bird cawed overhead, catching her attention, and her eyes returned to the edge of the forest where the stone walls of Camelot lay in smoldering crumbles. Everything inside was gone. The people had been turned to ash, and the castle lay in ruins. Her stomach turned bile rose at the back of her throat.

The boy peered through the smoke, but she still couldn't see him clearly. The tip of his blade, however, was clear and pointed right at the center of her chest.

All the air rushed from her lungs.

A bright light exploded.

Lina's eyes shot open as she dug her fingers into the tunic over her chest, right where the boy's blade had been. Around her, the wind whistled through the hazy treetops, and a nightbird sang in the distance. Above, twinkling stars poked through a velvet canopy.

She sat up, rubbing the sleep from her eyes and wiping the sweat from the bronzed skin of her forehead. Her gaze penetrated the shadows of the trees, searching for the town of Camelot in the distance. They were probably fast asleep inside their protective walls, completely oblivious to the danger she had been dreaming about for weeks.

She knew those walls would not protect them forever. Stone couldn't keep everything out. Especially not an army of fire.

And then she thought, *then let it burn.*

CHAPTER
FOUR

FIRE DANCING ON THE WATER. THAT WAS EVERYTHING left of Ren's father's legacy. His funeral pyre burned bright against the morning mist floating over the lake. Amber flames carried yet another knight to the place beyond. One by one they disappeared, and the glory of Camelot with them.

The other knights, along with Ren's mother, gathered on the bank of the lake as charcoal smoke swirled from the burning boat and the last bit of fire smoldered into the clear water.

Emeli squeezed Ren's hand, her skin warming his palm. There were moments between them when words failed, that all they needed was to exchange glances and the other would know what they meant. In this instance, her reassured look was meant to be a comfort, but there was little she could do to ease his aching heart. All the same, he squeezed back and allowed her to lean into him before she joined their mother on the rocky shoreline.

"He's with his brothers now. At peace," his mother stated, turning away from the water and meeting Ren with her hand on his arm.

He didn't know what to say to her. He'd replayed that night in his mind over and over, trying to figure out what he could have done differently. If he hadn't let Gwen distract him, he could have stayed and fought alongside his father. But no, he let his emotions carry him away. She had escaped, along with Morin and his men. What were they supposed to do now, wait around for another attack?

Ren's forehead tightened—not with sorrow but something else.

His mother pulled him into her chest, squeezing, before locking arms with Emeli, and together they walked away from the lake.

Ren stayed behind, staring at the smoldering boat through the mist until the last of the knights left. Geret hollered at him to head back, but he waved him off. When he was finally alone, the wave of emotion took hold, and he fell to his knees at the water's edge. Sobs shuddered through him like a violent storm, shaking his core.

He couldn't accept that his father was really gone. He had failed to protect him. It was if someone cracked the foundation under his boots and he didn't know how to make it solid again. The air left his lungs, and he couldn't breathe. Couldn't think. Couldn't be.

And then there was Gwen. He still couldn't accept what she did. How could she betray them like that? Betray *him*. She would have been a knight and Camelot needed her. But she gave up and allowed her anger to burn too bright. Now she was with the enemy.

Fire burned in his belly as he rose to his feet, fists clenched at this side.

He wiped the moisture from his cheeks and cleared the ache at the back of his throat. Ren turned from the lake as the sunlight pierced the gray sky, casting shadows through the trees. Dust particles floated in and out of the light, holding Ren's attention with their graceful dance. The air changed, and a lighter sensation overcame him. His shoulder blades relaxed into his back.

His gaze fell back to the lake, to the water lapping against the rocks. But then the sound stopped. The waves froze as mist crawled backwards, receding from the surface of the lake to the opposite shoreline. A ripple moved across the surface, splashing the rocks at Ren's feet. He was glued in place, eyes fixed on the opposite side of the lake where a figure emerged, dark and shadowed at first. But then the edges of his body came into focus and his boots floated over the water, moving closer.

The features of the man took shape—a head of auburn curls wearing a golden crown, a robe of fine, vibrant wool falling to the surface of the water around his body. Ren rubbed his eyes, questioning his own sight. The man tilted his head with the slightest upturn in his lips, filling Ren with a comforting warmth. The hole in his chest shrunk a little.

This was no strange apparition upon the water. This was not a trick of Ren's mind or a hallucination from grief. Standing before him now was none other than the lost King Arthur. Instinct forced Ren into a kneel, where he bowed his head in the presence of the king. Dead or not, his mother taught him courtly manners.

"Rise, Amren, son of Sir Bedivere, who was my oldest friend," King Arthur commanded.

He obeyed, rising to his feet.

Ren's lips fused together as he struggled to speak. "Are you really..." He cleared his throat, remembering all those years ago when he last saw the king on this very shore. "Are you really him?"

Arthur smiled, his face a gentle, comforting fire in a dark storm. "Yes. Like a shard from a shattered sword."

Ren gulped. "Why are you here?"

"I come to you, Amren, because Camelot is in great need, and you may be the only one who can save her from ruin."

His stomach tensed at the assumption. He was nobody, not even a knight. A shocking vibration ran down his spine as he remembered the echoes of Gwen's name being called at the knighting ceremony instead of his. He clenched his teeth, trying not to show his uncertainty in front of the king. This had to be a dream. The grief of losing his father was too strong and he had lost his senses.

"I assure you. This is very real." The king's eyes sparkled, as if reading Ren's thoughts.

Ren raised his chin, eyes focused on the king.

Arthur continued, "Excalibur. You must find the lost sword to unite the lands against our common enemy. The time has come again for Camelot to rise and become the shining place it once was."

The burning ashes of Ren's father still swirled on the surface of the lake, but he swallowed his sorrow. "I would do anything for Camelot, but I'm not a knight. I couldn't even save my father."

Arthur leaned in, resting a hand on his shoulder, the same way his father used to do. A warmth pricked at his skin, magic racing through him.

"The heart of a knight is not given. It lives in you. You don't become a knight. Knighthood is already within you."

Arthur smiled, floating back over the water.

Ren nodded, dropping his mouth open to say something, anything, that would make him appear more confident in accepting the king's quest. But there were no words. He was so far away from being ready, no wonder they hadn't chosen him for knighthood. Standing before King Arthur now, he wasn't sure he would ever be ready.

"Remember your worth, Amren Bedivere." The king drifted back into the mist upon the water.

"Wait!" Ren called after him, but the king had already vanished through the veil where he came.

Ren stared down at the mud caked on his palms. Twice now, he had seen the king on this shoreline—once, while he was small, crawling through the mud to get a better look when the king was dying, and again now. Both times, he came away with dirt on his hands.

⁘⊹⁓ ⁻ ⁃

REN WAS in too much shock to return to the castle, so he took his time wandering through the woods, stopping in a meadow his mother frequented to collect herbs. A blanket of purple swallowed the ground, weaving in between trees and other wild plants and emitting a perfumed fragrance into the air. Ren squatted in the field, gently tugging flowers at the root, tucking them into a hip sack. He wanted to give his mother something to lift her spirits when he returned home, and he'd seen her use these in her remedies before.

Thoughts of the funeral and of the king's request weighed heavily on his heart, but the more time he spent among the cool breeze and the rows of trees, the lighter he became. There was something about being away from the castle's walls—the expectations embedded in stone— he didn't realize was so confining until now. Here, there was warming sunlight and shaking leaves and little else. Here, things were simple. Swords and stones pitted against earth and light.

When everything had faded into a whisper, it all came barreling in again as frantic voices echoed through the meadow. Ren's hand went to his sword as he cut through the flowers and crept into the forest. Just beyond was the King's Road, frequently traveled by all sorts of people.

A crash sounded, and he drew his sword, moving through the trees and crouching behind a raspberry bush. The burst of bright red was just starting to bloom, emitting a ripe scent into the air.

On the other side, a cart lay on its side, its contents scattered all over the road. A crate of apples had cracked open, spilling the red fruit everywhere. Jugs of something sweet-smelling dripped their contents onto the ground as well. This was a supply cart. Probably coming from or going to Camelot.

Ren quieted his breaths and listened for the source of the commotion. Two beige horses stomped at the front of the cart, still strapped within their harnesses, but the driver's bench was empty.

A holler behind the cart sounded with the clang of metal. Ren headed toward the sound, readying himself to jump into a fight. He peered around the backside of the cart, spying two men surrounding a Camelot guard clad in crimson and gold.

One man had shaggy, tangled hair, which hung in greasy strands over his forehead. His trousers were soiled, and his cloak tattered, and he juggled a short sword between hands. Another man with muscled arms covered in tattoos drew an axe from his hip and let out a deep grunt.

Bandits. Of course. They had ambushed the supply run.

"What crown? There is no king to steal from." The tattooed man replied to what Ren assumed was a command to surrender. "The way we see it, these goods might as well be ours." He rolled the axe around with a flourish as if he was familiar with the weapon.

Sword at attention, the guard lunged forward, slicing at the shaggy-haired one. The tattooed one came back with a swift kick to the guard's stomach, knocking him back. The guard was skilled enough to keep his balance, but his breaths had grown heavy, and the bandits outnumbered him. He wouldn't last long.

Ren readied himself to jump into the fray when a girl with

dark hair and bronze skin charged from the trees twirling a dagger in each hand. She moved with quick finesse, almost like a dancer instead of a warrior. Glints of gold flashed in strands of plaited hair pulled behind her shoulders. She was beautiful, which threw Ren, freezing him in his steps.

Lunging at the guard, the girl nicked his arm with one of her blades, forcing him to drop his sword. She had her dagger to his throat in an instant as he pleaded for mercy.

Ren needed to do something. He darted from behind the cart, his presence surprising the girl enough for her to raise her blade from the guard's throat. As she did, the guard scrambled back on his elbows, reaching for his sword in the dirt. But the tattooed man was there, slicing at his side with his axe.

It happened so fast. The guard cried out and Ren jumped out in front. "Stop!"

The girl lunged, her blades clashing with Ren's sword. She yelled something to her companions that sent them retreating into the trees. But she remained, her eyes trained on Ren's, and he knew she wasn't going to give up so easily.

They danced, dodging, weaving, and kicking up dirt. She had better reflexes than him, moving with fluid grace and anticipating his every move. He'd spent years training with the other knights, but he wasn't prepared for the way she sparred.

He let out a frustrated groan, plunging his sword into air because she had tilted her shoulder at the last minute, dodging his blow.

A flash of a smile crested her lips, and Ren's cheeks flushed.

He couldn't let up, not for a moment. A thrill raced through his veins. Every attack with his blade was parried by one or both of her daggers. She twirled around him until his head was light and he stepped back to catch his breath.

"Not bad for a castle puppet," she said, studying him with narrow eyes.

"I make my own choices." Ren returned, rolling his neck over his shoulders and cracking the tension. This was his chance to do something good in the midst of a horrible day. The least he could do was bring these supplies back to Camelot. "You can't have them."

"Says who?" She spat on the ground.

Ren's mind went blank. He realized his name wouldn't mean anything to this girl

"What is it to you? They don't need them. They hold up behind their walls, stuffing their faces," she said.

"We..." Ren paused, clearing his throat as they both slid their boots over the dirt as they circled one another. "As a knight of Camelot, I can't let you take them."

The girl laughed. "You aren't a knight."

Ren clenched his teeth. How would she even know that? He thought he looked like a knight. All those insecurities swam up inside again. "And how would you know anything about knights? You steal what you want, only thinking of yourself."

"Are you serious right now?" she returned. "I know because there are only a few knights remaining in this forsaken kingdom. They are old and don't care for anyone outside their precious castle." She shot Ren a burning stare as if he was responsible. "Knights are a dying breed."

What did this girl know? Ren swallowed the rock at the back of his throat, holding back the wave of emotion threatening to crash over. His father was a knight. The best one.

He jumped forward, slamming his shoulder into her side. It was enough to knock her off balance, allowing him to get a leg behind her knee that sent her crashing to her back. The force expelled the air from her lungs and sent her coughing. In no time, he had placed the tip of his blade at her throat.

His eyes flickered over her figure, studying the golden ink stains running along her skin in symbols and patterns he didn't recognize. They ran down her neck, disappearing under the ruffle of her shirt. Lingering on the tattoos, his eyes lifted to her face again with a strange flutter in his chest.

He poked the blade further forward so that it grazed the skin of her neck.

She hissed, wincing away. "You think this is mercy, when really it's control."

Again, Ren was at a loss for words, but he had to say something. "I still can't let you take what isn't yours. And you are coming back with me."

She narrowed her eyes, wrinkling her brow like she was plotting a counterattack. Physical or verbal. To his surprise, she leaned back on her elbows, dropped her daggers, and raised her hands in surrender.

"Fine. Take the cart to feed your over-stuffed pigs while the rest of these lands starve." She grimaced and leaned forward. Ren followed her movements with his blade as she rose to her feet. "But I'm not going with you."

Ren pressed his lips together. "Yes, you are. Do you really think I'd let you go after what you and your group of bandits just tried to do? What's stopping you from attacking the next one?"

"Nothing. I won't promise you that, but do you see that man over there?" She flicked her gaze to the guard slumped against one of the cart's wheels. His breaths were shallow, his eyes drooping. A dark stain at his side oozed blood under his pressed hand, dribbling onto the soil in a black puddle.

"He won't survive if you spend any more time attempting to bring justice. I won't go with you easily, and he needs the attention of a healer. So, knight boy, you can either make me pay for this crime or save his life."

She tilted her head to the side and studied him.

Ren's face grew hot as a surge of anger burned through his veins. His sword arm trembled. Actually shook. He'd already lost too much. There would be no more funerals in Camelot if he could help it. It was what his father would do.

He dropped his sword to his side. "If you touch this stash before we come back to retrieve it, I will send all of Camelot out to hunt you down." It was harsh to say, but Ren was out of pity.

And with that, he kicked her daggers into the nearest bush and waved his sword. "Go."

She locked eyes with him—those dark, shining eyes setting fire to his skin. Then, twirling on her heels, she hopped through the bush, grabbed her daggers, and ran into the forest.

Ren's gaze lingered on the tree line to make sure she didn't return with the others, but after he was certain they weren't coming back, he rushed to the guard's side. Ripping his tunic, he banded it around the man's side and helped him to his feet.

They approached the horses, unlatching them from the cart. Ren slid the man onto the horse, mounting behind him. The guard thanked him in a weak whisper before they sprinted up the road, heading back to Camelot.

All the while, Ren thought about how the strange girl had made his aching heart race in a way only one other person had.... and that hasn't ended well.

CHAPTER
FIVE

GWEN

GWEN RODE WITH MORIN'S DARK KNIGHTS, THEIR crow flag flying the skies above their horse brigade like pirates on the water. The news of Morin's attack on the castle had cleared the route through once dangerous lands, so nobody dared stand against them. Even so, arriving in Orkney after days on horseback had left Gwen exhausted and sore. And stinky. She longed for a hot bath.

Castle Orkney, a crumbling facade chiseled out of the red sandstone cliffs with dark limestone pillars, was perched on a single sea stack jutting out of the water. Forming its own island, it towered a few hundred feet above sharp rocks and storming seas. Only a single rope bridge connected the towering castle to the mainland, making it nearly impossible to invade. This allowed Morin's grandfather, King Lot of Orkney, to hold reign over the surrounding land for centuries, even after his death.

Gwen cared not for any of that as she stormed through the front iron gates, meeting with glowing lanterns and the steady beat of drums deep in the heart of the castle. The noise vibrated the stone walls, fueling her steps. Arriving in a vast room exploding with scandalous frivolity only grew her rage.

Ignoring the dancers wearing nothing but chainmail as they gyrated around the room, Gwen strode past the candlelit crowd in search of Morin. A servant stopped her, offering a bright colored drink from a tray of exotic fruits and sugary pastries. She shooed her away, crossing the room to the other side where a grouping of velvet chairs sat with an army of people she didn't recognize.

She spotted him through a series of glowing balls of light that made the room spin and caused nausea to roll in her gut. Pushing it down, she headed straight for the center of the lounge.

Morin sat in an oversized chair padded in thick leather. One leg draped casually over the side, and he wore the tightest trousers Gwen had ever seen. In fact, she wondered if he was stuck in that position, and it nearly shook her from the storm raging inside. Nearly.

When she approached, the men and women fawning over Morin gave her no attention, and that was fine because her stare burned only in his direction.

"What the hell was that?" Gwen shouted over the noise. Now the others were paying attention, throwing glares her way, likely annoyed that her entrance had disturbed their careless existence.

"Ah! Gwendolyn. You've arrived. Safe travels I hope?" His smooth tone showed no sign of the chaos he'd left in his wake back in Camelot, further stoking the flames of her anger.

"I didn't help you escape the dungeons so you could kill the people I know and care about." Her words caught at the back of her throat as she remembered her fight with Ren and the bodies littering the ground when she fled. "You were supposed to storm the party. We had a plan. Nobody was supposed to get hurt."

"What are empty threats worth? Force was necessary, and I can't help it if their show of bravery got in the way."

"Show of bravery?" Her voice cracked as the fire consuming her belly threatened to burn her from the inside. Taking a steadying breath, she focused on Morin's smooth umber eyes. "You killed him. Ren's father."

She'd seen his body on blood-stained cobblestones. The knife that pierced her heart felt just as real. He didn't deserve it.

Morin lifted his chin. "A debt repaid."

It took Gwen a moment to understand what he meant, but the sharpness in his eyes and the vindictive undercurrent in his tone gave him away. "It was Sir Bedivere, wasn't it? The one who killed your general?"

Morin had told her about his father's loyal general who had stuck around after Mordred's death to command their army and work with Morin to grow it even further in the years that would follow. Even though Morin hadn't admitted as much, she got the sense that this general was more present as a parental figure than his real father had ever been. But she wasn't here for his revenge plot. "Why didn't you tell me?"

Morin clicked his tongue. "Some secrets are best kept close to the chest, don't you think? The same way you didn't tell me his son—Ren, was it?—was a friend?"

Gwen's chest tightened.

When she didn't answer, Morin furrowed his brow. "More than a friend, I see. Either way, don't worry about him. We accomplished what we set out to do. Now they know they aren't untouchable. Their idleness will be the death of them."

Gwen shook her head. "All the stories on the road spoke about the wicked son of Mordred, come to finish what his father started."

Morin's lip twitched. He turned to a woman with tight braids and a translucent slip dress tracing circles around the steel spikes on his leather shoulder armor. He brushed her off, and she floated away with a dreamy look in her eyes.

Morin stood, gripping a smooth obsidian cane and motioning with it for the others to leave as well. Once they were alone, he leaned in close to Gwen's ear and whispered, "And?"

Her blood froze and shivers raced down her spine. She blinked, trying to make sense of the nonchalance of his response. "I never signed up to slaughter my friends. I only wanted them to see that their knights aren't what everyone says they are... so we could tell them the truth." She let out a shuttered breath. The realization of what she'd done settled in her bones.

Morin wrapped an arm around her shoulders, pulling her into his side. The scent of his sweet breath and earthy musk made her head light. "You have lost sight of why we are here, beautiful one. Do you remember when we first met?"

Gwen nodded. How could she forget?

It was a feast night in the great hall, the snowstorm outside shut out by frosted glass and the stone inside warmed by the roaring fire. Laughter echoed throughout the room as the noble families gathered with members of the counsel. They announced their intention to name the next knight of Camelot, and since Ren was the eldest of the group, he was the favorite.

Even so, when two of the most spoiled brats Gwen had ever met from one of the other houses claimed Ren was the only one they would ever name, he stuck up for Gwen. He stuck up for all of them, exclaiming that any of them was better suited than he was. Ren was always like that. Looking out for her.

When she joined the group wearing a sparkling dress, her hair twisted into intricate braids and with jewels at her neck, the two brats had looked her up and down, twisting their mouths into sneers.

Edward, the oldest one, sporting perfect hair but reeking of his family's goat herds, stepped forward. "This is who you say is a better fighter than you?" His eyes roamed over Gwen, burning her skin. "She's a looker, but she'd be better suited on the arm of a knight, not fighting with one." He let out a laugh, as did his friend, whose name Gwen had already forgotten.

Ren surged forward, and Geret had to hold him back, but not before Gwen stepped in front, drawing her sword and pointing it directly at Edward's chest.

"Want to test your theory?"

Edward passed a smug look to his friend. "That wouldn't be fair... for you."

"Oh. Okay, how about I handle you both, then?" She tilted her head to the side, lowering her sword. "If you are afraid a girl will embarrass you, I understand."

That seemed to wipe the grin off his face and they both agreed to a duel in the courtyard.

Gwen smoked them of course, but it was what happened after that changed everything.

Edward was on his butt, mud soaking his pristine trousers and his now-not-so-perfect-hair flopped over his eyes. He growled, rising to his feet. "You think you are so good, but you will never be a knight in Camelot. Not after your father and mother soured their vows, betraying the greatest king we've ever had. That was the beginning of the end. Look where that got them. Looking where it got *you*. You are only an orphan taking advantage of everyone's pity." He spat on the ground, and this time Ren and Geret together leapt forward, but Gwen stopped them.

"They aren't worth it!" she yelled, pressing into Ren's chest and offering a sneer at a sour-looking Edward.

She convinced Ren and Geret to back down, and they returned to the great hall for the feast. Gwen pressed into the walls at the side of the room, letting the cold shadows swallow her. Even though she hated to admit it, something Edward had said struck her in the heart. They were right. Her parents were enemies of the kingdom, and she had grown up alone because of it. Of course they didn't want to name her. They could never.

Tears pricked at her eyes. She rushed out of the hall, traveling down, down, down, until she stood in the dungeons. Sitting against the cold hard stone, she let the despair take her, let its cold hands wrap around her shoulders until shivers overtook her body.

Her sobs echoed through the empty space. Then, somewhere amongst the steady drip of water coming from a leak in the ceiling, someone had coughed. She was certain of it. The sound stilled her heart as her eyes searched the dimly lit cells.

"Don't stop on my occasion. I too cannot stand parties." His alluring voice traveled from the furthest cell and Gwen stood, padding over the hard, stone floors and squinting into the shadows. On the wall, a torch flickered, but it wasn't nearly enough to illuminate the entire space.

"Who are you?" She retrieved the torch and swept it across the iron bars of the cell. In the corner, a figure sat on a cot, his arm draped lazily over one knee. But he didn't move when she approached; he simply turned his head away from the window.

Instead of answering her question, Morin continued, "I prefer more intimate affairs." That was a complete lie because Gwen knew Morin better now, but then again, his honeyed voice had drawn her in and she planted herself in front of his cell, studying his figure.

After a while, he swung his legs over the edge of the bed and rose to his feet. As he approached the front of the cell, Gwen's breath caught at the back of her throat, and she stepped backward. Dark hair fell over his shoulders and rough, uneven stubble peppered his jawline. His thin frame stood before her, his dark eyes tracking her movements.

A smirk played over his lips. "Why would a beautiful young woman have cause to cry all the way down here?" His gaze swept over her figure, though her dress was torn, and her hair had fallen from its plaits. But it wasn't unsettling as Edward's had been. It was pitied. That's when she noticed the redness around his eyes and the slight puffiness of his lips. Like he'd also been racked by violent sobs that night. They were quite a pair.

Suddenly self-conscious, she averted her eyes. "That is none of your concern."

"I see." He shifted his stance. "You come down here to my home to disturb my peace, and now I'm being rude?" He clicked his tongue.

Her eyes flicked up to his. "Nice home you have here. Do you host visitors often?" The brightness of the snow outside filtered through the barred window high above his cot. The stench of rot and urine and wet earth permeated the space, and Gwen had to hold back a gag, covering her mouth in the crook of her arm.

There was no telling how long he'd been in there. Depending on the severity of his crime, it could have been days or weeks. Years, even. She hadn't taken much interest in the happenings of the dungeons or in the laws maintained by the counsel and the knights. Perhaps she should have. If she had, she would have realized sooner how much of an outsider she was. That simple fact was becoming clearer every moment.

In the time her mind was occupied, Morin closed the space in the cell, now standing just out of reach behind the bars. Gwen's stomach tensed and she let out a gasp, stumbling back until her back pressed against the opposite wall. The narrow space between them was still too little, and every warning instinct she had fired inside.

But she couldn't look away because he was rolling a stone between his fingers, water dripping down his palm as if he had plucked it from the puddle in the cell.

"Everything you think you know about Camelot is about to change, Gwendolyn."

Her name coming from his lips stilled her heart, and she dropped open her mouth, whispering, "I'll ask again. Who are you?"

His gaze flicked to hers as the stone moved through his fingers faster and faster until it was a whirl of water and earth, and he flung it forward at the bars. Instead of crashing through as she expected, it melted into the iron, freezing each bar into an icicle.

She crept forward with curious steps, reaching a finger toward the shimmering substance. When she touched the glassy surface, it hissed, burning her finger. She snapped back her hand.

"I'm the only person who's going to tell you the truth," Morin responded with a mischievous spark behind his eyes.

With his arm still draped around her back in Castle Orkney, the memory faded, and Morin's voice brought her back to the present. "We did nothing wrong. They weren't ready for the truth, but sometimes it takes a tragedy to set things in motion. It will come out when the time is right, and when it does, both our names will be unsoured."

Gwen thought she detected a slight tremor in his voice, but when she opened her mouth to speak, Morin had reached into a leather pouch at his hip to grasp at a shimmering pearly powder, which he blew into her face.

Stunned, her eyes glazed over, and the room blurred. Then, the tension in her shoulders eased and a euphoric sensation took hold, causing her to forget why she was so angry. It was a welcome relief.

He leaned in with a hand to her waist, guiding her through the room. "My Gwendolyn. You are tired from the journey. We tested the strength of Camelot and found them wanting. If it weren't for that meddling sorcerer, we could have taken every-thing from them right then. But..." They arrived at a narrow stone stairwell at the far end of the room, and he took her hand in his. "More forces are required. In the meantime, my dear, go get cleaned up and have a rest. You've earned it."

Gwen nodded through her daze and turned to glide up the stairs, leaving Morin to his party with a strange ache in her heart.

CHAPTER
SIX

LINA

Lina took her time returning to camp, stopping at a gentle stream to watch the clear water move rhythmically over colorful rocks. The sound usually soothed her, but even the trickle of water couldn't douse the burning frustration swirling around her chest.

Sved and Drogo would be back at camp by now, empty-handed and with their tails between their legs. The supplies they had planned for weeks to intercept were sitting rotting in that abandoned cart, and there was nothing she could do to make it up. Supply carts only arrived every few weeks, except for this week, when Camelot needed a surplus for the lavish feast they were holding.

What a waste! All that food just for show.

They would have succeeded if it weren't for that boy who had interfered. If he had been alone, Lina wouldn't have worried but judging by his fine clothing and how shiny his sword was, she knew he was from Camelot. More would come, and she couldn't risk being arrested for thievery. Their numbers were already too few. Other druid clans had already abandoned these lands, migrated to other parts of the country, or traveled by boat across the sea. They were alone.

And she called *knights* a dying breed.

The boy's face flashed in her mind—hazel eyes, dimples softening his chiseled cheekbones, and that stupid, messy sandy brown hair that made it look like he had just woken up. Somehow, there was a familiarity to him, as well. It was something she couldn't place but gnawed at her insides like a wild dog with a bone.

Heat rushed her face, and she shook it away, pushing all thoughts of him from her mind. But they kept coming, fueling her anger.

Who did he think he was ordering her around? She hadn't seen him on patrol with any of the guards before. He was too young to be one of the knights, and why was he out there in the woods, anyway? Wasn't Camelot recovering from the attack the night of the feast? Didn't they have wounds to lick?

Letting out an exasperated sigh, she stood from the stream and noticed a rip in her blouse. She stuck a finger through and brought it back wet with blood. A nick. A small one, but a nick nonetheless. It was something hardly anyone could do because she was fast, and most fighters were too untrained or too slow. Or both. This boy had been neither. He was good. Too good.

She splashed water on her face, the cold stinging her cheeks. She then ripped the end of her tunic, tying the strip of fabric around her arm. Deciding she would not show up at camp empty-handed (unlike Sved and Drogo), she wandered upstream for a while, stopping at berry patches and collecting plump, wild raspberries and depositing them into a satchel at her hip.

She stopped at a part of the stream widening into a curve, fashioning a fishing pole from a sturdy branch and stringing together a line with a hook from her pack. Digging for worms, she attached one to the end of her hook and slid to her bottom at the edge of the stream, dropping her line below the surface of the water.

A cool breeze floated through the trees, and the songs of birds echoed along the bank. It was, by all accounts, a lovely day. Warm but not stifling. The air of spring carried the scent of fresh vegetation and perfumed blooms. This was the kind of day Lina normally spent out in the woods alone, hunting, or practicing her fighting footwork. She didn't mind moments of solitude.

Growing up with the druids was a communal experience, as they relied on each other for survival. They had to provide food for the group, hunting or trading for goods with small villages. They relied on one another for protection from neighboring bandits or the occasional drunken rogue looking for a fight. But far worse was the threat of those who viewed practicing the old religion as a dark art that should be eradicated.

While most had abandoned the kingdom of Camelot, the druids remained. This was her home, and she refused to leave because things had changed. She had a right to be here and so did the others.

She bobbed her line in the water, but still there were no bites. Letting out a frustrated growl, she dropped the branch.

Patience was not her strength. That's why their plan for seizing the food cart was such a good one. They would have to move camp soon, and stockpiling supplies would allow them time to find a better location, provide themselves with more protection, and settle into a daily rhythm instead of worrying where their next meal would come from.

Thinking of the boy and his lean muscles, she knew he didn't know what it was like to starve. He did not have to sleep on the ground in the cold or move from place to place out of fear. No, all he knew was a cushioned life inside Camelot's protective walls and a soft bed in which to sleep soundly.

Frustration took hold all over again, and she yanked her line from the water, snagging the hook in a bush.

She let out an exasperated groan. This couldn't stand. She needed to get back to camp so they could make another plan, one not so easily thwarted by chance. Because that's all it was. Chance.

The boy was lucky to come upon them and she would likely never see him again.

If she did, it would be too soon.

CHAPTER
SEVEN

REN LEFT THE INJURED GUARD WITH THE TOWN healer, who swore the man would live, but he could not motivate himself to return home after the day he'd had. Instead, he entered the Rose & Crown sometime around twilight when the shadows crept over cobblestones and all the good people of Camelot retreated to their homes. The good people.

Pushing his way through the grime-soaked jackets of travelers and stumbling over a burly, peg-legged man perched on a barstool with a flask in hand, Ren considered if he was a good person.

What that girl had said back in the forest still haunted his thoughts.

Knights are a dying breed.

What did she mean? Knights were the only ones still trying to keep the peace, and they were the only ones still providing aid where it was needed. Like his father with the fire in Willowdale.

His throat tightened as he realized that the fire in Willowdale couldn't have been a coincidence. Morin's knights were already within the walls of Camelot when the fighting broke out. Perhaps the fire in Willowdale had been started to distract the knights so the intruders could sneak in.

His father had always tried to do the right thing, but in this instance, it had made them vulnerable.

A curvy barmaid approached carrying a wooden tankard brimming with amber liquid and creamy foam sloshing over the side. In her other hand was a plate of crusty bread. "Coin?" she huffed.

Ren hadn't planned on drinking anything. He just wanted to go somewhere where nobody would notice him, but he needed a distraction.

Nodding, he reached for his leather satchel only to realize he'd left it in the meadow along with the flowers he'd wanted to bring home for his mom.

The woman gave him a tired expression. "You must buy something to sit. Now, get." She pointed a plump finger toward the door.

Ren sighed. He couldn't seem to do anything right. Why had Arthur chosen him at the lake? Why give this important, world-saving quest to someone who wasn't even a knight, and... what had the girl said?

Your kind, whatever that meant. He wasn't anything. He couldn't even afford a drink at this lowlife tavern.

Letting out a heavy sigh, he stood from the stool, distracted by a commotion at the front of the tavern—a skirmish between two men fighting over something. One was the shady fellow with the wooden leg and the other...

"If you don't think I will take that wooden leg of yours and beat you with it before I sprout a slimy squid leg from the hole, then you don't have a very wild imagination, do you?" Merlin fumbled with something in his pocket. He was dressed in the same fur-lined coat as the other night, with a yellowing shirt underneath and his long hair tied into a bun.

"Merlin! There you are." Ren rushed toward the skirmish, wrapping an arm around Merlin, who swayed into his side. "You didn't see me." He shot his eyebrows to the ceiling, hoping he would catch the hint. "We are at the back."

Ren guided him to the empty table, but Merlin turned, giving peg leg man a warning glare. The man seemed unbothered, though, and took another swig from his flask while rubbing his wooden leg, no doubt contemplating if Merlin really could make him grow a squid leg.

"I don't think squids have legs, by the way." Ren waved at the barmaid. "They have tentacles."

"That's what you think." Merlin said with a crooked smile.

The barmaid thrusted drinks into their eager hands and winked at Merlin, who gave her a sheepish grin.

"I don't want to know," Ren muttered, taking a swig of his drink.

"So, young knight. What brings you to the underbelly of Camelot? Girl troubles?" Merlin lit a short pipe with his staff-lighter-thingy and puffed a cloud of smoke at the peg leg. Somehow, the smoke shot through everyone else in the tavern, landing right on the peg-leg's head like a bucket of water. He didn't notice, too distracted with tickling the barmaid's side and tapping his flask on the bar for a refill.

"Don't call me that," Ren replied. "I'm not a knight." Then the truth hit him like a sack of grain to his gut. "And I don't have a girl, not anymore. I don't want to talk about her."

"Fine." Merlin took another inhale of his pipe.

"We burned my father today," Ren said aloud.

"Ah, yes. Sir Bedivere was one of the good ones. I knew him from the time he was a young lad as yourself, and when Arthur reigned. He was loyal to the end, your father. My condolences." Merlin tapped his cup on Ren's, signaling for them both to drink.

"Oh, and King Arthur had the nerve to appear to me afterward to send me on some quest to save the kingdom." Ren didn't know why he blurted it out, but he waited for Merlin's response.

With a straight face and the pipe dangling from the corner of his mouth, Merlin replied, "Yes, he tends to do that."

"What?" Ren's bottom lip dropped. He had expected a shocked response.

Merlin shrugged. "Do you think Arthur would have the balls to stay in the afterlife after all the work he put into shaping Camelot into the shiny coin it is? The work we did was exhausting. Arthur could be a real piece of work, you know." Merlin's eyes drifted to the wall behind Ren with a dreamy expression, curling his lips into an annoyed smile.

Ren glanced behind him to find nothing there. "He asked me to retrieve the sword Excalibur to unite the lands." He drained his cup, slamming it a little too hard on the table, rattling Merlin's staff-lighter-thingy.

Merlin eyed him suspiciously, covering the contraption with one hand and sliding it away from reach.

A slight buzz raced through Ren's mind, either from the tavern drink or the frustration growing inside. Why did Arthur choose him? Why not Galahad, Percival, or even Merlin?

Merlin twirled a small, blue flame within his fingers, fire springing forth and singing a piece of hair fallen from his bun. He blew it out, watching the smoke from his burnt hair with a sad expression.

Well, maybe not Merlin.

The wizard rose from his chair and retrieved two more silver goblets from the barmaid.

"Seems like you could use something a bit stronger, young knight."

Ren shot him a glare.

"Er... young Bedivere. Ren." He passed over the goblet.

Ren stared down at the thick liquid smelling of honey and rye, but he didn't drink. He was too upset and confused. Instead, he gnawed on a piece of stale bread while Merlin drank both goblets, and he helped his stumbling figure leave the tavern before heading back to the castle.

"AND THEN, this one time, your mother caught all the knights in a pissing contest—a literal pissing contest—in the middle of town square. She was so angry with your father, I don't think he returned to training for a week after that."

They both laughed. Merlin let out a giant hiccup, swaying into Ren as they entered the throne room. During the day, it would be filled with golden sunlight from the stained-glass windows lining one side. On the other, crest shields were mounted on the wall with colored banners from all the Knights of the Round Table. Crimson and white for Lancelot, purple and gold for Percival, royal blue and white for Kay, silver and red for Galahad, black and red for Bors, green and gold for Tristan, and violet and yellow for Gawaine, Geret's father. Lastly, there hung the yellow and red for Bedivere, which was Ren's house, but he wasn't certain if it still belonged to him now that his father was gone.

At the end of the room, Merlin ran a finger over the carved Pendragon figure etched into the wooden frame of the throne, chiseled from the finest dark wood and inlaid with gold. The seat, covered in a padded leather, had remained empty since Arthur's death. Now, a thin layer of dust coated the arms.

Merlin eyed the throne for a moment, looking like he was

about to slump into it and pass out, but his face sobered and he glanced at the sealed door behind the throne instead. Ren knew that door because it had always intrigued him as a child. There was no knob and therefore no lock, and it was always closed tight. He remembered one time while wandering around the castle after a nightmare, he found himself standing in front of it. He had leaned in, pushing as hard as he could to open it, but it never budged. Here it was, still closed, its mysteries forever kept secret.

Merlin wiped his hand over the brass rivets along the door, clearing the cobwebs and pressing his palm against the wood. Whispers filtered from his breath, and a golden glow radiated behind the door frame.

To Ren's shock, the door creaked open, and Merlin slipped inside with a devious smile.

A wave of musty air attacked Ren's nose as he covered his face in the crook of his elbow. The room was pitch black, and his voice echoed when he called out.

Stumbling over something solid, he cursed at the darkness, but still no answer from Merlin.

Ren's heart sped. The buzz he had acquired at the inn was gone, replaced by something different, something defensive. He gripped the solid mass in front of him, waiting for his eyes to adjust to the dark room. Then, there was a flicker of blue light on the other side, followed by a crack, and the lanterns ignited all around the space, illuminating the darkness.

Glowing spots flickered in Ren's vision before the room came into focus. It was as large as the feast hall, only this one was circular and fortified with stone arches. Dusty windows lined one side. A thick film coated the glass but allowed starlight to filter through the smudges. An enormous hearth, unused for a decade or more, sat on the other end of the room piled with a mound of black soot. When Ren noticed what he had in a death grip, he understood why.

A round table carved from stone and inlaid with fine wood stood in the center of the room. A thick dust covered the surface, and Ren swiped his hand across the top, revealing intricate carvings. Merlin stepped forward, his demeanor suddenly shifting. Gone was the goofy drunk burning his own hair. This Merlin was taller and looked older too, somehow.

"I don't think I need to tell you what this place is," Merlin said.

"No." Ren blinked his eyes in disbelief. It was a sobering moment.

Everyone thought the Round Table had been destroyed in the great war, Arthur's last battle at Camlann. But here it stood, right in front of him.

"I can't believe it."

Merlin flashed him a toothy smile.

"Why has this been locked away all this time?" Ren was still in disbelief. How could they hide away such a legendary thing all these years when it could have been used to help the remaining knights and bolster confidence in the kingdom?

"Do you see the number of emblems etched on the surface?" Merlin asked.

Ren's eyes darted around the table, taking a quick count. "Twelve."

"Yes, twelve. Twelve Knights of the Round Table. This table represents balance. With the king slain, and so few knights remaining, this table could not be used. It holds no power. The balance has been disrupted for too long."

Merlin overturned a chair, plopping down with a dust cloud and propping his feet up on the table.

Ren's mouth fell open. He shouldn't have been shocked. This was Merlin, after all. He did what he wanted, coming and going, disappearing for over a decade and then returning as if nothing had happened. Even so, this table was sacred, and Ren was certain whatever sludge lay at the bottom of Merlin's boots was far from sacred.

"Why did you bring me here?" Ren asked. He suspected he knew the answer, but he needed him to say it. He needed someone other than a ghost to tell him the years he spent training weren't for nothing, that not everyone who witnessed miracles during Arthur's time was dead. He needed someone to tell him that there were miracles yet before them, that Camelot was worth the fight.

Merlin let out a loud yawn like he hadn't slept for years. "Arthur was right, damn him. He always is. It is time to resurrect Excalibur."

The words hung in the air like heavy dust threatening to choke the air from Ren's lungs.

"And Arthur came to me because..."

"Because he believes you to be worthy. I don't think he is far off in knowing that the best of his knights weren't only those who won glory fighting by his side in all those battles. The best were those who remained at his side until the very end."

"My father."

Merlin nodded. "Noble knights are not born of chivalrous acts and good looks. Sometimes, the most worthy are those performing the deeds that go unnoticed by history done by those who hold everyone else up in their glory."

Ren swallowed against the scratchiness in his throat and fought back the stinging tears in his eyes.

"And I am his son."

Merlin nodded.

"Are there others?" Ren asked because there was still an empty throne out there. Someone had to fulfil that destiny too.

"I think he made himself quite known the other night, didn't he?" Merlin stated, and Ren already knew who he was speaking about.

"Morin." He hadn't meant for his name to come out in a growl, but it did. He was Arthur's blood heir. If it was anyone's destiny to retrieve the sword and claim the throne, it would be him, and Ren couldn't bear that.

Anger pulsed through him, and he pushed away from the

table, rising to his feet to pace the room. "We can't allow Morin to find the sword and take Camelot!"

Merlin picked at his teeth with a splinter ripped from the table. "That's the spirit!" He gave Ren an encouraging, though patronizing, fist in the air.

"He killed my father. His father killed the king. This must stop. Someone has to stop him!" Ren was fuming now. Heat swarming his chest.

"You tell him!" Merlin roused.

But then it hit Ren—the sword. Nobody had seen it since Arthur's passing. It had disappeared into the lake that day.

"Merlin, how do we get the sword?"

Merlin leaned back in the chair until one of the aging legs gave out from under him and he toppled to the floor. Wiping the dirt from his coat, he stood and cleared his throat. "Don't worry about that. Pack your things. We leave at first light. I know just who to ask," he said with a twinkle in his eye.

CHAPTER
EIGHT

REN AND MERLIN TRAVELED A WELL-WORN DIRT ROAD through Caledonian Forest in the morning mist. Merlin told him old stories about his father—stories he was glad Emeli was not around for, as they would have set her cheeks afire with embarrassment. They were stories of his romantic trysts before he met their mother, stories about his time with the other knights on hunting excursions, and stories about his bravery on the battlefield. Each loosened the knot in Ren's stomach a little.

He wondered if his father would approve this quest or if he would have found another way to defend the kingdom he had dedicated his life to protecting. Ren realized he would never truly know.

The knot wound a little tighter, and even with Merlin by his side, the loneliness crept inside like an unwanted visitor.

By early afternoon, the sky had turned gray, and gentle rain pattered on the treetops. Ren pulled his cloak from his bag, clipping it over his shoulder armor and pulling the hood up over his head. Despite that, the dampness settled into his bones as they continued into the darker part of the woods.

The worn path morphed into rock, and thorny, overgrown bushes stretched over the path, snapping against their horses' legs. Occasionally, one such tangle would jump out and snag a tail, and they would have to stop to free the poor beast. Eventually, it became easier to continue on foot, dragging the horses behind them.

A rustling in the bushes set Ren on high alert, and he drew his sword. Even Merlin reached for his pocket staff, igniting the end in flames, his eyes focused on the commotion.

Something large stumbled through a bush, getting his pant leg caught on a thorny branch. "Ouch!" the figure yelped.

Ren dropped his sword, letting out a relieved sigh. "Geret, what the hell are you doing out here!"

Geret fumbled with the tangled branch until a petite hand reached forth, releasing the branch from his leg, and Emeli stepped out.

"Not you, too!" Ren huffed, flinging his hands in the air.

"There you are. We've been tracking you two all day. I feared we would always stay a step behind." Emeli rushed to Ren, squeezing him into an embrace before slapping a stinger on his arm.

"Ouch!" Ren rubbed his arm. "You shouldn't be here. Go back!" Ren pointed in a random direction he hoped was toward Camelot.

Emeli rolled her eyes, crossing her arms. "Excuse me? When did you become Father?" Her eyebrows shot up. "You are the stupid one who decided to go out alone on some scavenger hunt while the rest of Camelot prepares for war."

"He's not alone," Merlin chimed.

Emeli shot him a fiery glare looking exactly like their mother. Merlin winced a little.

"Besides, who says you get to have all the fun," Geret added.

Emeli's nostrils flared. "Fun? Like the time you and Ren dragged me along to search for pirate treasure in that sea cave during high tide and we nearly drowned? That kind of fun?"

Geret backed up into the bush that snagged him, as it was less thorny than Emeli at the moment.

"Stop, you two. This isn't a joke," Ren interjected. "I wouldn't be out here unless it was important."

Emeli shifted her stance, tugging at the strap of her leather pack. Her eyes tilted toward Ren. "I'm sure you think it is, but you can't do this, Ren, it's not safe..." There was a slight crack in her voice that broke him a little.

He knew she was thinking of Morin, who could attack Camelot again at any time. But Ren couldn't retreat to the safety of the castle right now, not while he could make a real difference with the sword. Besides, seeing the Round Table again ignited something in him he was missing. A sense of adventure. Of duty. Something he could do to make his father proud. If the counsel didn't think Ren was ready to be a knight, he needed to show them how wrong they were.

He clenched a fist at his side before blowing a puff of air through his nostrils. "I can't go back, Em." Ren put both hands on her shoulders, lowering his voice. "This is something I must do."

Emeli chewed her bottom lip and sighed. "I don't understand. We can't just let you go into the wilderness with some mad wizard—"

"She has a point," Merlin interrupted, leaning his back against a tree trunk.

Emeli gave him a side eye and continued, "—With some mad wizard by yourself."

"Yes, I can." The edge returned to Ren's voice. "This is something I have to do on my own."

Emeli stomped her foot and snapped a branch, which echoed off the trees. "Says who?"

Ren looked at Merlin, who offered nothing useful but a shrug.

"It's just one of those things." Ren turned his back, continuing on his path. Maybe if he walked away, she would see how serious he was and give up.

"Wait!" Emeli hollered after, stomping much louder than necessary. "Ren! You stop this minute!"

"Go home, Emeli," Ren ordered, this time with a more commanding tone. He was done playing with his sister.

"Absolutely not," she argued, keeping his pace.

Ren groaned. His sister was not supposed to be a part of this. It was his quest, his burden. Having her around would only complicate things. Besides, he didn't think he could stand something happening to them. He'd lost too much already. "Geret, get her out of here." Ren swiveled on his heels and Emeli nearly ran right into him, stumbling over her feet to stop herself.

"Excuse me!" she fired back.

Geret sheepishly slinked behind, face red, but said nothing. At least he was smart enough not to get in the middle.

"Don't you understand what this looks like, Ren? We were attacked, Father is gone, and everyone back home spent an entire day arguing over what to do next. And here you are, abandoning us. Abandoning me!" Her voice cracked again, the freckles on her face reddening.

Ren let out a weighted sigh. "That wasn't my intention."

Tears sparkled in Emeli's eyes.

"They really spent the entire day arguing?" Ren asked, hoping the change in subject would stop the waterworks.

Geret jumped in, his face alight with excitement. "They found the room behind the throne and turned it into a war room. There was a map and everything. The elders showed up. They were counting allies."

Ren pursed his lips. "Really?"

"Kent, Nemeth, Deorham, and Cornwall. Those are the ones they are sure would come to our aid...or pretty sure," Emeli said, looking a little brighter. Though, Ren detected a hint of skepticism in her voice.

An uneasiness turned in his gut. He wasn't certain those alliances were as strong as they once were. They hadn't been tested since Arthur's time.

"And the table? Did you see it?" Ren asked.

They both shook their heads. "They pushed it aside and covered it with a dirty old cloth," Emeli said. "I'm not sure what Percival was thinking, but he, Bors, and Galahad had some secret conversation before any of it started. They think they are the only ones left who can make decisions."

Ren shook his head. Still, they refused to use the table, even after Merlin left it right there for them. He didn't understand it at all.

Merlin sauntered up behind them, twirling his staff, which was now extended and used as a walking stick. "Sometimes age does not denote wisdom."

They peered at him.

Then Geret's eyes grew wide. "Oh! I almost forgot! Galahad was asking for you."

Merlin tilted his head in an interested gaze.

A smile grew over Geret's lips. "He was pissed. You should have been there, helping them, I guess. He thinks you are held up in some brothel causing trouble."

Merlin's cheeks reddened. Emeli giggled, and they all relaxed their shoulders. It was just what they needed to lighten the tense mood.

Ren turned to Emeli. "Fine. You can come, but it could be dangerous."

Emeli nodded her head and turned to Geret. "Geret, too."

Geret flashed her a look of surprise. "Weren't you saying earlier you didn't want me coming with you because you didn't need chivalry?"

"I don't, but since you are the slowest runner because of your...bulk... you will prove a nice distraction if we're ever chased by wild beasts." She pressed her lips together to hold back a laugh.

Geret flexed one arm, a rippling muscle hardening. "I think what you meant to say was, because I'm the strongest I will be excellent protection for the group."

"Are you sure about this?" Ren asked Merlin.

Merlin's eyes lit up. "I don't know, but I believe there is something in that Knight's Code of yours that says, 'Stronger together.'" His brows shot up.

Ren dropped his head back, staring at the leaves swaying in the breeze overhead. A chill ran over his arms. He had to bring up the code, didn't he?

"You two better keep up. We don't have any time to waste," Ren directed, continuing onward along the path as Emeli and Geret jogged behind.

"Great. Now, what are we doing exactly?" Geret asked, and Emeli huffed an annoyed sigh.

Merlin's lips curled into a grin. "Adventure, young knights. Adventure!"

CHAPTER
NINE

THEY ARRIVED AT A FOREST GLEN TEEMING WITH GOLD petals and cobalt bell-shaped flowers. Tall green grass shot up from the ground, circling a small lily pond, and a stream emptied fresh water into the pond on one end. As Ren stared at the stillness of the water, something wasn't quite right about it. There were no ripples on the water, he realized. The lilies on the surface floated placidly, almost like statues, even as the stream emptied into the pond. No splashes. No sounds.

A chill raced over Ren's arms as he stared at the pond. Frosted rocks met with a layer of ice at the water's edge, but glancing around the glen, everything else was in full spring bloom. A floral sweetness and heady wet earth swirled around the space, but this pond appeared as though it were in the depth of winter, the ice stretching over the water's surface as if protecting it.

Merlin approached, picking up an icy rock and dropping it. He yelled a string of curse words and did a little dance, shaking his hand. The rock had left a pink burn in the palm of his hand.

"What the—" Ren was about to ask when Emeli shouted at Merlin.

"What are you doing?"

They all looked on in horror as Merlin eased himself into the pond, his body erupting into shivers. Wading into the center of the pond until it covered his waist, his teeth clattering together, he chanted words under his breath.

Ren bounded to the shoreline to wade in after him, but his feet slipped on the icy rocks, and he tumbled to his bottom.

As Geret helped Ren to his feet, Merlin lifted one hand. "Shh. You'll scare her away. Damn kids."

Then, bubbles rose to the surface in the middle of the pond— a few at first, but more simmered quicker and quicker until the whole pond was seething with them. Vapor clouds popped from the surface, freezing into glass orbs and shattering into tiny icicles. Slivers flew in every direction as Ren covered his head and Emeli and Geret cowered to the ground.

When the shattering ice stopped, they rose to find Merlin standing frozen in the middle of the pond. Small trickles of blood slid down his face and over the exposed flesh of his collarbone, but he stood his ground as a woman's head emerged from the depths. Swirls of shimmering silver hair surfaced first, floating around her as she rose. A silver crown graced her head with pearls and sparkling blue jewels. Her face was pale and translucent, almost liquid, like she was a part of the water. Icy lips and white eyelashes fluttered against dark, unnaturally wide eyes.

As she rose, the folds of her dress stretched over the surface of the water, pressing against her curves and taking shape.

Her wide eyes fixed on Merlin's face and blinked before she curled her lips into a smile of recognition. "Merlin. It has been many years since our lips last met."

The woman drew Merlin into her chest and pressed her mouth to his, sucking on his bottom lip.

Ren flushed, looking awkwardly away, as did Emeli.

But Geret had dropped his mouth open, gawking. "Ya know, he's kind of cool."

Ren shook his head, turning back to the pond. "Uh huh, but he's also an idiot." They hadn't spent as much time with Merlin as Ren had. They would see it soon enough.

Merlin erupted into a crazed laughter, pushing the woman away and stumbling back to shore. Water dripped from his jacket, hitting the earth in a billow of steam.

"Woman. You are the reason for our separation all these years."

"Of course." She pursed her lips into a sly smile. "How did you escape the caves?"

Merlin shot the group a skeptical gaze before waving off the question. "That is a story for my next visit. We have come for another matter. One of the utmost importance."

The woman's eyes fell upon the rest with a slight twitch in her lips.

"Amren and Emeline, children of Sir Bedivere and Geheret, son of Gawain." She announced their names as if they were entering a party, tilting her head forward with her gaze burning.

Ren looked at Emeli before stepping forward. "We need your help." He cleared the nerves from his throat. "Are you the Lady of the Lake?"

He suspected she retrieved the sword all those years ago when his father cast it to the lake. It made sense that Merlin would go to her now with the sword in question.

Merlin gave him a nod, confirming his suspicions.

The woman's face shimmered under the sun, ice crystals slithering up and down the side of her face. "I am."

"We've come for Excalibur. Do you still have it?"

She answered in a voice laced with honey but burning like bee stings. "I am the keeper of the sword, but I cannot help you."

Ren's stomach sank.

"Why not?" Emeli stepped forward and stood next to her brother.

Merlin's eyes turned wild, and he glared at the Lady of the Lake "Nimue. You must help with this. You owe me that."

"I owe you nothing," she spat back. "You served your time and balance is restored." Her lips pressed together, and her body hardened, the fluidness of the water seeping into her solid skin.

"You don't understand. Camelot is under threat and Arthur sent us to retrieve the sword. Don't you know what that means?" Ren pleaded but stumbled backwards when the woman rose higher in the water, shooting cracking ice bubbles in his direction.

The ice burst around everyone's heads, but not one touched them.

Ren's legs trembled.

"Be careful, young knight. Daring to question my knowledge of the world beyond the veil of Avalon is something few survive." She lowered herself back into the water, her face melting from the hard stone it had been. An orange fish swam up her dress, circling her neck and diving back down into the pond, disappearing into the depths.

Merlin chuckled. "You haven't changed."

A sly smile cracked behind her lips.

Ren didn't understand their relationship at all.

The woman, Nimue, spoke in a softer tone. "I would help you, but I cannot because I no longer have the Sword of Power."

Ren's eyes cast downward. She couldn't be convinced because she didn't have it. Looking to Merlin, a rock embedded in Ren's gut. Merlin's lips had pressed together in a line and the crinkles around his eyes deepened. He didn't know about this either.

Nimue continued, "The magic of Avalon is dying. Excalibur was no longer safe with us, so I hid it where nobody would dare venture."

Merlin's eyes grew wide, and a shade of green tinged his cheeks.

"And where is that?" Ren asked in a shaky voice, although he wasn't sure he would like the answer.

A shimmery frost circled Nimue's cheeks. "Merlin knows it well."

They all turned to look at Merlin.

He grasped at his coat like it was a comforting pet, stroking and petting the fur-lined edges. "You would do something like this," he bellowed in a not-so-playful, dangerous even, tone.

Nimue tilted her head to the side. "I'm sorry, but it had to be done. We had no choice." Her jaw flexed but the rest of her face remained hard as stone, except for the warning in her eyes aimed straight in Ren's direction.

Chills ran down Ren's spine. "What? Where is it?"

Merlin sucked in a breath and rolled his neck until it popped. "Nowhere good, I'm afraid. Excalibur rests in the one place I cannot help you retrieve it, as it is the one place from which I have just escaped." His eyes fixed on Ren's. "And it took me ten years to do it."

"The cave," Ren gulped. Everyone knew the story of how Merlin had been trapped in a cave somewhere under the mountains. He had thought it was only a story, though, something Merlin came up with to explain the reason he left the kingdom. Ren always assumed Merlin was traveling the world doing... well, Merlin things.

But the grave look in Merlin's eyes confirmed the truth of it.

They were screwed.

"The druids call it os-nàdarra bàs," Merlin said. The group

wrinkled their brows in confusion, so he clarified: "magical death."

Yep. Totally screwed.

Ren's chest squeezed and he looked at Nimue. "You are a sorceress of Avalon, aren't you? Can't you get the sword back for us?"

"Technically speaking, she's a Naiad, but we won't hold that against her." Merlin winked at Nimue, and she stuck her tongue out at him like a child.

Just like that, doom and gloom became playful flirting, which only made Ren's frustration grow. "Okay, but you can still help us retrieve the sword, right?"

Nimue's face melted, droplets sprinkling the surface of the water like tears.

"I'm afraid not. Once the sword left Avalon, I could no longer touch it, nor provide aid to anyone seeking it."

"Well, that's perfect, isn't it?" Geret, who had been suspiciously quiet, threw his hands in the air. Apparently, he was short on patience for these games, too.

Ren turned to the wizard. "Merlin?"

Merlin shook his head in despair. "She's right. She can't help us, and even worse, I can't either." He placed a hand on Ren's shoulder, leaning in. "I'm afraid you will have to complete this quest on your own. Arthur's intention, I suspect." He winked playfully. It was intended to soothe Ren's nerves but proved completely ineffective.

He breathed a dejected sigh, and Emeli squeezed his hand. A noble attempt, but it also failed to make him feel better. He had hoped for just a few days' journey to retrieve the sword, giving them time to mount a defense against Morin's next attack, but this wasn't going to be that easy. This was a quest for a real knight, and Ren still wasn't one.

Nimue's mesmerizing voice spoke in perfect harmony with the lapping waves. "I would also caution you, Amren Bedivere, that Excalibur holds powerful magic and could be a great asset to your kingdom. However, there is still much we do not know about it, and the consequences are beyond our sight. There was a reason your father returned the sword to Avalon when he did."

Goosebumps erupted on Ren's arms, and he rubbed his hands over them. As ominous as the warning was, what other choice did he have? He couldn't return to Camelot empty-handed. They needed him, and besides, he needed a win. "It's the only plan we have, and I intend on seeing it through."

"Very well. Good luck, Amren Bedivere." She bowed her head and sank back into the pond, disappearing below the surface.

The water went placid once again, and the ice crept over the surface until it covered the entire thing. As the group left, the trees closed in, shading the entrance and making it impossible to distinguish from the rest of the forest.

Even if he had wanted to, Ren knew he would never be able to find it again.

.·_¦·_ _ _

THE GROUP JOURNEYED to the end of the forest, stopping to make camp as a green twilight descended upon the trees and the glow of fireflies twinkled through the bushes. Merlin took a swig of something emitting a smell of burnt tar, passed it to Ren, and then to the others as a rabbit roasted over a campfire.

They passed the time telling stories until they were crying with laughter and ready to pass out.

"Why did Nimue trap you in those caves, anyway?" Ren asked, letting out a yawn and rubbing the chill from his arms.

"Oh. I killed her sister," he admitted, taking another sip from his flask and scrunching his nose at the taste.

"What?" Emeli exclaimed, falling off her stump.

Geret rushed to help her up, but she pushed him away, wiping the dirt from her riding trousers.

"You've heard of the sorceress Morgana, Morin's grandmother?" They nodded. "Right, so you know she deserved it."

"Well, that explains a lot," Ren muttered under his breath.

Geret sucked in a frigid breath and grew serious. "What is this beast thing guarding the caves? That's the story, isn't it, Merlin?"

Silence.

Well, not quite silence. The hoot of an owl sounded nearby, and the echoed snap of branches in the distance set Ren on edge. It wasn't like Ren hadn't considered what kind of terror awaited them, but he had hoped to delay the conversation for as long as possible.

"I'm not sure, actually," Merlin replied.

"What do you mean you aren't sure? Didn't you have to fight the thing to escape?" Emeli asked.

A mix of amusement and terror flashed over Merlin's face— quite a feat for a hundred-year-old-but-late-twenties wizard.

"It changes form with every encounter. What I had to escape may very well differ what you all will face."

Emeli gave a shifty glance in Ren's direction.

"How is that possible?" Ren's throat had gone scratchy thinking about the possibilities. Would this beast have sharp teeth and razored claws, or would it be something with poisoned skin that melted flesh from your bones? He shivered.

"It's a chimera," Merlin responded matter-of-factly, blowing a swirl of smoke into the fire, which took the shape of a winged lion with a cloven hoofed goat's body.

Geret looked the most confused of everyone with a twisted gnarl at his temple.

"Don't they teach you anything in lessons these days? A chimera is a monstrous enigma that could turn up as anything," Merlin explained.

"A what?" Geret moaned.

"Half-beast, half-human, half-goat, half-bird." Merlin counted out on his fingertips, a twisted confusion knotting his brow. "That's too many halves, but you get the point. Whatever form it wants to take in the moment is what it is. It mostly shifts shapes based on its opponents. Their fears, weaknesses, deepest subconscious thoughts."

Geret released his shoulders from his ears. "Oh, a half-goat doesn't sound so bad."

A sly smile formed on Merlin's lips. "It would be if that goat had rows of razor-sharp teeth, the speed of a lion, and an appetite for human flesh."

Geret gulped.

Emeli gripped her bow like it was going to spring forth from the fire right then.

"What form did it take for you?" Ren asked, again uncertain he wanted the answer and thinking he should probably stop asking these questions.

Merlin's face turned pale, and he frowned. "We don't talk about that."

Ren knew enough not to push the subject. Instead, he asked something practical. "Okay, so how do we get to the caves?"

Merlin sketched a map from their current location to the mountains where the cave should be, but then he gave them a grave expression. "I have a feeling there will be another journey taking place." He eyed the group, searching for someone to chime in with the answer. "One from the land of Orkney." His brows rose.

"Morin," Ren returned.

Merlin nodded. "I can't see everything, but I have a sneaking suspicion he also will be interested in this quest."

Panic flooded Ren's chest in icy waves. "But how would he know? Arthur only told me, and we only just learned where it is from the Lady of the Lake."

Merlin shook his head, handing the map to Emeli, who volunteered to keep it safe. Then he leaned back, observing the twinkling stars overhead. "Like I said. Perhaps I'm wrong."

Ren glimpsed the map before Emeli carefully stuffed it into her backpack. If Morin knew where to look, his journey would be shorter than theirs; his castle was far north along the coast with nothing between them and the cave but a few towns and a wooded forest.

Nobody was in a mood to tell any more stories after that, so they drifted off to sleep next to the crackling fire under bright stars. Sometime later, Ren awoke to a stirring in the distance. Something was sneaking through the bushes, and his breath puffed in the cold air as a shimmery frost coated the ground.

Approaching the sound, he found Merlin packing their horses. "You were going to sneak off, just like that?"

"Just like that," Merlin confirmed.

"What will you do?"

"Camelot needs me as they prepare for war. I suspect they are running around like chickens with their heads cut off without me."

Ren laughed under his breath, thinking about Percival attempting to rally the drunk and old people of Camelot to arms. They would need everyone to mount a proper defense. Worse, Galahad, who complained about training a bunch of teenagers, would have to train them.

Ren's amusement shifted to an emptiness inside. "We need you, too. I don't know how we will manage it without you." Ren stroked the mane of the beige horse, refusing to look Merlin in the eye.

"You are more capable than you know, young Bedivere. You will see."

Although the words were intended to provide comfort, Ren still didn't have the confidence everyone seemed to think he did. He had committed to this quest, yet what had changed? He was still not a knight, Camelot was still in danger, and now he had dragged his sister and his friend into the fray.

Merlin laid a hand on Ren's back. "Remember what I told you. Stick to the route and take caution. The chimera is not the only monster in these lands."

Not exactly the pep talk he was hoping for.

Merlin smiled, the light in his eyes visible under the starlight. "You'll be fine. Besides, who has the scarier quest, you or me? I have to stand next to Bors and protect not only the castle but also my dinner." He mounted, grabbed hold of the reins, and tugged both horses away until they disappeared into the thick forest.

A wave of anxiety wrapped around Ren's shoulders. Now they were truly alone.

CHAPTER
TEN

LINA

A COLD SWEAT CLUNG TO LINA'S BACK AS SHE AWOKE
with a start. Sitting from her bedroll, she dug her knuckle into her
temple where a dull ache pounded in her head. She'd had another
dream of Camelot. It was the same. A fire spreading. The piled
stones. And him, face obscured, watching her. This time, though,
instead of pointing the sword at her, he was trying to hand it to
her. But she refused, a racing panic flooding her chest.

Now she was sitting in her tent, the morning's first light not
yet casting a warm glow through the fabric. She shivered, rubbing
the chill from her arms and wrapping a wool cloak around her

shoulders. Spring may have been in full bloom, but the chill remained in this part of the woods, even during the day. It wasn't always so. The warmth of the world used to unfurl like a flower petal, spilling light through the trees. Now it was only cold.

Trying to fall back asleep proved useless, so Lina crept out of her tent to find a crackling fire nearby. A shadowed figure crouched next to the embers, warming their hands.

She wandered through camp past linen tents and drying animal hides. The chill spurred her pace until she stood at the fire pit. Nearby, stoneware and pots hung from trees and piled over a small, wooden table. They prepared all their communal meals here and it served as a gathering place to tell stories and sing songs.

An ache bloomed in her chest. Soon, they would have to move camp, just when this one was starting to feel like home.

"Morning," the gruff voice of Ragnor greeted her as he stood. His towering presence always made Lina feel small, even as she'd grown into a young woman. His hair was braided into a bun this morning, the silver streaks barely visible in the dim light.

"You couldn't sleep, either?" she asked.

Ragnor sank onto a tree stump next to the fire and sipped on something thick as tar that smelled bitter. "I never do, but not for the same reason as you."

Lina wrinkled her nose, joining him next to the fire. The warmth floated over her cheeks, and she let out a sigh, relaxing her tense shoulders under the cloak. "I don't know what you mean," she said, but she could sense his eyes wandering over her face, where heavy bags clung to her eyes. He always knew when something was bothering her. That's what happened when you raised someone as your own child.

"Still having those dreams, I see," Ragnor noted, taking another sip of the sludge in his cup.

Lina nodded but swallowed, saying nothing. She smoothed her hair back, working to braid it around one shoulder.

"You know that sight of yours should serve as a warning. I remember you used to have bad dreams as a kid, but I don't recall you having them as a young woman." He dropped the cup from his mouth. "Until recently."

"It's nothing. Like you said, just a bad dream." She forced a smile.

They sat in silence for a moment, staring at the flickering flames making shapes in the darkness and listening to the sounds of the forest waking from its slumber.

"I'm going hunting," she announced, rising from her seat, but Ragnor grabbed hold of her wrist. It was a gentle grip for such a large man. A familiar touch.

"I would be cautious, Adelina. Something is coming. I can sense it with the animal migrations, and now you are not sleeping. We should prepare ourselves."

"Prepare ourselves for what?"

Ragnor sniffed the air like a wolf before releasing her arm. "I do not know, but these things are never chance. The attack on Camelot. The supply run failure. Things are changing, and we must protect our own."

He gave her a warm smile, and she squeezed his shoulder in return.

"I will be back before sunset."

Lina packed her hunting supplies and left camp with a knot in her belly. Things were changing. Ragnor was right; she just didn't know what that meant for her and her people.

RETURNING to camp around hazy twilight, Lina had a successful day with rabbits strapped to her belt and fish dangling from her pack. Large game eluded her, but still she gathered wild mushrooms, berries, and other plants to make a tasty stew that would feed everyone for days.

She was feeling better. Proud, even. Until a gust of wind brought the smokey scent of roasting meat her way and a wave of chatter came from the fire pit. She approached, setting her pack down and unstrapping the rabbit carcasses from her belt.

"Lina!" Sved, sloshing something over the cup he was holding, greeted her, and the group that had gathered around the fire glanced up. They were all holding cups, and a sickening sweetness clung to the air.

Ragnor stood from his seat with his arm stretched out and brought her close to his side. Heat radiated from his sweat-soaked skin, and body odor assaulted her nose. Still, she forced a smile.

"You have returned to find us up on our luck, daughter." The scent of alcohol hung on his breath, making her stomach roll with nausea. Plus, he only ever called her daughter when he was drunk. So, great, they were all completely drunk. That's why their voices were so elated when she arrived.

"What are we celebrating?" She eyed the liquid in Ragnor's cup, deciding the syrupy texture had to be mead. They had little mead and usually saved it for special times. This must have been some news.

Ragnor swayed, dragging her toward the group. The clan sat in a circle, cups in hand—Sved and his two brothers, all the same thin, wiry figures with brown skin and pointed facial features, Drogo and his wife, Sigrid, a tall woman with thick, frizzed, blonde hair, and Fin, a younger man with fiery curls. Plates clanked together, and Lina could see they had devoured something meaty. Bones scattered all over the ground, and juices still smeared over their mouths.

She was hungry upon returning, but now she wasn't so sure, gripping the sides of her stomach and swallowing back the acid rising in her throat.

Ragnor handed her a cup with only a sip of mead left at the bottom. "You said we needed a new plan, and luck presented an opportunity today that will allow us to barter for everything we need with Camelot." His eyes scanned the faces of the others, who all lit up.

Lina wrinkled her nose, though, pushing the cup away. "With Camelot? What do you mean?"

She didn't like the sound of that. Their alliance with Camelot had ended with Arthur's death over a decade ago, hence the supply thievery.

Drogo belched, laughing. "I don't think she will believe it until she sees." His eyes flashed to Ragnor, who gave Lina a sly smile.

"Go and look for yourself. In the goat pens."

Lina gave them a shifty gaze before wandering away from the warmth of the fire and toward the other side of camp.

As she approached the pens, a small goat bleated, and all three goats that were normally kept inside were tied up to a nearby tree and munching on grass. Inside the pens, three indistinguishable lumps stirred.

Lina checked over her shoulder, and the sounds of Ragnor and the rest went back to making noise around the fire, talking and laughing. She crept closer to the nearest pen, peering through the bars. A body moved, rolling over and groaning. A young boy. Ruffled chestnut hair, dimples, and a face she cared not to remember.

He groaned again, fluttering his eyes open and rubbing this head. It took him a moment, but when his vision focused in the dark, he caught her eyes. "It's you!"

"It's you!" Lina returned, whispering and hushing him with her hand. "I knew you were stupid, but I didn't realize you were this stupid."

She crouched low to the ground and his eyes widened as he looked around the wooden pen. He scanned the area next to him where the others were rousing: another boy with dark skin and curls and a smaller figure, a girl, Lina realized, with flaming red hair.

What had they done? Lina's stomach dropped.

Returning to the boy, his hands gripped the wooden bars of the cage and shook it violently. "You can't keep us here!" The cage squeaked and groaned, and she quickly grabbed hold of his hands, intending to stop the sound. But when her fingers grazed his, an image flashed in her mind—the boy from her dreams, only this time his face was crystal clear because it was the same one before her now.

The image burned away as fast as it had come, and she found herself fallen back to the ground on her butt, beads of sweat burning her brow.

It was him. In her dreams. The realization made her head spin, but she didn't have time to think about it because the boy was at the other end of the pen now, stretching out through the bars.

"What happened, Ren?" the small girl squeaked from the far pen. "I remember setting out on the road and coming to a junction where we paused because you had a bad feeling."

"He was right about that bad feeling," the other boy answered from the middle.

"We were ambushed," Ren said.

"By them!" Ren pointed at Lina with a fire in his eyes, voice raised.

Lina jumped to her feet. "If you know what's good for you, you will shut up," she urged in as much of a whisper as possible, checking over her shoulder again. The ruckus from the fire still echoed through camp.

"Do you know her?" the girl asked.

"No!" Ren answered immediately. Then his eyes met with Lina for a moment before they flashed back to his friend. "I mean, we met. Once."

"Yeah, when you spoiled our loot on the King's Road." Lina leaned in through the bars.

"What? When was that?" the other boy asked.

Ren glared at Lina. "They were stealing. They are thieves."

Lina blew air through her nostrils and rolled her eyes. "You don't know anything, do you?"

She didn't know why she was entertaining any of this. She backed away from the pens and paced with her hands on her hips.

"I demand you let us free," Ren said in that arrogant tone, like he didn't realize the situation they were in.

Lina threw her hands up. "Yeah, okay."

Ren continued yelling at her back as she walked away, frustration burning inside her.

What was Ragnor thinking taking them? These were the children of the Knights of Camelot.

She stomped back into the fire circle, hands in the air and voice raised. "Have you all gone mad? Do you know what you've done?"

Sved ran a hand through his greasy hair. "We've saved us. You're welcome."

Lina shook her head, turning to Ragnor and hoping he would have some sort of explanation that made sense. "Well?"

"They were wandering where they shouldn't have been and started a fight. We ended it."

Lina crossed her arms over her chest, head fallen back so she could stare at the charcoal clouds floating overhead. Stars winked in and out.

"Don't you understand where they are from and who will come looking for them if they don't return home tonight? They are teenagers, Ragnor!" Her eyes met his again, but he could barely hold them open. He'd drunk far too much to listen.

"It's fine. Now we have leverage. We make a trade. Their knights for the supplies you failed to get. It's that simple."

A huff escaped Lina's lips. "Unbelievable. You think they are going to make that trade? What keeps them from sending their full army in here instead? We don't have enough people to defend against that. Who will die because of your stupidity?"

Ragnor's face hardened, and he ground his teeth. Lina immediately regretted saying it, but that didn't make it any less true.

Rather than wait for his lecture in front of everyone, she stormed off back toward the pens.

"Where are you going?" Ragnor called, his boots stomping on the ground behind her.

"Going to check on—" The doors to the pens hung open. Panic rose in her chest as her eyes searched the camp. They were gone.

Then, a few feet away, she spotted them rummaging through a cart where their weapons were piled.

Oh no.

"Hey, wait!" Lina hissed, but as they turned toward her sound, Drogo had his sword pointed right at them.

Ren raised his sword and lunged forward, knocking Drogo back. The rest of camp roused, and more people ran toward the commotion.

Lina darted toward the trees, circling around the backside. She had to stop this before Ragnor and the others killed a group of teenagers. All of Camelot would be upon them before they could flee, and that wouldn't be good for anyone. She didn't want to start a war they couldn't finish.

"Where do you think you are going?" Ragnor growled at the group.

Lina peered behind the closest tree, watching.

"I think we've worn out our welcome," Ren said, moving so his body stood between his friends and Ragnor.

He was brave, at least. Stupid. But brave.

"You've worn out your welcome when we ssssay you've wornnn out your welcome." Ragnor slurred his words as he pulled his axe from his hip.

"Ragnor. Go piss on a tree or something." Lina jumped between them, drawing her daggers from her hips. Ren and his friends were at her back, and everyone else in camp closed in around them. She didn't even know what she was doing, but she couldn't let them slaughter teenagers. And Ren... her dream... it wasn't a coincidence that she had run into him the other day. It certainly wasn't by chance that they ended up here now. She didn't know why, but they were important somehow. She felt that she was supposed to do something. What that was, she didn't know yet, but she would start by making sure they all made it out of this alive.

"Adelina. Traitor." Ragnor spat on the ground, squaring his shoulders but still swaying.

He was too drunk to think straight. She wouldn't be able to talk him out of this. Plus, she eyed the growing numbers in front of her. Fighting her own people wasn't something she wanted. She had to think of something.

Moving both daggers to one hand, she reached into the pouch at her hip and slid her fingers around a small sack of powder.

Ragnor's eyes widened. "I don't understand. Why help these strangers? Do you know what you are doing?"

"Not really," Lina answered, and it was the truth. "But there is something bigger happening. You said it yourself, and they have something to do with it. I just need to find out what it is."

Behind her, Ren grunted. "We don't need your help."

Lina glanced back. and the bigger one was holding Ren at bay, shushing him.

"What if this boy betrays you?" Ragnor asked, and Lina's gaze returned to the man who raised her, the only person who she was certain she could trust.

The image of Ren holding the sword out to her in her dream swam through her mind. Chills raced across her skin. She couldn't trust him, but she knew he had a part to play in stopping whatever was coming. She was tired of making enemies instead of allies. This way, she would know for sure what her future held because she would hold it in her own hands.

"I'm sorry, Ragnor. I have to do this." Without warning, Lina squeezed the sack of powder, whispering into her palm until a warm glow illuminated the dark. Then she threw it directly at Ragnor and the others, where it exploded into a blinding light and filled the space with dark smoke.

She tugged on Ren's hand, dragging him into the trees and shouting at the others to run.

The bewildered screams from camp fell away the further into the woods they ran. The darkness in the forest was blinding, but Lina knew these paths well. She led the others around obstacles, darting around trees and guiding them through as fast as possible.

Once they were far enough away, all sounds of camp disappeared, and they stopped to catch their breath.

"What... was... that?" Ren sucked in heavy breaths and the other two caught up, leaning over themselves.

Lina sighed. They had made it. At least for now.

"What?" Lina realized she was still holding his hand, dropping it instantly as cold air brushed against her palm.

They stood in silence for a moment and listened. An owl hooted in a nearby tree and the leaves shook in their branches in the wind. But there was nothing else. Ragnor hadn't ordered the others to follow. He had let them go.

Her shoulders relaxed. At least he had some sense or cared enough about her to let her choose her own fate. Either way, she now had time to think about what came next.

The girl with the others giggled. "Whew, that was close!" She swung a pack from her back, digging around inside until retrieving a small lamp. She used a fire steel to light a coil of rope soaked in oil, and it ignited in a whoosh. A soft glow illuminated the clearing.

Peering around the trees, everything seemed quiet enough.

Lina squatted to the ground, pressing her hand into the earth to steady her racing heart.

"What was that all about?" Ren was standing over her, demanding answers. Everything happened so fast, he was bound to be bewildered, but she wanted to play with him first.

"Again. What?" she replied with an innocent tone.

"What?" He threw his hands in the air.

"Were they going to cook us for dinner or something?" he asked, making it sound barbaric.

Lina rolled her eyes. "Maybe."

When he didn't look amused, she sighed "Of course not.

They wanted to barter with Camelot for those supplies you stopped us from taking. That's all."

"Barter?" the girl approached with her light, illuminating Ren's eyes with a glint of amber and green.

Lina turned to her. "Yes. That's all we wanted. They weren't going to hurt you... I don't think."

The girl gulped, looking at Ren. "Ren?"

He shook his head. "I still don't trust it. This could be a trap. How do we know she hasn't led us away from camp so they can surprise us in the dark and leave us defenseless."

"You aren't defenseless." Lina's eyes flicked to the sword in Ren's hand.

"You know what I mean. I don't trust you." He stepped forward, eyes set on hers with a scowl on his lips.

He was serious. Even after she helped them escape. She didn't blame him. *She* wasn't even certain what she was doing.

"Nor I you. Are we done?" Lina searched the ground for soft moss and sunk down onto her butt. It had been a long day, and the fatigue was settling into her bones. "I don't really understand why I helped you, but I thought they were making a mistake, okay? And now we are here. If you want to get out of this part of the woods by tomorrow night, we need to leave early. It's best if everyone got some rest."

The girl looked at Ren, as did the other boy. It was clear they were searching for him to lead.

When Ren didn't say anything, the other boy slumped against the base of a tree, his eyes drooping. "I'm fine to rest for now."

"Fine," Ren finally said, wrapping his cloak around his shoulders and sitting himself down a few feet away. "We'll get some rest and continue on at first light."

Lina huffed. Isn't that what she had just said?

After a few minutes. The crickets chirped a nighttime melody, and the moon appeared on the horizon, casting a melancholy light upon the group.

While the other two slept, Ren stared wide-eyed out through the forest.

"Call me Lina," Lina whispered to him.

"What?"

"My name. It's Lina. If we are traveling together for however short a time, you have to call me something."

He opened his mouth. "I'm—"

"Ren." Lina finished. "I heard. Ren?"

He nodded. "I would normally say nice to meet you, Lina, but—"

"It's not nice for me, either. Don't worry about it."

He pressed his lips into a line before digging around in one of their packs and tossing a blanket to her. "It could get cold."

Lina smiled to herself. If he only knew.

CHAPTER
ELEVEN

REN WOKE TO THE SOUND OF SOMEONE RUSTLING around. He sat up, blinking the fuzziness from his eyes. Emeli was busy stuffing items into her pack next to him.

"We are lucky we retrieved some of our things. I don't think I would have slept at all without a cover. It got cold last night." She rolled her wool blanket tight and tied it to the outside of a leather satchel.

A frosty sheen blanketed the forest floor, and a curtain of mist hung around the trees. Ren's breath fogged the air when he yawned, and he pulled his cloak close around his shoulders. He didn't want to tell her he didn't sleep at all last night. Actually, it had been miserable. Aside from the bone-chilling cold, he couldn't stop thinking about the druids and the girl who helped them. Glancing around the trees, there was no sight of Lina.

As he rose, Geret stretched his arms wide, groaning. "Well, I didn't sleep at all. I kept hearing sounds and thinking those fools were coming after us."

Emeli shot him a burning glare before securing her bag against the base of a tree, all packed and ready to go.

Ren's heart sped as he searched their camp for Lina. He still didn't trust her, and she could have fled overnight while they slept. He didn't quite know how he felt about that. She had helped them, sure, but though she seemed to have her reasons, it still didn't make sense.

Wandering through the trees, he caught something shiny glinting through the foliage and crept toward it. As he approached, he realized it was Lina crouching next to a small stream, the water trickling over shiny rocks. Cupping her hands, she dipped them underneath, bringing them up and splashing crystal water over her face. She wiped the droplets from her face with the hem of her tunic and turned, letting out a yelp. Her blade was at Ren's neck before he even saw her reaching for it.

"It's just me!" He exclaimed, showing his hands in surrender.

She let out a sigh and dropped her dagger. "Don't you know not to sneak up on people like that?"

"Sorry, I was making sure you hadn't run off. I'm shocked you're still here."

She wiped her hands on her tunic and frowned. Leather wrist cuffs wrapped her forearms, underneath, the golden ink of tattoos snaked over her skin.

"Not yet." She rubbed one of her temples with a knuckle. "You all are the greatest bunch of idiots I've come across."

"Hey!" he returned, but Lina wasn't even looking in his direction.

Instead, her eyes fixed on something invisible in the distance until she blinked away the daze, and her expression changed again. "I don't know anything about you other than you thinking you are knights of Camelot."

"We will be knights of Camelot," Ren corrected.

Keep telling yourself that, Ren.

She rolled her eyes and approached him. "Fine, but that doesn't change anything. I still don't know what I'm doing here. If it weren't for the—" She stopped mid-sentence, sealing her lips.

Ren quirked a brow. "Weren't for the what?"

She shook her head. "Too much to explain." She turned toward the stream again and ran her hand through the water.

Ren watched for a moment, but he soon felt as though he were intruding on something personal between Lina and the stream. She looked deep in thought. Maybe she truly was just as confused about helping them as he was. He stepped forward. "I guess we owe you our thanks for helping us. Whatever your reasons might have been, you didn't have to do that. Thank you. This quest is important."

She laughed. "Are all the people of Camelot so disillusioned by shiny quests? Promises of better worlds?"

Ren bit his lip. He didn't know how to explain it. She didn't know what the Camelot of his childhood was like. Maybe things had cracked slightly since Arthur's death, but that didn't mean they couldn't be mended.

"Because there is good in Camelot. Maybe it's not what you see, but I know there is." Ren meant it deep in his soul.

"It's not that simple. Camelot hasn't helped my people for ages. The other towns, either. What makes you so certain it can change?"

His stomach sank and his eyes fixed on the swirling water. He wanted to explain everything his father taught him growing up. Camelot was for the people and the Knight's Code was born so they could help protect that. But over the years the Knight's Code had faded—even Ren had to admit it. Shortly afterward, their numbers had faded, too. With no king and no knights, there was nobody to show them, but Excalibur could change all that. It was something the people believed in once upon a time. Even Ren. But how could he explain all of that to someone who didn't grow up there? Lina's life must be so different from his. Besides, he wasn't certain he should trust her with the truth.

She crossed her arms, eyeing him suspiciously.

He realized he had to tell her about the quest. She wasn't going to be fooled by vague answers. Plus, she could be useful. She clearly knew the forest better than they did.

Ren cleared his throat. "I can't make any promises, but I can tell you the truth. But you can't laugh."

"Why would I laugh?" Her hands moved to her hips.

"Because this is going to sound like another one of the mythical stories you don't believe, but you have to trust me when I say it's true. Otherwise, why would we even be out here?"

She pursed her lips, staring in Ren's direction for an agonizingly long time before nodding her head. "Go on."

He swallowed against his dry throat. "Okay. Here it is, then. I'm sure you heard about the attack on Camelot the other night?"

She nodded.

"Well, Morin wants the throne, but he would make a terrible king. He's selfish and arrogant and only cares for power, just like his father. When they attacked, many were killed. Good people." His throat swelled thinking of his father, but he decided to leave that part out. "He will return with an even bigger army. We must stop him."

"How are you and your friends planning on doing that? Are you going to fight against an entire army?"

"That's why we are on this quest. It's to retrieve the Sword of Power. Some people called it Excalibur. It's supposed to unite the lands and give the people something to believe in again. With the sword, we have a chance at saving the kingdom."

Ren wet his lips, studying Lina's reaction.

She didn't say anything at first, probably thinking about how ludicrous the story sounded. But to his surprise, she stood a little taller. "Okay, I will help you."

"What?"

"I will help you and your friends."

He couldn't believe it. She went from claiming Camelot was nothing but empty promises to offering help. "But...why?"

She sighed. "You aren't the only ones who believe in fate, Ren. Back at camp, when I touched your hand, I saw something."

"Saw something?"

"Something I keep seeing. I think it is a premonition. Only flashes, but there is fire burning the forest, chasing my people from the trees, and..." She bit her lip, and he could tell there was more she wasn't saying. "Let's just say I care what happens to these lands, and if I'm supposed to help you and your friends on this quest, as you say, then I will do my part."

A smile cracked Ren's lips. "You are full of secrets, aren't you? A premonition? Whatever that was back at camp—the explosion of light—I've never seen anyone do that before, besides sorcerers. Merlin, for instance."

Lina's eyes brightened. "You know Merlin?" She sat next to the stream, unlacing her boots and plunging her feet into the water. It must have been cold because she hissed on contact.

Most people knew stories of Merlin inside of Camelot's walls, but Ren forgot that people on the outside probably viewed him as more of a legend than a real person.

"He's back. He went away for a while, but I guess he knew Morin was coming and returned."

Lina's eyes softened, sparkling. They were beautiful, and he realized he was staring so averted his gaze, focusing on the tree across the river instead. A birch, perhaps, with pale bark and black eyes. Also watching.

"What is he like?" Lina asked.

Ren laughed under his breath, thinking about the clumsiness that was Merlin, but also how scary he could be while he wielded magic. "He is... exactly as they say."

"Huh," Lina mused.

"You are dodging my question, though. I told you about our plan. What about you?"

"I've learned a few tricks from the druids," she said as casually as one could, pulling her socks back on and lacing her boots.

"That wasn't a trick though. You have magic."

"I do?" A secret smirk grew on her lips.

"Okay, okay, I get it. I only thought it was impressive."

Lina looked away with a red flush blooming in her ears. Ren reached out, grazing her shoulder with his fingertips. He wasn't even sure what made him do it.

She let out an audible gulp, and turned from the clearing, away from Ren. "Are you coming or not? We need to get to this important quest and all."

Lina disappeared into the trees, and a coiled knot twisted at the bottom of Ren's stomach. He still wasn't certain telling her the truth was the right thing to do. The quickness of her offer to help and the fact she wouldn't talk about her magic. There was more to this girl than he knew. But what choice did he have? She was right. Even with Emeli and Geret, they were only three not-yet-knights going on a quest that could shape Camelot's future. And for Camelot, he would have to take a chance on her.

For better, or for worse.

CHAPTER
TWELVE

GWEN

MORIN LOOKED RIDICULOUS, GWEN THOUGHT. SHE SAT on a chestnut horse surveying the training field that sprawled along the rolling hills next to Castle Orkney. Morin, astride a midnight horse next to her, wore leather riding trousers, flashy knee-high boots adorned with silver metal clasps, a thin fluttery shirt, and a steely long coat. But the most ridiculous of all was the wide-brimmed hat with an outrageously large black crow's feather sticking out the side. The sun wasn't even out. It never was. Orkney was always under a constant cover of gloomy clouds and a wet drizzle. At least today was reasonably dry.

The waves crashed against sharp cliffs in the distance, mixed with swords clashing and men yelling orders before them. Gwen repositioned herself on her horse, flipping a gray cloak over one side. She had chosen a simpler ensemble than Morin—riding trousers and a stitched leather vest. There were no sparkly dresses in the castle. No bright colors, either. Every article of clothing existed only in shades of onyx and smoke. One of Morin's people had braided her hair into tight plaits today, weaving heavy beads and dark feathers into her golden locks. Splashing charcoal over her eyelids, she hardly recognized herself this morning.

She had to accept her choices, however. Change wasn't easy and Camelot needed to wake up. She needed everyone to see that things weren't as shiny as they appeared. So, she offered to accompany Morin to oversee the training of his army. But something was off about him (besides the ridiculous hat), and a moody cloud hung over him all morning. He hadn't made a single snide comment. To anyone.

They watched two young men in dark armor lunge at one another with swords and shields, each taking turns bringing fury upon their opponent. Their sweat ran down their faces, and angry, pink welts bloomed across their exposed skin. Gwen winced and turned to Morin, but his eyes were far off from the field before him.

"What is it?" she finally mustered the courage to ask.

He stared at her with his lips pressed into a line and let the question linger a little longer before finally answering. "They are going after Excalibur."

"Who? How is that possible?" Gwen's horse pranced in place, sensing her surprise. No one had spoken of the sword since Arthur's death. Everyone thought it had been lost. Nobody even searched for it. Why now?

"Your friends seem to have a source. They set out three days ago."

Ren? Gwen looked away, taking in a sharp breath, but Morin's eyes still burned into her.

"How do you know this?" she asked, her gaze as far off as Morin's now. A splinter had embedded into her gut ever since that night she returned to Orkney. The guilt festered over Ren's father's death, and her part in it.

"Someone in Camelot wasn't careful enough when calling for aid. They forgot magic carries echoes and that those echoes cast ripples for those who listen."

Gwen swallowed against a dry throat, pushing down her guilt. "What does that mean for us?" She glanced at him out of the corner of her eye.

Morin tracked the young men fighting in front of them. The smaller of the two struggled to beat his opponent. No matter how many times he lunged forward with his sword, a shield was there to block his blow. He stumbled backward.

Morin rolled his eyes, hopping from his horse and seizing the younger man's sword. He dove at the other one, but instead of bringing his sword down upon him as the young man did, he swept his leg under his opponent, tripping him. The man was so surprised, he lost his balance, fell to his butt, and abandoned his sword to the ground. Morin kicked the sword away, pointing the tip of his borrowed blade at the man's exposed throat as the man gasped for breath.

Morin drew the sword back, handing it to the younger one, and mounted his horse again. He turned his back to the training field and gazed out over the cliffs at his castle. "It means our plans have changed."

Gwen trotted up alongside with her brow furrowed. She didn't like the implication of a change of plans.

Morin whistled for the nearest guard. "Prepare our things. We head out at once."

"What about the men? The preparations for the siege?" Gwen looked back at the hundreds of men training on the cliffs with their canvas tents littering the rolling hills. It had taken weeks to amass everything here from across the country. Why was Morin thinking of taking a detour?

A serious crease etched into Morin's brow. "If they retrieve the Sword of Power, we don't stand a chance at rallying anyone to our cause. The people need a leader. They need a king, and whoever has that sword will persuade them to follow. It is written in history."

Gwen didn't like the idea of racing her friends to retrieve the sword, but she had to admit, it would give their cause an advantage. Perhaps with something that powerful, they would have an easier time convincing everyone to give Morin a chance. Because if what he had told her that day in the dungeons was true, she wasn't certain people would believe it. Arthur's reign was embedded into the very fabric of the kingdom like a golden thread weaved into fine silk. Its allure fooled everyone, including herself, but it was time to unravel that thread, piece by piece. Maybe the sword was the tool they needed to do that.

"Then," she said, "Change history."

CHAPTER
THIRTEEN

THEY MADE IT THROUGH A GOOD CHUNK OF THE wilderness in the first few hours—past cascading waterfalls, mossy caves, wildflower meadows, and hundreds of fresh pine and birch trees emitting the scent of tart citrus and moldy leaves.

By noon, Ren sipped from this canteen while handing pieces of stale bread to the group.

Geret took a huge chunk between his cheek and teeth, sighing and plopping down on a fallen tree trunk. "Now I understand why Galahad made us do hill sprints. My legs feel like sacks of grain after days of wandering."

"We aren't wandering," Lina chimed. "We are carefully navigating a safe path through the forest."

Ren nodded. "What she said."

"Well, I find it refreshing," Emeli said. "Think what we'd be doing back at the castle as an alternative." She upturned one eyebrow at Geret and waited for an answer, but he only shrugged. "We'd be polishing armor, sharpening weapons, stocking provisions. Basically, preparing for war. How is that fun?"

"Depends on your definition of fun." Geret stood with a huff.

"I like shooting things, but not people if I can avoid it. I definitely don't enjoy endless hours inside that dark, dank castle rummaging through our weapons stores."

"She has a point," Ren added. Sometimes he took his sister's side.

Lina snapped her fingers. "All the more reason to keep our breaks short. We have a long way yet to go." She took her lead position, urging everyone onward.

After days of travel, the daily strain settled in Ren's bones as his muscles acclimated to the distance. The mood of the group was harder to improve, as there was no acclimating to the long days. Their excited chatter turned into long bouts of silence. Even Geret's jokes were sparse.

Ren paid special attention to the growing anxiety fluttering around his chest and tried to battle it back by holding Excalibur in his mind. He reminded himself why they were out there. Why *he* was out there. He wanted to make his father proud and prove to himself he was worthy of the title of a knight. This was all he had left.

That night, a wall of clouds covered the twinkling stars, and the sky opened, lightning splintering the darkness. A low rumble shook the ground, and then the rain came pouring down in sheets for two miserable days. The relentless storm soaked them all to the bone until every piece of clothing they wore had grown heavy and emitted a moldy stench.

At night, the flames of their fire refused to catch on wet wood, forcing them into the shelter of a cave up on the mountainside. Emeli was so grumpy she didn't even fire a retort at Geret when he said something about a drowned rat smelling better. She didn't even roll her eyes. That's how Ren knew his sister was tired.

Then, a miracle—the sun rose on the third day, burning the mist from the trees and bathing the forest in a golden glow of warmth. They stopped to light a fire and hung their wet clothes to dry, one by one stripping to their undergarments.

Emeli flushed as she peeled off her heavy trousers, wrapping her arms around her midsection. She backed into the cover of the tree, digging through her sack until finding a damp blanket and draping it around her shoulders. Geret hung his tunic over a branch, averting his eyes from Emeli's direction. Ren smiled to himself and leaned against a tree away from the others, shivering. But Lina had strut toward the fire, hanging her leathers and blouse to dry over a pile of rocks. Underneath, nothing but a thin fabric barely covered anything. Then, she sharpened her blades on a rock like it was nothing.

Her lean muscles gleamed in the morning sun, her skin warm with a shimmer of gold where the fading tattoos stained her chest and thighs. Ren's cheeks heated as he realized he was staring. Again. He couldn't help it. As mysterious as she was, Lina was beautiful. Different from the other girls he knew in Camelot. He was beginning to see she was fierce and bold and—

"What?" She caught everyone gawking at her boldness. Her eyes shifted suspiciously around the others and landed on Ren. "Like you all haven't seen each other nearly naked before?"

"No!" Ren returned, and so did the others, all replying in unison.

Geret's eyes remained fixed on the space in front of him as Emeli turned beet red.

"Oh, this is too good." Lina laughed. "What kind of prudence do they subject you all to at the castle?"

"It's not prudence! It's proper." Emeli tugged on a nearby branch to cover more of her exposed skin.

Lina stifled a small snort. "Fine. I'll just have to enjoy this rabbit myself as you all shiver in the shadows because you are too 'proper' to join me."

She pulled a brace of gray, limp rabbits from a satchel and got to work cutting and skinning them with her blades. She blew on the hot coals of the fire, igniting the flames in a deep orange glow.

Ren's mouth watered at the sight of the rabbit. "Where did you get those?"

Lina didn't flinch or look in Ren's direction while preparing the meat. "While you sleepyheads were in a dog pile this morning, I went on a hunt."

Geret smacked his lips and grumbled something to himself before joining Lina next to the fire. Emeli glanced in Ren's direction, and he shrugged. Better to sit half-naked next to his best friend and sister and the girl they met, no matter how beautifully distracting she was, than starve to death and die of the cold.

Ren joined the group and Lina's eyes raked over him, completely unashamed for checking him out. Suddenly he no longer needed the fire's warmth because heat swarmed every inch of him. He was certain he would burn alive.

Emeli eventually followed, warming her hands over the flames before finding a seat on a log and pulling her blanket closer around her torso.

They all settled around the fire in silence, watching the dancing flames and listening to the popping wood until Ren reached his arms overhead, easing the tension in his muscles.

This time, Lina averted her eyes, poking a stick into the flames and dislodging flying embers into the air. "So, what should we do to pass the time?"

"I'm just hungry," Ren said, his stomach rolling, thinking of the hot, smoking meat.

Lina pouted her lips. "We have to wait for the fire to burn down a bit, but the rabbit will cook better that way on the coals. Plus, we've been a grumpy bunch of trolls the last few days, I need some fun." Her eyes flickered around the circle again.

They did look like a sad group. Geret hadn't cracked a joke since the drowned rat comment and that was hours ago. Maybe they could use some cheering up.

"Okay, I'm game." Ren cleared his throat. "What did you have in mind?"

Lina quirked a brow. "Since we don't know each other well, how about a truth game?"

Emeli picked her head up from leaning on her hands. "What is a truth game?"

"You know, we go around the circle and choose to answer a question truthfully, and if we don't, the person asking the question gets to make them complete a task. The more dreadful the better." There was a devious glint in Lina's eyes that made Ren lean in, while Emeli seemed to shrink further into the cover of her blanket.

"Let's do it," Geret chimed, looking as intrigued as Ren.

Emeli smacked the side of Geret's arm.

"Ow," he exclaimed. "This is supposed to be an adventure, remember? Like Merlin said. I'm not having any fun, are you?" He shot Emeli a burning stare.

The return of their banter gave Ren hope, at least. "Fine. Let's play Truth or Dare."

Lina jumped from her seat. "Oh, I like that. Truth or Dare. Who's first?"

Ren stood. "I'll go. Geret, Truth or Dare?"

Geret didn't even need to think about it before he responded with exuberance: "Dare."

Ren rubbed the stubble forming across his chin, his eyes scanning the distant space for an idea. The pile of rabbit meat sitting next to the fire caught his attention. Blood dribbled down the rock where they were piled and a smirk formed over his lips.

"I dare you to eat that meat. Raw."

Emeli let out a squeal, clasping her hands over her mouth. Geret stared intently at the meat and took a deep breath. He approached the pile, fingering through it until he found a small piece.

His lips opened to the meat—

"Don't you dare! You will get sick!" Emeli scolded.

Geret met her eyes. "Sorry, it's the game." Then he ripped into the meat with his teeth, chewed, and swallowed.

Emeli turned away, gagging.

Ren held his breath until Geret let out a loud belch and laughed. "Lame. Do better next time, Bedivere," he said, slapping Ren on the back.

"Okay, okay. That was just a warmup," Ren replied, sitting back down.

Geret cleared his throat and looked at Lina. "New girl. This was your idea so you're next."

Lina straightened her spine and lifted her chin. "Bring it."

"She has to tell a truth since she wanted to get to know us, yet we hardly know anything about her," Ren interjected because he really did want to know more about her. Mostly so he would be more confident in trusting her on the quest, but also because she puzzled him. He loved a good puzzle.

"That's not how the game works." She batted her eyes flirtatiously at Ren. "But fine. Truth."

Geret grabbed his chin in contemplation. "Ren told me you hate Camelot. Why?"

"I don't need to speak a truth to tell you that. Everyone hates Camelot. It's a fact. No secrets there."

"We don't hate Camelot!" Ren said, gesturing at Geret and Emeli, who nodded their heads in agreement.

"Gods, they really have kept you sheltered in that castle, haven't they? I won't need to explain this one; you will see it for yourself soon enough."

"That's not really an answer. I say you have to do a dare then," Ren added.

"Fine." Lina crossed her arms.

"I dare you to say something nice about each of us, though I know this will be difficult judging from your spiteful words since we met," Ren said.

Lina's eyes rolled over everyone before landing on Emeli. "Okay... you have beautiful hair, Emeli."

Emeli lifted a shoulder, pretending to throw her tangled hair back. "Thank you."

"And Geret, you seem the least stuck up of the group."

Ren hissed. "That's also an insult."

Lina rolled her eyes again. "Fine. Geret, you look very strong, and I bet you are good to have in a fight."

Emeli whistled through her teeth, and Geret's eyes darted in her direction while he threw his hands behind his head, leaning back into them. "That's right."

Then Lina turned to Ren. "And you..." She paused, forehead creasing like she was concentrating really hard. "You have lovely eyes, like soft springtime moss."

The circle went awkwardly silent, and all the air left Ren's lungs as a tingling sensation danced in his chest. He cleared his throat. "That wasn't so bad, was it?"

She bit her lip. "No. It was excruciating."

Geret coughed and Lina shook whatever daze took hold. "Right," her eyes flew from Ren's, but his cheeks still tingled from her burning gaze.

Lina turned to Emeli on the opposite side of the circle. "Emeli. Truth or Dare?"

Emeli lifted her chin a little higher. "Because nobody expects me to, I choose dare."

Geret let out a huff that Emeli ignored.

Ren took a sip of water to hide his laugh. Emeli and dares did not go together. This would be mighty interesting.

Lina looked deep in thought for a moment before pursing her lips into a devilish grin. "I dare you to kiss the big man over there." She pointed at Geret, and Ren nearly choked on his water.

"No!" Emeli immediately flushed the color of the fire, and Geret waved his hands in front of his face.

Lina narrowed her eyes on both of them, hands on her hips. "Why not? You are together, aren't you?"

Now Ren did spew the water from his mouth, causing Lina to burst into laughter so hard she had to hold her stomach.

But Emeli did not look amused, casting an awkward glance at Geret, who had become uncharacteristically silent.

"I can't believe you thought that," Emeli whispered.

"I'm sorry." Lina chuckled. "With how much you two fight, I just assumed. It was either that or siblings, but you don't look like siblings."

"Assume better next time," Emeli grumbled, grabbing hold of the edges of her blanket for support, no longer showing a brave face.

"Fine. I won't make you do that then. How about this: drop that blanket. The fire is plenty warm, see?" Lina did a twirl in her thin linen dress, and both Geret and Ren averted their gaze like the gentlemen they were.

Emeli shot Lina an annoyed stare before sighing, and she dropped the blanket to the ground, wrapping her arms around her midsection, her face red.

Satisfied, Lina flashed her a smile.

"Ren is next. Truth or Dare?" Emeli blurted. "It's only fair, brother," emphasizing the brother part.

Ren shook his head, smiling to himself. "Do your worst. Truth. You all know everything about me, anyway." But for a moment, he slightly panicked, remembering that Lina didn't know anything about him. He sucked in a breath, waiting for Emeli's question to come, hoping it wouldn't be embarrassing.

Emeli chewed her lip for a beat before her face hardened into a serious expression. "Do you miss Gwen?"

Ren's stomach sank. Anything but that.

"That's not fair, Em." He frowned. "I'm done playing."

He stood from his seat, leaving the circle and the comforting warmth of the fire. As he left, Lina asked the others who Gwen was, but he didn't catch the answer because he needed to get away from all of them. Right. Now.

He slinked into the trees until he was standing alone in a clearing of tall, wild grass that reached to his knees and slapped coldly against his bare skin.

Gwen. For a moment he had forgotten how much he missed her, but now it all came rushing back, twisting an ache in his heart. Walking with her in the shade of trees along the castle walls. Cuddling next to the fire while the winter wind howled outside. The way her head would find the space between his cheek and shoulder like it was shaped specifically for her. How her hair always smelled of sweet roses.

Anger swelled in his chest as he thought of her betrayal of Camelot. The death of his father. The way she rode away in the dark with the enemy. Why had she done that to them? Why had she done it to *him*?

He wanted to bury his feelings deep inside because what good did they do? He couldn't miss her, and he couldn't spend energy being angry with her, either. It was only a distraction from what he had to do. Right now, that was all that mattered.

Ren stood in the clearing, pacing, until the smell of roasting meat called him back.

When he returned, nobody said anything, and he was grateful for that. Emeli eventually handed him a leaf stuffed with juicy meat and squeezed his forearm. "I'm sorry."

Ren nodded. They didn't need to say anything more.

As they ate, Ren caught Lina eyeing him between bites, like she was waiting for him to crack or crumble. He knew Emeli and Geret had filled her in on the details, and he hoped it didn't change the way she saw him.

With dry clothes and the rumbling from their aching bellies subsided, the group headed out. Everyone was suspiciously silent around Ren for the first half of the day. Even Emeli and Geret gave extra distance between them on the trail. Emeli had wrapped herself tight in her cloak, and Geret trudged far behind.

Perhaps their little game wasn't such a good morale booster after all.

THE JOURNEY CONTINUED through fields filled with rainbow wildflowers. They crossed icy streams and passed small towns with thatched roofs and dried crops. Each town looked more decrepit than the last, buildings' facades crumbling and streets desolate.

As they trudged down a cracked, cobbled stone road through a town called Warwick, the weary faces of the townsfolk haunted Ren. Their bones protruded from under fraying, grime-soaked rags, their cracked, bleeding mouths and lifeless expressions frozen in place.

"What happened here?" Ren asked, mostly to himself, but nobody else seemed to have an answer. The group was eerily silent, as if their words would crack the fragile skin of those they passed. Ren didn't know people could live in such impoverished conditions. His father spoke of journeys to deliver food to neighboring villages, but a sack of grain wasn't fixing this problem. The knights had grown so few over the years. How could they possibly do enough?

A sickness rolled around his stomach as they stopped at the town blacksmith for Emeli to pick up supplies for her arrows. The blacksmith was more like a hovel—cracking wooden benches lined one side and sunlight filtering through a hole in the straw roof. A small, wrinkled man with a graying beard hammered away at a piece of silver, stopping to pump the bellows of a small fire, flaring it to life within a forge.

Suspicion laced his gaze as he spotted the group gathered at the entrance. Emeli greeted him with a shiny smile, handed him a piece of crumpled paper from her satchel, and pointed to the items scribbled in black ink. "Do you have these?" she asked, before reading the items on the list to him.

"Do you have the payment? I don't barter," he replied in a weary tone.

"Of course," she answered, digging in her pack and placing a stack of coins in the man's hand.

His expression shifted—his brows arched slightly, lifting his top lip into what Ren imagined was as close to a smile as the man could muster, revealing yellowed teeth beneath.

He tossed the flat piece of silver he was working with into a vat of cold water, and it spat and sizzled. Shortly thereafter, he disappeared into the back room.

"Not exactly like the blacksmith of Camelot," Geret commented, lifting up a thin fabric littered with holes from a small window letting in hazy sunlight. Dust particles swirled through the room, and the heat made beads of sweat gather on his brow.

"Shut up," Emeli scolded. "We are lucky he has the supplies at all."

The man returned with a handful of vials containing silver liquid, thin rope, and a small knife.

Emeli thanked him, and they continued through town until arriving at the square. A few tables with shade canopies circled the space where people sold goods, if they could even be called that. Bruised produce was stacked in cracked boxes and linens, and weathered leathers hung in the sun. There wasn't exactly a crowd of people like at Camelot's market—just a few groups wandering around looking but not buying anything.

A hunched woman wearing a soiled wool dress shook a bottle across the way, locking eyes with Lina. She moved toward the group and called, "Please! You need this. You practice the arts."

Lina waved her hands at the woman, shaking her head as her face reddened. "No," she whispered through the too-few bodies in between.

"I see your markings." The woman repeated, hobbling over. "Please. Avalon calls to you."

Lina shook her head again, catching hold of Ren's elbow and tugging him across the square, the pace of her feet quickening.

Somehow, the old woman caught up, shuffling in front of Lina and placing herself between the group and the exit to the square.

Lina's brow tightened, and she bent down to look at the woman. "I said no thank you," she said through clenched teeth.

It did nothing to deter the woman, who clawed at Lina's blouse while squeezing the bottle between her shaking, wrinkled fingers. "You must. You must. Here," she said, forcing it into Lina's hand.

Lina eyed the bottle with suspicion before digging into her leather pouch and pulling out a silver coin. "Wait. I didn't pay!" she hollered after the woman. But the woman had already gone, disappearing across the square and leaving the table empty where he kept her bottles.

"That was strange. What is that?" Ren leaned in, peering at the bottle in Lina's shaking hand, but she snapped it into her chest to cover the contents.

"I don't know, but we must go. I don't like this place, and its nearly sundown. We have a few more miles to travel before we can make camp," she replied curtly.

Ren's gut twisted. From the description Merlin had given them, there was only one final stretch through a wooded area before reaching the mountain. Beyond that lay the chimera in whatever beast form it would appear. Those knots turned to rot in the pit of his stomach. He didn't know how they would get past it.

Next to him, Emeli had filled a canteen of water at the well and sipped from it before joining Geret, who was resting against a stone wall. His head was tipped back, eyes barely open. Emeli handed him the canteen and forced him to take a drink before she sat cross-legged against the same wall and rummaged through her pack to organize the supplies she had purchased.

Putting his friends in danger made it all worse. He didn't

know how he would protect them. He didn't know how to protect himself.

THEY LEFT town as the early afternoon sun merged with the hazy blue of twilight, and the group came upon an old game trail in the forest just beyond the border of Warwick. A fine dirt path stretched one way, and something wilder with overgrown plants stretched in the other direction.

Lina stopped at the divide, staring at the woods beyond.

"Why have we stopped?" Ren squinted into the sun, which inched closer to the horizon. They still had a couple hours of daylight left until it would be too dark to continue. They should keep going.

"We don't come this far," Lina muttered, with her gaze burning into the trees ahead.

Ren exchanged a confused look with Emeli.

"What do you mean you don't come this far?" Ren asked.

"They are afraid of these woods." She sucked in her cheeks. "My people. This is the Brecheliant Woods. I can tell from the berries growing along the edge of the tree line. See?" She pointed to overgrown bushes with sharp, purple-tinged leaves and small, dark berries amongst a fluff of white flowers. "They call them pyracantha sìthean and they only grow on the border of these woods. Nobody knows why. And there are other things my people fear."

"Fear?" Geret gulped, peering into the woods.

"There are stories of hunting parties who trap around these woods, but once they travel into the Brecheliant Woods, they never come out."

Geret let out a long breath. "Perhaps they traveled through and made it to the other side?"

Lina didn't look at him, her eyes focused on the forest. "Perhaps. But there are safer roads around."

Ren studied the gravel path leading into the woods. If he remembered Merlin's map, this road would intersect with The King's Road, taking them into Bayard, east of the forest. "Yes, but those roads would add days to our journey, and we have wasted too much time as it is. What good will retrieving the sword be when we are too late to save Camelot? Or when there is nothing left to save?" Ren squared his shoulders, steeling his courage. "We must cut through."

"Perhaps the stories have been exaggerated throughout the years. It may be nothing but a few poisonous plants and a scary bunny or two." Emeli smiled sheepishly.

But Lina didn't look amused at all. Her eyes had grown alert, and her lips pressed into a scowl. "Let's hope you are right."

She stepped forward, taking the lead and gripping the daggers at her hip far too tightly.

CHAPTER
FOURTEEN

GWEN

"Ick. Why is everything here so sticky?" Morin bent over a bush with sharp-edged leaves, pulling his gloved hand back with a thick sludge stretched between his fingers.

Gwen rolled her eyes. Days. It had been days of listening to Morin's incessant complaining, and when he wasn't complaining, he was going on and on about what he would do when the crown was his. He'd show the people what a real ruler looked like by bringing back the fine art of sorcery. Not to be confused with that 'pagan stuff' the druids worshiped in the trees.

Morin wiped the sticky substance on the edge of his cloak and

Gwen wrinkled her nose in disgust, rubbing her palm along her jawline. Hours in these woods were making her teeth hurt. There was something here setting her on edge and she wanted to get through as quickly as possible. She glanced at the sky above and the inky darkness settling over the trees. Night was coming, and she didn't trust the echoed sounds in these woods.

As if on cue, a low howl sounded in the distance, and goose-bumps raced over her arms.

"Don't worry, darling. We are safe." Morin glanced around at the men they had brought with them on the route. Even though it was only a dozen or so, they still squeezed into the claustrophobic confines of the tight trees. Rows upon rows of twisted, thick pines shot up all around them, and in between every space was his personal league of dark knights.

The rest of their army was to continue on toward Camelot and ready themselves for the siege. It wasn't the worst plan, as it allowed Morin to chase the sword but still stay true to his original promises.

In a few days, this would all be over and Camelot could be reshaped, but relief was far from Gwen's mind as she surveyed the trees before them. She was beginning to think they were walking in circles. There was a distinctive-looking tree with barren branches shaped like wings she was certain she'd seen before.

Morin reached into the pockets of his long coat and retrieved a polished stone. He snapped his fingers together around it, but nothing happened. He did it again, this time with a grimace on his face, but only a small burst of sparks came from his palm.

"My magic isn't working," he grumbled as he surveyed the ominous fog creeping in through the woods.

Gwen shivered, pulling her cloak around her shoulders. She didn't like the look of that fog, and if Morin didn't have his magic to keep it back, she wasn't certain what horrors would follow.

Fires sprung up around them as everyone stopped for a break. Gwen took a seat next to Morin, hoping the flickering flames would combat the growing anxiety in her chest, but Morin ignored the fire. He continued to snap his fingers together again and again, a growing frustration rumbling at the back of his throat.

"I don't understand," he said, finally giving up and shoving the stones into his pockets.

"Something about this place isn't right," Gwen added, warming her hands over the orange glow of the fire. "It's unsettling."

A branch snapped in the distance, and everyone's eyes shot over in that direction. Morin gripped the sword at his hip, and Gwen unsheathed hers. Nothing came out of the hazy fog, though, and Gwen let out a breath. "Why is everything so loud in this part of the woods?"

Morin shook his head. "This is the type of magic that shouldn't exist. It's what happens when everything else is smothered. Magic needs somewhere to go, so it gathers in places like this until it becomes something else."

"Then why can't you use yours?"

He bit his lip. "I think, perhaps, that is the intention."

"Intention?"

His eyes scanned the trees, searching for something. "There is more to these woods than anyone knows."

"Okay. Can you be any more vague?" She let out a puff of air through her nostrils, settling into the ground and wrapping her cloak snugly around her shoulders.

"I am an open book," he said, retrieving a hunk of cheese from his pack and taking a bite. He broke off the edge and offered it to her.

She took it but snorted. "Yeah, right."

His hands shot behind his head so he could lean back. "Go ahead. Ask me anything."

The smirk on his lips dared her and she couldn't resist. Her eyes wandered over the intricate buckles on his vest and the shimmery embroidery on his black trousers. "What's with the fashion choices? I know you love the attention, but your magic tricks do that. Why show off?"

He snorted, straightening his spine. "Just because Camelot chooses modesty doesn't mean the rest of us can't enjoy life's pleasures."

"I had fine dresses back home." She ran a hand over her cloak, imagining the silky feel of the soft wool she had owned at home. This one was thicker, scratchier. Warm, yes, but heavy and dreary.

"I remember," his eyes roamed over her figure, causing a rush of heat in her ears.

She needed to change the subject. "What was it like growing up in Castle Orkney?"

His gaze left her skin burning, but he soon glanced away into the pines. "That's an easy one to answer. I didn't."

"What? Why not?"

As his gaze searched somewhere far off beyond the trees, a glassy ripple expanded in his dark eyes. "Father wasn't exactly thrilled when I arrived. He didn't want his enemies to have something to hold against him, so he hid me away when I was young. I was raised by a simple woman named Belinda in a small village as far north as you can travel. It wasn't until several years after my father's death that Grayson brought me to Castle Orkney to inherit my uncle's throne."

There was no flicker of amusement on his lips this time. Gwen often heard him talk about his army general Grayson like a father, and this confirmed her suspicions.

"So, you didn't really know your father?"

Morin shook his head.

Maybe he was right. They had more in common than Gwen cared to admit.

"It was a tragedy, what they did to my father and yours," Morin said, his eyes returning to their sharp form. "But the truth will soon set us free."

Morin smiled full-toothed, dropping his head back in his hands again. Gwen caught a different view of him. Perfect cheekbones. A pointed nose. Thick, defined eyebrows framing those dark eyes. He was handsome.

"Of course, we will correct those wrongs when I take the throne. That garish-looking hunk of wood is obviously in need of a serious makeover. I'm thinking plush velvet and perhaps a bit of gold?"

Handsome, yet still obnoxious.

FIFTEEN

LINA

THE FURTHER INTO THE BRECHELIANT WOODS THEY ventured, the more the landscape changed. The trees turned unusual colors—rich greens became coppery rust, and the sunbursts of light faded into an orange glow as the canopy thickened overhead. Clusters of mushrooms with wide, bright caps sprung up from the ground, and flowers, whose petals should have been curled open, were already tightly closed buds, as if they knew something the group did not.

Even the air shifted, growing dense but not rotten, as Lina had expected. It was velvety, which made her head swim. She didn't hate it, but she knew the deception meant this place was much worse than the stories portrayed. Jagged teeth hid behind a beautiful smile.

Her boots crunched on twisted branches as the dirt path disappeared, but she kept her stride, stopping to check for game trails and other evidence of a path, even though her confidence was waning. She couldn't allow this place to get to her. She promised to lead the group through safely.

Suddenly, her heart froze. The breeze rustled the leaves overhead and the call of a bird in the distance echoed through the trees. But then... nothing. The wind stopped and the bird song disappeared. Lina wasn't certain how long they all stood there listening, silently begging for the sounds to return. But they didn't. The only signs of life were the pounding of their hearts.

The emptiness pressed in, causing an uncomfortable knot to throb in Lina's brow.

"What is this?" Ren asked, standing still as a statue, even as Lina raised a finger to signal quiet. "What the heck is going on?" He raised his voice in a frustrated tone.

She sighed, turning toward the group, where panic edged all their faces.

"I can't be sure, but I think it's the forest."

"The forest?" Emeli stepped forward, eyeing the trees like they would come alive at any moment.

Lina nodded, sliding a dagger from her hip and holding it up.

"We need to keep moving. We don't know what is out here or how long it will take us to reach the other side. Stay alert." Lina took the lead, marching to her own orders as the rest followed.

After a few minutes, the boys trailed behind and Emeli pattered up next to Lina.

"You knew we shouldn't come in here. I wish we'd listened." Emeli said, glancing over her shoulder. "This place gives me the creeps."

"Ren was right. If we went around, it would have taken us days. As it is, we aren't even sure that Mo..."

"Morin," Emeli offered.

Lina flashed a crooked smile. "Right. We aren't certain if he's already made it there. We only had one choice. It just wasn't a good one."

Emeli let out a small laugh, shaking her head.

"What is so funny?"

"It's nothing, it's just that Ren and I always seem to find ourselves in trouble for making unwise choices. This one time, he insisted we go out on a hunt with the knights even though we were only seven. I thought we would ride around on horses and eat snacks, but the group ended up finding a stag and pursuing on foot. Since we were so small, we got left behind to watch the horses. But of course, Ren convinced me to follow them in secret."

"And?" An amused smile slid over Lina's mouth. It was nice to talk about something fun for a change.

"Well, we got lost, naturally. I came upon this peculiar part of the forest floor where all the foliage was stacked as if someone had arranged it like that on purpose. As I was stepping forward to inspect it, Ren came flying out of nowhere and pushed me out of the way, and he plunged straight down into the animal trap."

Lina gasped. "What happened?"

Emeli let out a laugh. "He missed any major organs, but a spike tore through his side, and he needed to be stitched up."

"Wow. You were lucky."

"Not lucky. I just have a good brother. Ren is always looking out for me. For all of us. He puts a lot of pressure on himself."

Lina peered over her shoulder, glancing at Ren with Geret walking behind.

"I'm beginning to understand that," Lina said, returning her gaze forward and nudging Emeli with her elbow. "Something has been bugging me about the whole Gwen thing and how everyone thought Ren would be the one knighted."

"What?"

"Why not you? You are twins, right?"

"Yes..."

"So, it was your birthday too. Why not you? Do they have something against female knights?" Lina scrunched up her face because of course Camelot would have something against female knights.

"No, not at all!" Emeli responded. "They named Gwen, remember? I wasn't a candidate because I told counsel I didn't want to be a knight."

Lina stepped closer to Emeli so she could lower her voice. "Why not? You grew up training with those guys, right?"

"Yes..."

"And I've seen you practicing with your bow. You are just as good as they are. Probably with a sword too."

"It's not about that. I never felt like I had the courage they have. I don't like to fight."

Lina nodded, pursing her lips. "Courage isn't the only quality necessary to fight. Besides, from everything Ren has said, it's more than being a soldier. They are supposed to help people, right? They protect with force when necessary, but they also care about people and lead by example. I can tell you have that in you. You're always worrying about everyone around you. You are strategic and smart, thinking things through instead of jumping into action. Camelot probably needs more of that and less brute strength...cough...Geret?" They both laughed as they stopped, waiting for the boys to catch up.

"Maybe you are right," Emeli said, offering a warm smile.

"So, are you talking about me?" Geret stepped in with his hands on his hips, catching his breath.

Lina and Emeli exchanged looks, bursting into giggles.

"What?" Geret consulted Ren but only received a shrug. Boys.

It was nice having friends her age. Lina had always run around with the druids who were much older. There were a few children, but none of them were old enough to talk to. This was new. And she didn't hate it.

THE SHADOWS BENT and moved as the sun dipped behind the horizon, and Lina let out a fogged breath. It felt like they'd been walking for days—Lina's legs were heavy and achy, her stomach turned with hunger, and her throat was so dry she could barely speak. The quiet closed in until it was suffocating.

As the dark stretched forth into the evening, they made their way through the woods with nothing sounding in the distance and nothing sounding behind them. The nothingness was all-consuming.

Ren stopped and leaned against a tree to dig through his pack.

"Uh-oh." His eyes frantically searched through the folds of the pack as he pulled out various items until reaching the bottom. "The food is gone."

"What?" Geret's eyes went wide, and he squatted next to Ren, grabbing at the pack.

"That's impossible. It was just here this morning before we entered the forest. I haven't been eating anything." Ren's face went pale.

A lightness swam in Lina's head. Something wasn't right about any of this, but she couldn't figure it out. Unless...

"That's what it wants," she said, certain the forest was responsible. "It wants us disoriented. Starving. Tired."

Ren locked eyes with her, jaw clenched. "Why?"

"I don't know." Lina scanned the trees as if searching for the sentient being watching over them, but no visible threat lurked in the shadows, at least that she could see.

"Do you think anything in here is edible?" Emeli bent down next to a cluster of mushrooms and poked her finger at their caps.

Lina breathed through her nostrils, dread coiling in her chest. "I wouldn't eat anything here unless we were dying and had no other choice."

Emeli gulped, rising to her feet and dropping the mushroom she'd picked.

"Our only option is to get out of here as quickly as possible, but I can't tell how long we've been walking." Lina stared through the trees at the stars, counting them and attempting to point out various figures in the heavens. Her stomach clenched. "They aren't there."

"What now?" Ren groaned, plopping himself against the nearest tree with his stuff from the pack still scattered.

"The stars. They aren't in the sky." Lina frowned. "I don't know how to get us out of here." She sat on the ground and dropped her face into her hands. If she couldn't trust the path in the forest, and she couldn't navigate by the stars she knew, she had no idea which direction was out. For the first time in a long time, she was lost.

Ren looked like he was about to be sick, and Geret and Emeli joined them in a circle, the lantern at the center casting a small halo over the ground.

"Why don't we take a break. I don't think our wandering around is helping," Ren said, scraping crumbs at the bottom of the pack and licking his fingers.

Lina shot him a furious stare. "I told you. It's not wandering, it's navigation." Even she caught the edge in her voice, but she wasn't sorry for it. They were in major trouble here.

Ren held his hands up in surrender. "Easy."

Lina's shoulders tensed, irritation crawling up her chest in a hot wave. She couldn't take being around everyone right now. She stood up, slinking into the trees. When Ren yelled after her to not go far, she yelled right back, "I'll be fine! I just need a moment!"

Heat burned her from the inside. The dull headache pulsing behind her eyes raged, causing nausea to roll in her stomach. As she bent over her knees, ready to throw up, she overheard Emeli and Geret bickering.

"If we are going to rest, someone should take the first watch. I'll do it," Emeli said.

"Oh no, you don't. If anyone is taking first watch, it's me," Geret's voice echoed back.

"Why? Because you are a man?"

"No. Because I'm not tired yet. If anything, my adrenaline is running high right now, and I can tell you are tired from those bags under your eyes."

"Excuse me!"

Lina could picture the look Emeli gave Geret and the corresponding flash of fear on his face. It might have been amusing if Lina hadn't been so irritated herself.

"I didn't mean that," Geret's voice responded in the distance. "Why do you have to be like that?"

"Like what?"

"Offended at everything I say. When did you become like this? We used to play together, remember? We would steal Sir Bor's fighting axes while everyone was feasting and cut off the heads of the straw dummies in the training fields. It was fun. Do you remember what fun is? Now, it's like I can't say anything to you without you getting mad."

Fun. Lina didn't know what that was like, either. For as long as she could remember, life had been about survival. Hunt. Eat. Move camp. Fight. Once in a while, when she was all alone in the trees and the echoed sounds from the forest indicated no threats, she could settle and practice her magic, reach into the earth and wait for it to send vibrations back. Those were times of peace, but not exactly fun.

Coming back to the present, Emeli's voice still trailed through the silent trees. It was as if their conversation was happening right next to her.

"I don't get mad at everything you say. You just put on this big show all the time and it gets old. I wish you would be like you used to be. Jokes aside. Posturing aside."

"I don't posture," Geret mumbled.

Lina shook her head, glad she had wandered off. Or rather,

carefully navigated away from the others. This was a conversation not meant for her ears.

"We are lost." Ren approached through the trees, shattering her solitude.

"Obviously," Lina replied, picking at the hard bark on the nearest tree. The sap underneath emitted a rich, honeyed smell, and she pondered tasting it.

"You aren't used to that, are you?" Ren asked.

Lina shook her head, refusing to answer him, but knowing it was true made her frustrated anyway. She wasn't used to getting lost, and she didn't know how to fix it.

"I'll take that as a yes," Ren said, inching closer as if sensing her growing fears.

"And what do you know of it? Emeli told me about the time you got her lost in the woods," Lina shot back, the irritation racing through her veins, making her skin itch.

Ren scrunched his brows. "What?"

"Never mind." Lina didn't know where that had come from. Emeli had told her to emphasize how good a brother Ren was, not how dumb he could be. Something was really bothering her. It crawled around inside, spreading like a sickness.

She rubbed her chest absentmindedly.

"Are you alright?" Ren asked.

"I'm fine. I just want to get out of here as soon as possible."

"Well, the others are resting. We can get them moving soon."

Lina nodded. "Alright. You better get back over there. I'll return in a second. I need another moment." She rubbed at her chest again with one hand, the other gripping her dagger tight. This wasn't good. It had already wormed its way inside of her, and she suspected it was affecting the others, too.

Then Ren's voice traveled through the trees. "Lina!"

She rolled her eyes. Couldn't they make it a moment without her?

"Lina!" he called out again, this time more urgently.

She ran toward the clearing, finding him standing next to the lantern, but Emeli wasn't there. Or Geret. "What happened?"

"They're gone."

"What do you mean they're gone?" She squinted into the shadows, heart racing.

"Emeli and Geret. They are just... gone," Ren said.

Lina's stomach sank. Getting separated in these woods was not a good thing. She clawed at the itch under the skin of her collarbone, the inky black spreading through her lungs.

Something—or someone—had snatched up Emeli and Geret, and she had no idea where to even look for them. This was something completely unknown.

This was not good at all.

SIXTEEN

GWEN

A CREEPING COLD SETTLED AROUND CAMP, AND GWEN'S teeth chattered. She awoke to the fire having gone out, leaving only a small curl of smoke billowing from the coals. She gathered branches, snapping them and wincing against the echoes. A few of Morin's men stood guard, but most were huddled together, resting. As she blew into the coals, igniting fresh flames over the piled branches, a whisper carried on the breeze.

Gwen.

Goosebumps erupted on her skin. She peered around the

trees. Morin was close by, but his eyes were shut, and he snored loud enough for it to amplify around them.

Gwen!

This time, whoever called to her did so with more urgency, the tone sharp and somehow familiar. She glanced around at the men on guard, but they did not stir. It was like they couldn't hear it at all.

She stood, drawing her sword, and wandered into the trees to follow the voice.

The fog thickened, pressing in against her skin and making it difficult for her to see.

Gwen. This time, the voice swirled around her like it was close. It was so distinct, she recognized the tone.

It couldn't be.

"Ren?" she whispered, searching the dense fog for her friend. When nothing answered, she shook her head. It had to be these woods. It was making her hear things. She shivered and turned to head back to the warmth of the fire, but she couldn't see the path. Velvety fog draped everything in a shroud, the trees becoming indistinguishable from one another. Her head spun as she squinted into the dark and her heart hammered in her chest.

Her footfalls echoed over the earth as she stomped in the directions from which she had come. At least, she thought she had come from that direction. Out of the fog, a figure in the mist jerked her shoulder backwards. There was the outline of a boy, too far to touch but close enough for her to recognize his features.

Ren's messy locks fell over one side of his face, and his clothes were soiled and tattered. A weary expression sunk into the lines of his face, and he looked older, like he'd been to some sort of underworld and barely made it out alive.

"Ren," Gwen called out to him, approaching slowly.

He said nothing, but he didn't run away. He stood there in a daze, his eyes locked onto hers.

Emotion welled in Gwen's eyes, and her chest squeezed.

Seeing him again was almost too much to contain. Guilt festered in her gut, thorny knots wrapping around her insides.

"You shouldn't be here, Ren. Turn around. Go home. It isn't worth it," she pleaded.

Ren frowned. "You killed him."

Gwen shook her head. "That wasn't supposed to happen. It wasn't supposed to go that way."

Ren's hand moved to his side and gripped the hilt of his sword.

Gwen froze. "Please, go back to Camelot. Things aren't as bad as they seem here. It's for everyone's good. I promise you."

Ren's face contorted, his lips forming a snarl, and he dropped his voice. "Your promises mean nothing. You betrayed me like your father did to Arthur. My father is dead because of you, and you think promising it will be better is going to make it right? You chose your side, Gwen."

The slice of his sword against the scabbard echoed in the fog as he drew it out, and Gwen winced.

"Please don't do this," she pleaded, gripping her own sword now. "I don't want to fight you. Not again." Her stomach clenched as the knots dug in.

"Let me pass, and this doesn't need to happen."

Her eyes rose to his. "I can't do that. We need the sword. Camelot needs change. Why can't you see that?"

But Ren didn't listen, lunging at her with his blade. She deflected the blow, but the sudden movement made her stumble backwards. Before she could recover, he was back, jabbing forward. She hopped to the left, and his sword ripped through the fabric of her cloak, barely missed her side.

She screamed out, energy surging through her blood as her training kicked in. This time, she was on the attack, grabbing her sword in both hands and swinging it in his direction. He was fast —much faster than he should have been—and he appeared suddenly on the other side of her. Her blade sliced at him but cut through empty fog.

A guttural laugh came from his lips that made the hair on the back of her neck stand on end. What had happened to him?

He came at her, swinging his blade. It met with hers, sending a metallic clang ringing out. The amplified sound pounded pressure into her ears, making them ache.

"Stop!" she yelled, dodging another blow and deflecting another. He was in front of her one moment and behind her the next, knocking a leg into her knees. She collapsed and rolled to the side to dodge his next blow as it came from above and slammed into the mossy ground.

She jumped back up, surging forward and meeting his sword with hers. He pushed her back, overpowering him until she ducked to one side, using the force of his blow to bring him crashing forward. She pushed again until his back was against a tree and she had him pinned with the edge of her blade at his throat.

"Ren. Please." She searched his face for that familiar gaze, for the softness in his eyes and the smile on his lips that always made her melt. But anger warped the boy in front of her. He was cold and determined.

"Do it," he hissed through clenched teeth. "Do it so I can join my father."

She shook her head, tears blurring her vision.

A jerk around her midsection caught her off guard as she struggled against the force. Looking down, a pair of hands had wrapped around her waist.

"It's not real," Morin's voice whispered into her ear suddenly. "Stop fighting. It's not real."

Her eyes darted back to the tree, but Ren was gone with nothing but a swirl of mist where he had stood.

She dropped her sword to the ground, and Morin released her waist.

"He was here!" She pointed at the tree, her eyes darting back to Morin.

His gaze dropped to the ground, and he ran a hand through his thick, dark locks. "I'm sure he was, but it wasn't him."

She didn't understand. He had been so real, as were the feelings festering inside of her. Then she noticed Morin's lip was bleeding.

Wiping the sweat from her forehead, she asked, "What happened?"

"We were attacked, but not by who you think. Come on. I think I know how to get us out of this cursed place."

The fog thinned and receded around them. Above, sunlight peeked through the thick canopies. She let out a heavy breath, picking up her sword from the ground and tucking it back at her side.

Looking back at the tree where Ren had been, the knot in her stomach tensed again, nausea rolling in her stomach. Perhaps the boy wasn't real, but the effect he had on her was. Which was much worse.

SEVENTEEN

"Anything?" Ren asked Lina as she plucked a leaf from a low shrub and rubbed it between her fingers and then sniffed it.

She wrinkled her nose in disgust, dropping the leaf. "No. Nothing." She peered around the trees, biting her bottom lip.

Ren had a horrible feeling in his gut. Losing Emeli and Geret was the worst possible thing. He and Lina circled the area multiple times, each taking turns venturing out into the trees and calling for them, but they always returned with nothing. Other than the glowing light from Emeli's lantern sitting where she left it, there were no other signs they'd been there. No footprints. Their packs were also gone. It was like they never were.

The sky grew darker, and the moon above cast twisty shadows through the canopy, making figures bend and move as if they were alive.

"Well, we can't stay here forever. What if something happened to them? We have to find them." The panic in Ren's chest took flight, making breathing more and more difficult. He could think of a hundred ways to die or get lost forever out there, and if that happened, it would be his fault. He had chosen to leave Camelot, to drag everyone out here. The weight of his decisions pressed his body deep into the earth, each step heavier and heavier.

Lina winced at his words. The deep bags under her eyes grew, her face permanently stuck in a scowl. "I know we can't stay here forever. Don't you think I've thought about that?"

"What do you propose?"

"I don't know, alright? Is that what you wanted to hear? I'm not seeing any tracking signs of them or of anything else, for that matter. We could continue walking through the woods, but I can't guarantee we are going to find them in that direction. Or at all. The best thing we can do is stay put and hope they find us. Otherwise, we are all lost."

The air left Ren's lungs, and he clasped a hand over his chest, where his heart raged. Hearing her say it out loud made it so much worse. He couldn't let this happen. "Fine. You stay here and I'll go." He slung his pack over one shoulder and stomped off.

Lina's boots pattered behind him, followed by a light illuminating the path.

"We shouldn't separate." She held out Emeli's lantern.

"Fine," Ren said, keeping his eyes tracking the dark woods ahead.

The more they walked, the more Ren couldn't breathe. Even as the moon slid into view overhead, casting everything in a pale glow, it all looked the same. There was still no sign of Emeli or Geret. If they couldn't find them, their best chance would be to meet up on the other side, but with the way things were going, he even wondered what hope they had of doing that.

Lina followed silently, occasionally rubbing a spot around her collarbone and rolling her neck uncomfortably around her shoulders.

Ren finally stopped, squatting to the ground and letting out a weighted sigh. His voice echoed off the trees much louder than he meant it to, and when he turned back to Lina, her eyes were wide.

"What was that?" he asked.

"That sound." She dropped her bottom lip, eyes searching the woods. Then, she snapped her fingers, and the sound reverberated off the trees so loudly that she covered her ears.

Ren surveyed the area, dropping open his mouth. "Whoa. You are right. The sounds changed. We must have traveled to a new part of the woods."

A spark of hope fired in his chest. They were making progress.

Their pace sped as they continued, carefully passing by trees and over little streams, each footfall echoing behind them as if an army were following close by. Shuffling through the trees, Ren's boot met with the sound of metal and his eyes dropped to the ground.

Laying in a pile of leaves was something shiny, and he bent down to pick it up. Brushing away the dirt revealed the long blade of a sword coated in a dark, slick liquid.

Blood.

The back of Ren's throat went dry, and he yelled for Lina. When she arrived, he pointed at the blade and reached for the sword's hilt, but vines had wrapped themselves around it, anchoring it into the earth. He tugged and tugged until a ripping sound echoed around them, tearing through the silence.

They both froze. Ren held the blade in his hand as they both listened. Lina snapped her fingers together, and the sound reverberated off the nearby trees, just as it had before.

"I guess we haven't made it past this part of the woods yet," Lina observed.

"You think?" Ren returned.

As if the woods were taunting them, a wind howled through the trees in a loud whoosh, shaking leaves from the canopies like rain all around them.

Once it calmed, Ren looked at the sword again.

"What is that?" Lina approached, her eyes on the blade.

"I don't know but look." He dipped a finger into the blood on the blade and held it out for Lina to see. "How is that possible? This sword was in the ground like it had been there for months."

Lina leaned in closer to examine the blade. "Weird. The blade has a green sheen to it."

Ren narrowed his eyes. Lina was right. Under the lantern light, an iridescent green wove its way through the steel. He'd never seen a sword like it. Wiping the blood from his fingertip onto his cloak, his hands went clammy.

"What if this is Emeli or Geret's blood?"

Lina grabbed hold of the hand he held the sword with, locking eyes with his. "It's not, okay? You said yourself, the sword was stuck in the ground. It's been here for a while."

"Then what is this, Lina?" his voice cracked. He dropped the sword, and it clattered to the earth.

"Let's just leave it for now and keep walking. The sounds in the woods are a good sign, remember? We are getting somewhere. This is nothing."

Ren knew her words were genuine, but the worry growing inside raged. He paced around in a circle, running his hand through his sweaty hair and adjusting the cloak around his shoulders. It suddenly felt too itchy, too hot, so he swung it off his shoulders, allowing a cold rush of air to wrap around him like an icy claw. His teeth chattered, and he looked to Lina, who was also shivering.

A cold fog crept along the forest floor as the temperature dropped again, sending a chill down Ren's spine.

"We should stop and light a fire," he said. It was mostly because of the cold, but he also felt on edge after finding the sword. Maybe he needed to rest and think for a moment. Doing so would help him come up with a new plan.

Lina agreed, and they gathered small sticks and deadfall for the fire. Before long, flames crackled between them as they gathered close around the warmth.

For a while, neither spoke. Ren let his mind wander with the dancing flames to Camelot and the fires in the great hall—thick furs draped over the chairs as mead flowed over the lips of goblets. Laughter echoed through stone from Bors, Percival, and even Galahad as they gathered and told stories of the old days. Little Elian would run through the chairs playing tag with the other children, and Ren's father was always there, holding his mother's hand under the table and tipping his glass to his comrades. Emeli, Geret, and Gwen would be there, too, and they would all join in the revelry inside the protected walls.

Ren didn't realize memories like those would be so precious. He now understood that their lives weren't what they thought. The world didn't exist only behind Camelot's walls. It was out here, in the wild places and the cold spaces between towns. It was filled with starving villages and thieves, with haunted forests, and with the mythological creatures he'd only heard about in stories from his father. The Lady of the Lake. Chimeras. All of them were out there waiting. Morin had been allowed to gather forces undetected, or if the knights had detected his intentions, they didn't take them seriously enough. There were probably other unhappy groups out there, too—kingdoms and villages who were turning against Camelot in the absence of a king.

"You look distressed." Lina finally broke the tense silence between them.

Across the fire, the light cast a glowing warmth over her face, softening her features and making her eyes shine.

"It's just not how I thought this would go." He sighed, poking the fire with a stick. Embers exploded and drifted into the dark sky.

"I tried to tell you."

He nodded. "I know, but I was so focused on the one thing my father has taught me since I was a child. And now..." He swallowed against the tightness in his throat. "Now he's gone, and none of it makes sense."

"Gone?"

He met her gaze. "He died that night when Camelot was attacked. It was Morin."

Her expression changed and her mouth melted into a frown. She stood from the rock and approached Ren and sat next to him so that their shoulders barely touched. She didn't look at him, and relief flooded his aching chest because he couldn't bear seeing the pity reflected in her eyes.

"I'm sorry," she said, her eyes focused on the dancing flames. "I never met my parents."

He turned to her now. "No? I thought that man was your father." He didn't know his name, and guilt swam inside.

"Ragnor? No. But he's about as close as I've ever had. They all are. They're my family."

"Oh." He didn't know what to say, but it made sense all the same. They were her family the same way Geret and Gwen were his family.

"Did you always live with them in the woods?" Ren asked.

"The druids? Yes. Or at least as long as I can remember. Ragnor says they found me abandoned in the woods, so they took me in, taught me to survive, and trained me to protect myself. I owe them my life."

"So, you don't remember your parents at all?" Ren searched for the anguish in her face, the same expression he guessed painted his face when he remembered his father was really gone. If those same thoughts were in her mind, she didn't show it.

Her eyes narrowed and her jaw tightened at the mention of them. "No. I don't know everything, but Ragnor said they were killed when I was young." Her eyes darted to Ren. "Because of Camelot."

The air grew thick, and a lump formed at the back of Ren's

throat. He wanted to avert his gaze as heat swarmed his face, but he leaned in closer. "That explains your distaste for Camelot."

Her gaze burned, but instead of unleashing the fire, she unclenched her teeth, and her eyes softened. "Something like that. I didn't even know them. It's just..."

"What?"

She pressed her lips together like she was being careful with her words. "That's all he said, and every time I pushed for more, he would deflect. I do know Camelot is responsible, and that's enough."

Her eyes cast to the fire, and the absence of her gaze gave Ren chills.

"For what it's worth, I'm sorry." It was the only thing he could think of to say, even though he knew it wasn't enough.

He gave her shoulder a gentle tap with his and returned his eyes to the popping embers of the fire.

The darkness pressed in, and silence settled around them. But it was different this time. Somehow, things had shifted. Having Lina sitting next to him was a warming comfort. Despite the chill and the unsettled energy in the woods, he knew it would be okay.

HOWLS in the distance woke Ren. He arose with a start, his eyes searching frantically for the source of the sound. He didn't even remember falling asleep. Looking around, Lina was also stirring.

Deep growls shook the ground, and Lina sprung awake, daggers drawn.

"What is that?" she asked, eyes wide.

Ren searched the trees, but there was no movement. Not even a shadow. "Whatever it is, I don't think they are close. The echoes are distorting the distance."

He hoped that was the case because the hair on the back of his neck was standing straight up, and he didn't want to scare Lina.

"Even so, we stayed too long. We need to get going." Lina worked to cover the smoldering embers of the fire with dirt.

Ren's shoulders tensed. Lina was right, but he hoped the fire would help Emeli and Geret find them. He was out of ideas of where to look next.

Lina covered everything in dirt, but there was one last smoldering coal which she stomped with the heel of her boot. It popped, and a firework of sparks burst from the ground and flew in multiple directions. One landed on the ground and caught some dry kindling aflame. Another dropped into a bush, igniting it instantly. The bush hissed, sending charcoal smoke into the sky.

Lina and Ren jumped into action, each attacking the fire with whatever they had to extinguish the flames. This only spurred them on, sending the fire crawling over the ground and catching anything in its path in a red blaze. Before long, they were choking on smoke as the fire spread between trees, jumping from branch to branch.

Lina stood at the center, her eyes fixed on the burning inferno. Tears streamed down her cheeks. "It's all my fault."

"What?" Ren rushed towards her, tugging on her arm. "It doesn't, we have to get out of here before it traps us."

She turned to him, horror striking her eyes. "You don't understand. I've seen this. The destruction. It's because of me." Her voice grew more panicked, and her boots planted on the ground.

Ren's head swam and his eyes stung, but he had to get her to move. He tugged on her elbow again, but she fought against him, pulling her arm into her side.

Voices carried on the wind. Screaming voices.

"Help! Ren, please!"

His heart stopped. It was Emeli's voice. He was sure of it. He exchanged looks with Lina, but she appeared to hear nothing, her eyes still transfixed on the burning trees. She knelt to the ground, raking her hands through the strands of her hair, now slick with sweat.

Flames engulfed several nearby trunks, but they burned

slowly, the bark peeling away in a screeching pile. Still, they stood. He had time.

"Lina. Stay here. I have to go find Emeli. I'll be right back. Do you hear me?" He yelled, but her eyes only flickered to his for a moment before darting back to the ground where she clawed at the soil with her nails.

Emeli's screams pierced the woods again and Ren sprinted in that direction until it grew louder and louder. Landing in a clearing, he frantically searched for his sister, but there was nothing. He was far away from the burning trees, but their screeching, amplified by the strange forest, still pounded in his ears. He covered his head with his arms to filter out the sounds so he could focus on finding Emeli. But her voice was no longer there.

Instead, a voice—male this time—wailed, "Ren!" It was Geret's frantic tone

Ren took off running, following the echoed screams. This time, fire swept over the ground, the smoke thickening until his lungs burned. Still, nothing. No Geret. No Emeli.

His heart pounded in his chest, and a fit of coughs took hold until he doubled over struggling for breath. Sweat slid down his back, soaking his tunic. It was too hot. He searched for signs of his friends, but it was only their voices all around him. In every direction, they called out for help, but he couldn't follow them all. Lina. Emeli. Geret.

The fire spread, and they were all in trouble. Hot panic raced through him as the voices swirled around his head. He dropped to his knees and pressed his hands to his ears. It was too much, and he was failing them all, just like he failed his father. If none of them made it out of here, he would fail Camelot, too. He didn't deserve knighthood. Maybe Gwen was right. Maybe he should give up.

His heart pounded and his breaths came in rapid succession, so he squeezed his eyes shut trying to force the panic away.

Through the noise, the voice of his father cut through the haze.

We need good knights like you, son.

It was one of the last things he had said to Ren, and he clung to it. His breaths slowed and he peeked through his half-closed lids. The voices still spun around him, all of them and all at once. That's when he realized he couldn't save them all. There wasn't enough time, and he was only one person. The realization tied thorny knots in his stomach, but his head cleared enough for him to spot something strange.

Mushrooms. A cluster of them at the base of a tree. In the dark, iridescent sparks burst from their wide caps, floating into the air like sparks from Lina's fire.

The mushrooms. The spores from the mushrooms were everywhere, clouding the air. They had been breathing them in since they first entered the forest, since they first felt strange. The silence. The sounds. The disappearance of Emeli and Geret. And now this fire.

Ren stared at the nearest tree engulfed in flames. It roared and ripped right through it in a fury of whipping fire that peeled away the bark, but still it stood. The trees should have been crumbling, breaking off in pieces, and then crashing down, not standing in one piece as they were eaten alive.

It wasn't real.

Ripping a strip of fabric from the bottom of his tunic, Ren wrapped it around his mouth and nose, binding it against his head. He took a few deep inhales, ensuring he could still breathe, and then he rose to his feet and ran through the trees.

The further he went, the more the surrounding flames melted into the trees, eventually disappearing entirely. The smoke cleared, and the stars pierced the night again. It was as if it had never happened. More importantly, there were no longer any screams from Emeli and Geret. But Lina's? They remained.

When he arrived at the clearing where he'd left her, she was completely distraught. Her hair stuck out in all directions and sweat drenched her dark locks. Tear stains streaked down her face.

She had dug into the earth. Dirt piled all around her, and she was pleading to the dark. "Please. I can't lose it all. I didn't mean it. This can't happen."

"Lina!" Ren rushed to her side, wrapping his arms around her. "It's okay. It's not real."

She thrashed against him, but that only made him squeeze her tighter against his chest.

"It's not real, but I am. Please."

She sobbed, her breaths coming in ragged gasps.

"I am real. I am real." He repeated into her ear until her fight lessened and her body finally went slack in his arms.

After a moment, he released her and pointed to his face covering. "It's the mushrooms. They've been poisoning us this entire time, making us see things that aren't there." He remembered the screams in the trees, and shivers ran down his back. "They've been making us hear things."

Lina nodded, wiping the tears from her face and taking in a slow, deep breath.

They ripped another shred of cloth from his tunic to make her a face cover before venturing back out into the woods.

With the magic of the spores no longer clouding their minds, the path appeared before them as they followed it through the thick forest. Eventually the trees thinned, and the air grew light. Dawn peeked through the canopy, dripping light through the darkness.

They said nothing on their way out of the cursed woods. Ren suspected Lina also battled the inner demons brought to light on the path behind them. He knew his stomach still twisted in knots with the fear of never seeing Emeli and Geret again. If they made it out, the looming challenges ahead still held an uncomfortable uncertainty. Even if he couldn't save everyone, that didn't mean he wouldn't try.

CHAPTER

EIGHTEEN

LINA

Lina let out a deep sigh as they emerged from the trees, clawing at her mask around her face and breathing in the fresh air. Sprawling hills lay beyond, the rising sunbathing everything in a warm glow. For the first time since entering the woods, she smiled.

The heaviness in her chest lifted, and she was so relieved, she threw her arms around Ren and let out a laugh. "I didn't know if we would make it out of there."

Pulling away, she locked eyes with him. "Thank you for what you did back there. I don't know what came over me." The darkness of the woods still clung to the shadows of her mind, but she refused to acknowledge them.

Ren pressed his lips into a line, and she couldn't help staring. She couldn't believe she was even thinking it, but she was glad it was him. She wasn't sure anyone else would have been able to break her out of that horrifying daze. The fire—the all-consuming nature of the terror taking hold of her—it would never end. She wasn't ready to face it. Thankfully, she didn't have to because he was there.

Something else rose in the flecks of amber at the outer corners of his hazel eyes, pulling her in. Heat swarmed her cheeks as she cast her gaze to the ground.

"Lina, I—" Screaming from the woods drew both their attention.

"Ren!" Emeli's voice shouted from the distance, and her figure appeared from the trees. It wasn't a relieved scream but a frantic one. Lina's heart sped as she ran after Ren, who was already sprinting toward his sister.

The siblings collided in a tight embrace, but when Lina caught up, terror flashed in Emeli's eyes. "It's Geret," she managed to say between heavy breaths.

"What happened? Where is he?" Ren asked.

"We were attacked by some sort of wolves. It was dark, and they were so big." Her voice became flustered, and she dragged them toward the trees. "Geret put himself between me and the wolves and tried to fight them off, but he was already injured from the knight."

"The knight? What knight?"

"What? It doesn't matter. I managed to fight off the wolves with fire-tipped arrows. I had to do something. I couldn't let him die in there, but there was so much blood, Ren." She was talking so fast. Tears welled in the corners of her eyes, and all color drained from her cheeks.

Ren stopped her, squeezing her shoulders. "You did good. Where is he?"

She pointed behind a row of trees. "I had to drag him toward the end because he lost all his strength to walk, but I couldn't get far. Thankfully I heard your voices. Come on!" She sprinted into the trees and they both followed.

Arriving out of breath, the sight of Geret's limp body made Lina's stomach turn. Slumped against a tree, Geret's eyes fluttered open and closed. His chest rose and fell, but his breaths were shallow. Crimson soaked his tunic, and his armor hung loose around his shoulders.

Emeli shook her head, covering her mouth with shaking, blood-soaked fingers.

Meanwhile, Lina stood over him, frozen, her eyes glazed over. Death was close. He needed medical attention, but they were nowhere near any town that would have a healer. This was worse than she could imagine.

"Lina!" Ren snapped his fingers in front of her, and she shook off the daze. "Can you help him?"

She dropped to Geret's side, peeling his sticky tunic from his side to reveal a bloody wound. He let out a moan and dropped his head to one shoulder.

Running a hand over the wound, Lina assessed its severity, but sickness rose at the back of her throat. "I don't know if I can save him." The words were cracked and broken. She couldn't get a hold of them.

"Please, you have to!" Emeli shrieked, falling into Ren's side as Ren wrapped an arm around her.

"I..." Lina shook her head. She'd never healed anyone this badly injured before. She had barely even practiced healing magic at all. She didn't know if she had the skills to do it. Plus, flashes of the fire spreading through the woods rose at the back of her mind.

Her fault. This was all her fault.

She shouldn't even be here. This was beyond anything she could do.

Her hands shook as she stood, and she turned on her heels to create some space. While she paced, her fingers instinctively went to the pouch at her hip as she felt for the smooth, comforting touch of the vials inside.

She didn't have the right ingredients. Or the strength. The woods had left her weak and unfocused.

Then, her fingers met with a small glass vial. She pulled it out and examined the iridescent liquid inside. It was the one the woman gave her in the market. Something inside her snapped together, and she knew this was exactly what she needed.

Emeli knelt beside Geret, pushing his hair out of his eyes. Looking at Lina, she whispered, "Please. You have to do something."

Lina squeezed the vial in her palm, and her instincts took hold as she knelt next to Geret. She ripped the tunic from the wound and bunched it between her fingers. "This is going to hurt."

Emeli squeezed Geret's hand as Lina dumped the liquid from the vial onto the cloth and pressed it onto his wound.

He yelled out in pain as sweat poured from his forehead.

This would help heal the deep wound, but she needed something to seal it.

"The flowers. I need the Pyracantha flowers. Can you find some?" Lina directed Ren.

Ren obeyed the order and sprinted off through the trees.

Emeli paced the area now, her eyes wild. Geret's moans had stopped, and his breaths had slowed.

"Come on," Lina begged, still holding the cloth into his side.

Luckily, Ren wasn't gone long, returning with his pockets full of the white petals. Lina pinched them between her fingers until they were slick with the flower's juices.

She rubbed her palms together, whispering into them until a warm glow seeped between her hands "Stand back!"

Emeli stepped back behind Ren, both their eyes upon her.

Lina kept chanting, closing her eyes and concentrating until the glow from her hands burned with blue fire. She lifted the cloth and replaced it with both hands. Geret yelled, his back arching away from the tree. He fought against her, but she pressed even harder into the wound. Ren jumped in, helping to hold him down.

All at once, Geret's body went still, and he let out a heavy breath before sinking back into the tree.

Lina released her hands and backed away, but she stumbled over exhausted limbs until she fell to her knees.

Emeli squatted next to Ren. "Is he…"

The seconds passed with agonizing slowness as Lina held her breath, pleading with Avalon to bring him back. She couldn't be responsible for his death.

Finally, Geret's chest puffed, and his breaths returned.

They all let out sighs of relief, especially Lina, who dropped her shoulders and stood with her hands on her hips.

Emeli dropped to Geret's side, and he fluttered his eyes open. "The baddest…"

"What?" she asked.

"Who is the baddest knight you know back from the dead?" he said, coughing and trying to sit up with a grimace.

"Bad is one word for it." Ren supported his shoulders, easing him into a sitting position.

"Don't do that ever again!" Emeli yelled, slapping Geret's shoulder.

"Ow!" he howled. "Haven't I been through enough?"

"It's all your fault! If you hadn't stepped in front of that wolf—"

"You're welcome, m'lady." Geret gritted his teeth and then assessed the damage to his side.

A slight smile crept onto Emeli's lips. "I told you I didn't need chivalry, stupid."

Lina shook her head. She wondered what it would be like to know someone that well. Her eyes flicked to Ren, who was examining Geret's wound. The skin around the wound was inflamed and beet red, but it had closed, leaving nothing left but a pink scar and scattered bruises.

Ren caught Lina's eyes.

She leaned all her weight against a tree, fluttering her eyes shut. The magic had taken a toll, and she needed rest.

"Are you alright?" Ren approached.

She merely nodded, too tired to speak.

"How did you do that?" he asked.

She lifted her head with one eye open, peeking at Emeli as she helped Geret to his feet.

"It's not my magic," Lina responded, stepping away from the tree and reaching into her sack for her last strip of dried fish. She gnawed at it as the salt melted over her tongue. "To heal. It's not mine."

"What do you mean it's not your magic? I saw you do it." Ren pressed.

Lina sighed, too tired to explain, so her eyes scanned the horizon instead. "I would really like to get as far from these woods as possible, wouldn't you?"

Ren looked slightly annoyed at her deflection but followed as she strode forward. Emeli and Geret trailed behind at a slower pace.

After a while, the tension of the woods lifted, and the group resumed small talk, including Geret recounting a story of when he fought off a bear in the Caledonian Forest ten times the size of the wolves who had nearly killed him.

Emeli laughed, and Lina caught herself smiling, too.

However dangerous the road ahead, at least they would face it together.

NINETEEN

SEVERAL HOURS OF BUSHWHACKING THROUGH overgrown thistles and sinking into swampy marshlands left Ren with a dozen stinging cuts and exhaustion weighing on his bones. They finally emerged at the base of the mountain amongst craggy rocks, and at least there was hope with the Silver Mountains finally in view.

They decided to stop for the night, making camp in a grove of narrow, pointed trees. The wind howled, shaking the barren branches which had not yet sprouted their spring foliage. Up here, the air was thinner, the temperature colder.

Ren hissed as he poured water down his arm, watching the clear liquid turn pink. His arm was on fire. He tried shaking out the sting, but that only fanned the flames.

"Here." Lina pulled a handful of leaves from her satchel and handed them around the group. She wrapped one around Ren's forearm until the sticky surface pressed against his skin.

He winced against the sting, but after a moment, the plant's syrup sent a cooling sensation spreading up his arm. He sighed in relief. "What is this?"

Geret pressed one against his neck, letting out a groan and fluttering his eyes shut. "I don't care what it is, it's heaven," he mumbled, sliding down the base of a tree and dropping his head between his legs.

"I found them in the Brecheliant woods," Lina said.

Ren's eyes widened, and he ripped them from his arm. "I don't want anything to do with those woods."

Lina chuckled. "They are healing. Why does it matter where they came from?"

Geret opened one eye, peering at Ren, and Emeli shook her head while applying more leaves to her arms.

"Because we can't trust anything that came from those cursed woods?" Ren was still shaken from his experience in the fire. His friends' screams still echoed in his mind, and he shivered.

Lina pressed her lips into a line and dropped her eyes.

They didn't talk about it, and Ren wasn't sure if he ever wanted to share what he experienced out there. Neither did anyone else, as they all seemed to have their own demons from the forest.

Lina blinked and continued wrapping her inflamed skin with the leaves.

Ren frowned and glanced at everyone wearing relieved expressions, leaning against trees, or resting on the ground. The stinging still surged up and down his arm, and he eventually gave in. Wrapping the leaves around his exposed skin, the relief was instant, and he decided it was worth it, cursed leaves or not.

"Where did you learn this stuff? Healing, tracking..." Ren eyed Lina as she brought an armful of kindling and worked with Geret to get a fire going.

A soft, playful smile edged her lips. "It's amazing what you learn living on your own outside the comforts of a town or the stifling stone walls of the castle." She winked, blowing on the fire and igniting the flames higher as they popped and shot sparks into the air.

Ren couldn't bite back anymore. The more he was away from the castle, the more he realized he had a lot to learn about the world. He questioned all the lessons they had sat through growing up—the history of the kingdom, the legacy of the knights, the stories about how Arthur brought peace to the lands. He realized that peace was only temporary, and the stories they were told had only been half truths.

A deep ache bloomed in Ren's shoulder as tension crawled across his back. He rolled the shoulder back, letting out a groan. These long days of travel and sleeping on the ground were not doing him any favors.

Lina caught his eye. "I can help with that."

Not realizing he was massaging his old injury, he dropped his hand and puffed out his cheeks. He's seen what she had done for Geret, and this was nothing in comparison. Maybe she could help. He nodded.

Lina's fingers traced the belt at her waist. Digging through a pouch, she found a tiny vial of velvety sand with a shimmer to it that glowed in the dimming light.

She sat next to Ren, edging a little closer before sliding her fingers along the collar of his tunic and gently tugging it down to expose the bare skin of his shoulder.

Goosebumps ran over his skin and his eyes instantly averted her gaze, focusing instead on Emeli and Geret huddled together and chatting over hot pine tea on the other side of the fire. Emeli briefly looked at him but quickly returned to Geret, where she had been pretending to be interested in one of his stories. Ren knew she was pretending because she was nodding her head and laughing. Laughing! Even though Geret had told this story multiple times on this journey already.

"Do you mind if I touch you?" Lina asked.

Heat rushed Ren's face as his attention returned to Lina. He noticed how close she was to his face, that her fingers were still wrapped around the fabric of his shirt. Flutters erupted inside him, but he played it off, nodding casually. "Sure."

She poured a bit of the sandy substance from the vial into the palm of her hands and rubbed them together, whispering so quietly under her breath, one might have mistaken it for the wind. A soft glow radiated from her pressed hands, and she placed one on the front side of his shoulder and the other on the back.

Her touch did things to Ren he wasn't expecting. He shifted in his seat, his gaze jumping to look up at the sky, which was turning shades of plum and burnt orange. It was beautiful.

"Does that hurt?" Lina asked, leaning in closer.

Ren's throat went dry, and his body tingled. "Umm... No."

"Good." She applied more gentle pressure.

Lightness filled Ren's head, but not because of his shoulder. This close to Lina, pine and other floral notes drifted from her hair. Her warm breath tickled the side of his neck, and the air in his throat hitched.

She let out a quiet giggle but said nothing. Maybe she was thinking the same confusing things.

"Magic isn't a cure, but it can help." Her voice interrupted the swirling thoughts in his head, and he cleared his throat, wetting his lips.

A numbing sensation spread under her pressed hands, and it seeped into his skin, penetrating deep into the muscles around his shoulder.

He let out a relieved groan. "That feels nice." He fluttered his eyes shut. His shoulder wasn't always in pain, but there was always a slight discomfort to it. The scar tissue underneath had healed, but it was sensitive at times. Right now, there was none of that. It was just warm and comfortable.

"Ren." Lina's voice shook him from whatever form of sedation he was in, and he realized he had melted into her side as his entire body relaxed. He quickly jolted upright, and she released her hands from his shoulder.

Across the fire, Emeli snorted.

Geret didn't even bother hiding a laugh. "You okay there, buddy?"

Ren shot them both glares before turning to Lina. She was still sitting next to him, and he was highly aware of the places where their bodies touched.

"Sorry. That was amazing. Thank you," he said.

"You're welcome. Like I said. It helps." She offered a smile.

Ren's eyes lingered on her lips. He imagined what they would taste like pressed against his. A flush rushed the back of his neck, and he slid ever so slightly away from her.

You can't do this, Ren. Focus on the quest. She's helping. That's all this is. She's just this beautiful stranger who has magic and is an amazing fighter. Her tracking knowledge is useful on this sort of journey.

When he met her gaze again, she stared back at him with those big, rich, warm eyes, and his mind went blank.

You're in so much trouble.

"You said magic isn't a cure." He needed to change the subject, but he also was truly interested to know.

"No. It takes too much as it is," she responded, tucking the vial of sand back into the pouch at her hip.

Ren's eyes lingered on her hips.

He coughed, his breath fogging the air. "And the same for Geret?" He looked to his friend who was, thankfully, fully engaged in telling stories to Emeli again. Neither was paying attention to them.

"He will be fine, but that wound will never go away. Scars

fade, but trauma like that stays trapped in the body. No magic can take it away," Lina replied.

"Oh," Ren whispered, his eyes locked on Geret.

Was she referring to the physical side effects of his injury, or the ones that would stay locked in his mind long after he healed? Ren knew which one would haunt him more because they were the same ones that still haunted him from that night in Camelot with his father. Again, in the Brecheliant Woods, the ones that crept into his nightmares at night, leaving him on edge.

He hoped for a better recovery for his friend.

TWILIGHT BROUGHT a crystal sea of stars overhead as cold air enveloped their camp. They fed the fire dead wood until the sparks disappeared into the sky. The quiet amongst the group settled around them. At the base of the mountain, so close to the os-nàdarra caves, the unsettling energy was palpable. Even Geret's usual flapping mouth pressed into a solid line as he observed the popping fire.

Lina disappeared somewhere into the forest, stating that she would be back. Meanwhile, Ren found comfort observing Emeli preparing her arrows. She balanced on a log, smoothing pieces of wood into slender shafts with a knife. Next, she pulled out the tiny glass pot with a corked lid she purchased from the blacksmith. She swirled around its contents and studied the iridescent color. Satisfied, she popped the cork and, one by one, dipped her arrow points inside, bathing them in the metallic liquid silver. The blacksmith had mentioned he got it from the market in town, but now Ren wondered if it was from the same woman who gave Lina the vial that saved Geret.

Emeli continued, floating the tip of the arrows over the burning fire, she then doused them in water from her canteen.

They sizzled, hardening into solid tips. To finish, she ran a coarse wool cloth around the edges, polishing them to a gleaming point.

Watching his sister make her arrows had always been calming for Ren, but not tonight. Tonight, he had a tough time stifling the anxiety clawing at his insides. He had worrying thoughts of the chimera guarding the cave. He wondered if Morin was close by. Worst of all, he experienced the sharp guilt of bringing his friends along for the whole thing.

His eyes darted to Geret, who was still suspiciously quiet while observing Emeli's preparations.

"It's not too late, you know." Emeli said. "We can still return home. We could take the safe road around the forest and join the others in the castle as they prepare for the battle. Nobody would think anything of it. They didn't even know why we came out here," Emeli commented, securing her new arrows in her quiver.

"Merlin knows. And Arthur. We can't fail them, Em."

Emeli nodded, not countering this time, but Ren caught the slight tensing of her shoulders. Guilt gnawed at him again and worry wormed its way inside over concerns about protecting her.

"Besides, this is more than just a sword. It's a chance for us to write our own names alongside our parents." Geret's voice shattered the tension, and they both threw glances in his direction.

He shifted in his seat. Wincing against his side, Ren was certain his injury still bothered him even though it was healed.

Silence.

Then, his eyebrows shot up. "What? You think you are the only one who needs to prove something to Camelot? We all have stakes in this quest."

Ren dropped his bottom lip, then closed it, unsure of how to respond.

"I've never heard you talk about that before." Emeli commented. "This quest, or your parents."

It was true. Geret hardly ever spoke about his parents, particularly his father. The couple who raised him were kind and generous, and Ren knew he always considered them his real parents.

But he supposed the stories of his father, Sir Gawaine, followed him like a shadow. The same as Ren's.

Geret sealed his lips and studied Emeli. His hand dropped to his side and pressed against the phantom wound.

"Almost dying changed things. It made me think about what I'm doing here."

This time Emeli's eyebrows shot up. "I thought you were here to make sure I made it home safe. That's what you said when we left Camelot to look for Ren."

Even in the dark, Ren could tell Geret's cheeks were on fire.

"That hasn't changed. Someone has to make sure you aren't eaten alive by monstrous wolves again."

Emeli nodded, whispering. "Or killed by green knights."

Geret averted his gaze, poking the fire with a stick as a cluster of embers popped into the sky. He didn't say another word, and even though Ren wanted to press further about the knight they encountered in the woods, especially because he remembered the sword he found taken over by foliage, he sensed Geret wasn't ready to talk about it. Maybe he never would be.

They sat in silence for a few more minutes before Lina returned. They all prepared for sleep, tucking into their blankets around the fire. Ren's eyes remained wide open as he stared up at the glittering stars.

If the forest taught him anything, it was that he couldn't protect all of them. But if they accomplished what they came here for, maybe he wouldn't have to.

THE NEXT MORNING, their pace quickened as they ascended the mountain. The goal of reaching the destination beat urgently in their hearts. A faint animal trail was the only path guiding them through loose rock and alpine tundra. Blotches of deep red moss with small white flowers grew between loose gravel, but that was the last of the vegetation as the tree line shrunk smaller and smaller behind them. The higher they climbed, the thinner the air became and the more difficult it was to breathe. The howling wind blasted them from every direction.

"Ah! This is a good one." Emeli beamed at the sight of a long, silky gray feather with tan stripes caught in a rock. She was the only one who seemed to have a positive spirit amongst the shadows of mountain giants. She ran a fingertip along the edge of the feather's vane, and it snapped back into stiff formation. "Strong and beautiful." She tucked the feather into her leather pouch and took a sip of water.

"Sounds like someone I know," Geret commented.

She rolled her eyes but then smiled when he was no longer looking.

"So..." Geret stopped next to Ren, planting his hands on his waist to catch a breath of air. Surveying the looming mountain peak ahead, he asked, "How is this plan of yours going to work exactly?"

"We'll approach from the west entrance like Merlin explained." Ren pointed to the back side of the mountain peak. "We have to hope the beast is protecting the front of the mountainside since that is the safer road." Then, he pointed to the other side as Geret squinted into the sunlight, beads of sweat forming upon his brow. "Once inside, we retrieve the sword and get the hell out of there before it knows we've been there."

Geret nodded, pursing his lips before taking a swig of water.

"And if the beast isn't guarding the front, and he blocks our only way in instead?"

"Then, we do what we've been trained to do. We fight it and make sure we win." Ren cleared his throat at that part, pushing down the uncertainty bubbling in his chest.

After hours of trudging up the mountainside, they arrived at a flat outcropping of sharp, flat stone peppered with small tuffs of alpine moss. Scanning the horizon, the flat stone shot back a few miles until it met with the mountain. It was difficult to see the entrance, but Ren knew it must have been there from Merlin's description of the landing. Above, the sun hung high in the middle of the sky, and his heart fired in anticipation of reaching the cave and finding what they came here for.

Their pace quickened on the flat surface until they reached the mountainside. There was a dark arch of sorts, a carved shadow out of the side of rock, but there was also something else blocking the entrance—Morin, flanked by dozens of dark knights.

"Well, fuck," Geret exclaimed.

CHAPTER

TWENTY

Leave it to Geret to say what everyone else was thinking. Ren hoped they could still beat Morin here despite the setbacks in the Brecheliant Woods but now that he was standing here with a small army in front of him, he realized that was wishful thinking. A rock sunk in his gut.

Morin's voice echoed across the mountain. "You didn't think I was going to let you and your little friends have all the fun, did you?"

Ren was too far away to see the smirk on Morin's face, but he knew it was there. Ren's jaw tightened and boiling blood raced through his veins.

He turned to the group. Emeli's mouth hung agape and Geret looked completely dejected. After what they'd already been through, staring down a dozen armored men blocking their only entrance to the cave was a hard blow.

But did Morin already have the sword?

"So that's Morin?" Lina's sharp gaze surveyed the entrance as she retrieved the daggers at her hip, twirling them between her hands.

"Oh, don't be such a sour sport," Morin cried. "We can take it from here, little knights. Your quest is over. Return home to your kingdom and know that you've done everything you could."

Ren shook his head and ground his teeth. The more Morin talked, the more he wanted to cut that grin right off his stupid face.

"That's who attacked Camelot?" Lina asked. "He doesn't look that bad."

"He's bad enough," Ren muttered, his head racing through ideas about how to get past this. Morin's men had them outnumbered, and they were already at the cave's entrance. They had the advantage.

Geret drew his sword and Emeli nocked an arrow in her bow, ready to aim. Ren nodded at the rest, squaring his shoulders as he lifted his sword. What choice did they have? They couldn't give up when they were this close. They had to try.

When the group was ready to charge forward, a shriek boomed overhead, and a flash of lighting and smoke poured down. Everyone froze with their eyes locked on the blue sky. Another shrieking growl sounded, this time deeper and longer, and instead of lightning, a barrel of fire shot from a bank of clouds.

The chimera.

Ren stepped in front of his sister instinctively, but she poked him in the shoulder blade with the tip of her bow. "I can't see, move!"

She pushed Ren forward, aiming at the shadow behind the fire and letting loose her arrow. It sailed through the air, disappearing into a ring of charcoal smoke clouds.

A shriek cut through the smoke, followed by an enormous figure tearing through the haze and swooping down on the group. They ducked, covering their heads just in time for the snap of claws at their backsides. The creature came into focus—a four-legged body covered in hairy scales. Golden, silky fur framed its face, and a set of giant wings shimmered under the sun. It zoomed over them again, and they ran to escape the snatch of bird-like talons attached to each padded foot.

The chimera did another sweep over the other side where Morin's men assumed fighting formation, and it caught an outlier with its talons, flinging him across the mountain. Next, the monster's sharp eyes and hawk-like beak turned toward Ren and the others.

When Merlin told him the chimera could take many different forms, a flying bird from hell was not something he imagined.

As they braced for another attack, Morin and his men advanced in fighting formation, running down the hillside and meeting with Ren and the others.

Ren went into fight mode, his body instantly reacting after years of training. He sliced at someone with his sword, elbowing another in the ribs coming at him from behind. Geret hollered as he punched through a couple of men. Lina twirled around with sharp blades, dashing in and out of the fray, while Emeli retreated to higher ground, perching on a pile of boulders and picking off Morin's men one by one.

They were so busy fighting each other, they didn't notice the barrel of fire shooting toward them in a cloud of heat and smoke until there was hardly any time to jump out of the way. Luckily, Ren did, somersaulting into the dirt and slamming into a jagged boulder. Pain shot through his bad shoulder as he stood, massaging out the burn.

He groaned, scanning the sky for the chimera, but it had disappeared for the moment. That's when a boot met his gut, stealing the breath from his lungs and sending him crashing to the ground. Morin peered over him, his sword pointing to his throat, and laughed.

"I don't understand why Camelot means so much to you. It's not your destiny to rule. Why burden yourself with the task?" Morin said. A gash along the side of his face dribbled blood over his pale cheek.

"You don't know my destiny." Ren clenched his jaw, edging up to his elbows while searching for the sword he had dropped.

"That's right, because I can't seem to recall any stories about your father during Arthur's time. Only the ones that matter are written, and the Bediveres are nowhere to be found. The sooner you learn this, the easier it will be for you."

Acid boiled in Ren's stomach as his fingers found the hilt of his sword, wrapping around the leather and gripping tight. "My father was a better knight than yours ever was. He was a better man, too." He swung his blade, slashing at Morin's arm, but Morin jumped back in time to dodge the blow.

"We'll see about that, Amren." He plunged toward Ren.

As they exchanged blows, Ren became more and more confident with each strike. He even tripped up Morin, sending him crashing to his knees. Morin's breaths were heavy. Almost weighted. Grunts of frustration had replaced the smug comments, and a vein throbbed in his temple. His jaw clenched every time he missed Ren and was met with the clang of his blade instead.

Ren was winning. He couldn't believe it. Every attack drew more and more mistakes from Morin, who was visibly upset. And then he had the opportunity to knock into Morin's unprotected chest with his shoulder. It sent him flailing backwards as he lost his footing, tripping over the sharp edge of a rock and landing on his ass.

Ren stepped forward with his sword pointing at Morin's chest.

The image of his father flashed in his mind—his bleeding body crumpled on the ground, and Morin standing over him with a smirk in this exact position.

Everything went hazy and his head went light as he swayed in search of solid ground.

The clang of another sword pulled him back as he slammed his own sword forward. In his daze, he peered at the person standing where Morin had been. In front of him was a familiar swirl of blonde locks and dressed in tight, black leathers.

Gwen stared at him through their crossed swords.

Ren's words caught at the back of his throat. He was still reeling from the image of his father, and now he was staring at a girl he didn't recognize. Charcoal paint splattered her face, and shiny crow's feathers weaved into the locks of her blonde hair. The expression staring back at him held no warmth of familiarity, only horror.

She seemed to be at a loss for words, as well, but it didn't matter because a wave of fire came barreling down between them as the chimera plummeted from the sky, scattering the clouds.

Ren jumped back, rolling out of the way from the wall of flames just in time. He choked on the smoke, searching for Gwen on the other side, but she was gone. So was Morin.

Morin's men re-grouped near the cave's entrance to focus on the chimera, and they sent a barrage of arrows flying at the beast.

Ren used the distraction to gather the others and fall back from the fight.

"Did you see Gwen?" Emeli said between breaths.

Ren's stomach tensed. "Yes. Is everyone okay?" He changed the subject because he didn't know what else to say. Seeing Gwen had pierced a hole in his heart, one that wasn't entirely unexpected but still left an uncomfortable ache in his chest. But what could he do about that? There were other things he had to focus on. He did catch Lina looking up at the mention of Gwen. She had been cleaning the blades of her daggers, but thankfully, she said nothing.

Geret had his hand pressed against the healed wound at his side, wincing, but he nodded, also at a loss for words.

"What are we going to do now? We can't keep this up. There are too many of them." Emeli took a seat on a rock, dumping water over her face and gurgling what was left at the back of her throat.

Ren scanned the field. Morin and his men were still blocking the entrance to the cave as the chimera circled, shrieking, above.

They needed to get inside the cave. It would protect them from the chimera and give them a fighting chance against Morin's men, who would be forced to narrow their numbers once inside. It would even everything out, but how would they make it inside?

"We need some sort of distraction," he said.

The group exchanged confused looks, but Lina dropped her eyes and let out a heavy sigh.

"Give me a feather." She thrust her hand into Emeli's quiver, ripping at her arrows.

Emeli squealed, pulling her quiver from her shoulder and tugging it away from Lina's grasp. "What the heck!"

Lina blew air out of her nose and outstretched her palm, nicely this time. "I don't have time to explain, but I have an idea. I've only ever done this once before, but it could work. I just need one of your stupid bird feathers."

Emeli looked at Ren, but he had no clue what Lina was planning either, so he shrugged. Sighing, Emeli dug through her leather pack, returning a tan feather with dark stripes.

Lina accepted it and pulled a bag from her hip, in search of another vial of mystery liquid. She pulled one out that looked like liquid gold, and Geret's eyes went wide.

"What is that?" Ren asked.

"Don't worry about it. It's going to get us to the entrance. That's all you need to know."

Geret shot Ren a shifty glance, but they both eyed whatever Lina was plotting all the same.

She took the vial, leaning it over the feather and tapping it until all the liquid had seeped out and drenched the feather's veins. A vapor erupted from her palm, and they all jumped back, shielding their eyes.

Lina laughed. "It's not a party trick."

Within her palm, the feather glowed, dripping vapor through her fingers and spreading over her hand.

"Are you sure about that?" Geret joked as the vapor wrapped around Lina's arm and crawled up her collarbone and neck. "Because it's a good one."

"Lina!" Ren shouted, reaching out for her arm when the vapor swirled around her face. It was trying to suffocate her.

But she stepped back, allowing it to take hold of her entire body until they could no longer see her figure. Out of the vapor a shriek sounded, and wings sprung out.

A hawk emerged where Lina's body had been.

They all gasped as the bird flapped its wings and flew into the air.

The bird—Lina—said nothing as she launched into the air, flying straight for Morin's army.

Another flying creature in the sky confused everyone as they scrambled to their positions, shooting arrows in every direction. Luckily, Lina was just as agile in hawk form as in her human one, so she dodged everything with grace. Meanwhile, the chimera rose higher in the sky, befuddled by the sight of the giant bird in its territory.

Ren realized Lina had given them their chance, and he commanded the others to run as they all charged the entrance.

As Morin's men battled Lina, Ren, Emeli, and Geret slipped closer to the cave. He turned to look at Lina, who was tearing into one of Morin's dark knights, ripping through his tunic and scratching at his face as he yelled out.

At the same time, Morin fumbled with the buckles at his

chest, and Ren knew he was about to take his crow form. There were far too many birds in this battle.

"Lina!" Ren yelled. The hawk narrowed its yellow eyes on him and swooped through Morin's men before landing on the ground at his feet. It erupted into smoke, and Lina emerged in human form, grinning.

"I'm not even going to ask," Ren said.

"Good," she replied.

The small victory was short-lived, as a blast knocked them both backwards.

Ren and Lina lunged for the cave's entrance as Morin's voice rang out, "Loose!"

Something hard knocked into Ren's back, flinging him into the hard rock of the cave. Light exploded, followed by a shuttering boom vibrating the entrance of the cave. Then, a fan of smoke and everything went dark.

Ren inhaled, choking on dust but calling out for his friends.

Emeli answered first with a quiet whimper. "I'm here. I'm fine."

Rocks tumbled behind Ren, and a spark flickered against the wall. Lina crouched next to the entrance with a glowing ember in her palm. Making a torch, she wrapped strips of fabric from her tunic around a branch and dipped it against the ember in her palm.

"Geret!" Ren yelled out next, allowing his eyes to adjust to the hazy light. The air inside the cave was sour and somewhere far off, the dripping of water echoed off stone.

A groan came from behind, and Ren breathed a sigh of relief at the sight of Geret pushing himself from his hands and knees. Lina swept the torch light across the entrance to the cave. There was no outside light streaming through, only stone and a cloud of dust.

"He's mental!" Geret exclaimed, shaking his head as dust poofed from his hair. "Why would he want to trap us in here if he wanted the sword for himself? Now he can't even get in."

"I don't know," Ren whispered to himself as his insides twisted with a bad feeling. "All that matters is we made it."

That bad feeling took form in a huffing breath deep inside the cave. A gush of wind raced through the tunnel as they all turned around, backing into the rock at the entrance. The shadow of the chimera emerged, its talons tapping along the stone floor as he stopped in front of them and let out an ear-shattering shriek.

TWENTY-ONE

GWEN

WHEN THEIR BLADES MET, GWEN THOUGHT REN WAS another illusion until his eyes softened at the sight of her. Confused. But not as cold as the Ren in the forest. This Ren was real. She massaged the tension forming in her shoulders, rolling her head around, but it didn't help. The discomfort was there to stay, so what would she do with it?

Morin let out a shrill yell, kicking his sword across the flat rock. He fell to his knees in the most dramatic fashion possible, raking his hands down his face in frustration. His dark hair fell in a curtain of sweaty locks over his eyes and his shirt was still ripped open, his bare chest and crow tattoo on full display.

That was one way to handle the stress.

"Why didn't you use your magic if he was beating you so badly?" She stood over him, hands on her hips. The rest of the dark knights gathered to lick their wounds, which were mostly inflicted by the giant beast.

His eyes flicked up to hers. "I know you think me vile, Gwendolyn, but I do believe in fighting fairly and they didn't have magic. At least I thought they didn't. I wasn't expecting to see a druid girl with them."

"A druid girl?" The casual tone masked her concern. She also noticed the beautiful stranger fighting with her friends. *Her* friends. Although, she supposed they weren't her friends anymore. Even worse than this new girl possessing magic and fighting skills was the way Ren had looked at her. He was in awe. Gwen could tell because it was the same way he used to look at her.

"Hello?" Morin snapped his fingers in front of Gwen's nose. He was standing now and looking very bored. She'd been so lost in her thoughts that she didn't even see him move.

"I'm sorry... what?"

He let out an exasperated sigh. "Honestly, if you are reconsidering all of this, you can go home and just wait for me there."

She scrunched her brow. "Go home? I don't have one, remember?"

"Exactly. So perhaps you should pay attention." He dropped his hands to his hips, latching the buckles of his tunic back together and re-covering the bands of muscle underneath.

Why Gwen even noticed that last bit, she really didn't understand.

Morin caught her staring and flashed her a toothy smile. "The last time you looked at me like that, I was burning this thing onto my chest."

Heat flushed her chest in a race of tingles. Ever since the

forest, she felt like her mind was slipping and she couldn't concentrate. Noticing Morin's muscular features was only a side-effect. Nothing more.

Peeking over at Morin again as he finished the final buckle and tugged on his vest, she definitely knew she was losing it because a wave of disappointment crashed over her.

"Well, that was just part of the plan." She crossed her arms over her chest, averting her eyes and forcing those ridiculous thoughts from her mind.

"And a good one at that. This has proved useful since. In fact..." His eyes dropped down to his now puffed-out chest. "It's quite grown on me."

Gwen shook her head. It may have been useful now, but she could still hear his piercing screams echoing through the dungeons when he took the knife and carved the crow into his flesh. It was a mixture of ink, soil, and feathers plucked from a crow. Once inked, he had called forth his magic, transformed his figure, and flown right out the window of his cell.

"A means to an end," Gwen noted. "What if the druid girl helps them get the sword? Did you think about that before you let them inside?"

Morin shook his head. "It won't make a difference. Magic cannot lift the sword, and it won't get them out of that cave, either. Merlin proved that."

Gwen's eyes widened, the unsettled energy from her chest dropping to the pit of her stomach. "What do you mean?"

The corner of his lip turned up. "We sealed the only entrance." He tilted his head, pressing his lips together like he was waiting for her to say something. He threw his hands in the air. "Honestly. The only entrance and the only exit. They are going to be trapped in that cave for a very long time. Even if they retrieve the sword, it won't matter. And that's *if* the beast doesn't devour them first."

Gwen swallowed against the stones in her throat. What had she done?

CHAPTER

TWENTY-TWO

THE GOLDEN EYES OF THE CHIMERA NARROWED ON them. A piercing shriek erupted from its mouth, echoing in the narrow tunnel, and Ren crouched to the floor with his hands over his ears. He reached for the sword at his hip before realizing it wasn't there. It must have flung from his hands in the explosion. He searched frantically in the dark before spotting it just out of reach. With his gaze fixed on the creature, he stretched out his body and reached for the hilt of his sword.

The chimera inched forward, darting its eyes across the group, probably deciding which one of them it would eat first. Ren's fingers met the soft leather of the hilt, and he let out a sigh, wrapping his hand around the weapon. At least he could fight back enough to allow his friends a chance at getting away. He just needed to distract it for a few moments.

He stood slowly, sword in one hand and using his other palm to signal to the beast. When the chimera snorted a burst of air toward them, Ren backed into the piled rocks at the entrance, where a sharp edge caught his hip, tearing through his tunic and causing a pained shriek to burst through his lips.

It was enough to capture the chimera's attention but not in the way Ren wanted. Its body shook, and it stomped the ground, wings popping and straining to spread open. But the tunnel was too narrow, and the beast snorted again, folding its wings back into its body. Up close, tiny spidery veins shimmered through the translucent skin. Ren would have considered them beautiful if they didn't belong to the beast standing between him and the sword.

Ren edged forward, readying to attack, and Geret followed close behind. Even Emeli drew an arrow from the quiver at her back, but when she did, a small feather floated to the ground in front of her.

To their surprise, the chimera's eyes darted to the feather, and it reared its front paws into the air like a horse and pranced in place. Snorting again, its nostrils flared.

"Emeli, the feather," Ren whispered out of the corner of his mouth.

"What?" she returned in a hushed tone, the arrow drawn tight within her bow.

"The feather. I think it's interested in the feather."

Emeli's eyes widened as she lowered her bow to the ground and bent down to pick up the feather.

The chimera watched with sharp interest, nudging forward.

Hopefully it would serve as a distraction while he and Geret caught it off guard with an attack.

"Careful," he warned Emeli, and she nodded, shifting her eyes to meet his.

She raised the feather into the air, and the chimera tracked its movement within her fingers. She slid a foot forward, and the chimera stomped forward. Its hot breath steamed from the sides of its beak, close enough to warm Ren's neck. What he was mostly concerned with was the sharp talons tapping on the stone. They were close enough to slash out, and in a moment, this could prove to be an enormous mistake.

Ren gave the signal for Geret to attack at his command, and he raised his sword, his shoulders tensing.

Just as they were ready to leap at the beast, Emeli yelled out, "Stop!"

She reached forward with the feather in hand and the chimera blinked its beady eyes, cocking its head to the side.

"Emeli, don't!" Ren urged, but she never listened to him.

Instead, she offered the beast the feather.

Ren's heart stopped, and he sucked in a breath, holding it for what seemed like an eternity.

The chimera snapped its beak forward, and he was certain his sister was gone. But standing still as a statue, she smiled at the beast holding the feather between its beak as it blinked playfully.

She glanced at Ren before reaching out and stroking the chimera's mane. It shuttered under her touch at first but soon settled into her hand, bowing its head for her to get a better reach. The feather remained secure within its beak.

The room was silent until Emeli let out a soft giggle, easing the tension in the small space. "I think it's okay. He doesn't want to hurt us."

Geret still held his sword out, and Ren didn't blame him because this couldn't be their luck. But if anyone could befriend a ferocious beast meant to have them for dinner, his sister could.

"Are you sure?" Ren asked.

The chimera stepped back from his sister, stretching its legs in the cramped space.

"Of course not, but the alternative would be much more diffi-cult, wouldn't it?" She tucked the arrow back into her quiver and slung her bow around one shoulder. "You can still fight him if you want to, but I think your odds of survival are slim at best." She smirked, stepping forward as the chimera shimmied backward.

Its eyes locked on Geret's sword, and then Ren's, and the beast stomped in place.

"Put those away!" Emeli barked. "He will never let us pass if he feels threatened. Would you?"

They exchanged looks. Geret shrugged and dropped his shoulders. Ren lowered his sword first, and Geret followed.

The chimera cocked its head, squawked, and shifted its weight to the side of the tunnel, leaving a narrow space to pass.

Even though they seemed to have tamed the beast, it was still shocking to think this sort of luck had befallen them. Ren's eyes darted around the space as he waited for the cave to come crashing down or something. It couldn't be this easy.

Emeli slid past the chimera first, darting through the narrow opening. Geret went next, legs shaking and holding his breath. Ren turned to Lina, who had been leaning against the wall of the cave, torch in hand, silently watching. Black bags hung under her eyes, and they drooped heavily. The hawk magic she had performed must have taken a toll.

"Are you okay?" he asked.

She nodded, straightening her spine and snapping back to consciousness.

"You're next." Ren gestured at the opening alongside the beast.

"No freaking way," she mouthed, one hand on her hip.

Ren had no time to argue, and so far, the chimera had allowed both his sister and Geret through without incident. There was no reason to believe Lina would be any different.

He shot her a stern glare, pointing yet again through the passage in silence so as not to scare the thing. As it was, the chimera blinked at them, the feather still clutched tightly within its beak.

Lina let out a sigh, holding out the torch and gripping the hilt of her dagger at her hip with her other hand. She crouched alongside the animal, pressing her body tight against the wall of the cave, and then darted past, disappearing on the other side.

Ren let out the breath he'd been holding and wiped a bead of sweat from his brow. At least his friends had a chance. With or without him.

He eyed the chimera in the dark, attempting to read its expression to determine if it was safe for him to pass. Perhaps it didn't care if the others reached the cave, but this was his quest. What if it was saving his energy for Ren? A shutter ran through him, and he swallowed the lump at the back of his throat.

He sheathed his sword, hoping he wouldn't need to retrieve it, and took a cautious step forward.

The chimera didn't make a move.

Another step as his boot echoed softly on the tunnel floor. Still, the chimera remained still.

His heart raced and his mouth had gone completely dry. This had to be a trap. The monster had him exactly where it wanted him before going for the kill. He was certain of it. He could imagine those sharp talons ripping clean through his chest, the snap of its beak shattering his bones.

Gulping, he moved forward.

The chimera must have sensed his growing fear because it blinked, lowering its head to watch as he edged forward into the space between its body and the tunnel wall.

Warmth spread from his belly, heating the air. The cave was so dark and cold that the heat would have been welcomed if it weren't coming from a giant beast. As such, it only made him sweat.

As Ren slid forward, his arm pressed against the chimera's leathery wing. It shivered, retracting the wing, and energy surged in Ren's veins. He froze, waiting for the beast to make its move, silently saying goodbye to his friends on the other side.

But it still did nothing. A small grunt spilled from its throat, a sign of agitation, perhaps, so he shuffled past until fresh air and smiling faces met him on the other side.

They didn't speak of their relief until the chimera turned to face them, its sharp eyes softening.

"See?" Emeli beamed.

"I don't believe it." Lina brushed dirt from her leathers and re-braided her hair away from her face.

The chimera stood in place, blinking, but made no more nervous moves.

The anxiety in Ren's gut eased, and he smiled to himself, still completely in awe. He prayed their good luck would hold as they continued onward.

They had to walk in a single line because of the narrow tunnel passage. Ren went first, illuminating the path with Lina's torch, then Emeli, Geret, and Lina at the back, who gave shifty glances over her shoulder at the chimera trotting behind them like a dog. It looked much more ridiculous than a dog since it had to squeeze its fluffy body tightly against itself to get past some spaces, but Ren was continually amazed that it could fit through such tight spaces. It was much smaller without the wings and the fluff of its hair.

After a while, the tunnel widened, and a fresh breeze swirled into the space. The group pressed together once again, with the chimera keeping some distance behind.

Then Ren halted everyone, squinting at the ground and picking up a single midnight feather. His eyes went wide.

"What is it?" Lina asked, peering over Ren's shoulder.

"It's been bothering me. Why would Morin trap us inside the one place he was trying to go? And this..." He brought the feather to his face, one finger sliding over the individual barbs. His stomach tensed. "They've already been here."

"What?" Emeli gasped.

"That's why Morin was so upset," he continued, his theory gaining strength, "It was almost like he'd already been defeated. That's why he tried to close off the entrance. It's why, once we got past him, he thought trapping us inside with the chimera would be better than allowing us to leave with the sword."

The chimera squawked, nuzzling against Emeli's neck as she giggled in response.

"Because they have already been in here. And my guess is..." He continued down the dark tunnel and they rounded a corner, the passage expanding into a wide cavern.

"He couldn't retrieve it. The sword didn't choose him," Ren said.

He stepped inside the cavern, and the others followed close behind.

"That means..." Emeli muttered, laying a hand on Ren's forearm.

Ren's throat tightened as the air seemed to thicken. "Excalibur."

Inside, a single beam of sunlight shot down from a hole in the ceiling, illuminating a stone mound. At the center, a sword hilt emitted a faint blueish glow.

The air turned heavy, and the sudden weight of Ren's destiny threatened to crush him where he stood. It was one thing to dream of this moment. He had held this image in his head the entire journey, yet standing here, ready to grab hold of it, gave him a frenzied panic inside.

"Whoa! Merlin was telling the truth!" Geret's voice boomed through the cavern.

Leave it to Geret to shatter an important moment of destiny. Ren shook his head.

"Well? What are you waiting for?" Geret slapped Ren square on his back. "Go get it so we can get the heck out of here!"

Ren shrugged him off. "This isn't a game." He took a timid step forward. And another, and another, until the patter of his footfalls echoed around the cave.

As he approached the stone slab, the silvery pieces of crystal weaving through the dark rock came into focus. Around the cavern, the slow drip of water sounded in puddles, leaving a sheen of moisture clinging to the walls. The walls were a pale gray, but the rock mound was different. There was magic racing through the air. He could feel it.

The sunlight from the opening in the ceiling was blinding, casting the sword in an ethereal glow. Ren glanced around the space, trying to imagine Merlin here for years. Why did it take him so long to escape? As if on cue, the chimera squawked behind the group, causing a shutter to run through Ren.

Emeli jumped, clasping her hand over her chest. "Shhh!" She wagged her finger at the dragon-lion beast, and it stomped in place, throwing a tantrum before shooting off the ground. It flew around the space's impossibly high walls.

As Ren approached the sword, his stomach turned to knots. More accurately, his insides felt like the writhing squid Merlin had threatened that man with in the Camelot tavern. That felt like so long ago. Ren was an entirely different person from when he left.

He ran his hand over the hilt of the sword, a light buzz pricking at his fingertips. If there were any doubts this was Excalibur, they were diminished after experiencing the charged energy. This was it.

The weight of the moment pressed upon his shoulders, gluing his feet into the stone floor of the cave. His entire life has been preparing him for this, and he longed for the power radiating from the sword in front of him. He needed to know he was meant for more, that this entire journey had been worth it. But it also terrified him. Once he had the sword and fulfilled his quest, what would come after?

Doubt wove a constricting rope around him, all his muscles tensing, freezing his limbs in place. He glanced over his shoulder at his friends, who looked back at him with anticipation.

Running a hand through his hair, he rolled his neck and straightened his spine. They were all depending on him. He had gotten them into this mess, and he would get them out. He owed them that. His thoughts drifted to Camelot and those they left behind: his mother, Galahad and the other knights, the people in the town. They were probably preparing for war right now, and this would help them defend their kingdom. It would prevent so much tragedy and tyranny at the hands of a ruler who didn't care for anyone but himself.

Then the image of King Arthur came to him. He remembered the look of hope on his face. Warmth had radiated from the once great king, and he had placed that hope on Ren for a reason. If King Arthur believed in him, then so should he.

He couldn't let them all down.

He was ready for this and whatever came next.

Sucking in a weighted breath, he dug his fingers around the smooth leather surface of the sword's hilt. Letting the air release from his lips, his muscles tensed, and he pulled.

Ren stared at the sword's hilt held tight in his grip. Sweat slid down his brow, stinging the corner of his eye as he ground his teeth together. Yet it did not budge.

Gripping with both hands, this time, he planted his boots against the bottom of the stone, and heaved with all his might, but still, the word remained lodged tightly in the stone.

Panicked thoughts flooded his mind, oddly similar to the knighting ceremony.

He failed. Twice. And this time, the entire kingdom would suffer.

TWENTY-THREE

THE WEIGHT WAS UNBEARABLE.

Arthur's words whispered in the folds of his mind: *The heart of a knight is not found in a sword. It lives in you.*

Did he know when he sent Ren on this quest he would not be able to pull the sword? Morin couldn't pull it, and he was born by blood. King's blood. But even that wasn't enough.

His blood burned... if they couldn't get the sword, this entire quest would be for nothing, and Camelot didn't stand a chance.

"Ren..." A faint voice broke his delirium, and he turned toward his friends.

Emeli stepped forward and squeezed his shoulder gently. Tears welled in her eyes as if this were her pain, as well. "It's okay. We'll find another way."

"This was supposed to be it." He shrugged her hand away. "I'm sorry, but it doesn't make sense. Why would Arthur send us here?"

Emeli shook her head, her eyes falling to the ground.

Everything crashed in all at once. The knighting ceremony. A quest he was never supposed to go on. The deceptions in the forest. And now this. He kept failing at everything. Was he worthy of knighthood at all? What was all the training for? He couldn't save Camelot. He couldn't even save his father.

The room spun, and a tingling fever seeped into his mind. Sweeping his gaze over his friends for grounding, they all avoided eye contact. Emeli fiddled with the leather hand wrap around her bow while Lina leaned against the far wall, peering into the tunnel they had come through like she was ready to bolt at any moment.

Geret, however, met his eyes with a sharp gaze, gnawing on his bottom lip. No doubt a joke was ready to tumble out of his lips and Ren honestly would have welcomed that. He stepped forward. "I suppose each of us needs to try now. I'm the obvious next choice."

He strolled past, shoulders back and eyes on the prize. Ren remembered his comments by the fire when he said he also had something to prove. For a moment, Ren begged Geret to be successful. Even if it would make his head ten times larger than it already was, it was better than the alternative of failing altogether.

Without hesitation, Geret took hold of the sword, flexing the lean muscles of his biceps. He huffed and groaned, tugging with all his might, but nothing happened. Ren almost felt bad for him.

"I was only showing off, you know, making sure you all knew the proper posture and all that because Ren certainly didn't look fit trying."

Ren *almost* felt bad for him.

Geret dragged his feet back in line next to Emeli, and she gave him a reassuring squeeze.

Next, Emeli moved forward, and Ren held his breath. She never wanted this life, and he didn't want to put that burden on her. He closed his eyes, peeking as she was at the stones. She drew one finger down the grip and then wrapped her delicate hand around the hilt before pulling. Her muscles didn't tense when she did, and there were no audible grunts or groans of effort. She, too, had tried and failed, because when she lifted her hand, it was without the sword.

A heavy sigh escaped Ren's lips. Emeli shrugged her shoulders and headed for the side of the cave, sliding her back down until she was sitting on her butt. She wrapped her arms around her knees and flashed Ren a worried look.

"What do we do?" Geret asked.

Ren rubbed his temple with a knuckle to release the pounding headache behind his eyes.

They couldn't leave the sword here unprotected. What if Morin came back for it? What if the sword could change its mind? He would probably come up with a clever idea for using magic to retrieve it, and with the sword, Morin would be unstoppable. He'd win favor with any lands who were undecided about their allegiances. Ren couldn't let that happen. There was too much at stake.

"Wait!" Emeli jumped from the ground. "We aren't done here. We still have hope!"

Her enthusiasm was both alarming and annoying.

"I know you try to look at the bright side, sis, but this... this is grim," Ren returned.

"No, stupid. We haven't all tried to pull the sword, have we?"

The group exchanged glances. Geret wore a sheepish grin while Emeli's eyes shone bright. They all cast their gazes on Lina.

Lina. She'd been casually watching everyone make fools of themselves this entire time without saying a word.

Lina's eyes widened as a cat in the dark, and Emeli flashed her a toothy grin.

"No." Lina put her hands up in surrender, leaning toward the tunnel behind her.

Emeli bounded over and tugged at her hand.

"No, no, no..." Lina continued, snapping her hand back and shaking her head.

"Come on!" Emeli whined. "You have to. We came all this way."

She grabbed hold of Lina's hand again and dragged her across the stone floor.

Lina's face turned a pale shade of green.

"You are our last hope," Emeli said, dropping Lina's hand when they were at the stones.

Lina shook her head again. "This is *your* thing. Not mine. I agreed to help you get here so your war wouldn't spill into my people's lands. But this..." She glared at the sword like it was a poisonous snake about to strike. "This is too much. I'm not playing your games."

She turned on her heels and stomped back toward the tunnel, leaving Emeli standing alone, dumbfounded.

Ren had to do something. Emeli was right—Lina should try too. They had to be certain they had done everything they could to get the sword. For Camelot.

"Wait! Lina!" he hollered after her, but the patter of her footfalls grew fainter in the darkness in the tunnel.

He exchanged looks with Emeli and Geret before following through the arch of the exit.

Meeting her in the dark passageway where the route narrowed significantly, he reached out for her hand, and the warmth of her touch sent tingles over his skin. "Lina, I know this isn't what you expected, but..."

Her lip twitched and she released her other hand from a clenched ball at her side. "No, Ren. I didn't agree to this. I can't take that sword. None of us can. It will only lead to more destruction."

"What are you talking about? This will save the kingdom. Look what has happened without this sword and without a king to wield it. You saw the towns. Everything has fallen apart since Arthur died and Excalibur was buried."

She met his eyes, a flicker of dancing flames from her torch sparking in their reflection. Those wild, beautiful eyes. But now worry raced through them.

"You don't understand," she said. "That vision I told you about, the reason I helped you back in camp. It wasn't only the forest that was on fire. It was Camelot too. Everything turned to ash, and the people..." her eyes welled with moisture, "The people were all dead. I can't be responsible for that. Nor should you."

"How do you know what you saw is related to this sword?"

Her gaze flickered to the dark corridor ahead, the one leading to the exit buried by rockfall. Maybe she wanted to escape. She could use her magic and free herself from all this. Leave them behind. But when her eyes returned to his, there was a softness there, flecks of amber melting in a sea of umber.

"I don't know for sure, but I think I saw the sword. And there was someone else..."

She stopped herself, swallowing hard.

Ren gripped her shoulders, and she relaxed under his touch.

"I'm sure whatever you saw could be true, but I have to believe we are doing the right thing. That's what I know. Right here. This. Us being here against the odds. There has to be a reason for that, too." An ache gripped his throat, and he swallowed back the emotion. "Plus, I know it's what my father would do, and he was the best person I knew. I trust that."

Lina's eyes fell to the slip of Ren's fingers trailing down her arms until they wrapped around her hands.

"Please, Lina. We have to try."

She looked past his shoulder at the glowing cavern behind them. "Fine, but it won't make a difference. You'll see."

Tugging her hands back, cold air sunk into his palms as she sauntered past him.

The others followed Lina's steps when she approached the sword. Ren's stomach turned to knots. The others wouldn't say it out loud, but if Lina couldn't retrieve it, they were all royally screwed with a capital "S."

Lina stopped at the stones, looking over her shoulder at everyone before letting out a breath and bracing herself. Then, she took hold of the hilt with one hand and pulled.

"See? What did I—"

A gasp escaped Ren's lips that echoed loudly against the cavern walls.

"No way," Geret exclaimed under his breath.

"Cool." Emeli grinned.

Lina's eyes widened as she moved her wrist, the blade of the sword coming with it, and she held it up into the air in front of her face.

A faint glow pulsed from the blade, swirling around her entire body as the shock registered on her face.

Ren didn't have the words, but something bubbled in his chest, rising at the back of his throat until it stung.

A small smile befell Lina's lips as she moved the blade back and forth, touching the steel with the tip of her finger. This was a good thing. Lina wasn't power-hungry like Morin, overly confident like Geret, or lacking courage like Emeli. If it couldn't be him, he was glad it was Lina.

"Hail the Queen of Camelot," Emeli announced, dropping a knee to the ground. It took Lina completely by surprise because she dropped the blade of the sword toward the rock below her feet so that it hung limp in her hand.

Then Geret followed as well.

Ren locked eyes with Lina. There was a dull shimmer to them he didn't recognize, setting a swirl of discomfort in his chest, but he joined the others on one knee.

"To the Queen of Camelot."

CHAPTER
TWENTY-FOUR

LINA

THIS COULDN'T BE HAPPENING. SILENCE SETTLED IN the cavern save for the slow drip of water and the pounding of Lina's heart.

She lifted the blade from the ground, but it felt far too heavy. What was this thing made of? Lead? She was accustomed to the light airiness of her daggers, not this hulking piece of metal making her arm burn. She couldn't do this. She shouldn't have let Ren's puppy dog eyes drag her back in here.

"Here." Ren's voice startled her, and she shivered, suddenly realizing how cold the air was in the cavern. He fiddled with the buckles on the harness where he kept his sword at his back.

"You need a way to carry it. It's heavy," he said. "Plus, it will be safer this way in case we are attacked on the route home."

Home. She should have listened to her gut and stayed back in camp all that time ago. How long had it been, anyway? Days? Months? How long had she been chasing clarity from her dreams to follow this group she barely knew? It was all messed up. She shouldn't be holding this sword. Ren should. It was his quest.

As Ren released the harness from his shoulder and handed it to her, she stared back at him and the familiar curve of his jaw, at the one dimple in his cheek that only showed itself when he was happy. She had gotten to know him over this time. He wasn't a stranger, anymore. None of them were. It had been her choice to join the quest. Nobody made that decision for her. She had to start owning her decisions.

She examined the worn leather of the harness, allowing her fingers to seek the places still warm from where it pressed against Ren's body. "How will you carry yours?"

"On my hip." He pointed to the scabbard still hanging at his side. Lina only saw him use it when he was getting ready to use his sword. It was easier to draw his weapon that way. Like her daggers.

Nodding, she slipped the harness over her shoulder, tugging at the strap to tighten it because Ren was much taller than her, but it didn't work. She couldn't quite figure out how all the pieces connected.

"May I?" Ren offered to help, stepping closer and taking the harness from her shaking hands. "It's going to be alright," he said. She didn't know why, but she believed him.

Ren took the strap and wrapped it around one of her shoulders, following the leather down her back and leaving a trail of goosebumps under his touch. Then, he directed her to turn to the side so he could grab hold of the other end. She turned slowly until they were face to face. He glided the strap tight around her hips, and heat flooded her chest. Giving it one final tug, he strapped the buckle together, and his eyes dropped to the floor.

It sat comfortably against her body like it was made for her, save for the extra leather at the ends, which she folded into a loop and tucked in so it wouldn't get caught on anything.

When she lifted her eyes, Ren was still close, their noses almost touching.

"Thank you," she whispered, forgetting all about the others in the cavern. In that moment, it was just her and Ren, their fates woven together more than ever. She was painfully aware of the pulse of energy coming from Excalibur, but it didn't matter at that moment because she knew his words were true. It would be alright as long as he was by her side.

This was new for Lina. She was independent—she had to be to survive—but this level of comfort with someone was new.

"Ahem." A grunt sounded behind them as Geret cleared his throat in the most obvious way possible. "Have you forgotten something? How are we going to get out of here?"

Ren stepped back with a flush on his cheeks, clearing his throat and wetting his lips. She tried not to think about how much she was thinking about those lips.

Peering around the cavern, the hard truth of their situation came rushing back. Geret was right. There was no easy way out. No additional tunnels existed aside from the one they had originally come down, and that exit was blocked by the rockslide. They could try and dig their way out, but that would take a long time and there was no guarantee Morin wouldn't be waiting for them when they emerged.

Her eyes traveled along the walls of the cavern. They were solid, stretching so high up she couldn't even tell where they ended. She didn't think they could climb them; it would be too dangerous.

With some effort, Lina sheathed the sword to her back as the others searched the space for an exit they might have missed.

The chimera launched into the air, shrieking, and Lina

followed its path. It beat its wings higher and higher, blocking out the light beam illuminating the now-empty stone.

"Of course!" Ren cried out, and he met her eyes. While the idea made his face light up with excitement, she thought she was going to be sick.

"We fly," Ren announced.

Everyone sent their eyes to the ceiling, and sure enough, the hole at the top appeared large enough for the chimera to fly through.

"I was afraid you would say that," Geret gulped.

"Brilliant!" Emeli beamed, whistling with her fingers between her lips. The sound caught the chimera's attention, and it swooped down, landing in front of her. She patted its mane for a moment as it let out a chirp from the back of its throat.

"Ugh." Lina sighed, sickness rising in her throat. She was fine flying when she was in control of her own wings, but being at the mercy of the ridiculously large bird creature was not sitting well with her. "Anyone else have any other ideas?"

Everyone shook their heads.

Darn. It had been worth a shot.

Emeli approached the chimera first, sliding her palm along the silky fur at its back. Gripping the mane, she motioned for help, and Geret lifted her foot up so she could swing her other leg over like the thing was a horse. Lina didn't much like horses, either. Too little control and they should be free to run wild.

Emeli steadied herself on top, wobbling at first, then leaning into the mane and squeezing her legs around its sides. It appeared safe enough.

"Okay, who's next?" Emeli asked.

Ren and Geret exchanged looks, their faces gone pale, but Geret volunteered anyway. It took Lina and Ren both to hoist him up and over and he slid behind Emeli while leaving plenty of space in between.

Lina helped Ren next, and he took up the cavernous space between Geret and Emeli before offering his hand to her. They pulled her up in front of Emeli, and she leaned over the creature's neck, finding a place to lock her arms together. All the while, she pushed down the nausea rising in her throat.

It's just like a horse.

Once they were all situated, Emeli patted the beast's neck, and commanded, "Go!"

Lina squeezed her eyes shut as the chimera let out a squawk as it pranced in place.

It's just a very large horse that could snap us in two or burn us alive with its dragon fire. That's it. Nothing to worry about—

Without warning, the chimera launched into the air amid an eruption of screams, headed straight for the streaming sunlight in the ceiling.

Only when a blast of fresh air fired over her face did Lina dare open her eyes, but she immediately wished she hadn't.

⁘⸻

"Never again!" Lina rambled through the trees with her hands flung above her head, hair sticking out in every direction. It was too long of a ride on a flying beast, and she nearly lost the contents of her stomach several times. The landing proved especially challenging, as she wasn't expecting a sudden crash through the trees as everyone hung on for dear life. "Next time you all want to drag me along on anything involving beast-slaying, please remind me of the idiocy of your hair-brained schemes." She bent over her knees, steadying herself on solid ground.

Ren huffed when he dismounted, waddling around after straddling the giant dragon-lion beast. It nearly made Lina laugh if dizziness hadn't been swimming around her head.

Emeli let out a heavy sigh as though she'd held her breath the entire way. "If I never have to ride anything again, I will be happy."

Ren shot Geret a warning stare, shushing him with a finger to his lips.

That did make a small laugh bubble at the back of Lina's throat.

A sudden beat of energy raced down her spine, and she realized the sword was still strapped to her back, the weight of it pressing down on her shoulders. She was a part of this now—tied to Camelot, whatever its fate—and she still didn't know how she felt about that.

The chimera squawked, startling everyone as it took off into the sky, circling the meadow and sailing off into the horizon.

"I didn't get to say goodbye," Emeli pouted.

"Are you kidding?" Geret replied. "How about saying good riddance!"

"Hey, he saved us when he could have had us for dinner. We owe him our lives. The code demands it," she said.

Geret grumbled and lay flat on the ground. "He wasn't very good at his job. We got the sword, didn't we?"

"Maybe he wasn't there to protect the sword from us, did you ever think about that?" she replied, readying herself to explain further.

"Shh, you two!" Ren interrupted. He flung his hand in the air, one ear angled in the other direction, away from the group. A low clatter sounded in the distance. "Do you hear that?"

Lina wasn't certain what she'd heard, but her senses were on high alert now.

Ren crept through the trees until arriving at the edge of the forest, peering into a bright meadow beyond. Lina followed, crouching behind a bush with a burst of pink blooms.

Squinting into the sun, Lina's stomach plummeted when she saw what he was staring at. Dozens of black fabric tents scattered the once golden meadow, now trampled by an army. Smoke billowed from campfires as men gathered around roasting meats and drinking ale. They all wore a black crow insignia upon their armor.

But it wasn't just Morin's army. Banners in blue and gold also fluttered in the wind. Other house crests, too, most of which Lina wouldn't recognize but she suspected were enemies. There were multiple armies here.

"We are too late," Ren said, breathless. He sunk behind the bush, averting his eyes from everyone.

"Camelot has an army though, right? And allies. I'm sure they will have enough men to defend the city and castle," Lina said.

Ren shook his head, all color drained from his face, all hope gone from his eyes.

"Yes, but not large enough to defend against this. The entire point of going after the sword was to give us a chance to convince our allies to go to battle, but that takes time. I never thought Morin would attack this soon. He must have been plotting this for years."

Lina searched for commentary from the others, but they all echoed the silent defeat.

"Surely there is something we can do. This sword isn't useless." As Lina said it, the sword thrummed energy behind her, unnoticed by the others. The power was growing stronger, and it made her chest tighten. What good was it for her to carry this powerful sword if they couldn't use it to save Camelot from the fires and her people from the corruption of Morin's reign? It would spread like blight over a harvest.

Ren dropped his head between his legs. "Excalibur can only save us if those who wield it band together. It's what my father always said about the rule of King Arthur. The sword alone is only a weapon. It's a powerful one, but it can't save an entire kingdom."

His voice trailed off as if he were lost in thought, and Emeli squatted next to him, grabbing hold of his wrist. "We did the best we could."

The disappointment was palpable. Lina knew how defeated Ren must have been. It was something they all shared. and Lina didn't know what to do with this sword if Camelot fell. The druids would have to move their camp as planned, travel somewhere far away where Morin's couldn't reach them.

She peered around the group, emotion welling inside. What would happen to them then? As much as she hated to admit it, she'd grown close with all of them over these weeks. She never thought it possible for druids and Camelot knights—well, almost knights—to work together toward a common good. It had been over a decade with this chasm between them, and she was just starting to see a connected path.

Suddenly, Ren jerked his head up, muttering to himself. "Excalibur can only save us if those who wield it band together."

"You said that already," Geret replied, his eyes exchanging a worried look with Emeli.

"No!" Ren stood from the bush, rushing back toward the trees, his voice growing louder. "Don't you see?"

As everyone hustled after him, he spun around suddenly, a light sparking in his eyes. "Lina, you have the sword."

She wrinkled her nose. "Yes..."

"Are you okay, buddy?" Geret patted him on the back.

Ren shrugged him off and focused his gaze on Lina, making her uncomfortable.

"Don't you see? We aren't alone. We never were." His eyes pulled at her attention, waiting for her to understand. But she was still lost.

After a moment of silence, Ren added, "If we had the druids by our side, we may stand a chance against Morin's armies."

Something pricked at her gut like a sore set aflame. "No. No way!"

Ren approached, grabbing hold of her shoulders this time. "But you have the sword. You can convince them to follow you if you ask."

She shook her head, lips pressed firmly together.

Her fate was tied to Camelot because it was her choice, but she wouldn't risk her people for this war. She wouldn't drag them into this.

Ren's eyes searched hers for an agonizing moment until everything else faded away like it had in the cavern. Images of the fire spreading in the forest invaded her mind. She saw her people fleeing as the walls of Camelot crumbled. Was that their fate if she agreed to this?

"Please, Lina. You have to consider this. It's our only hope," Ren whispered, sending goosebumps racing down her arms.

Or would it happen if she didn't?

She couldn't believe it, but she was actually considering it. Even though her dreams warned her this would happen, hadn't she been trying to figure out how to stop it?

The answer was already forming in her mind. She'd come this far...

Dropping Ren's hand, she turned on her heels and headed back into the trees.

Ren yelled after her, "Where are you going?"

"To recruit Camelot some new allies!" she answered back, not slowing her steps for even a moment because she feared if she did, she would lose her nerve.

She couldn't allow fear to chase her because she was tired of running from her fate.

CHAPTER

TWENTY-FIVE

LINA

LINA HADN'T SEEN REN LOOK THIS UNCOMFORTABLE since they were squeezed into the cave's entrance with the chimera. Ren, Geret, and Emeli were all cornered into a tree, sweating, as Drogo, Sved, and Sigrid pointed weapons at their chest. Meanwhile, Lina had taken a spot off to the side to watch, enjoying the show for a bit.

"How was this a good idea again?" Geret asked Ren.

"You talk when we say you can talk, boy." Drogo pointed the tip of his axe blade at Geret, exchanging a flirtatious smile with Sigrid.

Geret straightened his spine and swallowed. "Why is she not suspect? She led us in here!" He pointed at Lina, and she shook her head, finally stepping forward. She'd had enough laughs.

"Oh, calm down, Drogo. I told you. They aren't the enemy. The enemy is out there." Lina pushed through the weaponry, pointing out into the forest where, just beyond, Morin's camp was gearing up to march toward Camelot.

The man let out a gnarled rumble that sounded something like "stupid witch," and that was something she wouldn't stand for. She lunged forward, daggers in hand, and he stumbled backward, tripping over his feet until his butt was on the ground.

As Sigrid was helping him up, Ragnor strolled in. "Adelina. The savior has returned to us. What do you have there?" His eyes were on the sword hilt jutting out from the harness at her back. He had never seen her wield a sword.

Lina stepped in front of the group, turning slightly to the side to shield the sword from Ragnor's view. "It's not your concern. What is your concern is the war at your back, yet you do nothing."

Ragnor let out a bellowed laugh. "Since when have the affairs of Camelot concerned us? They do not care for our people. Why should we care for theirs?"

Lina rolled her eyes. This was typical of Ragnor, and she should have expected he would react this way. How could he not see the impact this would have not only on their people, but on all the towns in the kingdom? There wouldn't be anywhere safe they could go. Any trading routes would be rendered useless.

She paused. Here she was, arguing to help Camelot when weeks ago she would have been at Ragnor's side, laughing with him.

Behind her, Ren watched everything closely.

How much he'd changed her. Her eyes swept over Emeli and Geret's faces, as well. They had all changed in their time together.

She stepped closer to Ragnor, lowering her voice. "You must listen to reason. When have I ever knowingly deceived you? What cause would I have for not speaking the truth? This is happening and we have to be a part of it. Otherwise, can we really call ourselves part of this kingdom? Do we even want to be?"

Ragnor's lips upturned before his jaw clenched. "You left us," he said, his eyes glassy and his face's wrinkles more pronounced than she remembered. He'd aged in the short time she had been away. "You choose your side. What makes you think we wouldn't treat you the same way we treat all our enemies?"

A heaviness sunk in Lina's stomach. She'd wounded him when she helped Ren and the others escape that night. She had turned away from her family to follow a fate she wasn't certain was even set, but she had to believe it was the right thing to do. Ragnor couldn't see it because he was stubborn, so she had to show him.

She stepped back, reached behind her, and gripped Excalibur by the hilt. A warmth spread up her palm, and she grunted, tugging the sword over her shoulder as the others jumped back to give her room. She slid backward to be shoulder to shoulder with Ren. "Yes, I have chosen a side. I've chosen the side that is willing to do something. I am choosing to believe there is still hope for our people, that we don't have to be enemies with Camelot. Not if a change is coming. And it is coming, one way or another. We can either help them choose a better path, or we can watch their enemies—our enemies—destroy the hope of a better world. I'm done hiding in the shadows of the forest. I'm done running."

Ragnor pouted his lips, looking at the rest of the druids gathered to watch. With a scowl, he leaped forward, axe in hand, and Lina raised her sword in defense. But he stopped before his weapon connected with hers. His eyebrows shot up and he... smiled.

"You always were disobedient, even as a babe." He dropped his axe, swinging his hand in her direction. When she took it, he swooped her into his chest and squeezed her tight.

Audible sighs echoed behind her from Ren and the others.

Glancing over her shoulder, she met Ren's eyes before stepping to the side so Ragnor could have access.

"And you? What do you have to say?" Ragnor's eyes landed on Ren as Lina knew they would.

"Me?" Ren's ears turned red

"Yes, boy. You are one of them, aren't you? You and your friends?" He glanced at Emeli and Geret next.

"One of who?" he asked.

"Knights. Of Camelot."

Lina let out a snort, and Ren shot her a glare. But he still straightened his spine and lifted his chin. "Not yet, but my father was."

"Why shouldn't we watch in joy as Camelot burns? Even if Adelina here says we should help, what is it to us?" He crossed his arms. He'd tested Lina already. Now it was Ren's turn.

"Because Morin only cares about power. He will try to enslave every town and every community, even yours, as far as his reach will go. Then he will want more. His father was the same. We can't allow it to happen. Besides..." He lowered his hand, wrapping his fingers around Lina's hand, the one that held Excalibur.

A flutter sparked in her chest. Ragnor's eyes widened, but Ren was undeterred. "You asked what this was? This is Excalibur. We were tasked to return it to Camelot, to unite the lands, not divide them. That starts now."

Ragnor leaned forward, his peppery eyebrows arched like caterpillars. "Then why does my Adelina wield it?"

Ren released her hand, stepping aside. "Because she pulled the sword from the stone. It is her destiny to wield Excalibur and, eventually, to rule Camelot." His eyes traveled to Lina's, but she averted them, focusing instead on the dark earth below her feet. "If she chooses to, one day," he added.

Hearing Ren say it in such terms immediately made energy pulse from the sword at her back and she shifted her weight uncomfortably between both feet. She couldn't get a grounded feeling, and she hated that.

Ragnor's shoulders fell from his ears, and the others around him whispered, an elated energy running through them. "That does change things," he said with sparkling eyes.

She wished Ren hadn't done that. She was not prepared for this. She didn't even want it. But the way Ragnor looked at them now with a friendly gaze instead of as enemies, maybe it was worth her discomfort to persuade them to their side. For now.

Ragnor whistled through the trees to signal the camp, and more druids emerged from their tents. There was Matilda, whose husband had died on a food raid months prior. She held a small child at her hip. Fin bounded over, sword at the ready. All the others approached with suspicion in their eyes.

"Sounds like it is time we join the fight!" Ragnor hollered and the crowd returned with excited cheers.

Ragnor leaned into the ear of Lunden, a tall man with dark, braided hair and furs wrapping his shoulders. After Ragnor whispered something, Lunden nodded, grabbing Fin by the elbow as they mounted two waiting horses, and trotted off through the trees.

"What was that?" Ren asked Lina.

Before Lina could answer, Ragnor wrapped his large arm around Ren much to his shocked expression and answered. "You didn't think this small community was the entirety of our people, did you? We have clans spread out throughout the surrounding lands, some in the forests, some choosing to live close to the coast with their ships and sea gods."

Ren smiled. "Thank you for helping us."

"Ah, we haven't been in a good fight in ages. This will give us stories to tell our grandchildren! Now, we must feast and prepare for the battle tomorrow!"

With that, Ragnor shouted at the crowd, and they cheered back. "To the gods!" He snatched a cup of ale being passed around.

"Now what?" Emeli asked. "We have to get back to Camelot."

"There is time," Lina assured them. "You said they were about a day out? They won't attack until dawn. It's too dangerous, they don't know these lands as you do."

"She's right," Ren agreed. "We should get some rest then. Where can we make camp?"

"Nonsense. You will join us in celebration tonight, and you will sleep after. If you don't realize the reason you are fighting, you won't have cause to do it." Winking, she led them to the edge of the camp where a tent waited for them. A girl brought them buckets and rags to clean up with, as well as dry clothes.

Lina ran her hand along the soft linen tunic. She sighed, realizing how grimy she had become on the road and how good a fresh set of clothes would feel.

"Well, I'm game." Geret said, stripping off his tunic and grabbing a bucket of water to clean himself.

"Ugh." Emeli sighed, slinking into the privacy of the tent to change.

Ren stayed outside with Lina, and for a moment they admired the orange glow of the setting sun hanging on the horizon. It felt like only yesterday they had set off on their quest. Now, after everything they'd been through... Lina reached over her shoulder, searching for the energy beating from the sword's hilt like a heart. Now, everything was different.

Lina's stomach twisted into knots. It was strange going to battle with Camelot after she swore to hate them forever, but when Ren cast his eyes to the sky with a hopeful smile playing on his lips, she couldn't help but feel hopeful, too.

TWENTY-SIX

Twinkling fireflies illuminated the forest with a soft glow. Ren, Geret, and Emeli made their way toward the center of camp, where a low chant had already begun in a mesmerizing symphony of sound. Druids spun around the glowing flames, their bodies shimmering in golden paint, casting dancing shadows on the ground. The air crackled with energy.

The closer they got, the more the strange words vibrated under Ren's skin, soothing him into a relaxed state. It was a welcome relief from the weighted pressure of their journey.

Maybe Lina was right about this. He exchanged grins with Emeli, who tugged Geret into the crowd and joined the dance.

Before Ren knew what was happening, two girls wearing soft linen dresses and deer antlers weaved with flowers dragged him to the side, forcing him to sit on a log as they ripped his shirt from his torso. A rush of cold air swarmed his exposed skin, and the girls laughed, tipping a warm, syrupy liquid to his lips. The fires cast a glowing light that made them look like creatures of the forest. Maybe they were, because the liquid they slid down his throat sent a comforting tingle exploding in his head.

Lina slinked out of the shadows wearing a flowing silver gown the color of starlight, gold bands snaking up her arms and wrapping over her bare skin.

She was definitely a creature of the forest. The most beautiful one he'd ever seen.

She held a clay pot with shimmering golden ink and wore a devious smirk on her lips. With a flick of her head, the girls holding Ren down danced away and joined the festivities by the fire. Lina didn't speak as she dipped her fingers in the bowl of ink, and she sat next to Ren so their faces were inches apart.

His breath caught at the intensity of her warm eyes locked onto his. A terrifying wave crashed through his chest. This might be the last night they spent together. They never talked about what would happen after the battle for Camelot. Ren knew he would return home, but would Lina? Would she rejoin the druids after everything? Would she move camps and forget this entire journey had ever happened? Would she forget about him?

He opened his mouth to speak. He needed to tell her how he felt, how the thought of never seeing her again was more than he could bear. An ache swelled in his chest. "Lina, I need to—"

But she silenced him with a finger to his lips. As if she knew what he was about to say, she replied, "You don't have to. All we need to think about right now is enjoying tonight."

Something cold touched his chest, and he inhaled a sharp

breath, looking down to Lina's fingers sliding wet paint in a pattern over his skin.

"This is what matters tonight." She smiled, dipping her fingers into the bowl again and tracing lines over his arms and down the muscles that flinched under her touch.

"What is it?" Ren's eyes cast to the bowl where the shimmering ink swirled and breathed, "Is it magic?"

Lina nodded. "It is of the earth. It helps us to feel connected to the source, so we can touch it, allow it to become one with our bodies."

She leaned in closer, lifting Ren's chin with one hand, and without warning she dragged the cool ink down his forehead with a finger, forcing him to close his eyes as it ran down his face. She then traced a line down his neck and along his collarbone. A flutter beat inside his chest, but his eyes remained shut. Would this all be a dream if he opened them?

When he did crack his eyelids, a glowing image of Lina was so close to his face, the soft warmth of her breath teased his nose. Her lips hovered just in front his, and his hand reached for her cheek, cupping it tenderly. He wanted more than anything to bring her mouth into his, to feel the warmth of a kiss between them.

But as he leaned in, a tug on their arms split them apart. Dancers lifted them from their seats, pulling them into the wave of bodies pounding around the fire. Music thrummed through the space and Ren reached out, snatching Lina's hand so he didn't lose her. Together, they chanted the words with the rest. It vibrated in his chest, filling him with intoxicating strength.

They stomped their feet, laughing, and let out battle cries. It was the release Ren needed before going to battle tomorrow. The energy and confidence of the collective surged through him. This was why they did this—it was a reminder they weren't alone. They were a part of something bigger. However small their numbers, they were never alone.

Then, all at once, the chanting stopped, and the music with it.

A quiet hush settled on everyone as they spun to face the back of the clearing where a man dressed in bear skins and carrying a staff approached the fires. Up close, the deep wrinkles on his face creased the paint on his skin. His gray hair was wrapped in cloth and bound at his neck. The crowd parted for him, bowing in reverence. Ren leaned over to ask Lina who the man was, but the quiet of the crowd commanded his attention.

"Tonight, we call upon the gods and the goddesses of the earth and of the sky." His surprisingly powerful voice carried over the crowd. "We call upon you to protect our people in battle and to fill their hearts with courage so they may overcome fear." Lina flashed Ren a smile, her eyes bright.

"Let the trees give you strength, let the ocean fill your veins with courage, and let all the creatures of the forest give you peace within your hearts. Avalon, hear us now, your children, those who feel your presence, guide and protect us. Let the magic of the old religion seep across these lands, blinding those who reject you, in shadow."

He slammed his staff into the ground, sending a burst of flames shooting to the sky.

The crowd erupted in cheers, and the music resumed. Everyone grouped back together to dance and drink.

Lina turned to Ren with a pout on her lips.

"Avalon?" he asked.

She nodded. "Yes."

"I thought Avalon was dying. That's what the Lady of The Lake said. She said they could no longer protect the sword because their power was dwindling."

"She is not wrong. It is. Has been for a while now."

"So why do you still call upon it for strength? Are they still listening?"

Lina's eyes wandered over the crowd at the dancing bodies and the orange flames of the fire. Sparks popped into the sky, where stars seemed to swirl in tune to the music. Turning back to Ren, she clicked her tongue. "Avalon used to be a very real place for the priests and priestesses to practice their magic. They protected and maintained balance. But now, you are right, the strength of Avalon is fading, but that doesn't mean magic is also dying. Magic lives within the earth—in the trees, in the rivers, within the soil in the ground. It's all around us throughout the natural world." Lina gestured at the trees surrounding them, to where the moon hung low in the sky on the horizon. "It's just..." She stopped, her eyes falling to the ground.

"What?" Ren asked, tugging on her hand.

"Men no longer look to the earth for support. They build their castles and their walls to keep the natural world out."

"They build castles and walls to keep their enemies out."

She huffed a breath through her nostrils. "Are they not the same thing? People are a part of the natural world. They are living beings connected to the creatures of the forest and the mountains just as much as each other. Everyone used to be able to do magic, but they have forgotten and now it's a rarity. I think that woman in Warwick recognized it in me somehow. She must have practiced herself, or else she wouldn't have known."

"Thank the stars she did because whatever she gave you helped to heal Geret."

Ren searched for his friend, finding him off to the side, sipping from a wooden cup and eyeing Emeli who danced with a muscley, half-naked boy wearing nothing but animal skins over his manhood. Emeli laughed and Geret looked thoroughly sour. Ren shook his head.

Returning to Lina, he still had questions. "So, your magic. I noticed you always use tinctures and powders to make it work."

"I use elements from the earth to make those. Plants, flowers, soil, bark, feathers— anything that still holds the magic of Avalon within."

"Is that why you said your magic doesn't belong to you?"

"I'm only a vessel. Magic belongs to the earth, not to any one person. Not even to Merlin."

Ren's eyes arched, and he wondered what cheeky response Merlin would have to that.

"Come on, let's join the others." Lina tugged on Ren's hand, pulling him into the crowd. "We may not get another chance after tomorrow."

And there was that thorny ache again, bringing Ren back to his anxieties about Lina. About all of them. They may not get to do a lot of things after tomorrow.

As his mind was about to spiral, Lina pressed her body into his, wrapping his arms around her shoulders as they swayed to the music. They allowed the thrumming energy to pound through them.

Her hands wandered up his bare chest as they moved, sending a tingling warmth through his belly that made his heart race. She pressed her face into the side of his neck, and they stayed like that for a while, wrapped up in each other's arms.

The night faded into a blur of music and stars until Ren stumbled back to his tent, taking note that Geret and Emeli were already asleep in theirs. Even though he collapsed into the warm, woolen linens of his bedroll, exhaustion heavy on his bones, his eyes remained open.

Tomorrow, they would fight for Camelot. His home. But it wasn't only his home he worried about. It was his sister and Geret in the tents next to him. And Lina, the girl who unexpectedly swept into his life, anchoring somewhere deep inside. Even the small towns they passed through on their journey—the people who needed more from the kingdom. They all needed them to win tomorrow because if they did, they could do better. They could be better.

But if they lost? He couldn't even imagine what that world would look like. And, at least for now, he didn't want to.

TWENTY-SEVEN

REN WOKE BEFORE THE SUN ROSE. THE HEAVINESS OF A late night and restless sleep pressed against his eyes, so he was grateful for the steaming tea left outside his tent. Around camp, everyone stirred, preparing to leave on the trek to Camelot. Their makeshift army sharpened weapons, dressed in battle gear, and whispered hushed prayers to the gods of the old religion. It was far from how Ren imagined the Camelot army was readying itself right now.

Geret and Emeli joined Ren around a fire, stretching their limbs and strapping on various pieces of the armor. The druids were kind enough to lend them extra pieces, but they couldn't spare much. A pang of nostalgia sparked in his chest when he thought about the armor he would use if he were in Camelot—a shined breastplate with Arthur's dragon emblem, a pair of gauntlets and greaves, and a steel helm with a special visor that retracted to allow better visibility. They were his father's, and he always imagined his first battle would include them.

Before long, they were moving through the woods, heading for the edge of Caledonian Forest. The plan was to surprise Morin's armies from the west fields and divert their forces away from Camelot. Alone, they didn't have the numbers, but with a divided army, perhaps they would have a chance.

As the soft light of morning glimmered on the horizon, they arrived at the edge of the fields bordering Camelot. In the distance, the low roar of waves pounded against the shoreline, and a comforting warmth spread through Ren's body as he arrived home.

The relief was brief because standing between him and his home were multiple armies, amassed and advancing on the walls around the city. Lines of men marched forward with siege ladders alongside enormous trebuchets dragged by horses. Along the walls of the city, a line of archers held their positions, but nothing fired yet, as they would need to wait until they were within range.

But missing were Camelot's allied armies.

"They didn't come," Ren whispered with a sinking, awful feeling embedded in his gut. He couldn't believe it. Camelot was alone.

Geret bounced nervously on the back of his heels. "Now?" he asked, drawing his sword.

"No," Ragnor interjected. His gray hair was tied into a bun, and he wore fighting leathers with his chest plate stitched with runes. "We wait until the time is right."

"And what time is that? When Camelot is taken?" Geret huffed.

Ragnor gave no reply. Lina flashed Geret a warning stare before turning to Ragnor. "Do you think they'll come?"

His eyes tracked the field where Morin's army carted in stones thatched with grass, easing them into the trebuchets. Nearby, torch men stood at the ready.

Even Ren's nerves danced around his chest, and he didn't know how much longer he could wait. Stopping the attack earlier seemed like a better plan than waiting for reinforcements that would arrive too late or perhaps not at all.

A roar sounded from the field as the stones within the trebuchets ignited in bright flames. Heat raced through Ren's veins. He couldn't stand there and watch Camelot go up in flames.

"I really think we should—" But as he edged toward Ragnor, a whistle sounded across the field on the other end of the woods, commanding everyone's attention.

For a moment, nothing happened, until shadows emerged from the trees. The figures were dressed in leathers dyed pine green, and they had animal furs latched to their shoulders. Weapons were strapped to their bodies, yet they did not draw them. Ren counted their numbers as they approached but quickly lost count because there were so many.

An enormous grin spread across Ragnor's face as he stepped forward, his arms outstretched in greeting. "Bearach!"

"Ragnor." A man with dark yellow paint splattered across his face greeted him with a deep voice, rolling the R in his name with his tongue. "It's been too long. Why do you wait so long to venture to our lands to the north?"

"It's a dangerous crossing these days. I am grateful you were already traveling and answered our call." Ragnor clasped Bearach's shoulder.

"We owed you for coming to our aid with the Viking raids last spring. Now, we are even."

Ragnor flashed his teeth. "Of course, my friend."

"Now, where is this daughter of yours? I hear she is the new queen of Camelot?"

Ren's stomach twisted. Did Ragnor's men tell him this? Or were rumors already passing through the towns? He looked to Lina, but her eyes were downcast as a flush bloomed in her cheeks. Ren knew the term *queen* made her uncomfortable, but it would take a lot more than Excalibur to sit on the throne in Camelot. The counsel had a say now, as did the people.

Ragnor let out a barrel laugh. "Ah. She is here." He grabbed hold of Lina's shoulder and pulled her to his side proudly.

"I am not queen," she said.

"Well," Bearach returned, "with that sword, you soon will be. I hope you will remember us then." His eyes traveled to Lina's hip, where she had Excalibur secured in a new harness. He wetted his lips with his tongue, sending heat surging over Ren's skin.

He didn't like the way Bearach looked at the sword—and Lina—like prizes to be won. The politics of the crown had already begun, and they hadn't even entered Camelot yet. That's why the clan answered the call so fast. They had something to gain. He supposed that's how it had always been. He just had never witnessed it.

Lina nodded, averting her gaze from Bearach.

Ragnor pulled Bearach aside to discuss strategy, while Lina joined Ren, Emeli, and Geret at the edge of the trees. Ren's eyes cast to the field to watch Morin's armies form lines in front of the trebuchets. Black smoke billowed over their army like a dark cloud.

All the while, Ren searched for Morin and Gwen, but it was difficult to distinguish anyone with their midnight helm and armor with the same charcoal tinge. Even the armies displaying different emblems on their flags wore coordinated colors.

Ren laughed to himself thinking of Morin dictating orders for matching fashions. "We mustn't clash; it wouldn't be good for my skin tone."

"What is it?" Lina asked, eyes lighting, sending other thoughts fluttering through Ren's chest.

"Nothing." He cleared his throat, embarrassed now for even thinking such a thing on the brink of battle. Luckily, Geret was there to bring everyone back to reality.

"Why are we still waiting and catching up with old friends when Camelot is about to burn? We should attack now!"

His frustration was palpable and sent a heavy wave of panic through Ren's head. He glanced back, and Ragnor and Bearach still huddled together, talking enthusiastically and exchanging laughs. Lina had joined them, catching Ren's gaze with a 'sorry about this' look on her face.

Okay, enough of this. Ren moved toward Ragnor with a mind to tell him to knock off the nonsense when Emeli tugged on his tunic, pointing to the far end of the field that curved around the castle walls, meeting with the ocean cliffs. Two galloping horses charged right for them, and Ren drew his sword, yelling, "Incoming!"

Emeli nocked an arrow, drawing her bowstring back. "Should I shoot?"

Behind them, Ragnor and Bearach, along with dozens of others, drew their weapons in a barrage of noise cutting the air in a bone-trembling sound.

"What are you waiting for?" Geret asked Emeli. "Shoot them!"

"No, wait!" Ren said, squinting into the sun. The colors on the lead horse were familiar somehow.

"Ren..." Emeli urged in a nervous tone as the two riders slowed to a trot.

A tall man wearing bulging shoulder armor and a silver helm sat on the lead horse. His tunic was in shades of blue and silver, stitched into a pattern Ren couldn't see clearly. But again, it seemed familiar. Behind him sat a smaller-framed figure on a graceful white horse. It was a woman, Ren realized, her blonde hair cascading in waves down her back.

As they approached, the woman's face came into focus, and Ren realized who it was. Silver strands weaved into her blonde hair. Wrinkles creased the edges of her lips. She was much older than Ren expected, perhaps around her father's age, which made sense given the time that had passed from the last time he saw her. Even so, he recognized her blue sparkling eyes, as they were the same color as the sea on a cloudless day. Also, because they were the same color as Gwen's.

But the other figure?

The man removed his helm, revealing wavy locks falling over his face in chestnut and gray. Ren immediately recognized him as he had hardly aged at all. Ren was only a boy when he last saw him, but he was one of his father's closest friends and frequented their supper table, so he would know him anywhere.

Lancelot.

Emeli let out a gasp and Geret bowed his head, tapping his chest plate. They were both well known, even now.

Lancelot and Guinevere dismounted their horses and extended their hands in greeting.

Guinevere immediately leaned over to Ren, taking his chin in her hand and studying his face.

"Amren Bedivere. It's been so long, and you are now a man. I hardly recognize that bouncing, young child who used to run around our feast hall giggling and chasing my ladies' daughters."

Ren's cheeks flushed. "My lady."

He bowed, unsure of the proper greeting for a former queen.

As she moved on to hug Emeli and Geret, Ren looked to Lancelot. "What are you doing here?"

"We have watched Camelot suffer from afar for too long." Lancelot's voice rumbled in a familiarity that could only be described as legendary. "Plus," a smile played on his lips, "you have a resourceful mother full of surprises."

"What did she do?" Ren pictured his mother helping the army prepare in the castle. A pinch squeezed his heart. He missed her.

Lancelot exchanged a knowing look with Guinevere. "Let's just say we've kept in contact over the years. She has her ways."

Curiosity would have pressed Ren to ask more questions, but a rumbling from the field drew his attention as Morin's armies marched toward the walls.

"Thank you," Ren said, returning his gaze to Lancelot. "Thank you for coming back." Seeing Lancelot here filled a gigantic hole in Ren's chest and gave him the reassurance he needed going into battle. Even though he had trained for this, he'd never been in a battle and the presence of a senior knight was more welcomed than he could imagine.

Lancelot nodded, but his face tightened. "I am sorry about your father, Amren. He was a good man. Perhaps the best of us all."

Ren's throat closed as emotion swelled behind his eyes and he pressed his lips tight.

"Where is Gwendolyn?" Guinevere's eyes searched the ranks before returning to Ren's.

His heart sank. "She's not with us," he said, unsure how to break the news. He still did not want to accept it himself. Their encounter at the caves still weighed heavily on his chest.

When Guinevere's eyebrows arched, he knew there wasn't time to explain the entire story, so he just said it. "She's with Morin's army."

Guinevere passed a knowing look to Lancelot, and she cleared her throat. "I knew your mother was hiding something in her message." A tear slid down her ivory cheek. "Then she has made her choice."

Noticing Guinevere had a sword strapped to her hip between layers of silky fabric and chain mail, Ren took the opportunity to change the subject. "Are you fighting?"

"What do you think I've been doing these past years, knitting?" She let out a gentle laugh and Lancelot beamed, brushing his fingers against hers. "Besides, Lance is an excellent teacher."

"You two have been together this entire time?" Emeli asked.

They exchanged looks, a warmth radiating from them both, but their lips remain sealed.

Ren glanced over his shoulder at Lina, who watched the reunion from a grassy hill as she clutched the hilt of Excalibur. She tucked it into her side, as if trying to shield it from view. He wanted to tell Lancelot about the sword, but seeing Lina's protective stance, he thought perhaps he'd keep that secret for now.

After Lancelot, Ragnor, and Bearach had grown acquainted, horses were mounted, and battle gear was made ready. A roar tore across the field as the first flaming stone launched from a trebuchet, crashing in front of Camelot's gates and igniting the grass in flames.

"Are we ready?" Lancelot asked, drawing his sword from astride his horse. The air of excitement dancing behind his eyes was that of someone who hadn't been himself for a long time but had finally found home again.

It made Ren's heart swell.

"Finally!" Geret exclaimed, thrusting his sword into the air.

A sense of hope settled in their company. With Lancelot and Guinevere by their side, and with Ragnor and Bearach's army at their back, they were as ready as they could be.

Ragnor gave the signal to his men, and they all marched forward. Energy surged through Ren's veins as he followed with his friends, his eyes locked on the field before them.

As they surged forward, a whooshing filled the air when Camelot archers released a wall of arrows that rained down onto Morin's armies. Their sharp points pierced several men on the front lines but bounced off the shields of many more. Then, a flash of light exploded, an unnatural burst of energy deflecting the remaining arrows and shattering them into a hundred pieces.

Magic.

A man stepped out in front of the lines to survey the destructive power. He wore midnight armor, his dark hair flowed freely in the sunlight, and his piercing eyes bored a hole through the mass of bodies. Right at Ren.

Morin had joined his army.

Even from afar, Ren could tell he was pissed.

TWENTY-EIGHT

"Now!" Lancelot and Ragnor yelled in unison, shooting shifty glances at one another. Ren guessed neither man was used to taking commands from anyone else.

With the command, everyone took off running. Confused, Morin's army scrambled before realizing what was happening and could form a line to face their attackers. A black horse carrying Morin broke formation from the siege line, followed by another figure astride a horse next to him. It was Gwen, wearing form-fitting midnight armor, her hair braided tightly behind her head. Ren's chest squeezed at the sight. He hoped she would have stayed behind instead of marching in with the rest of the army. Her commitment meant she was past the point of no return. She really was lost.

Ren wanted to grieve the loss of his friend. He wanted to rage at her decision—a decision that pitted them against each other on the battlefield. This wouldn't be like the mountain. They wouldn't have time to hesitate out here, not with blades and bodies and blood. This time, if they met, at least one of them would have to truly fight, and he didn't want to make that decision.

Ren noticed Morin at the front of his men lifting his sword and giving a signal. The trebuchets launched their burning balls of fury at the Camelot walls, smashing into sections and slamming into the ground. Meanwhile, Morin's men readied themselves with siege ladders and grappling hooks. They were trying to break through the walls, and Ren knew he couldn't let that happen.

He yelled for Lancelot and the others to push through their lines. They needed to focus on the front lines at the walls, but the Camelot army released a new round of arrows that didn't distinguish between friend and foe. Ren reached for a discarded shield and covered himself from their raining points. When it was safe, he joined back in the fight, thrusting his sword into someone's chest. It went through easier than he expected, and he yanked it out in time for another person pushing from behind.

Everyone was so close together it was difficult to identify allies or Morin's men. It was so much different from the fighting he'd already been a part of on this journey. Battles were a different beast.

Ren deflected blows, kicking and ramming his shoulder into people to clear the way. While on the field, he searched for his sister and Geret but quickly lost sight of them. A familiar panic bubbled in his chest—the same one he'd had in the Brecheliant Woods. His instincts told him he had to find them. He had to protect everyone. But in battle, he couldn't do that even if he'd wanted to. There wasn't time. He had to trust that their training would keep them alive and that he would see them again.

Pushing down the panic, he turned his focus to the dark knights standing between him and Camelot. And there were many.

AFTER HOURS of battling in front of the walls, Ren had a newfound respect for his father and the other knights. Sticky sweat and blood covered every inch of him until he was no longer certain what belonged to everyone else and what might be his. So far, he had managed to avoid any major injuries, but his muscles ached, and his sword arm burned with exhaustion.

As the fighting broke off into smaller skirmishes, Ren finally caught sight of Emeli and waved her over for a momentary break just outside the walls. She jogged over, squeezing him into her chest.

The tension immediately melted from his shoulders.

"Geret?" he asked.

"Everyone is fine," she returned, sucking in a breath. "I've managed to stay on the outskirts, but I haven't found a good vantage point to use my bow yet." Her eyes scanned the walls, and Ren knew she wished she were up there instead of down here.

"I'm just glad you're alright. Stay away if you can. Only fight those who come after you," Ren instructed. Emeli rolled her eyes.

"I know, I know. You don't have to protect me, little brother." She knocked into his shoulder with hers.

From the walls, a pair of horses galloped toward them, followed by a dozen Camelot guards.

Emeli sucked in a breath and planted her hands on her hips. "Looks like they know we're here."

"I wonder what mother thinks," Ren said.

Emeli laughed. "I don't think she will be very happy with us."

Ren shot her a grimace, wiping deep red blood from his sword on the edge of his tunic. "I'm not sure who I'm more afraid of, Morin's army or her."

But Emeli didn't have time to answer because the barrage of men arrived, and Ren spotted Galahad astride one of the horses with a scowl on his lips.

"Amren. Emeline," he addressed them as the men behind him halted. "Your mother ordered your retrieval. We saw an opportunity, but we don't have much time. You must come with us." He offered a hand to Ren, but Ren took a step back.

As appealing as the protection of the castle walls sounded, Ren couldn't even think about retreating now. They had fought hard to get here, and Lina was still out on the battlefield somewhere with Ragnor and his men. They were all risking their lives for Camelot. He couldn't abandon them now.

A disappointed frown melted on Emeli's face like she already knew what he was going to say.

"I can't go. Not yet." He squeezed her arm, and prepared to say his goodbyes, but she stepped forward instead.

"We can't come with you." She caught Ren's eyes for a moment, nodding. "Our place is out here."

Ren grinned, adding, "We can't abandon them." He pointed to the druid army forming a new line against Morin's men at the walls.

Galahad straightened his back, his lips forming a line far from a scowl. In fact, it looked dangerously close to an approving smile. "I don't think it's wise, and your mother will be furious."

"I don't care," Ren interrupted, surprised by his own boldness. "As much as she may not like it, you and I both know she understands our duties. Besides..."

Ren's eyes scanned the group of soldiers surrounding them, assessing if he should say the thing he knew would convince everyone, the thing they'd been holding on to for the right moment. Looking at the size of Morin's army, maybe now was that time. Everyone could use a reason to keep fighting, including himself.

He cleared his throat. "We must also protect Excalibur."

The vibe instantly shifted, and a series of murmurs rumbled through the men. Galahad creased his brow while his horse shifted its weight and let out a huff. "That is impossible," he said.

"He's telling the truth," Emeli replied, beaming.

"Even more reason for you to come with us," one of the soldiers next to Galahad urged.

Ren searched for Lina's brown locks amid the druids in the field, but he couldn't find her. There were too many people and too many battles. She could be in any one of them. He had faith she could protect herself one-on-one, but this was different. What would happen if she was captured and they discovered what she carried? What if she was injured or worse?

He rubbed the back of his neck, forcing the thoughts down his dry throat. He couldn't think that way. She would be fine, but he needed to join them out there and do his part. He needed to find her if he could.

He turned back to Galahad. "We don't have the sword."

"What?" Galahad asked. "But you just said—"

"You heard him," Emeli stepped forward and approached Galahad's horse, stroking his mane.

Galahad leaned down so only Emeli and Ren could hear him. "You'd better have a good reason for this."

"I don't have time to explain, but we do," Ren returned, stepping away and stretching out his arms. He twirled his sword in one hand and squared his shoulders. "Camelot needs us."

The soldiers exchanged worried looks behind Galahad, and one of them removed their helm, tucking it under his arm. "We will join you," he said, and the others all nodded in agreement.

Now, Galahad really did smile, showing his teeth. "Whatever you need." He dipped his head into a bow. It was the first time he'd ever done that to Ren.

Warmth spread through Ren's chest as he nodded in return. "I was hoping you'd say that."

221

THE SKY TURNED a deep auburn as the sun dipped closer to the horizon and thick indigo clouds drifted overhead. Ren was exhausted, as were the rest of their forces. They'd been fighting for hours, and while they kept Morin's army away from the walls of Camelot, they couldn't keep it up. Wounded fighters were carted off the field, and the lines had begun to break. Despite that, Morin and his huge army kept pushing forward.

He spotted Lina fighting alongside Ragnor and a few other druids. She dipped in and out of the fray as she always did, daggers in hand. Ren's stomach fluttered as he approached, relief flooding his system. When he got to her, instead of pulling her into a strong embrace like every part of his body ached for, he offered a smile, as his eyes awkwardly scanned the faces of the others around. Ragnor gave him a deep, penetrating stare. He was also mud-covered, and his hair had fallen around his shoulders in tangled strands. But he still had energy. They all did.

"Having fun yet?" Ren said, sliding in close so that his back pressed against hers. A tingle raced down his spine at their touch, but fighters were still coming at them. He couldn't let up, so he raised his sword to block the blow of an oncoming blade.

"Tons," Lina responded between breaths as she squatted to the ground after pushing a man into Ragnor's waiting arms.

"Who are your friends?" She nodded at Galahad and the other Camelot soldiers whose presence was helping them overcome the fighting in this area. They made slow progress, but inch by inch they put more space between Morin's army and the Camelot walls.

"They were sent by mother," Ren responded, using the break in the fight to turn toward Lina.

"Your mother?" her eyebrows quirked.

"She thought we'd like to come home." He laughed, but then

he realized it probably wasn't funny. The weariness was affecting his mind.

Lina tilted her head.

"Behind the walls," Ren clarified.

"And you didn't go?"

"No," Ren huffed, ducking a blade from a rogue man racing toward him as Lina dug her dagger into the man's neck. As he collapsed to the ground, she frowned at Ren.

Lina's lips upturned slightly. "Maybe I misjudged you, Ren Bedivere."

Ren leaned in, running his fingers along her arm. He wanted so much for more, but their break ended when a loud boom sounded as another fiery stone crashed into the Camelot walls.

Morin's knights surged toward the opening, and Ren's heart raced.

"I have to go!" he yelled, running in that direction as Lina shouted something back to him, but he couldn't hear it over the increased tempo of the fighting.

Ren coughed through the smoke billowing from the fires along the walls. He searched for the others but only caught the back of Galahad, who had been sucked back into the battle. A group of Morin's knights made their way to the gate and were fighting over the stone crumbles.

Ren ran forward with his sword outstretched and crashed into the fight, but there were too many dark knights surrounding him. A boot to his chest knocked the wind from his lungs and sent him falling to his back.

Gasping for breath, a shadowed figure hovered above him— an enormous man with silver hair and sharp eyes. His boot slammed down on his sword hand until he released the hilt from his grip.

Ren called for help, struggling against the weight of the boot on his wrist, but everyone was too busy in their own fights. Everything slowed as he took in the horror of the surrounding battle. Piles of bodies scattered the ground, and dark stains soiled the once golden field. Wildfires burned over the grass, sending black smoke billowing into the darkening skies. A distant clattering of swords and a heavy crack sounded behind him from the gate.

They were breaking through.

His stomach turned to knots as the figure above raised his sword, readying to pierce his chest.

Ren said his silent goodbyes, clenching his fists into the ground and squeezing his eyes shut.

"Sorry, father," he whispered, readying himself for the final blow.

TWENTY-NINE

GWEN

GWEN DISMOUNTED HER HORSE, SLAPPING HER ON THE side so she would gallop far, far away from the mayhem happening at the gates. A part of Gwen wished she could go with her, but she knew the guilt twisting her insides into hard knots would follow her anywhere. As much as she wanted to hide, she had to see this through. At the end of everything, she hoped the rest of the kingdom would see how much better they were for it.

A shattering echoed over the ground as Gwen turned to find dozens of dark knights hauling a battle ram to the front gate. They grunted and hollered as the wheels on the cart crunched over gravel, the wood creaking under the enormous weight of the ram.

"Bring them down!"

Gwen recognized the voice. Sir Bors was manning the walls overhead, leading the archers in a melee of flying arrows aimed at the battling ram.

She didn't have time to think, so she swooped up a discarded shield and took cover as a barrage of arrows rained down upon them. Screams echoed at the gate, and bodies fell, their flesh penetrated by the sharp teeth of the arrows. They pushed toward the gate as another set of arrows whizzed through the air. This time Gwen had to leap out of the way as one nearly missed her backside. It was pure carnage.

As she pushed herself from the ground, a flash of chestnut hair passed through her vision. She spotted a shiny set of shoulder armor she knew all too well because of the many hours she had spent sparring with the boy wearing it. Ren was several feet away, battling through several dark knights at the gate. He took a kick to the center of his chest, which sent him crashing to the ground.

Gwen bolted across the space, pushing through bodies and blocking sword blades swinging in her direction. By the time she arrived, the silver-haired man wearing Morin's colors had Ren pinned, his foot crunching down on Ren's arm. Scarlet streaks and mud splattered Ren's face, and he ground his teeth together. Even though he struggled against his assailant, he wasn't strong enough to push him off.

A giant crack echoed across the field as the first smash of the battle ram crashed into the gate, sending splinters in all directions. Gwen couldn't watch because in front of her, the silver-haired man raised his sword, readying for a death blow. She didn't think, only bolted forward and slammed into the man's backside.

She didn't even realize she had lodged her blade into his back until Ren groaned from underneath. Gwen rolled off the pile, pushing the dead body from Ren's chest and yanking her sword back. Ren let out a gasp of air.

Gwen's blade pointed at Ren now, her arms shaking. This was the second time they had met this way, and she was, again, at a loss for words. Her insides squirmed with guilt, and heat swarmed her chest. She didn't regret her choices but facing him in battle was not something she had ever considered with this plan. It was inevitable, though, that she would face her friends, her family, even. But not like this.

He raised his hands up in surrender, blinking his eyes as if trying to confirm what he was seeing.

Withdrawing her sword, she offered her hand to him instead.

His jaw flexed, eyes wide for a moment, before he grabbed hold and let her pull him to his feet. Wiping the blood splatter from his forehead, his green eyes locked with hers.

Gwen's throat tightened. She had so much to say. She wanted to tell him she was sorry for leaving him trapped in those caves. She wanted to assure him that she had planned to go back for them if they didn't make it out. She wanted to tell him all the ways this plan had gone so wrong, but she was still angry at Camelot for making it come to this, for their idleness and their lies. For not protecting her and Ren better.

Instead of saying any of that, the sounds of the battle came into sharp focus all around them. Swords clashed. Arrows whizzed overhead. The battering ram took another swing at the gate and the wooden frame cracked and groaned against the pressure. It was only a matter of time before it would break open, allowing Morin's forces to swarm inside.

She turned back to Ren, whose eyes searched the battlefield as well. As he was bolting from the spot, he managed to say two words: "Thank you."

It was enough to fill the smallest of cracks between them.

As Ren disappeared back into battle, another crash sounded at the wall, drawing Gwen's attention. But this time it wasn't the battering ram. An explosion fired above the gate, and a figure appeared out of the smoke.

Merlin chanted into his glowing palms, dropping what looked

like a dragon's egg at the men below. It exploded into bright light, emitting a thick plume of smoke that swallowed the men manning the ram.

Fits of coughs took over the men fleeing the area.

Merlin caught Gwen's eye, and yelled, "Now!"

Out of the front gate came a barrage of Camelot soldiers leading the charge. They battled back the dark knights remaining and cut the ram loose from its cradle. The giant tree rolled off the cart, slamming into the ground. Cheers erupted, but only briefly, as more knights emerged from behind the gate with Merlin astride a beige horse. After the last person came out, they closed the gates and locked them tight.

Gwen took this as her cue to jump back into the fighting. She searched for Morin and spotted him at the end of the walk. But he wasn't alone. Merlin also found him and dismounted his horse. The two sorcerers stared one another down. Around them, everyone else broke out into fighting.

Merlin wore tight battle leathers clinging to every curve, and a barrage of talismans jangled over his stitched vest. But the most striking piece of his ensemble was a golden armor plate adorned with sparkling jewels over one shoulder securing a plum wool cape hanging to the side. It was a blatant mockery of Morin's own signature shoulder-plate-and-cape battle attire. Gwen knew that for certain.

Morin didn't look amused, and his mouth formed into a sneer as he caught Gwen's gaze, commanding her to join him.

She couldn't resist. "Look at that. You are a trendsetter." She cackled. It had been such a tough day, and seeing Ren had left her shaken. She would have done anything for a moment of reprieve, and taunting Morin was quickly becoming one of her favorite things.

"Whose side are you on? Because I'm not certain anymore," Morin noted, giving her a side eye.

It was a loaded question. One she didn't care to answer. Instead, she took her stance, sword at the ready.

"Gwendolyn, you shouldn't be here," Merlin said.

"You don't give her orders," Morin replied.

"And you do?"

"Nobody does," Gwen hissed at them both.

"Alright, then." Merlin unleashed his staff, springing it to life in a burst of blue sparks.

Morin sheathed his own sword, dipping his hand into the pouch on his waist belt.

Now she was wondering if she should actually be there.

Without warning, Merlin threw his staff forward, sending a bright light in their direction. Gwen let out a shriek as she shielded herself with one arm. But the crash came and went, and she'd been spared. The smoke cleared, leaving Morin kneeling to the ground. In one palm, a glowing stone had projected out a shield around them, protecting them from the blast.

Gwen let out a weighted breath, swatting debris from her shoulders and smoothing her hair back. She definitely shouldn't be here.

"That's pretty. Learning to skip rocks, are we?" Merlin jested.

"You have your toys. I have mine." Morin retrieved two more shimmery stones, rolling them between his fingers.

At this stage, Gwen rolled her eyes and stepped off to the side. Even sorcerers had to whip their magic around in some sort of masculine show, and she wasn't about to be a casualty of their silly game.

With the small talk completed, both sorcerers unleashed all their fury upon one another, exchanging explosive balls of light and smoke. Morin should have been quicker than Merlin, his swift movements besting most other opponents, but Merlin anticipated his every move, dodging and issuing counterattacks. They danced amongst the haze left from their fiery magic.

At one point, Morin drew his sword, using it to slash and jab at Merlin between explosive forces. Eventually, Morin launched a blast that hit Merlin square in the chest and knocked him backward. Gwen was about to jump in, but Morin shook his head, motioning her back.

With his sword tip pointed, Morin lunged forward, but as Merlin was pushing himself off the ground, a flash of a body blurred by. Galahad had joined the fight and was charging after Morin.

"Galahad, no!" Merlin cried, but he still slipped by.

Morin was ready, blocking Galahad's blows and issuing a counterattack with his blade. This time, Gwen did lunge forward, clashing swords with Galahad. All those training sessions were paying off in unexpected ways, as she already knew all of his moves. Gwen could tell by the irritated expression on Galahad's already sour face that he knew it too.

It was working. Together, they pushed Galahad back until Merlin issued another magical blast that sent everyone flying. Gwen's sword slipped through her fingers as she crashed to the ground, expelling all the air from her lungs.

Morin charged forward furiously in front of Gwen, deflecting the blade of Galahad's new strike. Gwen didn't think Galahad would have killed her, but she knew battles could be messy.

On the other side, Merlin chanted into his staff, and smoke rose from the crystals at the top. A flock of birds arose in a cloud of smoke. He was about to send them flying when Morin caught Galahad off guard as they dueled, sweeping his leg under his knee like he'd done to the young knight on the training field. But Galahad was better trained and leapt into the air to avoid the trip, which played into what Morin knew he would do. Instead, he sent a blast right at him.

The force crashed into Galahad with a booming crack, sending him flying backward into a pile of boulders. His body broke against the rock and dropped limp onto the ground.

Gwen's stomach dropped as a sickening bile rose in her throat. She never wanted anyone to get hurt, especially Galahad. It was all practice, all training, but of course that was false. This was a real battle where real people got hurt or killed.

When Merlin rushed to Galahad's side, the flock of birds he had conjured shattered in the air. He shook Galahad's body, but the knight wasn't moving. Even from afar, Gwen could see blood streaming down the side of his head where his skull had struck the rockface.

Gwen wanted to run over to them and help, but Morin had her by the elbow and was tugging her away.

She growled at him, jerking away from his grasp.

"I won't do this anymore," she cried, her eyes frantically staring at Merlin trying to wake Galahad with his magic.

"This is a battle. You can't have sympathy for every one of them," Morin said.

Nausea rolled in her belly. It wasn't sympathy. It was people she knew. Galahad was her stepbrother and was the only family she had left. This had gone too far. Morin had gone too far.

When she turned to him with a storm firing behind her eyes, he ran a hand down her spine, leaving a shiver over her skin.

His eyes softened. "It's almost over."

Was it? She surveyed the battlefield where so many had already fallen—Camelot soldiers she knew, grew up with, trained with.

Sickness rose into her throat, and she bent over her knees, emptying the contents of her stomach. Her legs shook, and she thought she may pass out.

It was too late.

THIRTY

Twilight crept over the field in shades of shadowy blues as Morin's knights retreated into the protection of the forest. A few scattered fights continued over the field, but between the Camelot army and the druid armies, they managed to hold back the dark knights from the walls. So far. Tomorrow, they would have to fight again. Ren couldn't bear the thought.

He poured a canteen of water over his face, propping himself up against an outcropping of boulders. Emeli and Geret joined. Red blood smeared across Emeli's forehead where a gnarly gash streaked through her pale skin. Geret winced as he approached, clutching at the side where his fatal wound nearly ended him. But both were alive, and that was all Ren cared about.

"I don't know about this, little brother. Do you think we should make a break for it? Get fresh weapons and a couple of hours of sleep before the next attack? Mom is probably freaking out." Emeli peered over the boulders, her eyes fixed upon the glowing lights of the castle, and Ren wondered if she regretted her earlier decision to stay.

Maybe he did, too, a little. A soft bed, a warm fire, and a hot bowl of stew sounded so good to him that it made his stomach rumble. He wanted more than anything to go home but looking out over the field at Ragnor and his men, along with those left from Bearach's clan, he knew he had to stay for a little while longer.

"I don't know, Em," he said, directing his gaze to his sister's pleading eyes. "Our priority is to protect the sword, and that work isn't done. If we go back now, do you really think they will allow us to rejoin the fight? Mother will have a million excuses why we must stay protected, and without Galahad to speak for us, I doubt the other knights will argue with her."

Emeli's eyes fell to the ground. Geret opened his mouth to say something but sealed his lips and slid silently down a rock to his bottom.

Lina was still among Ragnor's group, glancing in their direction. After spotting them huddled together, she walked over with a plate in her hands. She offered the food, giving what little they had to share. Ren was grateful for the gesture and took a piece of dried fish.

"How have you fared?" he asked her, searching her eyes for the answers he was toiling with.

Lina glanced over her shoulder at her people. "We've lost many men. Bearach has, too."

Ren frowned. "Us too, I think. Although there is no telling how many more wounded we have inside the walls."

"Is it difficult to be so close to home, yet feel a million miles away?"

How had Lina known what was in his mind without him having to say it?

He nodded as a rolling ache bloomed inside.

"I think your father would be proud of what you have done here," she said, wrinkling her nose and mustering a smile.

"I hope it's enough."

"It will be." She grabbed hold of his hand, a gesture that sent a warm tingle over his skin.

"What the..." Emeli choked, spitting out the water she had just sipped, catching all their attention.

Lina snapped her hand back, her face flush.

"Look over there!" Emeli peered over the rocks and pointed toward the cliffs behind the castle walls.

Lights flickered in the dimming light, and a dark line crept along the base of the wall.

Snapping to attention, Ren yelled, "They are trying to take the back wall! Hurry!" Grabbing hold of his sword, he sprinted toward the walls of Camelot. A scuffle of voices and boots followed him, along with a clattering of dishes and weapons.

Ren's body ached as he moved through the field, running over bodies and stumbling over discarded weapons. His burning muscles were heavy, but there was no option but to push through the fatigue. He scooped up a shield and held it in front of his chest.

By the time they reached the cliffs, he was out of breath and sweating. Heaving in air, Emeli arrived behind, followed by Lina and the others. Geret hobbled over and leaned against a rock. He didn't look too good, but Ren knew he wouldn't sit this out even if asked. He was just as stubborn as Ren.

The lights were torches carried by a dark line of men. They gathered at the base of the wall, some already scaling the steep stone barrier, cloaked mostly by shadow as the last bit of sunlight disappeared in the west. Ren approached the nearest cliff and peered over at the thrashing waves below. His jaw dropped. An entire fleet of ships had anchored about fifty feet from shore. Rune symbols and other emblems painted the sails. They were images Ren didn't recognize.

There were no black crows in sight. He squinted at the men scaling the walls. They wore rust-colored armor over red tunics with dark chain mail dripping down their arms.

"These aren't Morin's men," Ren said, heading back to the group.

"Who are they, then? Allies?" Emeli gasped.

"Whose allies? Ours or his?" Geret pointed toward the field where Morin's army stirred. Their silhouettes moved, dowsing fires and yelling commands across the field. They had finally noticed the strangers.

"There is no time!" someone shouted from behind Ren, and a barrage of bodies charged toward the wall.

"No! Wait!" Ren yelled, but they were already knocking him from behind, the number of men joining the charge increasing with every moment.

Nobody was listening. Emeli steadied him with a hand on his forearm. If they stayed, they would watch their army break against the new lines. If they joined in the fight, they faced an unknown enemy before learning any information about them. And everyone was still exhausted. It was risky.

"I for one haven't spent all those sweaty early mornings under Galahad's barking orders to watch strangers take our home." Geret twirled his sword and steadied himself on his feet. Emeli flashed him a smile and drew an arrow, aiming her bow at the wall.

Ren took a deep, steadying breath. What choice did they have? They couldn't give up now. Unknown enemy or not, the fighting would be the same. He glanced around at the determined faces of his friends. It was time for another battle.

He nodded at Emeli, and she inhaled a sharp breath, squinting with one eye down the shaft of her arrow. Then she released it, sending the projectile flying toward the wall. It found its mark, sinking into the back of one man scaling the wall. He fell and crashed to the ground.

"Nice shot." Ren elbowed her in the side. He drew his sword and joined the rest of the men running at the wall.

When they arrived, the clashing battles sounded all around. This new army's fighting was different, as they moved in short bursts, jabbing into the fray then retreating. Morin's army was all strength. These soldiers were ghosts. Ren couldn't adjust to dueling with a short soldier wearing rust armor and red colors like the rest. None of their faces were visible beneath slim-fitting helms.

Ren backed out of the fight to survey the scene. While their forces pulled several men from the wall, there were even more scaling the cliffs below, joining in numbers. It was impossible this many men had arrived right under their noses. Where did they come from?

Camelot wasn't prepared to defend this part of the wall.

To make things worse, Morin and his dark knights had joined the fray, and smaller fights ignited along the walls like wildfire.

Ren was certain the new army was not with Morin because they were kicking everyone's ass. Dark knights and Camelot soldiers either fell or fell back, allowing more and more of the army in red to swarm the cliffs like insects.

The only way they stood a chance was by assembling formations and driving synchronized attacks, but chaos ruled all around them. Even with Lancelot leading his group, Ragnor leading the druids, and Morin attempting some sort of strategy, the new army beat them all back one by one.

Ren was so busy tracking colors he didn't notice the figure creep up behind him until the sword blade sliced across his shoulder. He yelled out and stumbled as his hand grasped at the wound. Examining his fingers covered in sticky blood sent his stomach plummeting, and lightness rushed his temples.

A tall figure sporting the same armor as the rest of the army withdrew his sword and circled Ren. A crimson cape billowed behind him as he approached. In likeness, he was the same as all the others with one exception: sitting on top of his slender helm was a crown made of bones. Something about him turned Ren's stomach sour.

Ren lunged with his blade, but the red knight swatted it away like a cat would a mouse.

The wound on Ren's shoulder sent a searing pain down his arm, and he groaned as he fell to his knees. Using his sword to balance, he pushed himself up and stared wide-eyed at the crowned knight who stalked toward him.

"Who are you?" Ren asked, out of breath and in pain. He ground his teeth together to stay alert. He refused to go down like this.

The figure stopped and studied him through slits in his helm but said nothing.

"Amren!" a voice yelled out, turning Ren's attention. Lancelot had rallied men together and was fighting against a group of red knights. Behind them, he spotted Geret carrying Emeli away from the fray.

Ren bolted, leaving the crowned knight behind him.

"What happened?" he said, catching up with Geret and Emeli.

"I'm fine, it's just my ankle." Emeli groaned.

"Are you sure?" Ren examined her foot as Geret moved. Her boot was off, and it had swelled to twice its size. A deep bruise was already spreading up her leg.

"She wanted to stay. Can you believe this?" Geret huffed.

Emeli rolled her eyes. "Like I said, it's just my ankle."

"Yeah, and what do you think happens when you can't move on the battlefield? It will be your head next," Geret returned.

Now Ren really was going to be sick, but it was Emeli's eyes that went wide when she caught sight of the blood spreading down Ren's arm. She scrambled out of Geret's hold, landing on her one good foot and clawing at his shoulder. "What happened? Are you alright?"

The wound burned, making his head spin, but he sucked in a breath and clenched down his teeth. "I'm fine. It's just a scratch. Now go! I have to get back out there."

He slapped Geret on the back. "Take her to the druids. Their camp is inside the woods, and they can treat her. She will be safe."

Geret lifted one of Emeli's arms around his shoulder.

"Ren!" Emeli yelled, but Ren had already turned from them and was running back to Lancelot, ignoring the image of Emeli's horror-stricken face.

This was a nightmare. Visibility was low, and these new knights blended in with the shadows, surprising groups on all sides. It was a bloodbath.

He found Lancelot and his men joining the fight.

"Who are they?" Ren asked between breaths. He searched for the crowned knight, but he had vanished from the field.

"I've never seen them," Lancelot returned, smashing two knights out of his way with a powerful blow from his sword.

Morin was nearby, fighting back the red knights. Ren searched the crowd for Gwen, but the red knights were closing in fast, surrounding their group from all sides. He was having a hard time telling everyone apart.

"There are too many!" Ren panted, jabbing his sword forward but missing his opponent as they darted backward. Then they were back again, swinging a long sword right at Ren's head.

Ren ducked in time, but the wound on his shoulder split apart, sending a burning warmth down his arm. He cried out and doubled over.

Lancelot was there, covering his back. "You need to get out of here, kid. You're injured."

Ren's eyes lifted to Lancelet. Gashes and deep bruises marked his entire body as well, and he looked much older than this morning.

"We all are. That doesn't mean we give up." Ren straightened his spine, ripping the bottom of his tunic and, with Lancelot's help, binding his shoulder. He didn't know if it would hold, but it was the best they could do in a pinch.

More red knights spilled over the cliffs ahead of them, splitting apart so that half worked to scale the walls while the other half formed a protective barrier against the other armies.

"They keep multiplying. How is this possible? Where did they come from?" Ren turned to Lancelot, but his eyes were fixed on the approaching figure of the crowned knight who had returned to the battlefield.

Ren grimaced against the pain in his shoulder, but he readied his sword as he stared wide-eyed at the red knight king. If he was going to go out, he would go out fighting, just like his father.

As Ren moved forward to meet him, a shadow crossed over. Lancelot stepped out in front, shielding him from the red knight's view.

The two did not speak, squaring off in a singular battle among the surrounding melee.

Ren fell into a fight with one of Morin's men—a muscled soldier covered from head to toe in tattoos and sporting steely piercings in his ears. While he was busy fighting, Lancelot lunged at the red knight with a battle cry that echoed over the field.

The two sparred, their swords crashing together in a thunderous storm. Some fighters stopped to watch the loud spectacle, Morin's knights included.

Ren had his opponent on the ground with a slash to the back of his legs, so he turned his attention to Lancelot. Even at his age, Lancelot was nimble, using what he lacked in enormous muscle to his advantage by going on the defensive, parrying every attack. The crowned knight appeared to grow tired, stopping to catch his breath between blows.

Finally, Lancelot took an opportunity to counterattack after blocking another strike, jamming his sword into the red knight's stomach. The knight groaned and sank to his knees. Cheers—actual cheers—erupted on the field. Ren couldn't tell if they were Camelot's or Morin's army, but it roared over them all the same.

Lancelot let out a heavy breath and turned from his fallen opponent. Ren stepped over to join him, when a voice rang out nearby.

"Father?"

Gwen stood several yards away, panting, the braids in her hair having come undone so that strands frizzed in all directions. Her face was covered in grime, and she limped a little as she moved through the crowd.

"Gwen!" Lancelot returned, his eyes brightening as a wide grin spread over his face. But then a sickening gurgle came from his lips, all the color melting from his flushed cheeks.

Sticking from his chest was the sharp blade of a sword, with the crowned knight hovering behind him.

"No!" Gwen let out a blood-curdling scream, pushing through bodies until Morin was there, snatching her back with arms around her waist. Chaotic fights broke out again, and Morin and Gwen disappeared into the crowd.

Ren's heart stopped when the blade slid from Lancelot's chest. His body sagged, sinking to the ground and landing with a thud.

The crowned knight studied Ren through the slits in his helm before lifting it from his face. A curly head of chestnut hair fell over his dark eyes.

Ren stared wide-eyed at the man he recognized instantly. He had warped into something grotesque and twisted, as hollow cheekbones set into pale skin, and writhing shadows snaked around his neck like they were alive. An open gash along his side dripped sticky blood to the ground, but he seemed completely unaffected by the wound Lancelot had inflicted just moments ago.

Sickness rolled in the pit of Ren's stomach as his mouth

dropped open. This couldn't be happening. The man standing in front of him wasn't real.

"King Arthur," Ren gasped. All remaining hope drained from his body.

CHAPTER

THIRTY-ONE

LINA

"Impossible." Horror struck Ren's face.

Lina peered over the edge of a pile of boulders, having watched the scene unfold. Lancelot had been slain. Ragnor's group was busy at the wall, but as Arthur's army emptied their ships, they pushed the druid armies farther and farther back. Things looked grim. More than grim. They looked hopeless.

King Arthur was coming for Ren. Could it really be him? It felt impossible to even consider it, but the sword had seemed impossible, too, yet here it was, in her hand.

Ren swayed on his feet, the wound on his shoulder spilling

blood down his arm. The color of his skin had turned a ghastly shade. Lina knew she had to help, but she was transfixed on the king, as was Ren.

Arthur stepped over the body of Lancelot, twirling his sword playfully. "Haven't you learned enough of this world by now to know that anything is possible with the right variables in place?" His lips curled upward, but the smile was not warm. Cold chills ran down Lina's spine.

Ren opened his mouth to speak but said nothing. He could only wipe the sweat from his brow as his eyes fluttered open and shut. He had lost too much blood. He needed help.

Lina moved closer to the edge of the rocks, sliding one leg over and creeping downward.

"I don't understand. You wanted us to save Camelot," Ren said. "You wanted me to retrieve the sword." His legs trembled, and he used the hilt of his sword to support his weight.

There wasn't much time. Lina hopped from the rocks, slinking as silently as possible toward the pair as Ren continued.

"I trusted you. My father trusted you. He was loyal until the end." His voice shook, and Lina could sense the pain in his words. She knew how much the quest had meant to Ren, how fiercely he had wanted to retrieve the sword to help Camelot.

Arthur twisted his face, his eyes rolling in their hallowed sockets. "Your father betrayed me. Even as I spoke my last words with my dying breath, he showed me his allegiance, and it wasn't to his kingdom."

"What do you mean?" Ren asked.

"I asked him to bury me with Excalibur so I would never die, but he ignored my wish and cast the sword of power to the depths of Avalon. He let his king perish. That's what your father's loyalty meant."

"You are wrong." Ren shook his head. "My father was loyal to Camelot. He just wasn't loyal to you."

Lina crept closer, ducking behind a cart with piled bodies. It reeked of death, and she had to hold back a gag as she squinted around the wheel to keep watching. If Ren could keep talking, she could still surprise Arthur, but she needed a higher vantage point.

Her eyes followed the pile of bodies towering above her, and her insides twisted. It would have to do.

Wisps of shadow whipped around Arthur's billowing cape, and his lips pressed into a hard line. "Lucky for you, little knight, Camelot now has its champion. Without your help, they wouldn't have their king back."

Ren's face twisted with confusion. Lina didn't understand it, either. She climbed onto the cart, holding back the gag threatening to give her away. Once on top, she steadied herself and reached carefully for her daggers.

"You, Amren Bedivere, retrieved Excalibur, untethering my soul from the afterlife. I owe you my gratitude, in righting what your father wronged. You had the strength to do what he could not."

As Arthur kept talking, Ren's eyes finally caught hers and he dipped his chin slightly down like he wanted to communicate something. She squeezed her daggers, and Ren's lip twitched.

No. Not the daggers. The sword. He wanted her to use the sword. She wrapped her fingers around Excalibur's hilt, squeezing tight as a thrum of energy climbed up her arm. Sliding it slowly from the sheath at her back, she hoped Ren could district Arthur for a moment longer.

"What army would follow a dead king?" Ren asked, as if already knowing what she needed. He had been so intuitive with her from the start. Goosebumps raced over her skin as she recalled her dreams. Ren being there, handing her this sword. This was it.

"There are worlds beyond these lands." Arthur answered. "Worlds hungry for power and riches. I can give them those things once I am back upon my throne."

The wound at Arthur's side continued to ooze bright blood. There was no way anyone alive could still be walking around with that. This must indeed be Arthur, risen from the dead. She didn't know how such a thing was possible, and while she gripped the sword in her hands, a sickening thought twisted inside: It wasn't possible, so what kind of power could be responsible for this?

Lina leaned over the cart just a few feet away from where Ren and Arthur were talking.

"Immortality strikes fear and awe in weak men's hearts. While you embarked upon your little quest to retrieve the sword, I was busy gaining allegiances. They took very little convincing in the end. Now, I ask that you return Excalibur to its rightful owner. If you do, I will let you and the rest of your friends live."

Ren's eyes caught Lina's again, and he smirked. "But I didn't pull the sword."

"I did!" Lina leaped from the cart with the sword in both hands as Arthur whirled around. But he wasn't fast enough, and she sunk the blade deep into his chest before her feet had even hit the ground.

Arthur screamed and staggered backward, clutching at the sword buried in his chest.

Lina and Ren exchanged satisfied looks, but then something else twisted in Ren's face—shock.

A smoldering black smoke billowed from the sword in Arthur's chest as he yanked the blade from his own body with a sickening crunch of bone and tearing of muscle.

His shattering laugh erupted. "You can't kill me. I'm already dead!"

He clutched Excalibur in one hand, while still gripping his weapon in the other one. Now he had two swords, though one would have been powerful enough.

Ren shot Lina a frantic look. She didn't know what to do but retrieve her daggers and pray to the gods for help.

In the distance, chaotic commands traveled over the field. "Retreat!"

A wave of men rolled toward them, some in Camelot colors, but also Morin's dark knights.

They had been overpowered. They were giving up. Lina searched for Ragnor and the druids, but it was pure chaos now.

Bodies flew in every direction, and small fights ignited across the field.

Ren stood frozen in place as the king closed the space between them.

"Come on! We have to go!" Lina yanked on Ren's elbow, but his feet still wouldn't budge.

"We can't! The sword... we have to get it back." He stumbled, and his hands hit the ground.

Lina helped him to his feet, looking over her shoulder where Arthur was lunging toward them, two blades in the air. She grabbed hold of a discarded shield and heaved it at him. It worked, smashing into his torso and knocking him back. It gave just enough time for her to heave Ren out of the way.

His legs shook, and she had to support his weight with his arm around her shoulder, but they were able to meet up with a group of druids who had retreated into the woods.

Once they were far enough away, she stole a glance back at the castle walls where King Arthur stood at the base of the stone, eyes alight with fire. He caught a rope, swung it upward, and scaled the full height of the wall with the rest of his army before perching at the top like a gargoyle. With the flicker of his cape, he hopped over the edge and out of sight.

They had failed. *She* had failed. But this wasn't how her dream had gone. She had thought that everything finally made sense, but she found herself more confused than ever.

Then a thought crashed through her body like a powerful wave, knocking all the air from her lungs—the dream wasn't about Lina saving Camelot and her people.

It was about destroying them.

CHAPTER

THIRTY-TWO

WHEN REN WAS A SMALL BOY, THE DYING KING summoned his father to accompany him to the lake. His father hadn't realized Ren followed him, using the trail of crimson blood marking the earth like footprints to guide his way. They were footprints to the final resting place of the greatest king the world had ever known.

Arriving at the sacred shoreline, Ren watched his father lay the king down at the water's edge. Arthur groaned, stretching to move but unable to do so. Ren crouched behind prickly bushes, peering through the leaves. Even at a young age he couldn't tear his gaze away from the king. None of them could. Arthur had an otherworldly compelling presence.

Arthur reached for Ren's father, pulling him near to his chest, and with a dying breath he whispered something into his ear. Ren's father never spoke of what he said. It was a secret he took to his grave.

The golden armor over Arthur's chest rose and fell. Ren's father's face tightened. Reaching for the sword at Arthur's hip, he gripped the hilt.

Ren held his breath for an eternity.

The sound of Excalibur unsheathed echoed over the water in a thunderous slice. Holding it into the air, sunlight glinted off the blade, and energy pulsed outward in a wave, pounding against Ren's chest. He'd heard stories of the sword but had never seen it with his own eyes. Wet tears clung to his small eyelashes as he realized Arthur would never use the sword again, and it broke his young heart.

He crawled through the mud-soaked earth to get a better view as his father returned to the king and placed his fingers over his lifeless eyes, forcing them closed.

Turning toward the water, his father waded in until it soaked his trousers to his knees.

Ren rose to his feet now, not caring if he was seen, but his father was concentrating too hard to notice. He squeezed the sword's hilt with both hands and studied the blade before closing his eyes. Whispering to the lake, he tossed the sword into the air, watching as it sailed through the gray sky and then plummeted toward the surface.

Ren expected a splash, but an icy hand shot from the water instead, catching the sword by the hilt and dragging it into the inky black.

Ren's father puffed his chest, then let out a long sigh. The hard lines of his face melted into what Ren assumed was despair.

Now, as he remembered the moment, Ren knew it was not despair, but relief.

Relief was the farthest thing from Ren's mind as he watched Camelot under siege, her walls violated by Arthur's army. Ashy smoke billowed from inside the market square, where Ren knew the villagers were under attack. More death. More blood. And Lancelot... the weight of his death was too heavy to bear.

Was it all a lie? The quest. The sword. Was this Arthur's plan the entire time?

Ren hyperventilated, holding his hand over his chest as he struggled to take in air.

"You need to hold still," Lina spoke softly into his ear. She held a needle and thread and tugged as she stitched up the wound on his shoulder. A sharp pain shot down his arm, and he winced. He had forgotten about his physical discomfort. His mind wouldn't allow one more thing to hurt him.

"Lancelot is gone. Like my father. Like all the others," Ren whispered through the pain.

One by one, all legends die.

Lina didn't respond. She'd also been depressingly silent since the retreat. Ren noticed her hand kept moving to the empty sheath at her hip.

A piece of ash landed on his cheek, and he wiped it away, imagining a charcoal streak staining his skin. Glancing around the trees, he found Merlin hovering over Galahad, shooing away healers and whispering incantations. The usual gleam was gone from his eyes, replaced by a panic that cast an unsettled energy around him.

Somewhere behind them, the pained wail of Guinevere shook the ground when they brought Lancelot's body back on a cart. Ren couldn't look. He'd already seen him out there, all color drained from his face, his eyes lifeless.

Next to Ren, Emeli propped her leg up on a log, her ankle wrapped tight with bandages as she sipped on an herbal tea the druids had made. Something for the pain, they said, but judging from her empty expression, it may have contained a sedative, as well. Ren almost wished he had accepted the cup now.

Anything to dim the swirl of emotions threatening to burst from his chest.

Arthur had betrayed them. Not only that, but he made a fool of Ren. It was Ren who had made the decision to go on the quest. He was the one who had pushed Lina to pull it from the stone. He was the one who had brought it back to Camelot and right into Arthur's hands.

"What do we do now?" Emeli asked, her round eyes pleading, searching for a glimmer of hope. Ren didn't have the answer, and he definitely didn't have hope.

Even Geret shook his head, dowsing his dark locks in water and taking in a deep breath.

A warm tingle raced over Ren's shoulder as he realized Lina was working her healing magic on him. Letting out a sigh, he fluttered his eyes shut for a moment.

"Are you alright?" Lina leaned in and he caught a whiff of the herbs she was using still fresh on her hands, and he inhaled the scent, letting it soothe his nerves.

"I'll live," he replied.

"That's not what you said five minutes ago when I had to use the last bit of Ragnor's liquor to clean your wound. You cried out like a baby," Emeli joked and Geret burst out laughing. After a moment, so did Lina. But Ren couldn't. Not now.

He grabbed hold of Lina's hand, pulling her over to his side. Emeli and Geret conveniently brought up the weather, which was even more ridiculous because it was nighttime, bright stars shimmering obliviously in the sky.

"Thank you for what you did back there," Ren said, wanting desperately to focus on something other than the horrible situation they were in. Lina was still here, still taking care of him, still by his side. That meant something.

But her eyes fell to the ground as her hand once again fiddled with the empty sheath at her side.

"It's my fault he has the sword now," she whispered. "I failed."

"No." He pulled her in close, taking her chin in his hand and lifting it so she had to look at him.

"It wasn't your fault. We didn't know he was immortal. Using the sword was the right thing to do. It just didn't work."

She shook her head, eyes welling with moisture.

"You saved me out there. He would have killed me, and it would be my body on that cart with Lancelot."

"That was King Arthur, wasn't it?" Lina asked, and Ren nodded, all the air rushing from his lungs.

"It was Arthur who killed him?" Guinevere's voice traveled over to the group. She stepped out of the trees, her eyes swollen and red, scrapes and bruises littering her porcelain skin.

"Yes. It was him leading the red knight army," Ren confirmed.

Guinevere's eyes went wide. "If this is true, that means someone has the sword."

Knots twisted in Ren's throat, threatening to strangle him. "About that..."

Guinevere's eyes turned sharp.

"We have it. Or we did, rather."

Guinevere's hand snapped to cover her mouth. "You don't realize what you've done."

Ren stood, rolling his newly healed shoulder back as a dull ache pounded under the skin of a long wound stretching from the top of his shoulder bone to the blade in his back. But the tenderness was nothing compared to the ache inside.

"I have a pretty good idea." His thoughts were on the cliffs above the ocean where Arthur's men had arrived, their ships still floating over the break beyond the thrashing waves.

A look of panic spread over Guinevere's face. "No." She shook her head. "There was a reason your father cast the sword into the lake. He couldn't let Arthur keep it. It was too dangerous."

Dangerous? Ren remembered something Arthur said on the field. "He said the sword tethered him to the afterlife. Is that what you mean?"

Guinevere shook her head. "Yes, but I don't think you fully understand. We had to get rid of the sword... and Arthur along with it."

Ren's pounding heart froze. "*We?*"

Guinevere's eyes traveled to where Ren expected Lancelot's body was wrapped in cloth, waiting to be burned. "We did what we had to do. To protect the kingdom."

The truth barreled through him. Shocked expressions flashed over Geret and Emeli's faces, as well. None of them expected this. "You mean... you all killed him?"

Guinevere bit her lip, pausing before responding, "We all did."

Ren didn't know what to say. His own father had told him about Arthur's death, but he'd kept this from the story. "My father, too?"

She nodded, confirming the grief eating him alive. "Mordred's sword delivered the final blow, but it was done at the knights' command. A deal had been stuck. Kill the king, take the throne."

"What?" Ren shook his head. All this time he'd thought Morin wanted the throne because he wanted power, but what if he was fulfilling the promise to his father all those years ago, a promise the knights had made to get rid of Arthur?

His stomach grew sour.

"That can't be true. My father told me the truth. Arthur was good. Mordred wasn't. They wouldn't do that."

Guinevere steadied him with her hands on his shoulders. "Those stories were only partially true. Mordred was corrupt, but so was Arthur. In the end, at least."

Ren's eyes lifted to hers, searching for anything to make this make sense.

"They had to do it. Arthur had gone mad. The sword he loved was also his undoing. He had to be stopped for the good of the kingdom."

Ren rubbed his temple with a knuckle to ease the pounding in his head. He couldn't believe what he was hearing.

"And my father? He knew? Before the end..."

Guinevere lowered her eyes. "They all were in on it. That's the real reason Lance and I..." She cupped her hand over her mouth, choking back a sob. "That's the real reason we had to flee Camelot."

The knights had conspired to kill their own king. Ren's heart sank to the pit of his stomach. This was not what he expected. Then he remembered something Gwen had said that night when Morin first attacked Camelot.

You don't know the truth, Ren. Nobody here is innocent.

At the time, he thought she was talking about her parents betraying the king, but now he wondered if she knew the truth. Morin must have told her about the deal with his father. Kill the king, take the throne.

The realization made Ren dizzy, and he swayed on his feet for a moment until Lina's voice cut through the haze.

"Arthur has the sword again. What will happen now?"

Guinevere steadied herself against a tree. "We don't know, but it can't be good. It's the source of his power, and if it brought him back from the dead, I imagine it will only make him stronger."

Ren had already witnessed Arthur's strength when he battled Lancelot, and it gave him shivers. He couldn't imagine how much harder it would be to defeat him now.

"We need to get the sword back. Otherwise, there is no hope," he said.

Hope felt so far away. They were outnumbered and now Arthur had the advantage of the protective walls. Word would spread of Arthur's return, gaining him allies because nobody knew the truth about him. They would think he either miraculously returned from the dead or that his death was a coverup all those years ago. Even if the knights told the truth, who would believe them? Arthur's rule was a golden age, and ever since his death, things had deteriorated.

The more Ren thought about it, the more frustration burned inside.

He let out a growl, kicking a discarded helm on the ground. Scanning the field, he spotted Morin's dark army, who had retreated to the far side of the forest. They piled their dead at the tree line and tended to their wounded. As did Camelot.

They'd spent too much energy fighting each other, leaving the perfect opportunity for Arthur to strike. It was too easy for him to take what he wanted while the rest of them bickered like children over the throne.

He gazed around at his friends drenched in sweat and covered in grime and blood. They were innocent.

Or at least they used to be. Before he ever wanted to be a knight, Ren's biggest problem was staying awake through lessons. How he longed for those sunny days spent with everyone joking and coming up with ways to trick Galahad into letting them finish early.

He longed for those days of lounging in the grass with Gwen. Kissing and dreaming about the days they would become adults and how they would rule the kingdom. They didn't know back then what it would really be like.

All this time, they had thought Morin was the prince of deception, but he seemed like a child compared to Arthur. A spoiled, entitled child who only wanted to play king.

Ren ground his teeth and paced around the space while the others settled into a defeated silence.

Morin came to collect on the promise Camelot had made to his father, but he hadn't earned it. Not really.

Ren's father did, though, and he had died for it by Morin's hand.

Ren wished Morin would turn into one of his crows and fly away.

Morin...

Ren froze in his tracks, eyes locked onto Morin's army again.

The idea stuck him, and it turned his blood cold.

Geret was on his feet, swinging his sword and stretching his muscles. Emeli's eyes were closed, her face upturned toward the starry sky where the moonlight bathed her in a pale glow. The effects of the tea had apparently taken hold, yet her bow sat tucked into her lap, ready to be used.

Even after the day they had, they were still ready to fight. Ren needed to be, too. He couldn't let them down.

The idea took shape, and he couldn't believe he was actually thinking it. After hearing the truth about what Arthur's knights had done, how they conspired with their enemy to stop him, this felt eerily like history repeating itself. But they were out of options.

Ren cleared his throat and Emeli cracked one eye open to peek at him. Several others also directed their attention toward him and his stomach turned with nerves. "I have an idea."

The hushed silence threatened to smother him, and it made his head spin. "It might sound mad."

Geret and Lina had gathered around, too, as did Guinevere. Even Merlin lifted his gaze from several yards away. It was the first time he'd taken his eyes off Galahad.

Lina lifted a brow. "So? Let's hear it."

Gulping, he squared his shoulders and lifted his head. "We can't defeat Arthur's army alone. They are too strong, and they now have the defense of the castle walls to their advantage."

Everyone frowned, acknowledging the shared truth.

"But that doesn't mean it's over," Ren continued. "We have the strength of two powerful armies to take it back."

"What are you saying, brother?" Emeli asked, both eyes open and attentive now.

Ren pointed across the field at Morin's camp, and murmurs raced through those who were listening.

"Seriously?" Emeli gasped.

Lina watched, brushing mud from her leathers.

He had the attention of more soldiers now, and several groups of druids approached. This idea was gaining power.

"I know who they are, and I know what they've cost us." Ren's eyes cast over the field stained with blood where bodies lay motionless, piled on carts. "We have to put all of that aside now. Things have changed, and there is a larger threat. King Arthur."

When he said his name, bile rose at the back of his throat.

"Arthur is the real enemy. We learned that today. His army is stronger than ours, but we can't let him win. He can't have Camelot." He wanted to mention the sword, but too many people were listening, and that part was best kept a secret for now. "He isn't worthy, but we are."

Ren looked at his friends, and the other soldiers gathered around, searching for support.

"Amren is right," A low voice sounded from the crowd as Ragnor stepped through, clasping him on the shoulder the way his father used to do. "We must put aside our hatred for this one fight. Otherwise, what was it all for?"

A few people nodded, and whispers echoed through the growing crowd.

Lina looked to Ragnor, who beamed down at her.

"All this is well, but who is going to convince Morin of this plan?" Merlin sauntered through the crowd with Galahad's blood still caked on his hands. His lip twitched. "He will not be easy to reason with."

The crowd nodded, whispering to themselves as Ren searched for the answer.

"It needs to be someone who could be escorted through their camp without being killed. Someone with a friend on the inside." Merlin's eyebrows rose, a light returning to his face.

To Ren's horror, all eyes fell on him.

⁌ ─ ─

As Ren prepared himself for the journey to Morin's camp,

Merlin hurried over with a frenzied look in his eye. "Ren, there is something I need to tell you."

Ren's stomach sank. "Is it bad? Because I'm not certain I can take any more bad news."

Merlin's lip twitched again but he didn't smile or make a joke, his face going eerily still.

Great. More bad news.

"Guinevere was right about the sword. It's tethered to Arthur."

Merlin waited for Ren to respond, but honestly, he was too tired for it, and he crossed his arms, letting out a sigh through his nostrils.

"But it's not the only thing."

Something twisted deep in Ren's gut as he waited for Merlin to continue.

"The same magic that forged Excalibur was used to create two more objects. Objects of Arthur's rule."

Merlin paused and the anxiety in Ren's stomach intensified, its claws outstretched and digging into his insides.

"Are you going to make me guess, Merlin, because we don't have time for this—"

"You do have time for this, young knight." He pressed his lips tight, eyes cast to the ground. "What matters the most is for you to know that the same magic used to forge Excalibur is tied to Camelot. In ways you cannot possibly imagine. And the consequences dire if we do not retrieve that sword."

Ren could only guess what Merlin was hinting at, but they were out of time here. "I understand. That's why I'm going to Morin's camp to somehow convince him to help us."

Merlin nodded, the depths of his eyes hiding other secrets, but ones Ren suspected he wasn't ready to reveal yet. "Anything else?"

It was worth a shot.

Merlin paused, twirling his pocket staff through his fingers anxiously. "I didn't want to tell you this before you go over there, but there is a reason why the sword doesn't answer to anyone else. A reason why Arthur was the one to pull it from the stone when nobody else could. Because the magic that runs through it is mixed with Pendragon blood. And with that blood, the sword's power is fully activated."

Ren's mouth went dry. "Okay... so..."

"There was a group of us, in the old days," Merlin said, "those who believed in Arthur's vision of Camelot. We wanted to ensure his crown would last, so he would go on to rule, in this life and the next. The once and future king. And as long as he rules, Camelot will be safe."

"But you just said we needed to get the sword back..." This didn't make sense and the vein in Ren's temple was starting to pulse.

"Pendragon blood, Ren." Merlin said.

Ren's brow twisted in confusion until a thought pierced his mind. Clear as the lake from where Arthur has risen. "Merlin. There are only two Pendragons, and we can't let either rule Camelot. Not today. Not tomorrow."

"I know. So, you see the problem here." A sad smile passed over Merlin's face.

Nodding, Ren swallowed the ache. Only Arthur and Morin had the power to activate the magic in Excalibur, the force that could protect Camelot into the future. And without it?

"Are you ready Ren?" Emeli's voice snapped Ren back to reality and he felt like he was going to be sick.

At least the drowsiness was gone from Emeli's eyes, and she was bright and alert now, despite the limp from her injured ankle.

Passing a knowing glance to Merlin, he turned to his sister. He couldn't fail her. There was so much more they had to consider, but for now, the plan to defend Camelot would depend upon getting Excalibur back from Arthur and somehow driving his army away. They could figure out the rest later. Pendragon blood or not, Arthur couldn't rule. And neither could Morin. They had to be another way.

But first? It all hinged on getting Morin to agree to the plan.

"Great," Ren whispered to himself, using the anxiety circulating in his blood to propel him forward, across the field, and right to the edge of Morin's camp where he hoped they wouldn't strike him down before he had a chance to save everyone.

THIRTY-THREE

GWEN

WHEN THE MESSENGER ARRIVED REQUESTING GWEN TO escort a representative from Camelot to speak with Morin, she wanted to refuse. When she arrived at the edge of camp and saw it was Ren, she wanted to run away. Far, far, away.

Her eyes were swollen and tender from grief, but it was guilt that draped itself around her like a shroud, heavier than ever. Having to face Ren only made it worse.

She approached, nodding to him to follow, and led them through camp.

As they passed dark knights, small groups growled and threw

obscenities at Ren. Gwen kept her hand gripped on the hilt of her sword, shooting each of them warning stares. She was with Morin, and he gave the command for them to pass through without incident. Ren wasn't to be harmed, and she dared anyone to make a move.

The long walk was agonizingly silent, and if Gwen didn't say something, she was going to explode. "Are you okay?" she asked, her eyes roaming over the crimson-stained tear in Ren's tunic

He looked at his shoulder and moved it around. "I am now. You?" His eyes examined her neck, where she knew a nasty bruise wrapped around both sides. Someone had tried to choke her on the battlefield, but she had put her sword through his side, and he flopped to the ground like a dead fish.

She moved her neck, hissing through her teeth. "I'm fine. You should see the other guy."

Ren didn't flash her a smile as he used to do, and she needed the warmth of his smile now more than ever. Seeing her father on the battlefield had given her a jolt of hope she didn't know she needed, but then Arthur had killed him. All of that hope had transformed into a storm in her chest. An endless horizon of darkened skies.

It's not like she'd had a relationship with Lancelot; he'd been gone from the kingdom her entire life. The only childhood memories she had of him came in short bursts between his quests or battles, but the other knights told stories of his bravery and his kindness. Especially those from her stepbrother because, unlike Gwen, Galahad was old enough to go out with the other knights on their missions. He was the one who'd had a relationship with their father. Not her.

Despite all of that, the grief of losing him before they'd had a chance to reconnect was sharp and biting. She couldn't even share that grief with her stepbrother because he was far away from her, seriously injured and possibly dead. She could hardly bear to think about it.

Chewing on her nails, she turned to Ren and asked in a shaky voice, "Galahad... is he...?"

Ren glanced at her. "He's alive."

She let out a heavy breath.

"But barely," he added, jaw flexed.

Nausea rolled in her stomach. She didn't want any of them to get hurt, but things had gotten so messed up and she didn't know how to make it better.

"Emeli and Geret?" she asked.

This time, the vein in Ren's neck pulsed. "What are you doing? Now suddenly you care about us?"

She dropped her bottom lip to speak, but the words weren't there. She couldn't say, "Yes, I still care about you" to the person she was escorting through an enemy camp. Not when there were dead bodies still out there on the field waiting to be burned.

"I can't imagine what you must think of me right now—"

"What I think?" Ren interrupted. They stopped walking and stood next to a fire smoking a charcoal cloud into the air. "I think you conspired with our enemy to siege the throne. I think you stood by and watched my father die. I think my best friend betrayed me in a way I didn't know she could." His voice shook. "I'm so angry with you, Gwen, and I don't know what to do about it."

Red surged through his cheeks and his fists clenched by his side. A glassy sheen swam in his eyes, and he struggled to control his breaths through his nostrils. She knew him, and he was doing everything he could to hold back his emotions. She knew what must be lurking behind the strong facade.

She was the cause of his pain, and she didn't have the right to be sad in front of him. Wiping the moisture from her cheek, she whispered, "I know. I am so sorry about your father. That wasn't supposed to happen. None of this was supposed to happen. I wanted change. I wanted the truth to get out, but not this way. I didn't realize what it all meant. I was foolish and naïve, and I am so sorry for betraying you. And Emeli and Geret. For all of it."

Her eyes cast to the ground where she stomped down an ember that had popped out of the fire.

Ren said nothing for what seemed like a lifetime before finally opening his lips.

"We need this plan to work, okay?" Ren said. "We have to put it all aside for now. The plan is the only thing that matters if we are going to stop Arthur."

"Plan?"

He nodded, searching the path ahead where Morin's large tent loomed. "We have a proposal for Morin, but I'm not certain he's going to like it."

Gwen was most certain he wouldn't if it was coming from Ren, but she wouldn't tell him that. "He wants the same thing we do, you know."

Ren's brows furrowed as he waited for her to elaborate.

"They told you, didn't they? About what the knights did to Arthur? What our parents did?"

"Yes." A pained expression passed over his face. Gwen wanted nothing more than to wrap her arms around him to provide the comfort she once had. Instead, his fingers fanned toward hers ever so slightly, but not close enough to grab hold of them. It wasn't enough, but it was all she could hope for at that moment.

"Morin knew all along. Not everyone is as good as we were told, and not everyone is as evil as they appear. Not even his father, Mordred, was wicked from the start, and neither is his son." She pleaded with Ren, hoping he would come to see it. Even though she didn't like going to battle against her friends and family, she still knew things could never go back to the way they were before she met Morin that day in the dungeons. Camelot couldn't go back either.

Ren didn't respond, and Gwen would have to be okay with that. If it took him a lifetime to forgive her, she would wait.

"Whatever you need, if I can help, I will," Gwen said, stepping forward.

She glanced back over her shoulder, and his face had softened just a little. "I'm sorry about your father, too. I know what he meant to you."

Tears welled in her eyes, and she nodded, focusing her gaze on the tent. "Come on. He's waiting."

A lifetime spent earning Ren's forgiveness started now.

THIRTY-FOUR

"I took you for a half-decent warrior, but never the court jester." Morin let out a high-pitched wail of laughter as his men echoed his amusement.

Ren stood in Morin's lush tent as warmth radiated from a popping fire in a hearth at the center and a smoky haze filled the space. Rich fabrics in plum and crimson adorned chairs and carpets while Morin sat next to the fire wearing nothing but a leather skirt barely covering his manly bits. Healers surrounded him, dressing his wounds and rubbing salve on a blooming, purple bruise along his rib cage.

Ren ground his teeth. "There is nothing funny about this."

Morin winced as a young girl wrapped a pale cloth dressing tightly around his arm. He swatted her away, and the girl bowed, ducking out of the tent along with the other healers and Morin's guards. That left Ren, Morin, and Gwen in awkward silence.

Morin wandered to a small table and poured dark liquid into a goblet.

Gwen sat down in the corner, observing them with pale blue eyes. She gave no indication of their previous conversation. Not a twitch of her lips, no brightening of her irises. It was as if it never happened, and she was a statue again. Morin's statue.

Only, her comments about Morin still lingered in Ren's head. She believed there was something good in him.

"Drink?" Morin shoved a silver goblet into Ren's face, and he tore his gaze away from Gwen.

"Oh, come on. If you've come all this way to grovel, the least you can do is enjoy yourself."

Ren really didn't see any good at all. In fact, the longer he stood in front of him with that sly grin across his face, the more resolved he became that Morin could never, not in this life or the next, rule Camelot. Ren would rather die first. Pendragon blood be damned.

He pushed away Morin's hand with such a force that it caused wine to splash over the side, which stained a beige fur rug. Morin eyed the spilt wine with a sad expression. "Tsk, tsk." Shrugging, he handed Ren's goblet to Gwen, who took a sip, the liquid staining her pale lips red.

Ren hated seeing Gwen like this. A deep ache bloomed in his chest. He longed for things to go back to the way they used to be when they were friends. Instead of this weird enemy thing they had going on.

He had to forget about her. "I haven't come to grovel." He shook his hands in frustration. "We don't have a choice. We lost. Both of us."

"Says you," Morin returned, crossing his legs and sipping from the goblet of wine.

"We lost," Ren said again, with emphasis this time so he could get it through the man's arrogant head. "Even you can't deny that. He tricked you, too, made your army do all the dirty work to distract our forces so he could sneak in. I don't see your pretty little ass sitting on the throne in Camelot right now, or is this all another one of your illusions?" He waved his hands around the tent.

"You think I have a pretty ass?"

This guy was infuriating.

The smallest twitch in Morin's lip made Ren think he felt the loss all the same. He was just trying to hide it.

"We must do something. Arthur has taken Camelot, and neither your army nor ours has the strength to take it back alone. You can't win if you aren't even in the game."

"That's what you think. We are just getting started. Taking Camelot from you would have been easy, but this only slightly complicates matters." Morin took a long sip from his goblet, gulping down its contents and letting out a satisfied "Ahhh."

He was still deflecting, and as much as Ren didn't want to use it, he did have one card left unplayed.

"He has Excalibur," he stated bluntly.

Morin's shoulders tensed and his eye twitched as he cast his gaze to the empty goblet. "What?"

Ren let out a sigh, his eyes searching Gwen's as she watched them.

"You heard me. And if we don't do something, he will grow stronger and use that power to overtake both our armies and this entire kingdom. He will be unstoppable," Ren said.

Painful silence followed as Morin stood from his chair slowly, letting out a long breath through his nose. Through clenched teeth, he said, "What do you propose?"

"We work together, join our forces, and storm the castle."

Morin shook his head. "If what you say is true, we don't stand a chance at winning. The castle is fortified with strong walls and Arthur's men will overpower us before we can penetrate her."

Ren ran a hand through his knotted hair. Then, an idea sparked behind his eyes. "What if we don't take it by force? What if we got inside in secret?"

Morin's eyebrows rose and he tilted his head. "I'm listening."

"We know all the hidden entrances. If we can get inside, we can open the gate and let the rest of our forces in. From there, we could overpower their army with our combined numbers." Ren paced the tent with a buzzing energy racing through him.

"Am I supposed to trust that you will simply let us in through the front door?"

As much as it hurt to admit—and it really, really hurt—they needed Morin's army if they had any chance at beating Arthur.

Ren clenched his teeth. "Yes."

Morin studied Ren's face for a moment, appearing deep in thought. "And after it's done? Who would sit on the throne?"

"Is that seriously all you care about?" Ren threw his hands up in the air. He couldn't believe Morin was still on this throne thing. Despite what Ren had learned. It wasn't happening.

"Yes," Morin admitted.

"We can't just hand over the kingdom if that is what you are asking. Right now, we have to get the sword back from Arthur and prevent him from taking everything. It's the only thing that matters."

Rising from his chair, Morin approached Gwen, brushing a piece of her hair against her cheek as she leaned into him. Her eyes shimmered gold before she pulled away with a smile. It turned Ren's stomach to watch. Morin was using his magic on her, and even worse, she was letting him.

"I won't give up, you know," Morin added. "Even if we defeat Arthur. Even if we win this battle. We aren't allies. I still want what I want, and this doesn't change that."

"I know." Ren's stomach seized. This battle was long from over. Morin's blood powering the magic of the sword was something they would have to deal with later. After Arthur was defeated.

Morin nodded, thrusting his hand toward Ren. "Then we have a deal. A temporary alliance to recover the sword and kill Arthur."

Ren bit his cheek. "*If* Arthur can be killed. Either way, we need the sword, and Arthur won't be the one sitting on the throne of Camelot when this is over."

A flash of amusement washed over Morin's face. "Right. Let's hear the plan."

As Ren ran through the plan with Morin, he snuck a glance at Gwen. The slightest upturn of her lips was enough to give him hope that this entire thing might actually work.

THIRTY-FIVE

STOMPING THROUGH THE DENSE FOREST IN THE DEAD of the night with no light was not fun. In a single-file line, Geret led the way because he knew the tunnels best from using them as kids to sneak out of lessons. Ren followed, then Guinevere, and a few dozen other Camelot guards. Emeli stayed behind because of her ankle, much to her protest.

Meanwhile, Morin's army would storm the front gate as a distraction while Lina, Ragnor, and Bearach's men waited in the forest until Arthur's men fled out of the open gate to meet them.

That was the gate Ren's group was supposed to open. If all went well, their numbers would give them a chance.

"Hold!" Geret exclaimed, holding his arm in the air to stop the train of footfalls.

"Shh!" Ren whispered.

Geret crouched to the ground, tugging at overgrown shrubs and tossing sticks every which way. "I thought it was here," he said, his voice growing more unsure by the second.

Squatting next to him, Ren searched for the markings they all knew as children. Geret wasn't the only one who had snuck out of lessons.

Without light, though, it was useless.

"Did we take a wrong turn or something?" Ren asked.

Geret grunted while crawling upon his hands and knees. "Found it!"

Ripping a thorny bush from a smooth stone, he cleared away the remaining foliage. He slid his hand along the edge of white sandstone carved from the Camelot cliffs ages ago. Engraved ruins decorated the stone, worn down by the years and barely visible, but they were still there under their fingertips.

Geret grinned, and Ren patted him on the shoulder as the others gathered around the stone, using their combined strength to lift it from the earth.

A musty rot wafted from the hollow entrance. Carved stairs descended downward into the black pit, and Ren's stomach took a turn. They hadn't used these tunnels in years, and he wasn't sure they still provided a clear path into the castle.

Ren's father used to lecture the counsel about leaving Camelot vulnerable to enemies. He guessed he never knew his own children used these tunnels to escape. Now, here they were doing the one thing he had warned against.

He would be amused, though. Ren was certain of that.

Very clever, my son.

An ache pounded in his chest. He missed his father more than ever. He hoped he would have been proud after everything. He still wanted to prove that he was worthy of the knighthood his father always believed him capable of.

One by one, they made their way down the steps until stopping on solid ground at the bottom. Geret lit a torch, and a dim glow moved across the damp walls of the tunnel, scattering bugs on the floor and illuminating moss crawling up from the cracks between stones.

"Onward," Geret announced with a big gulp.

THEIR STEPS WERE swift now with the light. Besides, they had no desire to stay in these tunnels any longer than they had to. The air grew thick with their body heat, and echoing booms crashed overhead. Morin must have started the siege upon the front gates. The shattering sound gave Ren hope. Morin had actually stayed true to his word. So far...

With the distraction, the group quickened its pace, knowing this was the moment they needed to surface unnoticed. They arrived at a split in the tunnels, and Geret gave pause, rubbing his chin and muttering nonsense to himself.

"It's this way." Guinevere stepped around him, pointing to the tunnel on the left.

Geret shot her a confused expression.

"You don't think you were the only ones who needed to sneak out of the castle, did you? Some of these tunnels have been around since I was brought here as a young girl."

Ren laughed to himself as he stepped past Geret, along Guinevere's path because he was still shaking his head to confirm she was right. But of course, she was, because they arrived shortly after at a narrow, wooden door.

Ren glanced back at the group, and they all listened for movement on the other side.

Silence filled the space.

Sounds of the siege still rumbled distantly, but there was nothing else.

Ren pressed an ear against the rotting wood to be certain but heard nothing, so he pushed it inward, letting light flood the tunnel.

The group filed into what resembled a storage room filled with excess pantry items and cleaning supplies. It smelled of mold and vinegar, turning Ren's stomach sour.

"This is the servant's quarters." Geret whispered to the group.

Ren peered through the door at the empty hallway ahead, sword at the ready. "They aren't here," he said.

"Maybe they fled, escaped when Arthur's army infiltrated the walls," Geret offered.

"Let's hope so," Ren returned, uncertainty swirling in his gut.

As the group moved through the quarters, the booming outside continued, followed by yells and something crashing into stone. If they did manage to succeed at defeating Arthur, would there even be anything left of Camelot? Ren shook the fears away. He needed to focus on finding the corrupt, immortal king and defeating him. Everything else could come after.

They entered a hall lined with bed chambers, and still nobody swarmed them. Ren was starting to doubt Arthur had made it inside the castle at all, but that didn't make sense, either. Whatever men stayed behind in the castle during battle would not be enough to defend against Arthur's army. So where was everyone?

A soft cough sounded from behind a closed door. Ren stopped his footfalls, listened, and leaned into the doorway. With sword at the ready, he plunged through the door and was greeted by a series of shrieks. A group of ladies had huddled together at the far end of the room with Ren's mother, sword in hand, guarding them.

Her eyes softened and she dropped the sword to the stone floor, rushing across the room in an instant and squeezed Ren into her chest.

"Mother!" he returned, his voice muffled in the layers of fabric of her dress.

"Sorry," she said, releasing him from her tight hold. "I can't believe it's really you." She took his chin in her hands, examining the lines of his face. "I don't recognize this man standing before me."

Ren's cheeks flushed, and he forgot about the others in the room because he was so relieved to see her again. She was alive, and there was a piece of Camelot still intact after everything.

Geret cleared his throat, and her face lit up again as she gave him the same tight squeeze. She'd always treated Geret as a son. War be damned, that would never change.

After releasing poor Geret, who had clapped his hand to his chest to get a breath, she scanned the room, as her eyes searched for another. "Where is Emeli?"

Ren patted her arm. "She's alright. Just injured. Nothing serious, though. She stayed behind in the care of some good people."

Worry lines etched his mother's face and she frowned. Ren knew how much she probably ached to see Emeli, too.

"Lady Bedivere." Guinevere gave a short bow, interrupting the moment of reflection. Ren's mother was not having it at all, ignoring all courtesies pulling her straight into an embrace as well.

"Queen Guinevere. What a surprise."

"Former Queen." Guinevere corrected.

"Once a Queen, always a Queen."

Ren's mother's eyes scanned the room again. "And Lance?"

A heaviness settled amongst the group, and Guinevere's eyes teared up as she shook her head.

Ren's mother didn't need the words to understand; it was obvious from the tone of the group what had happened. Ren didn't know if he could get through the explanation, already feeling his throat tighten at the mention of Lancelot.

"Then he is with my husband and their fallen brothers. It is good company to keep."

Ren stepped in and rubbed a consoling hand on his mother's

back. "I'm sorry, but we don't have much time. What happened to everyone?"

She broke away. "Most everyone fled when the walls were breached. Some got out, but I'm not certain about several others." Her eyes darkened, and she glanced at the group of handmaidens huddled in the corner who had been watching with wide eyes. "I stayed behind to make sure everyone escaped, but it was too late by then and we were forced to hide."

"What about Bors and Percival? Were they still defending the wall?"

"I don't know. I'm sorry, dear. Things have been chaotic."

"What about Arthur?"

"Arthur?" She raised her eyebrows.

"King Arthur was the one leading the army from the sea. He's the one who laid the final siege to the walls."

Ren's mother glanced at Guinevere as though sharing an unspoken secret.

"I was afraid this would happen. I'm assuming you retrieved it? The sword?" she asked Ren.

He dropped open his bottom lip to respond but didn't want to admit it. How could she even know that? With her eyes boring into him, he confirmed. "Yes, but now he has it."

"I can't believe Arthur actually did it. Your father had his suspicions, and it haunted him until the day he died. If this is true, then we are all in danger." She stood and clasped her hand on Ren's cheek. "My brave boy. I am so sorry. I wanted to protect you from this, but I should have known fate isn't something we could easily manipulate." Her eyes bore sorrowful shadows that made Ren emotional.

Something swimming in her eyes bothered him, though. He guessed it was guilt, but it wasn't her fault they pulled the sword and brought back Arthur.

"Mother?"

"It was me. I convinced the counsel to choose Gwen over you."

I thought it would keep you away from these burdens." She pulled him in, kissing his hair.

A manic laugh escaped his lips, and she pulled back with a bunched forehead.

The knighting ceremony was so long ago, he had forgotten it entirely. It all seemed so silly now. It didn't matter in the end. Knight or not, they still had to deal with the battle and with Arthur.

Gathering everyone in the room, they explained the tunnels, confirming they were clear to pass though. Ren's mother argued to stay with the group, and then she argued for Ren to go with them. Ultimately, she agreed to lead the others to safe passage away from the castle.

Ren blinked the emotion welling in his eyes watching her go but focused on the task at hand—finding Arthur, retrieving the sword, and winning back Camelot. If they couldn't do all of that, nobody would be safe, including his mother.

⟶╬⟶

MORE EMPTY HALLS and hushed sounds met them as they passed through the rest of this wing of the castle. When a handful of men charged them in the courtyard, it was only an annoyance. Surveying the yard, Ren had a sickening thought.

"The throne room." His throat was raw, and he wished he was sitting in the great hall with a refreshing glass of water instead of out here in the chilled air roaming around empty courtyards. Through the great hall, he would find the hallway leading to the throne room.

"Or the keep." Ren gulped down the sharp-edged rock at the back of his throat. That would be worse than the throne room.

Geret gave him a worried look. "If they made it to the keep, they could be up there for days. Weeks even. Especially if it had been stocked and supplied before the battle.

Ren nodded. The keep was designed as the last place of safety within the castle walls, and Arthur would need a safe place to recover after battle. But the sword would speed his recovery and perhaps even bring back his former power, if what Guinevere said was true.

He didn't want to entertain the idea of the keep just yet, so he decided on the throne room option first. "We have to hurry!"

They sped across the courtyard and into the great hall where they were met with yet another ghostly empty room.

Bloody rags and turned-over medicine bottles littered the space. Bitter herbs and sickness hovered in the air, churning the acid in Ren's stomach. He covered his mouth with his forearm while searching for any clues. Had Arthur even passed through here? His mind wandered over the tables as he imagined the chaos during the battle. This is where his mother would have tended to the wounded with her tinctures and herbs. By the look of all the blood puddled on the floor, there had been many casualties. Sickness rose in his throat, but he choked it back down.

Then, a pair of Arthur's knights rushed through the far door with swords in hand, and they clashed with their group. Fighting ensued, and Ren did his best to push through and arrive at the other end.

Geret shouted from the fray. "Go! We can hold them off here. Find Arthur!"

"I'm not leaving you!" he returned.

"We'll be fine," Guinevere chimed as she slashed down a man double her size with her sword.

"What she said," Geret added with a smile on his face. He seemed to be enjoying himself as he kicked one opponent in the gut and slammed into another with his shoulder.

Ren didn't have time to argue. "Get to the gate when you have a chance. Morin's reinforcements should be there, and the druids beyond. Stick to the plan!"

Geret nodded as Ren darted through the doors, his muscles tensing at the thought of finding Arthur in the next room.

Dark shadows draped the throne room in eerie patterns. Moonbeams burned through the stained-glass windows, but the torches that normally kept the room alight had burned out. He scanned the space, finding the throne at the far end empty, as well, as it always had been. He let out a breath and relief flooded his veins. He half-expected to find Arthur sitting on his old throne.

But he had hit another dead end. If Arthur wasn't here, where was he? A shadowy figure moved against the opposite doorway, and Ren sprung into fighting position.

Morin locked eyes with Ren, casually stepping inside the room. "I already checked the war room. Nothing but an old relic." He referred to the room behind the throne. The one unlocked by Merlin.

Ren's jaw clenched at the insult to the Round Table. Morin's eyes flicked to the shadow of the empty throne, licking his lips. Ren stepped forward with his sword held out in front of him. Morin did the same, sliding over the stone floor. Both swords aimed at one another as the two men slowly approached the center of the room until they were nearly touching.

"What are you doing here? I thought we agreed you would stay with your army outside the walls," Ren said.

"And miss all the fun? Come on, I thought you'd know me better than that by now."

They both inched forward again, eyes glued to one another's steps. All the while, Ren was on high alert searching for any sign of attack. He still didn't trust him.

Meeting in the middle, they both lowered their swords.

"He's in the keep, isn't he?" Morin had already guessed what Ren suspected. It was the only other place he would be without hiding in one of the living quarters. Ren didn't think Arthur was the hiding type.

"He has to be," Ren returned, an unsettled energy pulsing through him.

"That is not good." Morin said.

Ren rolled the tension from his shoulders. "Yeah, no kidding."

Morin pursed his lips. "We won't be able to get inside. They already raised the ladder. We are on his terms now. He won't come out until he's ready."

"You think I don't know that!" Ren groaned, eyes rolling.

"We could just wait." Morin raised his brows.

"Giving you time to regroup your own army so you can attack us again while he watches? I don't think so."

The clash of the fighting from the great hall grew distant, and Ren hoped that meant Geret and Guinevere had moved on to the gate.

While searching the room for answers, Ren studied the banners hanging from the rafters belonging to the knights. His eyes paused on the Bedivere's banner. A familiar ache twisted inside. Was it really Ren's house now? After learning everything, he wasn't sure he even wanted it anymore.

A fiery urge arose in his chest, making him want to rip those banners from the beams and burn them. Even though the thought took Ren by surprise, it still gave him something.

He met Morin's eyes. "I have an idea."

REN AND MORIN ran from the throne room with black smoke at their backs, coughing and sweating from the blaze. They were met with Geret and Guinevere and the other Camelot guards in the hallway.

"The gate is open but Arthur's army is still nowhere to be seen. Morin's men are standing by," Geret said.

Guinevere's eyes landed on the smoky haze behind Ren.

"The smoke should flush them out," Ren said. "Everything is connected. The great hall, the throne room, and the keep. Even with the doors barred shut, it can't keep smoke out. Not for long.

"Smart." Guinevere said, smiling.

"So, we just wait?" Geret huffed.

"Yes, but outside," Ren added, covering his mouth from the thickening smoke.

The flickering glow behind the stained-glass windows meant the fire was spreading. Ren observed the windows from the courtyard and prayed his plan would work.

"I must admit, Amren. Burning down your own castle is extreme, even for me," Morin added while leaning lazily against the stone wall.

"Why the heck is he here again?" Geret added, pointing at Morin.

Ren shrugged, eyes still locked on the smoky haze billowing from the windows ahead.

Time passed and the fire seemed to simmer inside the great hall, which was sending gray plumes into the keep. Yet there was still no sign of Arthur and the rest of his army.

"Something isn't right. Why haven't they shown themselves yet?" Ren asked, staring up at the keep. Light flickered inside from lit torches, but there should have been movement also. More than that, there should have been bodies fleeing the keep seeking fresh air.

Morin studied an abandoned helm, tracing a glowing light around the etched dragon shape on the side. "Unless they never were in the keep," Morin whispered to himself, but they all heard it.

Ren and Geret exchanged worried looks.

Outside the walls, the screaming and clashing of swords intensified. Scanning the gates, he couldn't tell if Morin's army was still outside, but he certainly didn't hear anything that indicated a large battle outside the gate. But there was smoke somewhere beyond the gate, perhaps in the forest. There was too much smoke.

The voices of the others faded as Ren's focus shifted from

inside the walls to outside of them. There was a battle raging out there, but not at the gate. It was happening in the forest.

Bile crawled up the back of his throat. "It was an ambush," Ren said, and everyone's eyes fell upon him. "Arthur never meant to stay inside Camelot. He got what he wanted—the sword—but he still needed to find a way to split us all up and cause chaos so he could escape. He drew us inside on purpose."

"And the others?" Geret asked, panic flashing in his eyes.

Ren looked to the forest again. "Lina is in there. And Emeli. With Ragnor's men."

"We fell right into his trap."

Ren nodded, anger burning his insides. It's like Arthur knew exactly what Ren would do because it's what his father would have done. And Arthur had known his father well.

His hands clenched into fists at his sides. He had to fix this.

"I'm going after him." Ren's legs moved toward the front gates, but his torso remained in place as Morin's hand gripped his shoulder.

"If you are going after the sword. I'm coming, too."

Ren slapped his hand away. "I'm not going after the sword. I'm going after Arthur and to find my sister and Lina. They are alone out there."

"Find Arthur, find the sword. I'm coming," Morin said more sternly now.

Ren exchanged exasperated looks with Geret, who shrugged. "He could be useful."

Raking his hands down his face, Ren let out a groan. "Fine but remember our deal. We work together to defeat Arthur."

Morin lifted his hands in surrender, and a swirl of glowing smoke rose from his fingertips.

Showoff.

"Geret, you go with the others to counter the rest of Arthur's army at the gate. We can't let them all get away. They will come back stronger next time. We have to stop this now."

Ren's eyes tore across the swirling smoke over the castle steeples and hoped someone would make sure the flames they set were put out. Otherwise, there wouldn't be a castle to come back to.

Then, they ran. Ren knew another way out, but they had to hurry before anyone noticed. He didn't know where the energy came from, but it burned like fire and fueling his steps until they were outside the walls, through the fields, and finally at the tree line.

Inside, the sounds of battle ripped the trees apart.

He just hoped he wasn't too late.

THIRTY-SIX

LINA PACED THE TREES, HER GAZE LOCKED ON THE smoke billowing from within the castle walls. Flashes of her vision played behind her eyes, and she had to steady herself against a tree. It was exactly the way it had happened in her dreams. Fire in Camelot. All this time, she'd been afraid of how she fit in with all of it, and now she wanted no part. Ren tried to convince her to go with them to retrieve the sword, but the truth was, she didn't want it. She had never wanted it.

She took a steadying breath to clear her head.

A loud bang sent a shudder through the ground. That would be Morin at the gates. His men were busy providing the distraction they promised. Somehow, Ren had somehow convinced Morin to ally with Camelot forces. He had a way with people and always knew the right thing to say. He had a gift for finding the hope buried inside, even with her.

Lina's gaze darted to the walls again. Still no fighting inside. Something was wrong. Ren should have caught up with Arthur by now, but the only sounds of fighting were coming from the front gate where Morin's men clashed with whomever was left. She couldn't tell if they were Camelot soldiers or Arthur's knights, but she was certain it wasn't the sound of an entire army. Something was missing. Or rather, someone.

"What are we to do? Stand here and hope your friends are successful?" Ragnor paced between the trees, swinging his axe at unsuspecting plants and slicing their tops clean off.

"Can't you have patience? They will come out. You'll see." Knots coiled tightly in Lina's stomach, though. The longer they waited, the more doubt seeded itself in her gut.

She secured her daggers at her hip, tightening her leather armor and striding out from beneath the trees to get a better look. But she never made it because a barrage of screams echoed behind her, followed by metal clanging and the sounds of fighting ripping through the trees. Armored men ran at her and nearly missed taking her head clean off with an outstretched blade. She tore a vial of powder from her satchel and launched it straight at them with an incantation.

The blast knocked her back as well, and she coughed through the haze as she pushed herself up from the ground. Her head spun. She had never used magic in battle. It was too sudden and took too much energy, but she had no choice this time.

As the haze cleared, Ragnor rounded up the druids, who attacked the red knights. This was Arthur's army, and if they were out here instead of inside the castle...

She darted into the trees. He had tricked them. Arthur

didn't want to hold the castle against two armies; he wanted to get the sword and flee with it. But he couldn't do that with so many men standing by. Now the only force stopping him were the druids because their armies were split between the commotion at the gate, those inside, and what small forces remained in the woods.

She couldn't let Arthur escape with the sword. She had to find him. Fast.

Lina ran through the woods, meeting with multiple groups fighting in the melee. The druids battled back the attack, and Lina did her best to jump in where she could. However, their numbers were few, and Arthur's knights swarmed the trees like fire ants.

She ran into Fin, who was dueling two against one. They were wearing him down, so Lina threw an explosive powder at Fin's opponents, who flew forward to their bellies, their faces buried by debris. It was the last of her magic. She fell to her knees as the trees swirled around her. Fin squatted by her side and lifted her to her feet.

She leaned into him for a moment until her legs stopped shaking, and she pressed away. "I'm fine. You need to go to the gates and warn Morin's army about Arthur. We need help."

Fin nodded and took off through the trees.

"It's not going to help." Arthur's voice traveled on the wind, sending chills over Lina's arms.

The resurrected king stepped out of the haze, Excalibur in-hand.

Lina ground her teeth and gripped both daggers tight in her palms, wishing she had saved some of her magic. She was going to need more than her will to stop him.

Arthur's eyes dropped to the sword's blade where a faint blue tinge pulsed from the steel. The energy called to Lina in a familiar hum.

"Miss it?" Arthur asked.

Her eyes locked onto the hollow depths of his. "Not even a little."

He pressed his lips together and dipped his head. "If you say so."

Lina couldn't stand another word, so she surged forward, leaping into the air with daggers pointed. When her blades came down, Arthur raised his sword, which connected directly with her weapons. The force knocked her back, sending her flying. She landed hard on the ground, and pain shot up her spine as she groaned and rolled over to her hands and knees. But Arthur was already next to her. His towering figure cast a shadow over her, and Excalibur glimmered in the moonlight.

The power of the sword made him ten times stronger than when they had last met. Her heart sank. If he had beaten her so easily then, what chance did she have now? Searching for support through the woods, she found none. Everyone was busy with their own fights. She was alone.

Arthur clicked his tongue. "Didn't you feel the power of the sword when you held it?"

Lina had felt that power. It called to her still, but there was no way she would admit it to him. She wouldn't give him the satisfaction.

Pushing herself from the ground, she raised her blades and squared her stance. Metallic saliva coated her tongue, and she spat, her blood marking the ground. "You are mad."

"Am I? Even still, I am right. When you held it, you could feel its pull, couldn't you? You know the way it can make your blood tingle." Arthur closed in, taunting her with the sword.

She wiped the blood from her lips and stepped backwards, but the back of her boots knocked against the trunk of a tree.

Arthur tilted his head, studying her. "You feel it still. It calls to you."

She shook her head, holding back the emotion.

"It's alright. It's not bad. It's in your blood, after all."

Lina opened her mouth to respond but the words wouldn't come as her mind raced with the possibilities.

Arthur's upper lip curled over his teeth. "I wasn't sure myself until I saw you wielding Excalibur, the melody of it in your hands, how it sang the same song as your heartbeat."

No. It's not true.

A cold smile crept over his mouth as he closed the distance between them.

"It still sings to you, doesn't it... daughter."

CHAPTER
THIRTY-SEVEN

Stars pierced the canopy overhead as Ren and Morin crept into the trees. The sounds of fighting swirled from every direction. Their plan had worked too well, it seemed, as everyone was engaged in the fight. Ren spotted a group of Ragnor's men battling with Arthur's fighters as Morin's dark knights surrounded them both. Whether they were helping was something Ren couldn't wait around to see as they moved through the forest swiftly, ducking behind bushes and dodging the fray.

When someone would get too close, Morin would blast them with his magic, which sent bodies flying from their path.

Maybe he was useful after all.

But none of this progress was getting them any closer to finding Lina. Or Arthur.

Ren halted Morin for a moment to listen to the muffled yells of battle, but none of them were voices he recognized.

"If you just let me, I can find—" Morin started.

"Shh. I can find them, just give me a moment to make sure I'm not skewered like a pig, please."

Morin rolled his eyes but did as Ren asked, scanning the surrounding fighting groups for anyone who dared to glance in their direction with ill intentions.

Ren closed his eyes, placing a hand to the earth like he'd seen Lina do when she was tracking. He had an inkling that if he could stop and listen, if he could call to the earth the way she did, it would help him find the path. At least he hoped it would.

Come on. Give me something.

He concentrated, creasing his brow and pressing his hand into the cool earth.

He silently felt the energy of the earth, the way Lina explained when she used her magic.

Magic belongs to the earth, not to any one person.

If that were true, maybe he could grab hold of it for a moment if he quieted everything else. It was a long shot, but searching the entire forest through the fighting would take them too long, and by then, Arthur would've already escaped.

"Please," he whispered, letting out a slow breath.

Above, Morin's gaze shifted to Ren in an expression of disbelief. He could have asked Morin to do this, but he would've rather died.

Then, his palm pickled slightly, and a pulsing blue light swelled under the earth. If the darkness hadn't been descending from above, it may have been too faint to see, but it was mirroring the twinkling of the stars like they were staring at a still body of water.

Ren blinked to be certain he wasn't imagining it.

"You are full of surprises, Amren Bedivere," Morin whispered.

Satisfied, Ren stood with his sword in hand. "It will lead us to Lina, and hopefully Arthur, too."

"How do you know they will be together?"

Ren paused. It was a gut feeling more than anything, but he knew he should trust his gut after everything he'd been through. If he'd had more confidence before, maybe Arthur wouldn't have the sword right now. None of this would have happened. "I just know."

Morin lifted a hand, gesturing for Ren to lead the way.

THE LIGHTED PATH stopped beyond an outcropping of aspen trees. Echoes of distant fighting still rang through the forest, but there was an eerie quiet settled here. Too quiet.

Until it wasn't.

Cries rang out, and Morin and Ren hurried into the clearing, meeting up with two people. Lina was on one side, both her daggers drawn and a fierce expression hardened on her face. On the other side was Arthur with Excalibur in hand. A blue glow radiated from the sword as he held it out, but the man himself looked different. Gone were the hollowed holes around his eyes. His face had grown plump where jagged bones had once been visible. Most noticeable of all, no wound poured blood from his side.

They were too late. The sword had already brought him back.

"Lies!" Lina hissed, not noticing the presence of Ren and Morin.

Arthur smirked, his eyes flashing to the new figures. "It's true. Amren can verify, can't you?"

Lina turned to them. Her eyes snapped right to Ren, and a fire erupted over his skin.

"I was just explaining to Adelina why she was able to pull this sword." Arthur held the blade out, studying its features. "But she does not believe me."

"It can't be true. Ren?" Lina's mouth dropped open, her eyes pleading.

Ren's jaw tightened as he remembered when Lina pulled the sword. It was a crushing moment of defeat for him. But for Lina...

Merlin's voice echoed inside.

There is a reason why Arthur was the one to pull it from the stone when nobody else could.

Pendragon blood.

His heart stilled as he stared at Lina. She was breathing heavily, and her eyes were painfully dark with a deep pain swimming behind them. And now Ren knew why.

"You are her father, aren't you?" Ren addressed Arthur, turning away from Lina with a hole in his chest.

Arthur broke into a smile and nodded.

"Welcome to the family," Morin grumbled, and Arthur's eyes landed on him for the first time with a flash of amusement.

Lina gave no response, instead directing her frustration at Ren. "You knew? How could you not say anything?"

Ren took a step toward her. "I didn't know. You have to believe me. Not until this moment." What he didn't want to tell her was what this meant. For Camelot. For her future.

Her eyes filled with moisture, even as her face hardened again, that projection of strength armoring her against the pain.

"Lina, listen," Ren responded. "It doesn't matter."

"It matters to me!" Lina's voice broke.

It shattered Ren. They'd never had a chance to talk about why Lina pulled the sword and what that meant. He'd been so blind to the truth that was right in front of him this entire time. Too distracted with his own emotions. Powered forward by the completion of the quest so they could defend Camelot. He should have seen it. He should have known.

Lina still stared at him with a broken expression. This must hurt more than he could imagine. She'd grown up without her parents. Even though she always projected strength, those wounds must have burrowed deep. He'd seen it with Gwen and Geret, too.

All Ren wanted to do was comfort her, but Arthur had crossed the clearing, demanding attention. Morin withdrew his sword with one hand and ignited a billowing fire in the other. Ren was forced to tear his gaze away from Lina to square his stance into defensive formation.

"As much as this reunion warms my dead heart, I have a kingdom to rule." Arthur charged forward with a powerful blow, meeting both Morin's and Ren's swords, knocking their weapons to the ground with an energized blow.

Lina leaped to the side, her eyes trained on Ren and Morin as they rose to their feet.

Morin sheathed his sword and retrieved another glowing stone. "Screw a fair fight."

Morin thrust both hands forward with an energy blast right at Arthur, but the blade of Excalibur shielded him, shattering the magic.

Red knights filtered into the clearing. Ren and Lina jumped into the fray, battling them back and trying to pierce their defense. Camelot soldiers joined, too, as did Morin's men, moving at his command. Fights broke out all over the clearing, but Ren's eyes tracked the glowing blue of Arthur's sword through the bodies. Occasionally, someone would get close to Arthur, attempting to strike him down, but every attempt failed as the assailant was beaten back or struck to the ground. Nobody could touch him.

Morin's magic smoked through the trees until a cloud of haze lingered in the air, making it difficult to see. That's when Ren called for Morin, who was dueling with Arthur amid flashes of light. Ren joined in, swinging his sword and clashing with the sword of power. He learned to brace himself for the blows by planting his boots into the ground and deflecting the strikes, but the force was wearing him down. He didn't know how long could keep this up.

Lina was in and out, doing her best to fight back any red knights swarming the area.

One of Morin's blasts deflected off Excalibur, shooting back at the sorcerer and hitting him square in the chest. Morin landed on his back and was left gasping for air. Ren attacked next, taking advantage of Arthur's momentary distraction by jabbing his blade into the king's side.

Arthur screamed as he turned his own sword back at Ren, but Ren ducked out of the way as an audible crack sliced through the air. He didn't know where the armored red knight had come from until he had crashed into Ren's bad shoulder. The blow knocked him to the ground, the impact creating a pop, followed by a sharp pain shooting from his shoulder. Lina stood next to him and pushed the knight back.

Ren knew immediately his shoulder was dislocated, and a heavy sense of defeat crashed over him—heavier, even, than the pain itself. Lina shuffled into the fight, dancing around Arthur and avoiding his attacks until Arthur found the right moment to land a blow to Lina's daggers. The force sent her backwards, and she crashed to her bottom.

Ren stood, groaning in pain and bracing against the throbbing in his shoulder. All he could do was watch Arthur turn to Morin, smiling, as a chill creeping into the clearing. They battled back and forth for a while. Ren did his best to beat back any red knights who had jumped into the fray, but with only one good arm, exhaustion was setting in.

A sharp scream rang out as Arthur's blade sliced right through Morin's left bicep, and the smoking stone he'd been holding dropped to the ground. Morin fell to his knees.

"Like father, like son. Say hello to him for me, will you." Arthur sneered as he raised his sword above Morin's head to take a killing strike.

Panic flooded Ren's chest, and he locked eyes with Lina in a desperate plea.

We must keep fighting.

She understood, and she rose from the ground, grunting with effort.

Ren dug deep, searching for the strength he had carried with him on the quest for the sword. He tried tapping into the motivation that had driven each step along the journey. All those years of long days training and watching his father leave on missions with the other knights. This couldn't end right here. Not like this.

He gritted his teeth, gripped his sword tight, and adjusted his bad shoulder to lock it into place. He would have to avoid using it for a bit longer but would manage. He had to.

Meanwhile, Arthur was too enthralled with taunting Morin to notice the arrow whizzing through the trees until it struck him right in his sword arm. Letting out an agonized scream, he dropped Excalibur to the ground.

Ren stole a glance behind him, catching Emeli leaning against a tree a few yards away. She lowered her bow with a wince, hobbling over her pained ankle. Ren let out a sigh of relief at the sight of her, but a loud boom sounded, and he turned as Morin hit Arthur's unmanned sword with a blast of magic.

The stones in Morin's hands smoldered as he dropped them to the earth.

Excalibur flew away from Arthur's scrambling reach and tumbled over the ground before landing right at Ren's feet. He froze and stared dumbly at the sword. Bending down, he gripped the hilt, and a hot surge of energy pounded through him. The pain in his shoulder numbed, and his body filled with intoxicating strength.

Arthur was already coming at him using someone's discarded sword. Lina jumped in front of Ren, forcing him back with her blades. It was enough to give her a chance to join Ren's side.

Dark shadows bloomed in the king's eyes, the plumpness from his face melting away into hollow caverns. He moved forward, stumbling over his feet. The strength of the sword was already leaving him.

"You are a disgrace to Camelot and this sword." The anger

burned in Ren so fiercely his body shook as he held the sword upright.

Arthur's pointed teeth flashed in the starlight. "I built Camelot, boy. She is mine forever, as is that sword." He lunged forward with a growl, but another arrow sliced through the air, landing at Arthur's feet, forcing him to jump back.

That's when Lina jumped in, the point of her dagger slicing through Arthur's thigh. Blood dribbled down his leg. Then, more spilled on to the ground, but not from his leg. The gaping hole at his side was back, growing the dark crimson stain on his tunic.

Arthur circled them both, and they all clashed—Ren wielding the power of Excalibur with every blow. But with only one good arm, his movements were slow, and Arthur was not, anticipating his every move. Lina was there too, weaving in and out to distract Arthur, but it only went so far because the red knights were back to defend their dead king.

Arrows whizzed through the clearing, some meeting their mark while others just missing. It gave Lina a chance to leap over to Arthur, where she kicked her boot behind his knee and sent him crumpling to the ground.

As Lina caught her breath, Arthur stood far quicker than he should have been able to do, ready to fight again.

Ren and Lina gasped for air, both sticky with sweat and desperate for time to recover, but Arthur still had energy. Even without the sword, the power of it still fueled him, and he seemed able to meet every move with strength. More red knights swarmed the clearing as Arthur stalked around them like prey.

An arrow cut through the treetops far above any of their heads, causing Ren to direct his gaze back to Emeli. She wasn't alone. Multiple men were barreling down upon her, too, and while she fought back, her movement was impeded by her injury.

Ice ran through Ren's veins as he caught Lina's eyes. He had to help his sister. He couldn't watch her be overcome by red knights.

"Go!" Lina yelled, as she ducked an incoming blow and

slammed her dagger into the neck of the knight before her. "Help her!" she urged, sending a boot to another knight's side, forcing him to the ground.

Ren turned on his heels and prepared to sprint toward Emeli, but another arrow cut through the air, landing in the back of a man battling with Lina. Emeli was on her feet again, bow in hand, drawing her next arrow. Next to her, Geret was battling back anyone who got too close to her position.

Ren locked eyes with Emeli from afar.

I'm okay. She let him know with their twin intuition.

"Thanks, Geret," Ren whispered under his breath, wasting no time jumping back into the fight alongside Lina. Ren jabbed his sword through the last man standing between them and Arthur.

Ren snuck a glance behind him again where Emeli had nocked an arrow. If he could distract Arthur for a moment longer, maybe she could strike his heart.

"What will happen once you take the throne? What will be the cost of your unnatural rule?" Ren asked Arthur, hoping he was in a talking mood.

Arthur spat. "These lands? None of them matter. You clearly haven't learned how the world can betray you." His eyes flashed to Lina. "How those you trust most can betray you. But you will, and when that day comes, you will understand there is only one thing in this world worth protecting."

"Camelot means nothing without the rest of the world," Ren replied, side-stepping around Arthur to drag his gaze away from the rest of the fighting.

"What do I care of the world?" Arthur laughed.

Then, the arrow Ren had been waiting for whizzed by his ear, landing right in Arthur's chest, directly into his heart.

Ren let out a breath and relaxed his sword arm, but to his horror, Arthur merely snapped the shaft in two, leaving the point inside his flesh and continuing like a sharp arrow hadn't just pierced his heart. Something that would have killed anyone else.

But Arthur wasn't just anyone else. He was already dead. And he couldn't be killed. Not like this.

Arthur's voice stormed through the clearing. "I would stand on a fiery river and watch the world burn to have Camelot again." His voice was a low snarl belonging to something not of his world, and it made the hair on the back of Ren's neck stand on end.

Ren and Lina exchanged disheartened looks.

Bright blood trickled down Lina's temple from a fresh wound, and her breaths came in ragged gasps. The ache in Ren's shoulder pounded more painfully than ever, even with the sword numbing the worst of it. They were both worn down.

Still, Ren couldn't give up. However shattered or beaten he was, he owed Camelot the breath in his lungs, the strength in his body.

He looked at Lina again, and he sensed she felt the same.

They were ready to give it all, even their lives, if it meant stopping the dead king from taking control of Camelot.

"Camelot can't stand alone," Ren said, and out of the corner of his eye, a shadow crept behind Arthur. Morin had risen from the ground, one hand pressed against the oozing wound on his arm. He appeared paler than ever as he wielded a fireball in one hand. One last trick.

A spark of hope flickered in Ren's chest.

Keep him talking, Ren.

"What are you going to do, little knight? Kill me? I've already risen." Arthur snarled, and a raging fury burned in the depths of his empty eyes.

Ren smiled. "No, I'm not."

Morin launched the fireball directly at Arthur's back and a boom sounded. The force tossed Arthur's body like a rag doll, but it also sent Ren and Lina flying backwards.

Smoke bloomed in the clearing as Ren pushed himself from the ground, shaking his head to make sure he still had all his senses. Searching for Lina, he found her groaning an arm's length away as she scrambled to sit upright.

He spotted Arthur several yards away, rolling from his back and choking on black smoke. Most of the skin had peeled off his face, leaving a haunting, skeletal figure, but he was still alive.

Despair turned to a throbbing headache behind Ren's eyes. They had tried everything—magic, an arrow to the heart, every drop of their own blood and sweat.

Ren turned his back from the king, approaching Lina while she propped herself up from the ground onto her elbows.

His eyes dropped to the sword in his hand.

No. Not every drop of blood...

Ren squatted next to Lina, and for a moment, everything else blurred. Reaching for her cheek, he pressed the palm of his hand against her skin, warmth burning between them. Lina had something he didn't, and he knew exactly what they needed to do. "If his story is true, then you and Arthur have the same blood. The same magic. And that power also runs through the sword."

He pressed the hilt of Excalibur into her right hand, wrapping her fingers around the leather. "You have to wield this. It chose you for a reason."

She shook her head in protest, but that only made him tighten his hand around hers.

"You can do it. You just need to let in the power like you do with your magic."

Lina's lips quivered. "I'm scared. What if I end up like him?"

Ren leaned in so close that their foreheads pressed together. "I'm scared, too, but I promise I won't let that happen. Arthur pushed away everyone he cared about, but you won't do that. You aren't alone."

Lina's eyes swam with moisture, but she squeezed them tight for a moment and nodded. Ren let go of her hand and winced against the pain shooting through his shoulder again. At the same time, he felt as if an enormous weight had been lifted. It felt like letting go of the pressures he'd carried since he was a boy, all the expectations from his father about joining the knighthood. For the first time he could ever remember, he let it all go.

Lina stood, gripping both her hands around the hilt of the sword with a determined look.

This was what mattered now.

Ren bent to the ground, finding his own discarded sword and twirling it in one hand as its familiar weight molded back into him.

Together, they surged forth in attack.

Arthur blocked their blows at first, but Ren and Lina brought more, moving in unrelenting, coordinated steps. Ren led, charging with his sword, and Lina followed, matching his footwork. They danced like this for some time, finding small ways to trip up Arthur as his defenses grew clumsy. Ren jabbed his sword into the king's arm, and Lina swung Excalibur overhead, bringing it down, only to have Arthur twirl out of the way at the last minute.

A hard grimace befell Arthur's face. The open wound at his side had stained his entire tunic a dark color. He was once again a walking corpse.

Lina stopped for a moment to adjust her grip on the sword.

"You can do this," Ren mouthed.

She nodded, sucking in a deep breath as the blade pulsed a blue light, tendrils of energy wrapping around her arm. When she faced Arthur, a trail of glowing energy spidered through the earth, meeting with her feet. She let it in, just like Ren said she could, and everything melted into one, coming to a point at the tip of the blade.

They lunged forward again. This time, Arthur couldn't fight them back, and Ren plunged his sword deep into the king's chest, capturing his attention long enough for Lina to leap toward him. With the glowing sword, she ran it straight through the fatal wound at his side.

Arthur let out a shuttered breath as they both yanked their swords from his body. Arthur fell to his knees, coughing up dark liquid and vomiting it to the ground. Smoke swirled over his already charred face, and he grimaced. Because of the pain or the agony of defeat, Arthur finally appeared as someone who had lost.

"This isn't over." He mouthed before smoke whooshed up over his entire body, sending whatever was left of him scattered into the air like ash.

Ren and Lina stared down at the space where Arthur had been, but there was nothing left of the dead king save a puddle of dark blood staining the earth.

Relief washed over Ren as he turned to Lina. Her eyes met his, and they pulled him in like they had done this entire time. He couldn't fight it anymore, and he rushed to meet her. They crashed into one another, pressing their lips together as everything melted away—the battle, the pain, all the secrets unearthed. None of it mattered because they were entangled, Lina and him, in a web of destiny, woven together in silky longing. And it felt right.

"Insufferable." Morin's voice broke them from the spell, and they turned to find him leaning against a nearby tree with an exhausted expression. Saying nothing more, he stumbled off through the woods. Ren let Morin retreat knowing there was still more to be done with him another day, but that didn't matter right now. Right now, he was too tired, and Lina still had his hand in hers.

Bursting into laughter, they fell to their knees in exhaustion.

They survived. Together.

THIRTY-EIGHT

GWEN

IT WAS OVER. GWEN HAD HELD HER POSITION AT THE gates of Camelot as instructed, leading a band of Morin's dark knights, alongside Camelot soldiers, against Arthur's red army. The plan worked. Splitting Arthur's forces between the castle walls and the forest actually worked.

The fighting dwindled as the sun rose and light beams pierced the hazy air. Smoke still billowed from within the stone walls, the fields outside trampled, and blood soaked into the ground like heavy rain. But Arthur's army retreated to their ships, leaving Camelot's shores. Hopefully, for good.

Gwen's muscles burned, the bruises and wounds leaving her skin on fire, but she stood on her own, heaving in breaths, and wiped her brow with her forearm.

Even though the fighting was over, an unsettled energy rolled around her stomach. She'd imagined what would happen if Morin succeeded, but she never thought about failure. And definitely not like *this*.

She scanned the trees as groups of fighters emerged, battered and beaten, and they counted their numbers. But there was no sign of Ren and the others. She assumed they had defeated Arthur and retrieved the sword. Otherwise, his army would not have retreated, but their absence made her nervous. And Morin... her feelings about him were complicated. She couldn't quite identify what stirred inside at the thought.

"I'm not dead if that's what you're wondering." Morin's voice sounded behind her and she whirled on her heels, meeting his gaze.

His face was a ghostly white shade. Paler than normal.

"Are you okay?" Her eyes searched his figure, landing on the streaks of blood dried down one arm, and the ripped fabric of his tunic over his bicep. Her stomach turned.

"What? Don't I look it?" He swayed on his feet and stumbled forward as Gwen rushed to his side, catching him in her arms.

"You've lost a lot of blood. What happened?"

"Good old grandfather, Arthur." Morin's eyes darkened, and he pushed himself from her grasp, steadying himself on his feet again.

Gwen's eyes went wide, and she swallowed the knot at the back of her throat. "What do you mean? Did he... did he win? What about Ren..." Her words trailed off; mouth gone dry. If anything happened to anyone else, she didn't think she could take it.

Morin dug through the pouch at his hip until slipping a flat, smooth stone through his fingers and pressed it against the congealed blood around the wound at his arm. Blood still seeped from the wound, and he hissed when the stone pressed into it.

Gwen leaned over to help, but he waved her away, whispering under his breath as the stone glowed and smoked vapor. He winced again and then spoke through his clenched teeth. "They are fine. All of them." His dark eyes met hers again and there was truth there.

Relief washed over her, and she could breathe again.

"More than fine, I'd say, actually." Morin's lips twisted into a smirk as he stood up straight, dropping the magical stone to the earth. He sealed the wound, but it looked deep enough that Gwen was certain it would take more to heal.

"What do you mean?"

But he didn't answer, leaving his last statement to linger annoyingly in Gwen's head. Like always.

She lifted her chin. "Well, now that you are feeling better, you can tell me what happened."

"Ren has the sword. Well, Adelina has the sword... but details." He waved his hand in the air casually. "And Arthur is banished. For now."

Gwen quirked her brow, an uncomfortable ache twisting in the pit of her stomach. "What do you mean for now?"

Morin's jaw clenched, and he clicked his tongue. "Let's just say I don't think Arthur is done with Camelot yet."

Her gaze scanned the wall of the city with the steeples of the castle beyond bathed in the morning sun, making the stones shimmer like jewels. She always thought Camelot was most beautiful at dawn. And there it was—the ache burning alongside the guilt. Two sides to the same coin. She wasn't done with Camelot either.

Clearing her throat, she leaned in close to Morin, whispering, "what are you going to do?"

"Me? Don't you mean what are *we* going to do?"

Her eyes burned hot, and she sealed her lips, grinding the back of her teeth together. She didn't realize she already knew her plans. She dared to think it when she spoke to Ren last, but facing it now was entirely different. Everyone had been so brave to do what needed to be done. Even Morin, agreeing to go with Ren and the others. She knew how much that pained him, and no doubt she would never hear the end of it, but she had more left to do, too. It just didn't look like what she thought it would.

Morin studied her face through the depths of his dark eyes and then lifted his hand, brushing her cheek with the back of his fingers. "Gwen."

Shock rippled over her skin. Morin had never said her shortened name like that. Never. And the way the echo of his touch lingered on the edge of her jaw...

But the feeling was fleeting because the sound of galloping hooves quickly rose behind them as a band of Camelot guards raced over, shields up and weapons drawn.

Morin immediately took off running for the forest, tugging on Gwen's hand to follow, but she shook her head, planting her boots into the earth. She couldn't go with him. Not this time.

His eyes darted frantically from her to the guards as he bounded into the forest, crouching behind a tree and shrinking into the shadows.

The guards approached with the tips of their blades pointed in Gwen's direction and she dropped her sword to the ground, raising her hands.

Morin rose, retrieving his own blade but Gwen sealed her lips together, locking eyes with his from the distance, a silent warning on her lips. What she couldn't say aloud to him.

Don't

Morin's jaw tensed but he released the hilt of his sword as the Camelot guards dismounted their horses, closing in around Gwen.

"Gwendolyn Marie Lancelot, you are under arrest for treason against the kingdom." A tall guard approached, yanking her arms behind her back where he secured ice-cold shackles around her wrists. Even though she hissed through the pain, she didn't fight against him. She chose this. She deserved this. It was time she owned her decisions.

As the guards led her away from the forest towards the walls of Camelot, she stole a glance over her shoulder, hoping to see him, but Morin had disappeared. Turned into a crow or something and flew away. Far, far away from Camelot. From the ache of defeat. From Gwen.

A STEADY DRIP echoed over stone. The air was thick with humidity, and a moldy stench had permanently embedded in Gwen's nostrils. And why was it so cold? Even while the sun blazed outside, a beam of light burning through the small window overhead, shivers rippled over her skin as she rubbed her hands down her arms.

In the next cell, a man coughed and coughed, gagging on the stale air until he threw up bile in the corner. Gwen shielded her nose in the crook of her arm, trying hard not to think about the nausea rolling around in the pit of her stomach.

She tried to think of something else. A wild rose bush snaked around the trunk of a tree. Clusters of perfumed petals fluttering in the fresh breeze. The touch of Morin's fingers wrapped around her wrist. The depths of his dark eyes pleading with her to run.

But she hadn't run. That's why she was here, in the place where they first met. It was comical, really. The moment that changed everything would end up being her doom.

She wondered if Morin had made it back to Castle Orkney. Wondered if the wound on his arm had healed properly. How stubborn he'd been on the journey back. He would have viewed it all as a defeat, even though it wasn't his army that failed. Nor Camelot's. Arthur was back. And nobody was prepared for that.

Something thudded down the hall, like a body hitting the ground, followed by hurried footsteps.

Gwen squinted into the dimly lit hallway as a figure appeared. Voices filled the floor as the figure passed by every cell, to cackles and pleading. Then, the shadow of a man stopped in front of the bars of her cell. Gwen held her breath.

Stepping next to the bars, he waved a torch in front of his face, and Gwen let out a sigh.

Ren.

"Gwen," he greeted her, leaning his face as close to the bars as possible.

She hesitated, stepping away. Disappointment settled in her chest. For a moment, she thought it might have been Morin.

A manic laugh bubbled from her lips. What had she thought? That Morin was coming to free her the same way she had him? After all that time, had she really considered that he changed? He let her turn herself in, probably watched as they chained her, before fleeing. She'd been agonizing over it for days. Weeks. How long had she been down here? She'd lost count.

"Gwen?" Ren's voice shattered her thoughts, and he cleared his throat, gripping the bars between them.

The softness in the outer corner of his hazel eyes sent a flutter through her chest. Those familiar eyes she knew so well. It was a small comfort.

"Hi," she said, inching towards the bars and grasping at his fingers as they reached for hers.

She needed to forget about Morin and focus on what was in front of her. And here now was her oldest friend.

"How are you?" Ren asked, his voice cracking.

She straightened her neck. "Fine. They could be better at cleaning down here though. I'll have to speak with someone about that when I get out."

The blood in her veins turned cold. *When she got out.* What she should have said was, *if* she got out. They hadn't even set a trial for the prisoners yet and she didn't have any idea what hers would look like.

Ren cracked a sheepish smile before his eyes averted her gaze. It was probably hard for him to be here with her.

"So..." Gwen started, before wetting her lips and sliding down to sit on her ground. It was cold, and dampness seeped through her trousers.

Ren joined her, leaning his head against the bars so a fluff of his hair poked through, and she tugged on it. "Your hair is getting long."

He ran a hand through it before leaning back over and she met the side of his head with hers, the bars between them.

"You should have your mother cut it for you before training starts again. You know how sweaty you get out there." She let out an awkward giggle. This was hard for her too. She didn't know what to say or how to talk to him. Their conversation at Morin's camp was forced. Necessary. But this? This was just depressing.

Ren turned to look at her. "I saw your mother in town today."

"Oh?"

"She looked like her old self, helping, speaking with everyone who approached her. She was a good queen."

Gwen didn't know her mother as the queen. She was too small then to understand. But she ached to see her now. "That's good. I'm sure everyone needs a little light after everything..."

A twisty, thorned thing wrapped around Gwen's heart. She was the reason they needed light. Needed her mother to return to offer a helping hand. And Morin... her heart raged in her chest and her breaths came in long gasps like she couldn't get enough air. There wasn't enough air down here.

"Hey?" Ren's hand reached through the bars, grabbing hold of hers. "It's alright."

Was it alright? She could feel the hot tears well in the corners of her eyes and she took a long inhale, sniffing back the emotion.

She turned to meet his gaze. "It's not alright, though, is it?"

She needed him to be honest with her. She knew she would have to face the consequences of her actions, and she was ready for that, but this waiting down in the dungeon was not making it easy to meet her fate with grace.

"You are here aren't you?" Ren said. "You helped us when we needed you the most. That means something, okay? They will see it. Give them time."

Gwen nodded. "Fine." She gazed through the bars, snagging some of Ren's hair again and twisting it between her fingers. "You really need to cut this hair."

"Yeah, yeah." He shook her fingers loose, offering a smile. A genuine one. Not an awkward one because he felt sorry for her. She knew him better than that.

If Ren of all people could find a way to visit her despite everything, giving her the smallest bit of hope, maybe she would have a chance with the rest. A chance to make amends. A chance to return to the Camelot she knew.

The Camelot she knew she could love again.

CHAPTER

THIRTY-NINE

LINA

WHILE CAMELOT REBUILT, LINA TRAVELED THROUGH the woods to meet up with the druids. She took her time traveling from the golden fields into the shady cover of giant oaks and deep into the pine forest where the setting sun cast hazy shadows through the bright leaves. Her fingertips brushed the rough texture of tree trunks and thorned, flowering bushes. Taking in the rich, heady scent of wet earth, she stopped to appreciate every step over the moss-covered ground.

She was silently saying goodbye—goodbye to the woods, goodbye to the life she knew, goodbye to the person she had been before meeting Ren and the others. Before the sword gently pulsed at her hip like another appendage. Before, her future was so uncertain. She felt like a storm building momentum—wind howling inside, clouds darkening and casting everything in shadow. It was a bit dramatic, she would admit, but still true.

Seeking shelter from her thoughts, she approached the druid camp, but her stomach plummeted when she arrived. Tents had been packed away, supplies were piled on carts, and half the people she'd fought side-by-side with had already moved on.

They were leaving. She knew they would, but she didn't expect it to be so soon. A downpour of emotions crashed over her until her legs trembled and her stomach turned.

Spotting Ragnor sitting next to the crackling fire, she took a silent seat next to him, unsure what to say. They sat like that for a while, neither breaching the comfortable quiet. Eventually, Lina reached into the pouch at her hip, returning with a small vial and emptying the contents into the fire pit. The flames popped, then turned a rainbow of colors. It was silly magic, something she learned from an elder when she was young, but she still found it soothing.

Watching the dancing flames turn a shade of indigo, she finally spoke. "So that's it? You're still leaving like you planned?"

Ragnor didn't answer at first, stroking the fine strands of silver hair in his beard before turning to her. "It's what we do, Adelina. We've stayed here too long as it is. You know if we don't go now, winter will come fast, and we will lose our opportunity."

Lina pressed her fingers into her collarbone, scratching at the itch that never went away after the Brecheliant Woods. Something clawed at her under the skin, something she couldn't quite reach. "But so much has changed since you made those plans. You have an ally in Camelot now, and they won't forget who came to their aid."

He scrunched his forehead, returning his gaze to the fire. "You do not know that with certainty. We once had an ally with Arthur's Camelot, but his protections died with him, and we do not yet know how this new Camelot will be shaped. What we know for certain is we must protect our people, and to do that, we must go somewhere new."

"Merlin walks about freely with magic. Doesn't that mean things are already changing?"

"Not enough. Not yet."

Discomfort edged Lina's chest, and she twisted loose strands of hair over her shoulder. "Then I will go with you."

He raised his hand, eyes landing sharply on hers. "No. Your place is here now. In Camelot."

She'd been afraid he would say that. For days, she had put off leaving the house where she had stayed within the village, dreading having this very conversation with Ragnor. Her hand went to Excalibur at her hip instinctively like it always did when she felt lonely or afraid these days. The gentle beat of power flowed through the hilt, penetrating her palm. She took a deep breath.

She still didn't know how she felt about the sword or the power that thrummed through her so strongly. Whatever she summoned in the woods against Arthur, it felt good in the moment but left her with a hollowness inside. Unlike using her other magic, drawing from Excalibur cost her more than just energy. It wasn't borrowing from the earth; it was stealing from something else. Some*where* else. And she hadn't figured out where that was yet. A shiver ran through her, and she leaned over the fire, warming her hands and hoping the heat would banish the trace of magic left lingering on her skin.

"What if I don't want to stay in Camelot?" she asked.

Ragnor grunted. "You are chosen, and you can't waste the opportunity. If they want you to use that sword to sit on the throne, think of how you can reshape the kingdom. Perhaps someday soon the druids will be safe to stay in one place again. Besides..." Ragnor waited for Lina to look back at him, then threw a suspicious twinge in his eyes. "What about the others? Your new friends?"

"I care about them but that does not mean I am like them."

"You don't have to be like them, Adelina. Maybe that is why this is your destiny. The world needs someone like you to show them another way."

Lina rubbed her collarbone again, dropping her hands and exhaling. She knew this already, but hearing Ragnor say it gave her a small bit of hope. Camelot would always make her uncomfortable, maybe for good reason, but that didn't mean she shouldn't use the opportunity to do something good. Maybe life in the castle wearing confining clothes and walking through dimly lit corridors didn't always have to be such. Maybe it could be more than that. Maybe she had judged them too harshly without giving them a chance.

Then she thought of Ren and how his support in the battle helped her accept the power from the sword. He gave her strength, even when she was afraid of the sword. His constant certainty grounded her.

Her fingers danced around the hilt of Excalibur again, but she didn't grip it for support this time. She merely explored the tendrils of power pulling at her fingertips. Maybe this sword could be different, as well. Just because it brought Arthur back didn't mean it couldn't also be used for good, like it once had been.

She had Ren, after all, and the others. Maybe that's what made her different from Arthur, whose friends had all turned their back on him by the end. They didn't fight hard enough for their king. They gave up.

Ren's voice echoed in her mind.

I won't let that happen.

Ren would never give up on her. She knew that with certainty.

"You're right," she breathed. "You are always right."

Ragnor let out a belly laugh, snorting. "Of course I am, I am your father."

Even as the words left his mouth, a painful silence fell between them. The word had a different meaning now, and Ragnor knew it because Lina caught the sadness setting in the depths of his eyes.

"Ragnor?" she waited for his focused attention because she needed to ask this, and she needed him to tell her the truth this time. "Did you know my father was King Arthur?"

He cleared his throat. "No, I did not. But I did lie to you, to protect you."

Lina cocked an eyebrow, urging him to go on.

"When I told you Camelot was responsible for your parent's deaths, I only said it because I was bitter about how they had turned their backs on our people. I didn't want you anywhere near that castle or those people, so I made up a story. I am sorry."

Tears poked at the corner of her eyes, and Ragnor leaned over, wrapping an arm around her shoulder. Warmth radiated from the furs he wore, and she settled into his side. His embrace was comforting, safe. Being around him calmed her fears, but even so, he couldn't protect her from the world, not anymore. He couldn't protect her from her fate.

She pulled away, wiping the moisture from her cheeks. "And my mother? Do you know where she is? Who is she?"

Ragnor shook his head. "No. I am sorry."

She pressed her lips into a line, holding her breath. "It's just as well. It doesn't change anything." Forcing a smile, she stood alongside Ragnor when he rose from his seat.

"Come," he waved her on. "You can help us finish loading the carts, and then you must get back to Camelot before dark. The world is changing, and I worry about you out here alone."

"I can handle myself," Lina returned.

"That I know. Some things will never change."

Lina laughed, allowing her eyes to drift to the flickering flames of the fire, which had turned a shade of deep emerald. The color shimmered in her eyes, sending a wave of burning heat blooming in her chest.

Something just under the surface stirred.

And her collarbone itched.

CHAPTER

FORTY

As fall erupted in color and the air turned crisp and cold, Guinevere summoned Ren and Lina to meet her at the site of an old temple of Avalon deep in the woods. Ren hadn't spent a ton of time with Lina over the summer. Everyone was too busy rebuilding, healing, or trying to adjust to everyday life again. At least that's what Ren told himself. But Lina seemed to avoid everyone, traveling from the village to the woods, sometimes disappearing for days at a time. Every step away from Camelot felt like a step away from him.

So, when they reunited on a grassy hill overlooking a little glade protected by birch trees, the ache in his chest lessened a little.

"Good hunting?" Ren's eyes landed on Lina's pack from which dangled a brace of rabbits.

"Soon it will be too cold and more difficult to find them so..." her voice trailed off as she admired the shaking leaves of the tree grove they'd entered.

A narrow, boot-packed path guided them through the forest as they walked in awkward silence. Birds chirped in canopies. Twigs snapped as small animals bounded out of sight. It reminded Ren a little of the Brecheliant Woods, minus the toxic, hallucinogenic mushrooms.

When the silence was too much to bear, he blurted out the thing he had been wanting to say since the end of battle. "I'm sorry I didn't see the truth about Arthur. And the sword. When you pulled it... I wasn't thinking about that, and I should have." He stepped over a gnarled root, his gaze tracking the ground until he caught her eyes focused on him.

Her jaw clenched, and her feet stopped in their path. "It's okay. It wasn't your secret to reveal. Even if you had known before, I don't think I would have wanted to know."

The knots in the pit of Ren's stomach tightened. He was still keeping what Merlin told him a secret—there was more to it than just the power of the sword. That her Pendragon blood could be the key to protecting Camelot. He just didn't know how to tell her. She'd been through enough already and as she said, maybe she wasn't ready to hear it. So, instead, he let out a weighted sigh, responding, "I get that. I'm still sorry it happened the way it did."

"I know," she said, continuing down the path, and reaching out her hand to touch the golden leaves outstretched on a birch branch. "I kept something from you, as well."

She stopped again, but this time she didn't look at him. Instead, her gaze tracked the dusty clouds drifting lazily in the sky. "Do you remember my vision about Camelot burning?"

Ren nodded.

"Well, you were there too."

"I was?"

She turned, her eyes falling to his. "I wasn't sure at first, but when I saw you in camp that night, in the goat pens—"

He let out a laugh. "That was not fun."

She smiled. "I know. Sorry about that. But when I saw you there, it became obvious that my fate would be tied to yours."

"What does that mean?" Ren's throat went dry, his insides twisting with nerves.

She bit her bottom lip and shook her head. "I'm not sure yet."

They stood in silence for a moment, listening to the birds.

"I never meant for this to happen." Lina broke the silence this time, eyes cast to the sky again with a far-off expression. "I never wanted the sword. I wish you had been the one who pulled it, not me. You are more deserving."

Guilt rose in Ren's chest. There was a time he wanted the sword more than he'd ever wanted anything, but he'd never even considered that he wasn't meant to have it. Maybe he was always meant to help Lina. She never wanted this life, and in many ways, that must have been much harder for her than it was for him.

He was close enough to tug at her hand, so he wrapped his fingers with hers, pulling her in close. "Lina..." He searched for the right thing to say but realized there wasn't anything he could say to change things. He could, however, be there for her. "I'm sorry we dragged you into this. I'm sorry it's a burden you have to bear for a place you never considered home. For a place you hate."

She didn't respond right away, but her eyes sparkled. She squeezed his hand and drew him in closer. "You're wrong. I don't hate Camelot. Not anymore." Her eyes lingered on his for a beat as his heart pounded in his chest.

Parting her lips, a wisp of breath teased his neck, sending tingles down his spine.

He opened his mouth to say something, *anything*, and he was about to ask her if the kiss they shared in the woods was a mistake. He'd been out of his mind with longing since that night. He had missed her and wished they could have more time together, but he wasn't sure if she felt the same.

But he didn't have to ask any of that aloud because she lifted her face to his and pressed her mouth softly against his.

He was so surprised he stood there like an idiot before pulling back.

She offered a sheepish smile, biting her bottom lip. Heat surged his cheeks.

A piece of hair fell over her cheek, and he reached for it, tucking it behind her ear and allowing his fingers to brush over her soft skin. Then he leaned in with the confidence he should have had the first time and went for it.

Their lips touched in a deep longing like they were always supposed to end up like this.

He'd kissed girls before, but this was different. This was dangerous. It was as if he couldn't bear to part from her, like the moment he did, he wouldn't be able to breathe. She parted her lips further, deepening the kiss as their tongues danced with the same grace as Lina's fighting.

Yep. He was doomed. He couldn't let her go. Not now. Not ever.

Breathless, they finally parted. Her lips were flush, her eyes bright. She was the most beautiful thing he'd ever seen, but this time, he knew it wasn't a dream because he was still breathing.

Her cheeks flushed as she flashed him a smile.

The flutter of wings broke them apart as a flock of crows launched into the air somewhere close. Ren's hand went instinctively to the sword at his hip, eyes scanning the trees. But moments passed and nothing happened.

Lina squeezed his hand, tugging him along the path. "Come on. She's waiting."

But when she dropped his hand, leading on the path ahead, panic rushed his veins. One day, Lina may choose to leave all this behind, and if she did, he didn't know how he'd survive it.

THEY ARRIVED at an outcropping of stone slates arranged in a circle. The rest of what used to be an Avalon temple had crumbled, taken over by vines and wild bushes covering the stones. Light filtered through the overgrown trees in ethereal beams and an energy crackled out of reach. Ren wasn't sure how, but there was magic still lingering there.

Guinevere waited for them as they entered, welcoming both with tight hugs. She was a hugger like Ren's mother, and he had to say, he didn't hate it. The comforting embrace helped ground him after his moment with Lina.

"Thank you for coming. I wanted to see you outside the walls of Camelot, away from those weighted memories." Her eyes welled, but she pulled back the emotion, offering a warm smile instead.

Running her hand along a cracked stone, she said. "I've decided to stay in Camelot."

Ren and Lina nodded, but Guinevere flung a hand in the air. "Only if you allow it."

Ren's face burned hot, and he exchanged a confused look with Lina.

"What do you mean, if we will allow it?" he asked.

Guinevere clasped her hands together. "Arthur banished me many years ago. You were only a boy then, Amren, but it was written into the law, and only a pardon from the king will break it."

"But there is no king," Ren said.

"Exactly," Guinevere added. "In the absence of a king, this is the time to come back and be with my daughter. She needs me now more than ever."

Ren thought about Gwen down in the cold dungeons. She would need her mother when they conducted the trial. She would need all of them.

Guinevere continued, "I already spoke with the counsel, and they advised seeking the blessing from you both."

"Us?" Ren shifted his stance. The assumption that he and Lina held any kind of power made him uncomfortable.

Guinevere nodded. "Lina holds the sword of power, and you," she lifted Ren's chin between her fingers, "you helped save Camelot. They want to give credit where it is due, and I must say, it is long overdue."

Lina chewed her lip, looking even more uncomfortable with the idea than Ren did.

"Of course we want you to stay," Ren answered. Guinevere's presence was already a great comfort to the people in the village. He could tell by the way they admired her when she helped with the rebuild. She was a former queen, after all, and interacting with the people of the kingdom came as easily to her as breathing. If anyone had the experience necessary to help lead Camelot into a new age, it would be her.

Ren turned to Lina, searching for her approval.

"I don't have the authority to grant you a pardon, and I haven't been here long enough to say what is right or wrong, but..." Lina caught Ren's eyes, "if Ren wishes it, I trust his judgement."

Ren's cheeks burned. *Composure, Ren. Knights remain composed.*

"Thank you," Guinevere said. "I know you must have questions, and while I'm not certain I can answer all of them, the least I can do is try." Her brows flicked up as her gaze fixed on Lina specifically.

Lina leaned against a stone. "Arthur said he was my father, which would explain why I could pull the sword from the stone. Is it true?" There was a deep longing in her eyes. Ren was certain she'd been wrestling with this all these months.

Guinevere pressed her lips together. "I can't say for sure, but I suspect it could be true. Arthur was... not himself in those final years. He became erratic and power-hungry, and when he learned what Lance and I had done..." A sadness settled on her face. "The jealousy drove him mad, and he took to seeking out the company of other companions. For revenge or lonesomeness, I'm not certain, but it's possible you were born during that time. I imagine he wanted to keep you a secret. Your mother wouldn't have known what to do with a child of the king's born out of wedlock, so she may have given you up to protect you."

Lina's eyes dropped to the floor of the temple, where little cream flowers poked through the blades of browning grass. "That is what Ragnor admitted, as well." Her face twisted into a painful expression. "He lied to me all these years. He told me Camelot was responsible for my parent's death." She looked to Ren, then returned her gaze to Guinevere. "Do you have any idea who my mother was?"

Guinevere shook her head. "I'm sorry, Adelina, I don't know who your mother is."

Lina dug her boots into the ground. "I've been on my own my entire life. I guess this doesn't change anything."

"That's where you are wrong. You are a daughter of Camelot now." Guinevere approached, touching Lina's shoulder.

"What if I don't want to be a daughter of Camelot? What if I don't want this life?" Lina's eyes darted to Ren again, betraying her guilt over this admission. But her voice cracked, and Ren hung on to that. She may not want it now, but he could tell she was fighting something inside. Something, he hoped, that might allow her to think differently one day.

Guinevere leaned in and took both Lina's hands. "What do you want? Do you genuinely want better for Camelot and your people?" Guinevere pressed her lips into a stern line, lifting her head high.

"Ragnor asked the same thing."

"He knows you won't get this chance again. You've been given something you do not yet understand, and that can be scary. The path may be difficult, but that doesn't mean you shouldn't walk it." She released Lina's hands.

Lina bit her bottom lip and clutched the hilt of Excalibur at her hip. "Thank you. I will think about what you've said."

"Good," Guinevere said, casting her face to a sun-lit beam and letting out a weighted sigh. "It warms my heart to be back in Camelot. Now, I'm sure you are anxious to return to town. I hear preparations are already in place for the ceremony." With a wink she dismissed Lina but called out to Ren, "A moment?"

"I'll see you back at the castle," Lina said, rushing from the old temple. She couldn't get away fast enough. It was a lot to take in, and while he didn't want to see her struggle so much, Guinevere was right that she could make a difference here. He hoped one day she would accept it.

Once the sound of Lina's boots disappeared, Guinevere's face changed, a hardness lining the soft wrinkles around her eyes. "It's about the sword."

"The sword?"

"As you know, the sword is tied to Arthur and is the reason he came back from the dead."

Ren nodded. The sight of Arthur's hallowed face still haunted his dreams.

"There is more to the sword than you know. It did something to Arthur. There is a reason he changed in those final years. All the stories you've been told are true, up to a point. He was a great king, and he brought about change and peace to these lands. But then something happened. His desires grew, and his behavior became erratic."

"Okay..." Ren followed but wasn't certain he liked where this was going.

"Lance always thought it was the sword. There is no other reason for it. The longer he had Excalibur in his possession, the madder it made him. It corrupted his heart. Do you understand?"

Ren nodded wearily. "Lina has the sword now."

Guinevere shut her eyes in a pained manner, and a rock rumbled in Ren's gut.

Lina had been afraid of this. Ren had hoped it wasn't true, but Guinevere had confirmed the very thing they suspected.

"We have to make sure that doesn't happen," he said.

"Yes, we do, but it won't be easy. The sword is the key to Camelot's survival, but it could also bring about—"

"It's destruction," Ren finished the sentence, the truth of it clawing at his insides. Merlin hadn't mentioned that part, but of course, Merlin always spoke in vague sentences, only divulging partial truths.

Guinevere rested her palm on his cheek, forcing his eyes to meet the deep sapphire of hers. "Be careful who you fall in love with, Amren. Kingdoms have crumbled and crowns fallen because of love. I should know." Her eyes glanced into the vague distance behind Ren with a deep sadness.

Ren opened his mouth to respond, but he wasn't sure what to say. He couldn't tell her there was nothing between him and Lina because that would be a lie. Now that he knew the sword was dangerous, he wanted to be even closer to her so he could protect her from it, like he promised in the fight with Arthur.

Guinevere smiled sadly before leaving Ren amongst the crumbling stones of the Avalon temple.

There was still much Ren had to learn about the world. That terrified him and seeded doubt in the depths of his mind, heart, and soul. As if the stones sensed the same thing, a vibration shuttered through them, as the remaining pieces of stone cracked and crumbled to the ground. A cold shadow passed over him, sending a violent shiver down his spine and making him crave the warm fires inside the castle.

At least he could always count on the comforting fires of Camelot.

FORTY-ONE

THE DAY FINALLY ARRIVED FOR A NEW KNIGHTING ceremony. This time, they announced not one person, but four.

Ren entered the great hall to loud chatter. Everyone from Camelot gathered in their finest attire to mark the occasion. Silks and rich velvets in bright colors swept across the marble floors. Never in the history of Camelot had they anointed more than one knight at a time, and after the attempted siege, this was quite the momentous event.

Ren spotted Emeli, who shined in a moss-colored gown and mustard corset. Bronze arm bracers and a polished chest plate wrapped her body, and this time, Ren didn't even care how much she talked about the ensemble beforehand because she deserved it. She gave Ren's hand a squeeze, their twin reassurance. Ren didn't need it, though, because he had no doubt in his mind they all deserved this.

Geret wore his best tunic in bronze with shimmering green embroidery. His armored plates covered his broad shoulders and forearms, and he radiated joy, feeding off the energy of the guests. He always loved a good party. He approached, leaning in to whisper something in Emeli's ear that Ren couldn't hear, and she sucker-punched him right in the side. Ren chuckled as they split from him to mingle with the crowd.

When Lina entered the room, she stole Ren's breath.

Her fighting leathers had been replaced with layers of creamy silks in shades of burgundy. The dress had been tailored to hug her curves in all the right places with a slit up one leg. Cutouts along her waist teased bronze skin, and flowers wandered over her neckline.

Waves of warm brown hair cascaded over her shoulders as her eyes spotted him across the room while moving through the crowd.

"You have to stop doing that," Ren said, reaching for her hand.

"What?"

"Walking into a room looking so beautiful that I forget my name."

She blushed, but a frown formed over her rouged lips.

"Hey," he tugged her closer. "Are you alright?"

She gazed out over the crowd and cleared her throat. "I'm fine."

He'd been around her long enough to know when she was donning her emotional armor. "Is it this room?"

She shook her head, although Ren suspected she still wasn't comfortable inside the castle walls. She'd only been inside a handful of times since returning from the woods, and in every instance, her gaze swept towards the exits as she fidgeted with her hair or reached for the sword permanently at her hip.

"Then what is it? Is it the ceremony? Because I used to think it was a big deal, but the truth is, it's not. Not really. It's just a formality." Being a knight meant something different to him now. Before, he sought validation to prove himself worthy of following in his father's footsteps. He no longer needed a title to tell him that. He couldn't believe it had taken him so long to figure it out.

"Don't you say that Ren Bedivere, it is a big deal," she scolded. "I'm just not sure I belong up there with you, Emeli, and Geret. You've trained your entire life for this, and I just walked in. I'm an imposter."

Ren leaned into her ear, brushing the soft skin of her neck with the back of his fingers. "You belong here. The sword wouldn't have chosen you otherwise. Besides, we all agree that you earned it, too. As Guinevere said, Camelot owes you."

She nodded, biting her bottom lip.

"Breathe. I'm right here with you," he added.

She squeezed his hand, and they floated into the crowd.

Before long, a silence fell upon the guests as the knights filed into the room—Percival, Bors, and Galahad. The legendary Knights of the Round Table were down to just three. A pinch sparked in Ren's chest. It was hard to ignore that every time he'd dreamt of this day, his father was also there. He caught his mother's eyes on the other side of the room near the windows. She pressed her lips together and dipped her head.

Before the ceremony started, she had cornered him in the hallway, brushing her hand through his unruly hair in an attempt to make it stay down. But then her face turned serious, and she pressed a tender kiss to his forehead and squeezed his shoulders.

"Your father would have been so proud."

It took everything in him to hold back the emotion.

The knights lined up on the dais at the end of the room, commanding everyone's eyes. One by one they called out all their names—Ren, Emeli, Geret, and finally, Lina.

Ren kneeled along with the others in front of the knights as Percival tapped his blade on all their shoulders. When it was Ren's turn, the blade sent a tingle through his body. When it lifted, the heavy weight he had carried for as long as he could remember was lifted, too.

"Arise, Knights of Camelot," Percival announced.

They rose to a cheering crowd so loud Ren barely heard Emeli's joke to Geret about his "shining knighthood."

Jokes aside, they had done it. They were knights.

Afterwards, a feast rivaling the original ceremony took over the great hall. The wine flowed freely, and everyone stuffed their bellies with the most decadent foods. Even Lina. Throughout the night, Ren cast glances in her direction, silently checking if she was okay. To her credit, she appeared every bit the part, smiling and laughing with the rest. Even so, her hand kept reaching for the sword that wasn't there at her hip. They had decided to leave the swords behind for this one. Bad luck and all.

Even though it was only temporary, a slight twist in her lip or a knot in her brow made Ren wonder if she experienced a small pinch of pain every time she brushed the emptiness.

As quickly as it had begun, the day was over, and everything had changed.

EARLY THE NEXT DAY, as the kingdom nursed hangovers, Ren rose early, summoned to the Round Table room. The morning light cast colorful shadows through the stained-glass windows, and a fire crackled in the room's hearth. Once layered with grime, the floors were now polished to their original shine. It looked like a brand new room. That first night Ren and Merlin stumbled inside felt like ages ago.

Galahad and Merlin chatted in one corner of the room. Merlin touched Galahad's arm playfully, and for the first time since the battle, an enormous grin spread over Galahad's face. Ren chuckled. He hoped this new Galahad would go easier on them in training because his shoulder hadn't quite healed.

Percival, Bors, and Guinevere huddled near the windows. Next to them, two elders from the village sat in chairs, one with sagging wrinkles spidering his face, and the other with a long, white beard with breadcrumbs caught in the wiry mess. A striking woman with greying strands weaved into her chestnut braid watched over the room with sharp eyes. Ren recognized them all as council members, but why were they here now? He was about to head over to Merlin to ask what was happening, but an arm wrapped around his shoulder and slapped him on the chest.

Geret leaned in. "What do you think this is all about?"

Ren shrugged. "I'm not sure."

Emeli walked in behind Geret, but Ren hadn't spotted Lina yet. He found himself constantly checking the entrance for her figure.

Merlin strode to the center of the room, commanding attention. "I asked you all here today because we have a conundrum to solve." Eyes darted around the room where everyone looked just as confused as Ren.

Merlin stood in front of the Round Table. Its polished surface gleamed in the morning light, and the scent of fresh-cut wood hung in the air. Someone clearly had put some love into the "old relic," as Morin had called it.

Clearing his throat, Merlin continued, "We stopped our enemies from taking Camelot. For now. But it's time we resurrected old practices and filled these chairs with knights worthy of the name." His eyes cast to the twelve empty seats around the outside of the table.

A flutter beat inside Ren's chest. The first time he laid eyes on this table, it inspired him to embark on his quest, but he never imagined he would sit at it like his father once had.

"Sir Percival. Sir Bors. Sir Galahad," Merlin announced, gesturing at the empty places.

The men took their positions in front of their house-coat-of-arms etched into the table. It must have felt like coming home.

Next, Merlin announced the Lady Guinevere to hushed whispers around the room. She glided to the table, standing over a newly engraved crest in the wood—swirling scripts encompassing a wild rose. So that's why she wanted to stay. She wanted to take up Lancelot's seat at the Round Table.

Next to her was a blank space, and Ren couldn't help but think of Gwen. If she had chosen differently, perhaps she would be here now taking a seat next to her mother. A twinge of longing scratched at the back of his throat. Maybe one day she could make it right.

"Sir Geret, of Gawaine," Merlin said next.

Geret puffed his chest and grinned as he took his place in front of a carving of a shaggy bear. He winked at Emeli, and while she rolled her eyes, Ren also caught a blush on her cheeks.

Ren counted the chairs now. Percival, Bors, Galahad, Guinevere, and Geret. That was five. With him and Em, that would make seven.

Merlin cleared his throat loudly. "Sir Amren, of Bedivere, and Lady Emeline, of Bedivere."

Emeli nudged Ren in the side with a sharp elbow, and Ren realized Merlin was staring at him.

The title felt all wrong. Sir Bedivere was his father, not him, but it was something he'd have to get used to.

"Sorry," he said to Emeli as they both rushed to stand at their seats. Emeli's emblem was a graceful fox running through birch trees. Ren's was a lion sitting on a pile of stones. The beast's two fierce eyes stared back at him.

The golden mane of the chimera flashed in his mind. Merlin had said the chimera took its shape based on who it was facing. Now it all made sense.

"And finally, the house of the king, Lady Adelina Pendragon," Merlin announced.

The room fell silent as Lina stepped out of the shadowed

doorframe of the entrance. Ren hadn't even seen her there. As she tentatively walked under the stained glass to cross the room, the rainbow lights casting dancing colors over her skin left Ren breathless.

"Your highness?" Merlin addressed Lina, pulling back her chair from the table. Her hand fell immediately to the sword hilt at her hip.

"Only if you never call me 'your highness' ever again." She smiled, and her eyes met Ren's. He knew that title made her skin crawl.

"Of course. Your *royal* highness, then," Merlin corrected with a twinkle in his eye.

Ren laughed, even as Emeli elbowed him again and shot him a burning glare.

Lina sighed but stood proudly at the table. Carved into her crest was Arthur's pendragon symbol, but they'd altered it with the addition of a hawk flying overhead through wispy clouds, a sword gripped tight in its talons.

A dragon, and again, the chimera's scaly body and outstretched wings were hard to ignore. A lion and a dragon.

Something strange rumbled in the pit of his stomach.

"Now that we are all present. You see the conundrum, yes?" Merlin asked.

Ren's eyes flicked around the table. Eight. They had eight knights. That left four empty spots. "We need twelve," he said.

A sly smile slid over Merlin's lips. "Exactly." He turned to Percival.

Old Percival straightened his spine. "After much deliberation with the counsel." He looked around the room at the remaining people, including the two village elders, the stately woman, and two others who had traveled from two other villages in the kingdom. "We have decided to hold a tournament next summer with the four remaining seats as the prize."

Emeli leaned into Ren's ear. "Have they ever done that before?"

He shook his head. "No, the king always designated his own knights."

This was something entirely new, and Ren wasn't sure what to think. Knights were carefully chosen, not awarded.

Percival hushed the gossip buzzing around the room with his hands. "We also understand the Knights of the Round Table have lost a bit of their former glimmer, so we are adding another incentive. Something to entice the best of the best candidates from around the globe to make the journey to Camelot."

Ren held his breath, his boot tapping over the stone floor in anticipation.

Percival's eyes landed on Galahad. Who let out a heavy sigh. "That old relic?"

Percival nodded with a devious grin on his face.

"I nearly died for that worthless cup," Galahad added, and he crossed his arms over his chest with a sour expression on his face.

Merlin leaned over to Ren. "This just keeps getting more interesting, does it not?"

Ren shook his head. Interesting wasn't exactly the word he would use, but it certainly was a surprise. He couldn't be certain what relic they were referring to, but he had a good idea from his father's stories. If any of them were true, it was too important to give away. And besides, Merlin had mentioned there were multiple objects of Arthur's rule which were imbued with Pendragon blood magic. Items that could help defend Camelot from Arthur and whatever else was headed their way. Using such an item as a prize didn't sound right.

This tournament was sounding more and more suspicious by the moment, but what could he do? If the senior knights and the counsel had already decided, and Merlin agreed, he would have to accept it.

Circling the room, Merlin stood next to the flickering flames of the fire. "Now that we have that sorted, all will be right in Camelot again. Knights of the Round Table, you may take your seats."

With that, they all sat in unison with the sound of wood scraping against the hallowed stone floor.

Ren didn't know what he expected to happen once they all took their seats at the table, but nothing spectacular occurred. No glowing lights or surging energy. Just him, Emeli, Geret, and Lina, around the table, passing knowing glances as they took their hard-fought places amongst the legends of Camelot.

This time, things would be different. They would strive to do better than their parents. Perhaps they would even re-write the Knight's Code. But there was one thing he was certain of—they would do it together, and together they would add their own chapters as the descendants of the Knights of the Round Table.

Merlin cleared his throat, knocking his staff on the table. "Now, let's get to work. For fame and glory and all that nonsense."

EPILOGUE

MORIN

Blood slid down Morin's arm, and a sticky sweat coated his lustrous skin. Flying was dreadful, so he switched to horseback somewhere around Farhallow, the smallest horse-dung town he'd ever seen. But at least they had horses.

Perched on a stout, ebony-colored brood, he gripped the horse's mane and slumped against its neck. It was a position he held for half the day. Though he was able to speed up his healing before leaving the battlefields of Camelot, he still had a long way to go. His left arm was useless, making flying an embarrassing undertaking, and sorcery would be tricky. He needed a long, wine-induced, winter slumber next to a roaring fire while he plotted his next move.

Rounding the top of the hill, Castle Orkney stood below, but something wasn't right. Struck immediately by billowing smoke rising from the castle, he realized it was under siege by a fleet of ships at the shoreline. *His* castle. Fire erupted at the base of the island, and a black line of men scaled the dangerous cliffs with rope ladders like insects infiltrating a hive. *His* hive.

Waving in the breeze like a serpent riding the wind was a red dragon emblem blazoned on one ship's banner.

Shock barreled through Morin. "This cannot be." He turned his horse around to descend the hills for a better look.

Morin dismounted his horse with a groan, creeping over rock piles at the base of the cliffs. The ships unpacked weapons as they launched fireballs at his castle. An explosive boom sounded overhead as a cannonball engulfed in flames struck an outer wall, sending a barrage of stone tumbling downward. They crashed into the sea, sending the ships below thrashing against the high tide. But this did not deter them.

A figure dressed in dark armor disembarked a small dingy boat. Stepping out onto land, he scanned the shoreline and assessed the siege progress. Above the cliffs, the men had penetrated the outer wall, breaching the castle. Morin knew he should have left more forces to defend her, but he was blinded by his greed. No, not greed, aspiration to take the kingdom that should have been his all along. As a result, he had lost both Camelot and Orkney.

The brooding man on the shore turned toward the sun, and the light illuminated his face from the shadows. Panic rushed Morin's chest, and he ducked behind the rocks. It was the dark king Arthur. This was far worse than he imagined.

Arthur barked orders at his men. They unloaded hefty, wooden crates from the boat, lugging them up the shoreline where a path met with the road, then to the bridge connecting land to castle.

He's moving in, Morin realized. An icy chill raced down his spine.

The sight of his castle overthrown was too much for Morin to bear. He let out a wailing shriek and ripped at the buckles on his tunic. Flying be damned, he needed a quick exit. Burning from the inside, smoke transformed man into crow, and he lifted into the sky using his one good wing.

The distant wail caught the dark king's attention, and his eyes cast to the sky above the castle. Smoothing his chestnut curls behind his ears, he straightened the bone crown on his head and stretched his lips into a satisfied smirk.

ACKNOWLEDGMENTS

Writing a book is solitary, but being an author is not. I'm so grateful to all the wonderful people who have supported me over these long years. Firstly, to my parents who always encouraged me to dream and follow my passions. It was this foundation that gave me the courage to start writing all those years ago and never let it go. To my musician brother whose creativity and bravery inspire me every day. To my husband for supporting me during long hours, long days, and long months when I'm working on books. I know it's not easy being married to someone who always has one foot in another world, but I hope it's worth it.

To my editor Joel Brigham, thank you for helping me shape this book into a real book worth publishing. Your astute observations on character development and sharp eye for story, truly made this book shine. Ren, Lina, and Gwen wouldn't have been able to complete their quest without you. To Maria Tureaud, for helping me flesh out the opening chapters, you will always be my sister shield-maiden.

To my beta readers and critique partners for this book—Nadine Bells, Lindsay Barrett, Katrin, J.L. Fernández, Sarah Willis, Nicole Loos Miller, Gwenyth Reitz, and Elizabeth Soule, thank you for making the story better upon every draft and pointing out the good (and the ugly). You helped me become a better writer and I am forever grateful!

To Lisa Case Hill—I spent so many hours writing this book during our meetups. In the balcony at the Tattered Cover. In a cozy, dark corner of our favorite coffee shop. And at the library spending long sessions followed by a lovely lunch as a reward.

Thank you for your dedication and friendship. I cherish all the memories, and I know your books are going to make it into the world too soon enough.

To Lauren T. Davila, who was the first person to bolster my confidence in this book. And to the entire WriteHive mentorship class, especially Lindsay, Nadine, Katrin, and Christie, I am so grateful the mentorship brought us together. You have become good friends and are all super talented writers. Can't wait to see all your books on my shelves!

To the RevPit class of 2023—Gwen, Nicole, Liz, Melody, Megan, Misa—it's been a joy to go on this journey with you all. Your support carries me through the challenging times and your uplifting enthusiasm makes the wins that much more special. I'm looking forward to growing our careers together in the years to come.

To Kath Richards for answering my endless questions about self-publishing (I hope I didn't annoy you too much!). To my agent, Bethany Weaver, even though you weren't involved in the creation of this book, your relentless support of my self-publishing journey and my trad career means everything. To my agency siblings—thank you for cheering me on during this wild journey. I know when we are famous authors, we will look back on these times and laugh.

To Aes Munandi, for creating the wonderful cover and bringing my characters to life—I don't know how you did it, but you managed to capture the spirit of the story so well and I couldn't be happier with the end result!

And finally, to all the readers who enjoy Arthurian stories, thank you for giving my version of the tale a chance. I like to think every iteration of the King Arthur myth draws inspiration from all that came before, and with it, the once and future king lives on inside us all.

ABOUT THE AUTHOR

Kimberly Lynn Hanson writes atmospheric fantasy novels for adults and young adults, inspired by nature and myths. When she's not writing books, she works as a project manager and adventures in the Rocky Mountains of Colorado where she lives with her husband and furry children.

Learn more by visiting www.kimberlylynnhanson.com

instagram.com/kimberly_lynn_books